CHASING SALOMÉ

A NOVEL OF 1920S HOLLYWOOD

MARTIN TURNBULL

"CHASING SALOMÉ"
BY

Martin Turnbull

This book is dedicated to

JON PONDER

because without Nazzy we never would have met.

Copyright 2019 Martin Turnbull

All rights reserved. No part of this e-book may be reproduced in any form other than that in which it was purchased and without the written permission of the author. This e-book is licensed for your personal enjoyment only. This e-book may not be re-sold or given away to other people. If you would like to share this book with another person, please purchase an additional copy for each recipient. If you're reading this book and did not purchase it, or it was not purchased for you, please purchase your own copy. Thank you for respecting the hard work of this author.

DISCLAIMER

This novel is a work of historical fiction. Apart from the well-known actual people, events and locales that figure into the narrative, all names, characters, places, and incidents are the product of the author's imagination or are used fictitiously. Any resemblance to actual persons, living or dead, events or locals is entirely coincidental.

1

Alla Nazimova opened the mahogany-and-glass doors of the Ship Café with a flourish that sent her scarlet satin opera cape swirling around her. Years of performing in the theater had trained her in the art of the dramatic entrance, so she knew that the light from the crystal chandelier directly above would catch the sparkle in her sapphire necklace and bring out the violet in her eyes.

The maître d' was a rotund chap who looked like he enjoyed his brandies. "Oh, Madame!" He scurried out from behind his podium. "What an honor to have you dine with us tonight!"

"Thank you, Emile." Alla watched him count the number in her party. "My husband is unable to join us this evening." He didn't need to know that Alla had no desire for Charles to be there. She had someone else in tow that night—and it wasn't her husband.

The Ship Café was neither a ship nor a café. It was a restaurant that had been fashioned to resemble a Spanish galleon and lashed to the Venice Beach pier. It was one of those novelty places that Los Angeles architects had lately been conjuring with unfettered abandon. But with its sloping walls and low-slung ceiling striped with wooden beams, the overall ambiance was effectively nautical.

She had chosen it for tonight's celebration precisely because, like most things in Hollywood, it was not what it appeared to be. Adorned in their modish Paris gowns and tuxedos with black silk lapels, most people in Hollywood were not what they appeared to be, either, but in Los Angeles that was hardly a crime.

Emile collected an armful of menus and led them toward the center of the room.

As Alla zigzagged through the maze of tables, heads turned, eyes stared, mouths gaped. Earlier that day she had completed her fifth film in the twelve months since arriving in California to begin her contract for Metro Pictures. Every one of them had been a blazing success, so now she was recognized wherever she went. She smiled regally, her right hand fluttering like a captive dove until she reached the head of the table, where she took a seat and patted the right-hand-side silver setting for her new love, Jean.

Dagmar Godowsky, a dark, sleek, swan-like actress who had appeared in Alla's latest picture, slid onto the seat to her left. "I'm so glad you chose this place. Ever since that wretched Volstead Act started worming through Congress, it's been getting harder and harder to find a drink around this burg. The other night, we had to drive all the way to the Vernon Country Club, and you know how far that is. Don't get me wrong—the whiskey was terrific and the Paul Whiteman Orchestra was playing, so we had a great time. But brother, what a trek!"

"UGH!" Viola Dana exclaimed from further down the table. She, too, was a Metro star and a salt-of-the-earth type, the way girls from Brooklyn could be. "Imagine if it actually passes. Why even leave the house?"

"Of course it'll pass." Maxwell Karger was the studio manager at Metro. An okay sort of chap, but a little too weak-of-chin for Alla's tastes. "More than thirty of the forty-eight states are already dry. It's just a matter of time."

He was right, of course. Prohibition felt like a swarm of locusts massing on the distant horizon—close enough to hear the relentless thrumming that warned of a time when alcohol would become as scarce as fresh peaches in a Russian winter.

"In that case, let us *carpe diem* while we may." Alla raised her hand to attract the waiter lingering at their periphery. "Your finest champagne, please. Preferably Moët et Chandon or Veuve Clicquot."

He cleared his throat. "We've had quite a run on champagne of late and unfortunately we're out of both those labels."

"What's left? Taittinger? Mumm?" Alla ignored the evil eye that Karger shot her. She knew what he was thinking. *These labels are expensive. If you're assuming that Metro is going to underwrite your extravagant tastes . . .* She stroked his quivering cheek. "Fret not, *mon cher*. Madame shall be footing the bill tonight."

Alla had never figured out how the rumor had started that she wanted to be referred to as "Madame," but she liked the way it played into her *La Grande Dame* image. Broadway critics had hailed her as "this generation's foremost interpreter of Ibsen." And for her second picture, *Toys of Fate*, Metro had billed her "The World's Greatest Actress in Her Greatest Play." Somewhere in between Broadway's theaters and Hollywood's filming stages, Alla had become "Madame." And every time someone called her that, she would quietly chuckle to herself and wonder what her monstrous, bellowing Cossack of a father would make of it.

As far as she was concerned, when you start out life as a girl from a poor family in Crimea, you can reasonably expect to spend your life scratching out a living in a half-forgotten corner of the Black Sea. But if you end up the highest-paid actress in the world, you're entitled to be called Madame.

Karger's shoulders melted at the news that he would not have to part with any of his precious money. In all fairness, he was already handing over thirteen grand a week to have Alla emote in his photoplays. The least she could do was buy a few bottles of Laurent-Perrier, which was the best champagne left in the Ship Café cellar.

With the matter of refreshments settled, Alla ordered enough salmon mousse on Melba toast to feed the extras on a D.W. Griffith extravaganza. That done, she sat back and looked around the dining room.

Most of the tables were full, and the patrons were ordering booze like dehydrated fish gasping for their last drink. They were all good-looking ladies and gents whose fortunes had soared from the gobs of cash the studios were willing to throw at the flickers. Gay chatter filled the long room, and a few restive souls had ventured onto the elongated dance floor that split it in two.

Alla's gaze skipped from the glossy smiles to the glittering tiaras. *Who could ask for anything more?*

Almost instantly, she answered: *I could. I want more.*

The growl of her long-dead father's voice erupted in her head. *You greedy, ungrateful little worm. All this money and fame and success, and you're still not satisfied. PAH!*

The waiter arrived with two bottles of Laurent-Perrier thrust into pewter ice buckets. Alla was grateful for the distraction as he and a busboy darted around, uncorking bottles and filling champagne coupes.

Her director, Herbert Blaché, raised his glass. He was a dapper Englishman with a French name, a painstakingly trimmed mustache, and sharp eyes. His wife, Alice Guy, had once been head of production at the Gaumont Film Company in France. Alla could scarcely imagine how a woman had become the head of a film studio—nor could the French. As soon as Herbert and Alice were married, she had been forced to resign her job. God forbid a smart, well-read woman should be in a position to tell men what to do. But France's loss was Alla's gain.

"A toast, if I may," Herbert declared. "To Madame Nazimova. As ever, a joy to direct, even amid the bleakness of a cholera epidemic."

He was referring to the outbreak that propelled the plot of *Stronger Than Death*, the picture they had completed filming that afternoon. Alla played a French girl with a weak heart forced to dance in order to help quash an uprising somewhere near Calcutta. She winced at his words. She had been celebrated for her

Nora in *A Doll's House* and for her *Hedda Gabler* and would happily have continued her career on the boards except that these picture people had dangled a preposterously lucrative carrot in front of her. What was she supposed to do? Say no? So she hadn't. And now she was prancing around, pretending to be a dancer whose dicey ticker might be the end of her.

Surely we can do better than this nonsense?

Alla murmured her thanks and held her smile as though she hadn't a care.

She cast around the room again to see if any new or interesting faces had joined the bustle and her gaze lighted on a raven-haired beauty somewhat in the Theda Bara mold. She turned to Dagmar, who always knew everybody wherever she went. "Who is *that*?"

Dagmar only needed a swift peek. "She's one of those Ziegfeld Follies girls who've come west to make it in pictures. She goes by Nita Naldi, but I doubt that's her real name."

"Ziegfeld?" Yet another girl who thought a pretty face was the only required asset. "So she's not a real actress."

"Au contraire. She's filming *Dr. Jekyll and Mr. Hyde* at Famous Players-Lasky with John Barrymore. I've heard whisperings that she's put in a star-making turn. I don't know why she's bothered, though. My friend May Robson is working on that picture, and she told me that as soon as filming is done, Nita's returning to New York to be in a musical play called *Aphrodite*. It's based on that novel by Pierre Louÿs."

The name clutched at Alla's throat like Jack the Ripper. Pierre Louÿs was one of her favorite authors, not least because he wrote about people who lived on the fringes of society. It also helped that he was good friends with Oscar Wilde, whose work Alla adored beyond measure.

"*Aphrodite*, you say?"

The novel was about courtesans in ancient Alexandria and was the type of project Alla could sink her teeth into and relish every bite. But instead, she was supposed to be content with playing defective dancers frolicking around West Bengal while everybody in sight was dropping dead.

She let out a prolonged sigh. "How fortunate for Miss Naldi."

Beneath the starched white tablecloth, Alla reached toward Jean's leg. She wanted to feel the warmth of her thigh, to stroke it gently as a promise of delights to come later that evening.

Alla had met her on a recent trip to New York. At twenty-six, Jean had arrived a little late in the game to become an actress, but was attractive nonetheless. Alla had been in a tobacconist's on 67th Street. Perfumed cigarettes had become all the rage, so she had instructed the tobacconist to imbue them with the bespoke fragrance that Caswell-Massey had concocted for her. As she waited to be served, in walked this girl, her carob-brown hair snipped into a head-turning Castle bob.

A tentative conversation over the Cuban cigar counter had grown into a more intense exchange over macarons and passion-fruit tea at the French café around the corner, which soon led to passion of a different sort in Alla's apartment at the Hotel Des Artistes. Before anybody could say "Uncle Vanya," Miss Jean Acker had signed a $200-a-week contract with Metro Pictures and was sitting by Alla's side in an Atchison, Topeka and Santa Fe railcar back to Los Angeles.

But Jean's leg was out of reach, which did little to bolster Alla's flagging spirits.

Nobody had said a thing—not to her face, at any rate—but when viewing some of *Stronger Than Death*'s dailies, Alla had been galled to see that she had put on too much weight. On the way out of the screening room, she had told herself that she hadn't been too fat to seduce that young script girl, Dorothy Arzner. *She didn't mind your fleshier carcass.* But by the time Alla had arrived home to her mansion on Sunset Boulevard, she'd come to her senses. The camera was unforgiving. She had to slim down before *Heart of a Child* started filming; nobody would believe her as a hundred-and-thirty-nine-pound poverty-stricken waif.

Dagmar offered up a slice of toast she had slathered with

salmon mousse. When Alla pushed it away, Dagmar harrumphed. "What's up with you? You've been little Miss Down-in-the-Mouth all evening."

Alla deflected her question with an airy shrug. "You know what I'm like at the end of filming. Drained and depleted."

Dagmar shook her head. "That's a load of hooey and we both know it."

Alla lobbed back a wide-eyed look that said *It most certainly isn't*, but Dagmar wasn't buying. "I'm pretty sure I know what it is." She jutted her head toward Jean, whom Herbert had dragged into an earnest discussion about how Cecil B. DeMille had used his camera on Gloria Swanson in *Don't Change Your Husband*. That is to say, Herbert was lecturing and Jean was nodding.

"You do?" Alla asked.

"Viola told me all about it."

Hearing her name, Viola looked up from her menu. "I told you about what?" She read their faces and dropped her voice to a whisper. "You mean Grace Darmond, huh?"

Alla could feel defensive walls rise around her. "Isn't she with Vitagraph?"

"Was," Viola said. "She's now filming *The Hope Diamond Mystery* at some Poverty Row second-rater."

"Oh, my goodness!" Dagmar rose from the table, her eyes glued to something across the room. "I'll be right back." She scampered away.

Alla turned to see what had captured her attention, but Viola slid into Dagmar's vacated seat and stage-whispered, "My current paramour is filming *The Great Air Robbery* at Universal right now." Ormer Locklear was an accomplished stunt pilot, who was also married. But so was Viola, and in Hollywood, marriage vows were as rubbery as a French letter. "The scenarist is poker buddies with John Clymer, who wrote *The Hope Diamond Mystery*, and he told George who told Ormer who told me that their leading lady is a lady lover with a lady lover of her own." Viola drifted her movie-actress eyes past Alla and onto Jean.

Alla took great care to freeze her face. Nobody could label her a stringent moralist, especially when it came to marital fidelity. She had always seen herself as a free spirit, unconstrained by staid principles that equated "wives" with "goods and chattels." Her intimate circle knew that her own so-called marriage was a sham. But sometimes it was expedient to play by the rules. Even if you didn't agree with them.

So this news that Jean was sleeping with someone else shouldn't have prickled Alla like a corkscrew pressed to her flesh. If she could have been true to her moral code and waved away the news with a blasé flick of the wrist, she would have.

But she didn't.

She couldn't.

And that's because you're The Great Nazimova, so it never occurred to you that this girl fourteen years your junior would think of looking elsewhere. Let alone to an actress working on Poverty Row. You're forty, and that's the end of the road for leading ladies. Who do you think you are —Mary Pickford? You're an egotistical nincompoop who deserves a slap across the face.

The ensuing silence might have grown unbearable had it not been for Dagmar's well-meaning but ill-timed return with the man she had dragged through the restaurant with disconcerting zeal.

Alla guessed he was around Jean's age, but those swarthy continentals with their olive complexions were hard to pin down. He was not without appeal, though, with those sleepy-lidded eyes that slanted slightly at the outside edge, giving them a distinct come-to-bed quality.

However, Alla didn't need an introduction because she already knew who he was: an Italian taxi dancer who'd kept himself out of the gutter by giving lessons in the Argentine tango to neglected society wives. And only a fool would assume that dance lessons conducted in private homes were the only exercise going on before the hour was up.

Flashy hoofers-for-hire like him were a dime a dozen, especially in New York, where a while ago he had met a scandal-prone socialite, Blanca de Saulles, at whose divorce trial he'd testified. She had later shot her ex-husband at point-blank range, reducing the whole affair to a turgid melodrama, not unlike the histrionic pantomimes currently boring Alla to tears.

And now Dagmar was hauling this shameless would-be Latin lover toward her.

"Madame!" she exclaimed, prodding him forward. "I would like to introduce you to—"

"I know who he is!" Alla refused to look at him and instead focused her fury on Dagmar. Deep down—though not very far down—Alla knew that she wasn't playing fair. She was angry that she'd let herself get so pudgy. She was indignant that Jean was sleeping with another woman. And she was jealous of that Ziegfeld Follies girl across the room who got to act in *Dr. Jekyll and Mr. Hyde* while Metro had her playing Eurasian twins and destitute chorus girls.

Dagmar blinked. Alla's withering tone had caught her off guard. "But Madame, he—his—this is Rodolfo di Valentini, and he's been dying to—"

"How *dare* you bring that gigolo to my table?"

Dagmar and di Valentini exchanged scared-rabbit glances as every diner in a four-table radius looked up from their broiled squab and veal cutlets.

"I'm sorry, Madame," Dagmar stammered. "It's just that—"

If they want The Great Nazimova, I'll give them The Great Nazimova. Alla threw her head back. "Why is he still here?" She stared past Viola to the six-man house band, which had launched into "A Pretty Girl is Like a Melody." Alla counted to ten. "Have they left?"

Viola nodded. "They slunk away like wounded snakes."

"Good."

"Oh, come now," Jean said. "You don't mean that."

After what Alla had learned about that Poverty Row hambone, Jean was the ideal victim of her residual venom. "Do you even know who Rodolfo di Valentini is?"

"I read the newspapers just like everyone else."

If Alla had ever learned how to drive an automobile, she would have risen to her feet and swept haughtily out of the place. But she had never bothered, so now she was stuck at a table of people sitting awkwardly and studying their butter knives. *You're the official hostess*, she told herself. *This discomfort is wholly your fault and it's up to you to repair it.*

"I think that is more than enough commotion for one night," she said blithely. Both bottles of Laurent-Perrier were empty. Alla wriggled her fingers; their waiter appeared. "Two more, if you please, *mon bon garçon*. By the time you get back, we shall be ready to order dinner." She faced her woebegone party. "Has anybody seen *Broken Blossoms*? I hear Lillian Gish's performance is a revelation."

2

If Alla had known the fate of *Stronger Than Death*, she might have ordered a seventh bottle of Laurent-Perrier and taken the trouble to enjoy the evening at the Ship Café more. The picture had received a rapturous New York premiere, followed by a gurgling death rattle when the more malicious critics had issued a slate of purse-lipped reviews.

Stinging though they were, Alla couldn't disagree. She would never have believed herself as a dancer caught up in a native uprising during a cholera epidemic, so she could scarcely have expected her fans to do the same. Even her most ardent admirers would put up with only so much bunkum.

Her follow-up to *Stronger Than Death* was another potboiler, *Heart of a Child*, in which she played a Cockney lass who rises to become the wife of a nobleman through a series of ludicrous situations. At least in *Billions*, the picture after that, she'd played a Russian—but not a relatable member of the proletariat. She was a princess who escapes Czarist rule and moves to America where she falls in love with an impoverished poet. What drivel! What hogwash!

Her husband, Charles, had written the scenario, after which she had taken to her typewriter and rewritten the titles so that there would be some semblance of literary value to the whole mess. He had huffed and snorted at what he viewed as her slight to his writing skills. But it wasn't *his* face on the screen; it wasn't *his* name on the posters; it wasn't *his* reputation on the line if the picture flopped.

She could have coped better with her artistic ambitions being ground to dust if her personal life had been a sweet-smelling romp amid fields of rose petals. But there, too, life had poked her in the eye with an ice pick.

A month after the evening at the Ship Café, Dagmar had called Alla with the news that Jean Acker had gotten married. "To a man!"

Alla gripped the stem of her candlestick telephone like a dagger. "Do you know who she married?"

The heavy pause at the other end warned her that she ought not have asked.

"That Italian tango jockey, Rodolfo di Valentini."

The telephone had almost slipped from Alla's grasp.

She had enjoyed a sumptuous smorgasbord of lovers, free of the need to restrict herself to one sex or the other. There was delight and pleasure and satisfaction to be found in sharing a bed with someone, regardless of their gender. "I bed the person, not their privates." She had made that pronouncement at a dinner party a year after arriving in New York, and hadn't thought the idea particularly controversial. She was simply stating a fact, Russian-style, with no coy euphemisms to diffuse her meaning. But it had stopped the party cold, and it had taken all of Alla's conversational skills in a language she had only just mastered to get the dinner back on track.

But lesson learned: for all their declared love of freedom, Americans could be conventionally moralistic—even the theater crowd, who loved to wear their demimonde status on full display. After that night, Alla had grown a little more selective about how and when she expressed her passions—and with whom.

Experience had taught her that affairs with men or women

always followed a similar path. Some of them lasted a night, some a week. The good ones carried on for a month or two, while others struck a richer stratum of true emotion that took both participants by surprise. Going into an affair, the practical stratagem was "Never assume, never expect, never presuppose."

But still, affairs were one thing; marriage was altogether something else.

People constantly get married, she told herself as Dagmar blathered on and on. Sometimes for the very best reasons, and sometimes they're motivated by rational considerations. Alla understood that. She didn't own Jean. Nor did Jean owe her anything. But still . . .

Alla dropped into the wicker chair next to the telephone. "When did this happen? And how? And—why?"

"He's shooting *Eyes of Youth* with Clara Kimball Young—"

"I don't care if he's shooting Abraham Lincoln between the eyes. He's a gigolo!"

"Will you let me finish?"

Alla felt the heat of anger burning in her chest. Of all men to run away with, did it have to be that . . . that . . . dancer-for-hire? She fanned herself with the *Photoplay* magazine she'd been reading when Dagmar had called. She told Dagmar to continue but soon wished she hadn't.

A few days after the night at the Ship Café, Jean and di Valentini had run into each other at a housewarming party. Jean had explained how mortified she'd been over Alla's high-handed rebuff and begged di Valentini's forgiveness. His response had been to ask her to dance.

Alla throttled a snort. "I can only assume he is a remarkably gifted dancer, seeing as how they're now married after, what, a month?"

"Hold on," Dagmar said. "There's more."

Alla's bar lay within reach of her telephone cord so she poured herself a shot. But then reconsidered. Congress had ratified the 18th Amendment; the Volstead Act was now the law of the land. It was bad enough that the all-too-human impulse to drown one's sorrows now risked imprisonment, but vodka might soon be hard to come by. Wouldn't it be wise to ration?

It was gut-wrenching enough that Jean had chosen Grace Darmond over her, but now this third-rate Beau Brummel? Screw it. Vodka jolted her throat. "Go on."

The wedding party had taken place at the home of Metro Pictures' treasurer, Joseph Engel, with Maxwell Karger as the best man. It was as though Dagmar had reached through the telephone wire and slapped Alla. Then once again for good measure. Alla had only installed this infernal contraption at great expense a month or two before and was now regretting it.

"Anything else?" Alla hoped she could hang up now and polish off the vodka. Prohibition be damned.

"You'll get a kick out of this: Rodolfo booked a room at the Hollywood Hotel but Jean locked him out. He pounded on the door, begging her to let him in, but she refused. Eventually he slunk away, back to his apartment."

"Jean spent her wedding night alone?"

"Well, evidently, she . . ." Another heavy pause, followed by a hoarse whisper. ". . . sought comfort in the arms of—of—"

"Grace Darmond," Alla finished for her.

Alla thanked Dagmar for letting her know and made an excuse to end the conversation. She crossed her parlor to retrieve her cigarettes. Dropping onto her sofa, she lit one and took a deep puff. The Metro bigwigs had bent over backward to throw their marginally talented $200-a-week contract player a wedding party, but they couldn't find their most important star a decent script?

No. That wouldn't do. Not at all.

* * *

Alla knew that if she had showed up to her meeting empty-handed, Mister Maxwell Karger would dismiss her as a complaining shrew who didn't know when she had it good, and would send her away like the obedient little puppet he wished she was. She had to go into his office armed with a plan.

For weeks now she had been ruminating about the play Nita Naldi was heading to New York for. Pierre Louÿs's novel, *Aphrodite*, had been both criticized as the worst of literary excess and lauded as the finest example of refinement. But it was also the best-selling work by any living French author. Three hundred and fifty thousand copies was a lot of mille-feuille, no matter which way you sliced it. Alla had read the French edition of *Aphrodite* but had mislaid it during one of her many moves. Los Angeles was hardly America's epicenter of culture, so she'd had to make do with an English translation she'd found in a second-hand bookstore near downtown L.A.

The story more than held up; it had electrified her. The plot encompassed everything: courtesans, sculptors, Greek goddesses, ancient Egypt, statues, hemlock, love and betrayal, and all set against the Lighthouse of Alexandria. Exotic, yes, but in a grand fashion, ready-made for film. Monsieur Louÿs had confirmed his willingness to sell her the American screen rights and wasn't even asking all that much, so Alla was ready to put up her dukes, as Americans were fond of saying.

She strode into Karger's office on the Metro lot and said, "You're going to listen to what I have to say, and you will let me say it, without interruption, until I'm done."

He puffed on his cheap-smelling domestic cigar and nodded as though to say, *Take your best shot*. He always gave the impression that whether he was talking about overcoat buttons, cast-iron skillets, silk ribbons, or motion pictures, everything was a product to be packaged and sold. All that mattered was that they generated more money than they cost. Alla's proposal was more expensive than her previous releases, so she figured she had a battle on her hands. But to his credit, he puffed away on his repellant cigar until Alla had finished.

"Okay. Fine. Draw me up a budget."

Had she worn him down with her relentless passion? Or had

he figured the sooner he agreed, the sooner he'd get her out of his hair? Alla didn't care. She had her 'yes.'

She flew back to her office as though she'd been dipped in kerosene and set aflame. Images burst from her imagination, as luxuriant as a Maxfield Parrish painting: a bevy of courtesans, draped in white poplin, decoratively deshabillé, their gold-and-black eye makeup radiant in the roseate gloaming behind them, hands outstretched, goblets of gold, pitch-black eunuchs pouring wine from silver urns.

The scenario would have to weave the plot with the characters so seamlessly that the audience couldn't help but be swept up into the spectacle. The title cards would have to be alluring, suggestive, outrageous, witty, and perhaps even shocking. Alla rewrote them over and over. The days and nights blurred into a feverish haze. After a couple of weeks, she fell into an enfeebled heap of crêpe de chine, perfumed cigarette butts, and empty coffee cups, and had scant idea what day it was.

She called Dagmar and pleaded down the line. "I need help, *chérie*. I cannot do it all by myself."

"Of course you can't, you absurd ninny!" Dagmar gave a gentle laugh that revived Alla's spirits. "You think Pickford does everything all on her lonesome? Tell me, which department do you feel weakest in?"

"Costumes." Alla had made some drawings, but they fell woefully short of the outlandish splendor she had in mind.

"I have just the person for you," Dagmar said. "He's been working for DeMille. Not only is he a ballet dancer, so he understands how costumes need to move, but he's Russian. The two of you will be utterly simpatico."

The man who arrived at Alla's doorstep two days later was a brooding scowler who wore a guarded smile. "Theodore Kosloff, at your service, Madame."

Alla welcomed him into her formal parlor and opened the last of her vodka. Although there was no telling when she might see another, *Aphrodite* was shaping up to be a top-notch picture so she decided to take the risk that someone somehow would provide her with more.

As she explained the plot and setting for the film, and her overarching vision, he nodded and nodded until she interrupted her discourse.

"Perhaps you might like to take some notes, Mr. Kosloff?" He had arrived carrying no briefcase. "I'd be more than happy to fetch some paper and pencils—"

He waved away the offer. "Not necessary."

Having lived among garrulous Americans for nearly fifteen years, Alla found the company of a taciturn Russki almost comforting. A gentle wave of nostalgia broke over her. She could smell her mother's pirozhki, fresh from the oven, the cabbage-and-potato-infused steam filling her nostrils. Her childhood had felt like the plot of a Grimm Brothers fairy tale, so revisiting her youth was a pastime she seldom indulged in. On the rare occasions she did, she was quickly reminded why: she had been an unhappy child trapped in abysmal circumstances over which she'd had no control. What was to be gained by looking back?

She brushed away her passing wistfulness. She needed the help of this aloof gentleman and had no time to waste.

When she was done, he thanked her for the opportunity, and told her that he would flesh out some sketches and send them over in due course. He was out the door before Alla could ask him to clarify what constituted "due course." By the end of the week? This time next month?

She felt it best not to press him too hard. She understood an artist's volatile nature, but prayed he wasn't like that. There was room for only one temperamental creative type on this project, and she had dibs on that title, thank you very much, Mister Theodore Kosloff.

* * *

"Due course" meant twelve days, as it turned out. Alla was hammering away at her Underwood #5, typewriting the scenario for the umpteenth time, when a knock on her Metro studio office door yanked her out of ancient Egypt. She needed a moment to take in the apparition that stood in the open doorway like a ballerina waiting in the wings.

Glossy dark hair framed a symmetrical face blessed with an unblemished pale complexion that had apparently rarely felt the sun. The woman penetrating her with aquamarine eyes possessed an ethereal beauty, but at the same time looked as though she saw through everyone and everything. "Madame Nazimova?"

Alla rose to her feet. "And you are . . .?"

The woman took a purposeful stride inside the doorway. No delicate tiptoe for her. As she moved forward, Alla noticed her silk Japanese kimono. It was crimson, trimmed with black, and eddied about her like mist. Beneath it, she wore a plain teal tunic that hung to her knees, and beneath that, a pair of matching trousers. The swirling kimono and long tunic almost hid them, but in an era when women didn't yet have the right to vote, the spectacle of a female in menswear was enough to cause pedestrians to walk into brick walls and motorists to drive off the road.

Who is this? Whatever she wants, she can have it.

The woman thrust out her hand. "My name is Natacha Rambova."

Her grip was firm, her self-assurance enthralling. Despite her name, however, Alla detected no trace of a Russian accent. She was American, that much was obvious. But oh, that skin! Alla now was close enough to see that it was as immaculate as it had looked from across the room. How old was she? Twenty? Forty? Two hundred and seventy-three? She bore a timeless quality that only enhanced her impenetrable allure.

"Have we met?" It was an unnecessary question. Nobody who met this woman was likely to forget her.

Miss Rambova held up a brown cardboard tube. "I have your *Aphrodite* costume sketches."

Alla cleared away the scattered detritus from her desk and invited this unruffled creature to join her. "I was expecting Mr. Kosloff. I take it that you're his secretary?"

Rambova's eyes flared as she extracted loose leaves from out of the tube. "No. I'm his—" She broke off and continued to remove the leaves in silence.

For someone who took pains to articulate each word with such precision, her choice to not finish the sentence came as a surprise. Perhaps she wasn't sure what she was. Kosloff's secretary? Assistant? Lover? All of the above? None of them? No, Alla decided, she knows who she is and what she wants. She's choosing not to tell me. But that's fine. I'll figure her out.

Rambova pulled a dozen sheets from the cylinder and unfurled them on the desk. Off to one side stood a miniature wooden rocking horse, ten inches high and painted in blues and reds; she used it as a paperweight to anchor one edge of the top sheet and flattened a palm on the other.

Alla studied Kosloff's sketches of somnolent courtesans in cream-colored cambric, priests in floor-length black vestments trimmed with gold, geometric peplums for the eunuchs. Each design resembled the ideas that had existed solely in Alla's imagination. *How remarkable!*

The fourth sketch was for the lead character, Chrysis, a golden-haired Galilean proud of her skill at securing the servility of men. Kosloff had designed a robe of diaphanous gauze that gathered around the décolletage in thin leather straps that would accentuate the bust. Alla had never been the most voluptuous of femmes fatales, so it was impressive that Kosloff had taken the time to design a costume that would show her meager assets in the most complimentary way. He had added a tan sash around the waist that would enhance her curves, such as they were. Since recoiling from the sight of herself in *Stronger Than Death*, Alla had adopted a vegetarian regime and the pounds were falling off.

"This is breathtaking," she murmured.

The woman said nothing.

Alla pointed to the sash. "This costume will billow around me in the merest puff of wind, so might it not be better if we enhanced the effect by making the ends of the sash hang lower?" She ran her finger to the ankles.

Rambova selected one of the sharpened pencils Alla kept in a glass jar and bent over the sketch. With a few quick brushes of an eraser, she extended the ends to the mid-shin. "What if we were to attach a little trinket? Not too heavy. Something with . . . hmmm . . ."

Alla breathed in her perfume. Unlike most women who bathed in theirs, Rambova had applied it lightly. It was Chypre by Coty, which meant that she had money. Or came from money. Either way, what was she doing working for a guy like Kosloff?

"Gravitas," Rambova said finally.

Alla was still preoccupied with the fragrance. "I'm sorry —what?"

"The sash." She drew a little bell on one end and an Egyptian ankh on the other. "If we attach something to the ends, I think it would lend your character gravitas. Personally, I prefer the ankh."

Alla did too, but was curious to know her reasons. "Go on."

The woman smiled for the first time, quiet and knowing, but it altered her delicate face, lending it a dash of humanity. "Ancient Egypt is a passion of mine. Cleopatra, Ramses II, Nefertiti, Hatshepsut. I find it all so endlessly fascinating."

Of the four pharaohs she had named, three of them were women. Was this girl sapphic?

It wasn't as though Alla had any sexual interest in this woman. For all Rambova's sphinxlike qualities, Alla wasn't interested in dragging her onto the nearest mattress. No, no, she realized, the attraction here was intellectual. After the Jean Acker - Grace Darmond - Rodolfo di Valentini quagmire, Alla needed a respite from love affairs for the time being. She longed to know this enigma better—if Rambova would allow it.

"I agree with you about the ankh, but won't Mr. Kosloff be annoyed with you altering his designs?"

"He probably would—if they were his. But this is my handiwork."

"You did all this?"

Rambova nodded.

"Does Kosloff often present your work as his?"

Her smile turned wry. "Mr. DeMille thinks Theodore is very talented."

Alla tsked. "And I think it's time you stepped out from everybody else's shadow."

Those cool, blue eyes dilated slightly. "I was hoping you'd say that."

"I want you to come work for me."

"Seriously?"

"When can you start?"

"Tomorrow."

"So soon? What will Kosloff think?"

"He's been taking credit for my work for far too long. What Kosloff thinks is no longer my concern."

Alla smiled. "My dear, I think you and I are going to create magnificent things together."

3

*A*lla picked up the latest issue of *Motion Picture* magazine and pointed to its cover painting of Lillian Gish looking virginal in a red blouse with a ruffled lace collar. She had met Lillian several times and reckoned her to be in her mid-twenties, but here she came across like she was twelve and had wandered off Sunnybrook Farm. "Have you read this?"

Natacha glanced at the magazine and frowned in that serious-as-brain-surgery way of hers that still, after weeks of working alongside her, continued to mystify Alla. Natacha returned to the photographic proofs that the Metro photographer had taken of her *Aphrodite* costumes. "Generally speaking, I don't read magazines. However, I heard the other day that *Vogue* will be bringing out a French version later this year. *Vogue Paris*, they're calling it. I imagine I'll pick up a copy. But why are you asking about *Motion Picture*? Are you in it again?"

Alla had appeared in the May 1920 issue. Like every movie magazine article, it was a fluff piece arranged by the studio's publicity department—if one man with nine fingers and a tenacious case of dandruff could be called 'a department.' *Motion Picture* had sent a slim-hipped pixie of a girl, young and inexperienced but blessed with a bawdy charm that put even a seasoned star like Alla at ease. The resulting article made her next movie, *Billions,* sound like it was poised to become the next *Birth of a Nation* instead of the over-baked mound of twaddle that Alla knew it to be.

She flipped through the June issue, affecting an air of nonchalance. "There's a most extraordinary article about Hollywood's sex life."

Natacha put down the proofs. "What about it?"

Alla held up the magazine long enough for Natacha to read the headline— HOLLYWOOD'S BOHEMIAN ENCLAVE—and then began reading the two-page spread.

"'As one observer describes it, the law of the colony is that everybody is entitled to do exactly as he or she sees fit in all personal matters. If you don't like it, you may stay away but you must not knock it.'" Alla stared into that perfect oval face with its meticulously outlined red lips. "Has that been your experience?"

Alla knew she was being terribly forward, but this was the first time she had met anyone who had erected a wall around themselves that her celebrity hadn't been able to breach. The more this woman kept her own counsel, the more curious Alla had become, and more determined she grew to peek inside.

"Life out here in Hollywood is like nowhere else." Natacha smiled gently. "It certainly isn't like this in Salt Lake City."

"Is that where you're from?"

"My mother was a member of a prominent Mormon family."

If Natacha had said 'Shakespearean thespians' or 'European aristocracy,' Alla wouldn't have been the least bit surprised. But this statue of theatrical sensuality with her ballerina-erect posture, her loose silky chemises of scarlet and purple, her flat slippers and chunky jewelry *came from Mormon stock*?

Alla smothered her astonishment enough to reply, "You don't say."

"My great-grandfather was Brigham Young's right-hand man. He had sixty-five children by forty-five wives."

"Sounds exhausting."

"It does, rather, doesn't it?"

"So I assume Natacha Rambova wasn't the name you came into this world with?"

The gentle smile hardened slightly at the edges. "If you were lumbered with Winifred Kimball Shaughnessy, wouldn't you change it?"

A crack in the wall at last! Alla let out a long sigh, taking care to make it as silent as she could. She extended her hand. "Winifred Kimball Shaughnessy, my name is Marem Adelaida Leventon. Pleased to meet you."

Natacha took her hand and shook it firmly. "Likewise."

"I do like it," Alla told her. "Natacha Rambova—it suits you."

"Winifred always felt like a name that belonged to somebody else. I figured I was stuck with it until I began studying under Theodore in his Imperial Russian Ballet Company. I felt more at home there than I did back in Salt Lake or the south of France. And then one day I realized I could be anybody I chose to be."

"It's quite a revelation when that happens, isn't it?"

"As soon as I landed on the name Natacha Rambova, I knew it was the right one."

"I've found that reinventing oneself has both its advantages and disadvantages, but when you're forced to escape a restrictive upbringing, what other choice do we have?"

"I was lucky in that respect," Natacha said, picking up her *L.A. Times*. "My mother did the escaping for me when she divorced my dipsomaniac of a father and married a chap named Edgar de Wolfe. Everything changed after that, including summers in France with his sister, Elsie."

Alla blinked. "Elsie? de Wolfe? Is your *aunt*?"

Elsie de Wolfe was the world's most famous interior decorator. Her clients included Stanford White, Oscar Wilde, George Bernard Shaw, and Henry Clay Frick, not to mention half the people photographed in the rotogravure. But of even keener interest to Alla was that Elsie de Wolfe shared a New York house with her—ahem—close friend, Bessie Marbury.

Alla looked at this young woman with fresh and admiring eyes. Puzzle pieces started falling into place. The dispassionate self-composure, the measured timbre of her voice, and how she didn't walk across a room so much as glide through it like an ice skater. These were the hallmarks of someone who didn't like who she was and had set about reinventing herself into someone whose exterior more closely matched her interior. It was a process Alla Nazimova knew all about.

Natacha pointed to the *Motion Picture* hanging from Alla's fingers. "What else does it say?"

Alla recommenced reading out loud.

"'In these days of suffragettes and long-haired poets, bifurcated skirts and lisping ladies, it is hard to know who's who and what's what. It's getting to be quite the rage – this exchange of identities.'" Alla lowered the magazine. "I'd be curious to hear your opinion."

Natacha lifted a non-committal shoulder. "*Vivre et laisser vivre*, I always say."

Given Alla's louche reputation, it came as a relief to know that this woman was not about to condemn Alla for whom she lured into her bedroom but instead followed a "live and let live" creed.

In the time they had worked together, Alla had recognized that this was a kindred spirit and intellectual equal. And although Alla doubted that Natacha took after her renowned aunt when it came to domestic cohabitation, in all other matters Natacha Rambova and Alla Nazimova were an ideal match.

She laid the magazine to one side and picked up a sheet of photographic proofs. The costumes Natacha had dreamed up for the Alexandrian high priests were as eye-catching as everything else her bounteous creativity invoked. Designed with dark velveteen because it photographed with less sheen, the cassocks had broad shoulders and buttons the size of silver dollars.

"I do love these," Alla said, "but I'm concerned they might be lost during the night scene in front of the lighthouse."

"I thought about that." Natacha reached for a fresh drawing

Alla hadn't seen yet. "What if we changed the lighthouse to Carrara marble? I came across a photo of Michelangelo's Pietà in Rome. It's a grayish-white, so it would make a nice contrast—"

"You can forget it." Maxwell Karger's voice cut through their conversation like a machete. His bunched fists sat jammed onto his hips and his chin was thrust out like a boxer's.

"What can we forget?"

"The whole thing."

Alla hoped he meant either of her upcoming releases. *The Brat* was ready to ship to theaters, and *Billions* was being edited. Compared to *Aphrodite,* they were frivolous trifles and Alla couldn't give a tinker's damn about whether or not they succeeded. Only *Aphrodite* occupied her thoughts.

"Mr. Karger." Alla mounted her most affable smile. "Please, do come in. Natacha and I were—"

"We're canceling *Aphrodite.*"

God forbid the man should exercise a soupçon of diplomacy when delivering a deathblow like this. Alla's heart grew leaden and sank slowly in her chest. "But why?"

He had never said as much, but Alla suspected that he was the type who viewed giving women the right to vote was the first step down the rocky path to anarchy. He made a clicking sound with his tongue as though to say "I'm not required to defend my executive decisions."

"Oh, come now, Mr. Karger." Alla softened her tone to coax an explanation out of this tightwad she was lumbered with. "If you're going to abandon what is shaping up to be one of the most singular films to have ever come out of Metro, the least you can do is explain why."

She had to put up with an overdramatic sigh, but she got her wish.

"Yesterday, the Supreme Court ruled that motion pictures are to be defined as a profit-making industry and therefore are not covered by the First Amendment's guarantee of freedom of speech.

If charged with obscenity and/or immorality, we could find ourselves liable."

"That's ridiculous." Alla whacked *Motion Picture* against the edge of her desk. "How is what we do any different from journalism? Or literature? Or painting? Or sculpture? It's a form of art that—"

"We're not making art here—"

"Maybe *you* are not." Alla's fingertips trembled. "However, I can assure you that it's the goal of—"

"We're making motion pictures, Miss Nazimova." He skewered each syllable of her name with contempt. "We are a commercial enterprise, not a charity. We must—"

"Don't talk to me like I'm a child!" An edge of shrillness had crept into her voice but she was powerless to stop it. "I know what's at stake. This is my career, too."

"This conversation is pointless because the Supreme Court of the United States has made a ruling, and now we must live with it."

Natacha let out an indignant huff.

"Since the day you brought your *Aphrodite* project to me," Karger continued, "I've been more than a little nervous. I said nothing because I respect your track record at the box office."

Alla wanted to say "You respect the profits I've made for your minor-league studio," but this was not the time for a hostile retort. At least, not if her precious *Aphrodite* could be saved from the trash heap.

Karger pulled at his necktie. "The subject matter of your picture is provocative, to say the least. It was a different story five years ago, perhaps even as recently as two. But not in this new environment. No, no. It's too risky."

"It doesn't have to be." Alla injected into her voice as much perkiness as she felt she could get away with. "If it's the courtesan angle that worries you, we could play it down. We could make her a—a—"

"Hedonist," Natacha suggested. "A free-spirited voluptuary who passes her days—"

"It's already done," he said. "I've issued a press release stating that *Aphrodite* is not suited to the requirements of Madame Nazimova."

He had made a crafty move. He knew Alla would be upset at this news but wasn't so worried about her feelings that he'd be open to reversing his decision. However, he did dull the blow by making it seem to the outside world that Madame Nazimova was in charge and that she had decided that *Aphrodite* fell short of her lofty standards. But as much as Alla appreciated his token gesture toward face-saving, she could see from the steely look in his eye that there was to be no changing his mind.

"Thank you for coming to tell us in person," she said. His Adam's apple jiggled up and down like a tiny chipmunk trapped in a paper sack. "We bid you a good day." Alla picked up the photographic proofs even though they had been rendered obsolete.

The two women listened to the sound of Karger's footsteps recede.

Natacha slapped the top of the desk with her open palm. It was the rashest thing Alla had seen her do in the whole time they'd known each other. "What a cowardly little nothing of a man! I'm sick of him and every blowhard like him. How do men like that rise to such power and influence?"

"They are the automatic inheritors by virtue of their sex."

"But aren't you angry?" Natacha asked. "Disappointed? Frustrated? Disenchanted at the very least?"

With anybody else, Alla would have laid a placating hand on her arm, but Natacha wasn't the type who welcomed physical contact.

"I'm all of those things. But if we screamed and cried and threw this lamp out the window, we'd be labeled over-emotional children incapable of making rational business decisions."

"But I *do* want to scream!" Natacha burst out. "I *do* want to cry! I want to throw this lamp out the window as far as I can!"

The Tiffany lamp with its pyramidal shade had set Alla back nearly two hundred dollars. It was an opening-night present she'd given herself as a memento of her Broadway debut in *Hedda Gabler* in 1906. It had been an outrageous indulgence at the time, and so she felt very attached to it.

"Let's go for a walk around the block." Alla plucked their hats off the rack in the corner. "It'll help clear our heads, and, with any luck, soothe our disappointment."

Metro's studios sat at the intersection of Cahuenga Boulevard and Romaine Street. The city of Hollywood was a patchwork of concreted streets without sidewalks and dirt roads with clumps of fiddleneck weeds reaching for the sun. They trudged along Romaine in silence.

After a block or two, Natacha shocked Alla by taking her arm. Revealing their real names to each other had felt to Alla like an important step in the evolution of their friendship, but she wasn't sure Natacha felt the same until she hugged Alla's arm to her side.

"You were absolutely right back there," Natacha said. "Flickers are no different from literature or painting or sculpture. They're another form of art and deserve to be taken seriously."

"Enough with orphans caught in the storm and mousy little secretaries in love with their bosses!" A dry wind gusted down from the Hollywood Hills and blew a cloud of dust around them. "Why aren't we filming *Jane Eyre*?"

"Or *Middlemarch*?"

"Or *The Scarlet Letter*?"

"*Tess of the D'Urbervilles*."

"*Madame Bovary*."

"*Madame Bovary*!" Natacha gripped Alla's upper arm with a strength Alla would scarcely have guessed she possessed. "When it was first published, they accused Flaubert of obscenity and now it's one of the most influential literary works in history."

Alla blinked. Natacha had conveyed what irked Alla most

about Karger's decision. What had been obscene fifty years ago was now a literary masterpiece. Yes, *Aphrodite* teemed with courtesans, but hadn't women like that existed ever since men decided they couldn't keep their peckers in their togas?

"Why should we care if some narrow-minded stick-in-the-mud spinster from Chattanooga objected because she might catch a peek at the side of my breast?" Alla declared. They stopped under a pepper tree to shade themselves from the June sun. "Nobody wins when everybody aims for the lowbrow."

"Mr. Karger's cash register might disagree."

"I'm not interested in cash registers—his or anyone else's. I want my pictures to be beautifully crafted, elegantly mounted—"

"Like a Botticelli!"

"Exactly. Is that too much to ask?"

They laughed because it was clear from the events of the last half-hour that it was, indeed, too much. But if there was a place for the Fatty Arbuckles and the Buster Keatons and the Mabel Normands to mug their way across the screen, then there must also be a place for the sort of literary classics Alla wanted to make.

A Chevrolet touring car puttered into view. It would have been a deep clover green when it first rolled out of the factory, but it was now chipped and faded and emitted pops and whimpers and large billows of smoke. They watched it pass until it disappeared around a corner.

"You know who else shares our opinion?" Natacha asked.

"Who?"

"June."

June Mathis was an explosion of a woman. Not terribly tall or especially attractive—certainly not by Hollywood standards—she nevertheless won everybody over by the sheer force of her enthusiasm. She brimmed with ideas every moment of her waking hours and left people with the impression that her bottomless well of inspiration pervaded half her sleeping hours too.

She had only been writing for a couple of years when Metro had appointed her as the head of their scenario department. By the time Alla and Natacha were stomping through the dust, she'd already written five pictures for Alla. Granted, they weren't *Middlemarch*, but she always did her best to spin gold from the dreck they handed her.

"Do you think she knows about *Aphrodite*?" Natacha asked. "I don't suppose Karger's told her."

"I'd bet my last dime he never gave her a second's thought." They started heading back to the studio gate. "I'd much rather she heard it from us."

June was reading from the page curled into her typewriter when Alla and Natacha walked into her office. As usual, the debris of a thousand notions stampeding through her imagination littered her desk. Not once had Alla ever seen it cleared of papers, clippings, magazine covers, and notes scrawled on the backs of envelopes and utility bills. Alla had once spied an idea for a movie that June had scribbled on the inside of a Juicy Fruit chewing-gum wrapper.

She peered at the two women over the top of her spectacles and broke into a smile. "Ladies! To what do I owe this pleasure?" She noted the hesitation playing across their faces. "Or heartbreak?"

She took the news better than Alla expected. "How very typical." She picked up her fountain pen and tapped it against an armrest. "I don't suppose there's any way we could change Karger's mind?"

"He's already sent out the press release."

She planted her fleshy elbows on her ink blotter. "If they won't let us make *Aphrodite*, the least they can do is let you choose your next film."

"Try telling Karger that," Natacha said.

June fixed Alla with her dark brown eyes. "If you could have your pick, what would it be?"

"Goodness, June, there's so much to choose from. So many roles I haven't tackled yet. I need a pen and paper to—"

"Don't think about it! Off the top of your head, what title makes you tingle with anticipation the way *Aphrodite* did?"

Alla blurted out the first one that came to her. "*Camille*." She had read Alexandre Dumas's novel when she was a teenager and had always imagined herself a perfect Marguerite Gautier.

June clapped her hands together as though in prayer. "Oh, Madame! That's perfection!"

"I have to agree," Natacha said. "It's ideal."

Alla waved away their enthusiasm. "No, no, no. We can't do *Camille*."

"Why ever not?"

"Because Clara Kimball Young did it in 1915 and Theda Bara did it a couple of years after that. Twice in the past five years is far too soon to be thinking of another version."

Alla could see June's cogs and gears already churning. "But they took the traditional route," she countered, "setting their picture in eighteen-forty-whenever-that-was. But what if we placed the story in modern times? Made it relevant to today?" She snapped her fingers. "Camille is a New Woman!"

The term had been gaining traction lately. The idea of a woman being married by eighteen, pregnant by nineteen, a mother by twenty and trapped for the next forty years in a marriage she may not have chosen herself was falling by the wayside. New Women smoked in public and drank like men. They enrolled in college to become doctors and lawyers. New Women weren't content to be mute satellites of their fathers and husbands and brothers. And they were more likely to marry later in life—or not at all.

And that was especially true now that they had won the fight for suffrage. With women entering polling booths, the future now promised a world that their sisterhood from previous generations could never have dreamed of.

"There is a Parisian designer, Emile-Jacques Ruhlmann." Natacha's eyes took on a faraway look. "He conjures the most superb designs. And then there's Hans Poelzig. He's an architect in Berlin. His interior décor is like nothing I've ever seen. If we're going to give Marguerite Gautier a New Woman makeover, I know exactly how to present her."

Alla waved her hands in the air. "You're forgetting that *Aphrodite* fell under the guillotine because Chrysis is a courtesan. And so is Marguerite. If we tell Karger we want to do *Camille*, he'll spit in our faces."

"However!" June held up a pudgy finger. "In American pictures, harlots must perish. Conveniently for us, Marguerite Gautier dies of consumption. She pays for her sins."

The three women sat in silence, mulling over June's point, until it dawned on them that they had come up with the perfect project: a story drawn from classic literature with relevance to twentieth-century audiences, featuring a strong woman's part that satisfied the strict directives foisted on them by the Supreme Court.

And best of all, it would give Alla a death scene—and that was one thing actresses could never resist. She broke into a beaming smile. "I believe we have a winner."

4

*A*lla spent Christmas Eve scribbling last-minute cards that would fail to arrive at the doors of their intended recipients on time. Normally she was as organized as a stiff-backed secretary when it came to social niceties like cards and gifts. But the Christmas season of 1920 had slipped away as she worked long days absorbed in preproduction for *Camille*.

Alla had been relieved when June told her, "Leave Karger to me." Any chance that he might redeem himself after being the best man at Jean Acker's wedding had sputtered out when he had canceled *Aphrodite*. If June wanted to approach him with their idea, well, then, that was fine by Alla.

In truth, June was better suited to the task. She was five years younger than Alla but possessed a comforting maternal quality. Maybe it was the matronly swell of her bosom that invited people to turn to her for sage advice like the babushkas from Alla's Crimean youth. Practically everybody at Metro studios came to June eventually: cameramen, script girls, crowd-scene extras—even the front-gate security guard, Mick, a weathered old-timer who had served in the Boxer Rebellion and rarely gave anybody more than an indifferent nod.

If the job of selling *Camille* had fallen to Alla, she would likely have charged in like a battleship and harangued Karger until he said yes—and then he would change his mind, as he had done with *Aphrodite*. But crafty old June had strolled in there, casual as a Sunday barbecue on Santa Monica beach, and sat down with an oh-and-by-the-way air. "I have a suggestion that I think will make you and Madame happy, *and* will overcome the objections of those censors."

She'd walked out with Karger's approval to announce *Camille* as Nazimova's next production.

That was all Natacha had needed to hear. She launched herself into designing a fabulous wardrobe for their Marguerite Gautier, and equally enthralling sets with which to frame her.

Bored with writing out the usual Christmastime bromides, Alla drifted into a meditation on the creative life. One minute your picture is a hit and you're on top of the clouds. But let a tactless remark slip during an interview and your next effort is playing to empty houses. You start working on a project that throws open your creative floodgates, causing you to leap from your bed each morning, and then the project is ditched and you feel like shriveling up into a ball, never wanting to leave the house. And then you happen upon *Camille* and your mind is awhirl once more.

Alla tapped the nib of her fountain pen. *Any normal person would think that after a lifetime of riding life's highs and suffering its lows that I'd learn to temper my expectations. But I throw my heart and soul into what I am doing. I cannot operate any other way—nor do I want to. Spend my days pecking at a comptometer or standing behind a notions counter, a pink grosgrain ribbon tied in my hair as I maintain a vacant smile to hide my slowly decomposing soul? Hand me the hemlock right this very minute.*

Ray Smallwood walked into her office, derailing her reverie. He was a fastidiously dressed gentleman in his early thirties who had directed her in *Billions* and the recently released *Madame Peacock* in which she'd played a headstrong actress who abandons her family for the irresistible lure of the stage. They had developed the trusting relationship that a lead actress should foster with her director if there was to be any hope of an authentically realized portrayal. Despite *Madame Peacock*'s dismal performance at the box office, she had chosen Ray as her *Camille* director. From the tentative way he lingered, however, Alla could tell he was a reluctant herald.

She thrust her pen to one side. "Should I assume that you haven't come to wish me a warm and merry Christmas?"

He sat himself in a visitor chair. "I come bearing good news and bad."

"Let's start with the bad and get it out of the way."

"We've tested Raymond Bloomer from *The Belle of New York* but he's all wrong for Armand."

"And Jack Holt?"

"Too old."

"Wallace Reid?"

"Still recovering from the injuries he sustained in that train crash while he was filming *The Valley of the Giants* with—" Alla appreciated how he stopped himself before he identified Reid's costar. Grace Darmond was a name that still stung. "And anyhow, he wasn't right," Ray added, "He's a handsome rake, God knows, but too all-American to play a young French law student."

Alla drummed her fingernails against the desktop to blunt her growing despair. Armand Duval was the romantic lead and the only role still not cast. "We only had three names on that list."

"Which brings me to the good news."

"You're going to tell me that Douglas Fairbanks is so desperate to play Armand that he's willing to do it for free."

"Chance would be a fine thing. I'm here because June wants you to meet her in the screening room."

"When?"

"Right now."

Alla glanced at the clock on the wall behind him. "Four o'clock on Christmas Eve?"

"It'll be worth your while."

• • •

The screening room at Metro wasn't much bigger than Alla's formal parlor. It contained five rows of six seats, each of them as comfortable as a sack of frozen potatoes.

Alla walked into the fusty room expecting to find it empty—punctuality was not among June's virtues—but she had already installed herself in the second row.

"Madame!" The sterling silver charms on her bracelet tinkled as she waved Alla closer. "Do I have a treat for you!"

Alla dropped into the chair next to June's. "Ray told me that neither Raymond, Jack, Wallace, nor Douglas are right for Armand."

"Douglas who?"

"Private joke. Never mind. Tell me why I'm here."

June picked up the telephone to her left and told the projectionist that they were ready. The screen flickered to life and a title card appeared.

METRO presents
REX INGRAM'S production of
VICENTE BLASCO IBAÑEZ's
literary masterpiece
THE FOUR HORSEMEN
OF THE APOCALYPSE

followed by a second one,

Directed and Supervised by
REX INGRAM

and then a third.

Written for the screen by
JUNE MATHIS

The Four Horsemen of the Apocalypse had been a gargantuan undertaking by anyone's standards, let alone by a relatively small studio like Metro. Its budget was a staggering $800,000, and directing the picture was such a strenuous undertaking that Rex had needed fourteen assistants to help him corral twelve thousand extras. The ambitious artiste in Alla fought off the pangs of jealousy as the opening credits appeared. With so much at stake, Metro was planning to go all-out to build *The Four Horsemen of the Apocalypse* into a triumph. To be a part of an era-defining event was the ultimate dream of every performer, but Alla didn't appear in this picture, let alone at the center of it. Plus, she had other matters on her mind.

"June, my darling," she said, "I'm sure you're very proud of your work, but it's Christmas Eve and I've got—"

"I didn't ask you here to see the picture."

"Why am I here, then?"

"SHUSH!"

The preface appeared on the screen.

In a world old with hatred and bloodshed, where nation is crowded against nation and creed against creed, centuries of wars have sown their bitter seed, and the fires of resentment smouldering beneath the crust of civilization but await the breaking of the Seven Seals of Prophesy to start a mighty conflagration.

. . .

Alla didn't know what breaking the Seven Seals of Prophesy was or what it entailed, but this was not how she wanted to spend her Christmas Eve.

The next title card talked about the Argentine and toiling in vast grazing lands, but Alla wasn't paying much attention. Dagmar Godowsky had invited her to a house party near the Hal Roach studios in Culver City. Her father, the renowned pianist Leopold Godowsky, was going to be treating the guests to his dazzling technique and Alla wanted to meet him in the hope of convincing him to attend one of her Saturday night salons.

The opening scene revealed a lone gaucho wearing a checkered shirt. He sat astride his horse as he looked out across the pampas filled with cattle roaming the treeless countryside, scrounging for whatever sustenance they could find.

A couple of scenes later, the action changed to a smoky bar and the title card talked of a young libertine named Julio. The card gave way to a handsome cad wearing a dark bolero hat and taking a sip of his beer. Turning to his left, he gave the audience a chance to take in his striking profile, but only for a few seconds. He faced the camera again, offering the audience a second opportunity to drink their fill of his nakedly animalistic charisma.

As the couple on the saloon's dance floor launched into a tango, this Argentine rake sprang to his feet. He deftly supplanted the male dancer and, taking the señorita in his arms, proceeded to lead her in a wide circle as though nobody were watching.

June nudged Alla. "So what do you think?"

"Don't be silly, my little *lapochka*. The film has barely begun."

"I'm talking about the gaucho get-up with the tango hips. Photographs well, doesn't he?"

"He's got a special something."

"What do you think about casting him as Armand?"

Alla watched the roué glide and hop and float his partner around the smoky dance floor. The tango came to an end. The libertine from the Argentine escorted his señorita back to his table, where he offered her a drink as the camera pushed in for another glowering, lustful close-up.

Alla lurched forward in her seat, her fists clenched in resentment. *Him? Metro had cast this guy in the lead of their most ambitious picture?* "Do you know who that is? His name is Rodolfo—"

"He goes by Rudolph Valentino now, and he—"

"Do you know of his scandalous past? The Blanca de Saulles shooting, not to mention how he—he—"

More than a year later, Jean's snub still grated. On only the odd occasion did Alla permit herself to mull over what had happened. And when she did, she was powerless to overcome the morose tentacles of her Russian nature.

June pressed her hand to Alla's. "I know all about him and what happened."

Alla pulled away. "I don't think you do."

"It's not like Blanca de Saulles killed her husband out of love for Rudy. She killed her husband because she hated him. The poor schmuck was just an innocent bystander and was forced to leave town because of notoriety he didn't ask for."

Alla struggled to fit this nugget into her theory. "That may or may not be true—"

"He told me the whole story."

"There's more to it than that. There's personal history between us that I cannot overlook. I'm sorry, June, but this Rodolfo—"

"It's Rudolph—"

"Rudolph, Rodolfo, or Rumpelstiltskin—it matters not." Alla could feel her *La Grande Dame* persona taking over. Any moment now, she would gather herself together and stride from the room with all the outrage and indignation she could muster, which, it could not be denied, was substantial. "Even an actress of my range cannot hide abhorrence of a leading man," she told June. "It will show, plain as day, in our close-ups. So if you have brought me here to convince me to cast that philanderer, you've wasted your time as well as mine."

"He told me what happened that night at the Ship Café and

meeting Jean Acker and all about their rushed marriage. You need to know that he regrets it, all of it. He genuinely believed Jean was as in love with him as he was with her."

"In that case, he's a fool." Alla flew to her feet. "And I refuse to work with fools." The silhouette of her head blocked out di Valentini's face on the screen. *The less I see of him, the better.*

What unsettled Alla most wasn't that Jean had chosen Grace over her, or that she had up and married this amateur. Lovers, they come, they go. It was simply what happened when one lived life guided by one's passions. But what this business with Jean and Grace and Valentini had brought home was the inescapable slap in the face that this was what happened when a woman turned forty. *You can no longer beguile potential bed partners with your looks alone. Sooner or later you were bound to reach the point where being The Great Nazimova isn't enough.*

"That's the word he used: fool." June was employing her gentle maternal voice now. "Jean's rejection was thoroughly humiliating." She paused, then added, "I suspect you know how that feels." Alla felt *La Grande Dame* thaw around the edges, but pride prevented her from showing it, even to Mama Mathis. So when June wrapped her fingers around Alla's wrist, Alla didn't yank it away. She let herself be drawn back into her seat, where she mumbled and harrumphed and clicked her tongue disapprovingly but continued to watch the film unspool.

Another close-up. Another profile. Alla hadn't been following the story so she no longer knew what was happening, but she did know that this di Valentini, or whatever name he went by now, could certainly fill a screen with a mischievous wink or a sad smile.

June jabbed Alla's shoulder. "Here's what you need to do, Madame."

Alla raised an eyebrow. *And what is that, pray tell?*

"Take off your scorned lover chapeau and put on your hardheaded businesswoman helmet. You need to keep watching this picture clear through to the end before you reject the actor who is, in my estimation, perfect for Armand Duval. Can you do that?"

Alla uncrossed her arms, faced forward, let out a deep sigh, and continued watching *The Four Horsemen of the Apocalypse* with fresh eyes.

By the time THE END appeared, Alla was more won over than she could have predicted. Di Valentini's performance was so mesmerizing that it was no wonder June had become his most ardent booster. Alla had always admired June's knack for spotting nascent talent and finding the right property that enabled those gifts to blossom. Di Valentini shone like no previous male leading man, and it was obvious to Alla that he could become an overnight sensation when *Four Horsemen* was released.

He was also under contract with Metro, which meant they could get him cheaply. Once his star began its inevitable trajectory, however, the screen's newest heartthrob might complicate their budget. A sensible businesswoman would have known that she ought to put her feelings aside and make the obvious, sober, levelheaded decision. But Alla never claimed to be sensible. Nor did she claim to be a businesswoman, for that matter.

As the lights in the screening room came up, she continued to teeter-totter as she asked herself: *Could I make convincing love to the man who had made love to my most recent lover?*

June whispered, "Just say hello."

Alla let out a groan of resignation designed to remind June that one didn't get to be Hollywood's highest-paid actress by being as malleable as melted candle wax. "Set up a meeting."

June got to her feet. "No time like the present."

"Right now?"

As they stepped into the crisp evening air, Alla asked where they were going.

"My office."

"He's there? This Rudolph Valentino of yours?"

"Come on, he's been waiting long enough."

If anyone else had pulled a stunt like this on her, Alla would have marched away, spouting indignation and outrage. But June's intentions were always pure, and, Alla had to admit, her protégé did have a certain something.

June's office was only a short walk away. She ushered Alla inside, where a gentleman dressed in a sharply tailored suit of slate-gray serge was leaning against a filing cabinet smoking a pungent cigarette that Alla knew could not have been American.

He straightened up and rushed toward them. "Madame!" he exclaimed, his dark brown eyes dancing like wood sprites. "You saw *The Four Horsemen of the Apocalypse*, si? You liked, si? And my performance? I pray that you enjoyed it because your approval means more to me than my English will allow."

Even Alla, who had rarely been susceptible to manly sex appeal, had to admit that the guy reeked of it—on the screen.

In person, though, he was all unaffected boyishness.

He grabbed up her hand—not that she had offered it to him— and nattered about the advantages of living in Los Angeles over New York, and how one must moderate a stage performance for the demands of motion picture cameras. Without stopping to draw breath, he shifted to his love for homemade meatballs and how difficult it was to find decent chianti in California. "Ah!" he exclaimed, the fingers of each hand pressed together into a point, "but when you find it, all the memories of the home come rushing back. You must know what I mean, Madame."

His seven-minute monologue had rendered Alla mute. Where was that Casanova who had burned fiercer than a bonfire? Where was the lady-killer who could take the heart of any woman he wanted? In real life, this Valentino was nothing like the presence he projected on the screen. Which means, Alla told herself, the boy really can act.

He frowned at her, puzzled by the silence. "It is the same when you are drinking the vodka of Russia, no?"

Now and then, when Alla passed a restaurant, she would find

herself salivating over the memory of a dish of borscht or plate of pelmeni or a piping-hot knish, and suddenly Mother Russia felt like it lay on the far side of the moon. So yes, Alla Nazimova understood what it was like to feel homesick for a distant country. It appeared that she had more in common with this unassuming beguiler than with the fickle heart of Miss Jean Acker.

And more to the point, Mama June was right. Of course she was. She always was. It was time for Alla to put on her businesswoman hat. The smart choice was to cast this intriguing charmer.

Alla lifted her chin slightly. "Signore Valentino," she said, adding a subtle hint of Italian accent to her words, "I would be delighted if you agreed to play Armand Duval to my Marguerite Gautier."

5

*E*arly in the New Year, Natacha walked into Alla's office and held up a large sheet of white paper. She had sketched a glorious floor-length wrap made of diaphanous green-tinted gauze on which she had painted large mauve camellias. "What do you think?"

"Need you even ask?"

It hadn't taken the two women long to see that they were boon companions who desired to waste no time now that their paths had crossed. They would meet for cocktails at a Culver City speakeasy called The Hot Spot, or afternoon tea at Henry's Café, or hamburger dinners at Sternberger's on Vine Street and gab, gab, gab the night away.

Natacha was the first woman Alla had ever met who could talk about Nietzsche philosophy one minute and in the next, appraise the historical accuracy of the earrings Pola Negri wore as Madame du Barry in *Passion*.

One night at Hollywood Boulevard's newest in-spot, Musso and Frank Grill, she had talked about the recent Finnish declaration of independence from Russia, the work of Emmeline Pankhurst, the life of an Egyptian slave in the time of Cleopatra, and then reviewed the most recent rendition of the *George White's*

Scandals currently shocking Broadway audiences. And that was before their roast capons had arrived.

Natacha was also the first person who'd ever uttered the name "Coco Chanel" in Alla's presence. For that reason alone, Alla felt that the woman deserved her undying loyalty.

Finally, she had met someone who could see the same potential in motion pictures that she saw. They both wanted to imbue filmmaking with substance, explore the human condition, add to the collective understanding of what it meant to be a sentient being in the modern world.

Most Sunday mornings, Natacha appeared at Alla's doorstep, newspapers under her arm and dressed in Chinese silk lounging pajamas. Alla would make coffee and bake sweet rolls—her kitchen skills were negligible, but her sweet rolls were a source of pride—and they would sprawl out on the floor of Alla's parlor with their cups and cigarettes, quoting headlines and interesting tidbits to each other.

Until Natacha Rambova, Alla had met very few people with whom she could sit in the blissfulness of an easy silence and not feel the need to cram it with inane prattle. Her new friend valued the economy of words, rarely wasting them on any subject she hadn't given much deliberation. But when she did speak, it was always worth listening.

Alla took the sketch from her. "Oh, my!"

"It's for your first scene when you exit from your private box at the Paris opera. You need to be wearing a memorable outfit."

"It certainly is that." Alla ran a fingernail down the silhouette of the billowing train. "And underneath?"

"I haven't sketched it out yet, but I'm picturing a sheath. Quite tight, so it might be hard to walk, but it'll emphasize that slim figure you've worked hard to achieve." Alla had now dropped twelve pounds, thanks to her vegetarian diet. "With a hoop around the neck and a white camellia at the base of your throat."

Alla was about to tell her that she loved it when a snow-covered mountain explorer filled the doorway and pulled back the fur-lined edge of his hood. Tiny white flakes of shaved mica filled his hair. It had collected in the crevices of his ears and the edges of his mouth; a few rested on his enviably long eyelashes.

"Madame!" He smiled to reveal his row of gleaming white teeth.

"Signore Valentino, what a surprise to see you." Alla was glad that she had taken June's sage advice and cast Valentino. He had a disarming way about him that was part-naïve, part-flirtatious, part-pliable, and Alla could now see why Mrs. de Saulles might have shot her ex-husband over him. She waved a hand over his padded jumpsuit of dark leather. "Been out climbing Mt. Everest, I see."

He laughed easily, which was, Alla had discovered, a genuine and appealing trait. "The Arctic. But snow is snow, si?" He dusted mica from his shoulders; it floated to Alla's carpet. "We had a break in filming so I come to ask you where is my script?"

Natacha had been standing off to the side, blocked by the fur cowl. She brushed away a lock of hair. It was a slight movement, but enough.

"Oh, but please excuse me, ma'am. I did not see you." He spotted the sketch on the desk. "You are having a meeting and I burst in here like the Yeti from Nepal."

Alla raised a hand. "Rudolph Valentino, I'd like to present our costumer and art director, Miss Natacha Rambova. Natacha, this is Rudolph Valentino, who will be playing Armand Duval."

Rudy raised his eyebrows. "Miss Rambova, it is a pleasure."

To an outside observer unused to perceiving the subtle signals that Natacha threw out, it might have appeared that she was unimpressed by this robust slab of manhood who Alla felt was on the verge of redefining the male romantic lead in American pictures.

Her smile was perfunctory, her posture rigid, her hands immobile.

But Alla caught the sudden flaring of Natacha's nostrils and her intake of air. It was shallow and almost silent, but she detected it nonetheless.

"I'm sorry, Rudy," Alla said, "but June hasn't finished it yet. Once Metro pushed back *Camille* until your current picture—remind me what it's called?"

His eyes remained stuck on Natacha, who was looking over a second sketch she'd brought with her. "*Uncharted Seas*."

"Yes, of course. At any rate, Karger gave his consent to cast you in our picture but only if we were willing to hold off production until you were finished."

He pulled his gaze away. "I'm sorry if I caused you any inconvenience."

"As a matter of fact, it has given us some breathing space to get everything exactly how we want it. Isn't that right, *Natousya*?"

Natacha didn't look up from her sketch but instead nodded and let out an agreeable murmur.

"Thank you for stopping by." Alla guided him out into the corridor. "I'll have the studio messenger get you the scenario as soon as June and I have completed it."

"Thank you, Madame. And it was a pleasure, Miss Rambova."

"Likewise, Mr. Valentino."

Alla closed the door behind him.

"So that's the guy everybody insists will be the next big sensation?"

Natacha used a tone that was supposed to say *I don't get it*, but Alla could read the girl like a banner headline in the *L.A. Times*. Mr. Valentino had made more of an impression than he realized.

* * *

Alla and Charles's chauffeur rounded the corner onto Broadway in downtown Los Angeles and hit a headache-inducing traffic snarl. The red taillights ahead of them lent a rosy glow to Alla's husband's face. He craned his neck and tsked like an old spinster.

"For crying out loud! What the hell's all this?"

None of the motorcars lining Broadway were moving. The pedestrians packing the sidewalks had resorted to elbowing each other out of the way as they headed past Eighth Street to the Mission Theater.

Hardly an Angeleno over the age of twelve hadn't heard of the superheated splash Rudy had made at the New York premiere of *The Four Horsemen of the Apocalypse*. The press had covered acres of newsprint extolling his performance and how it had left even the most hard-bitten New York women tingling with his untethered sexual force, and how they had left the Lyric Theater with "their faces contorted with pent-up concupiscence." Alla had needed to look up the meaning of that last word and when she did—"A desire for sexual intimacy; Sexual lust; Morbid carnal passion"—she'd laughed out loud.

Not because it wasn't true, but because that naïve puppy with his sainted mother's spaghetti sauce recipe, his weakness for bespoke suits, and his unguarded willingness to please was nothing like that swoon-inducing lothario he played. But he underwent an ineffable transformation when he stood in front of a camera. He had the type of persona that encouraged fans to see what they wanted to see. If the New York papers were anything to go by, a great number of American women were sadly lacking in the fornication department.

And now it was Los Angeles's turn to fall under his spell.

When Alla had first watched the picture, she'd been too distracted by June's outrageous suggestion that they cast a notorious taxi-dancing gigolo opposite her, so she wanted to see it again and had cajoled tickets out of Maxwell Karger. She *needed* to see it again. The reaction in New York could have been an aberration. It wouldn't have been the first time that a picture had quickly sunk from sight beyond the five boroughs.

"The picture starts in less than twenty minutes," Alla said.

Charles grunted. "What do you want me to do about it? Get out and play traffic cop?"

When Alla had told him they had tickets to the *Four Horsemen* premiere, she had expected him to be excited to see the source of all the fuss, but he had instead reacted with crotchety impatience ever since.

She pushed against the car door handle. "We'll have to walk."

"To a premiere? But everybody will be there, not to mention the entire contingent of press this side of the Rockies. I will *not* be walking!"

It was times like this that Alla questioned why she persisted with this marital pretense. They presented to the world as though they were legally bonded in a state of matrimonial bliss. However, it had been born of a face-saving lie, convenient at the time but had gone on too long to correct.

God knows she had tried several times in both Russia and America to divorce Sergei Golovin, whom she'd married in haste in 1899; she'd immediately regretted it and had separated from him soon afterwards. But the mail to and from Russia was unreliable—especially as Sergei was an itinerant actor and hard to track down. She suspected that he secretly enjoyed the idea that he was married to one of the biggest stars in America and wasn't about to give up *that* status.

One day, during the run of her third Broadway play, a bunch of theater people had landed on the doorstep of her Hotel Des Artistes apartment overlooking Central Park. During the ensuing impromptu party, cocktails had flowed, tongues had loosened, and questions had surfaced about Alla and Charles. They had done several plays and had frequently been thrown into each other's company. By this time, she and Charles had slept together on a number of occasions. The sex was, well, it was fine, she supposed. Not the type to make her toes curl, but those sorts of lovers were rare and she'd certainly had worse. Sergei Golovin, for starters. But Charles was companionable and his conversation was congenial. So without thinking, Alla had assured everyone at the party that she and Charles had gotten married. Just a private ceremony, she had said. The two of them, a witness, and the justice of the peace.

Alla assumed that nobody gave a fig one way or the other. But within days, people were sending telegrams and cards, cornering her at suppers, congratulating her on the marriage, and hoping they were supremely happy. The rumor train had charged out of Penn Station at full steam and there was no pulling the emergency cord.

And then a most unexpected thing had happened.

She and Charles started getting invited to dinner parties and theatrical openings, art exhibits and invitation-only cocktail soirees. A cloak of propriety settled around Alla's shoulders as a whole new vista of doors opened wide and she found herself welcomed like a returning prodigal daughter.

She had only ever been on the outside looking in, so this new development had all been so seductive. First, a poor child—and worse, a mere girl—then a penniless student. Even when she'd arrived in America, learned English in less than six months, and conquered Broadway in *A Doll's House*, she was still an actress, which was a polite way of saying "harlot, hussy, and husband-stealer." She got plenty of invitations, but not into the homes of respectable society.

Suddenly there she was, and all because she was married—or so everybody thought.

It hadn't taken her long to find that, generally speaking, society people were insufferable bores with limited worldviews. They rarely ventured off their narrow paths through life, and so the same faces popped up over and over. None of them did anything interesting, and so their conversation revolved around nothing more stimulating than how hard it was to find good help. The whole scene was dull beyond endurance, so Alla stopped accepting invitations and threw out the RSVP cards. No more talk of opening night at the opera, the summer sailing at Montauk, or the latest celebrity debutante of the season.

Being liberated from New York society had felt like losing twenty-five pounds of useless blubber—but she was stuck with everybody in New York assuming that Charles Bryant and Alla Nazimova were man and wife. And when Metro had come calling, they had been forced to continue the charade.

But four years and ten movies later, Charles was starting to feel like a dead weight around Alla's neck. The cordial conversation and serviceable sex were now in the long-distant past, leaving them to be not so much a couple but two people who lived under the same roof. She had given him the director's credit on *Stronger Than Death*, not because he did any of the directing—Alla had done all that—but because a picture directed by a woman wasn't what people expected. This wasn't 1912 anymore, when men didn't care about the flickers and let the women do what they wanted. Films were now an industry. They made tons of money. So naturally the menfolk had elbowed the women aside, telling them that they could go back to baking cakes and darning socks. We'll take it from here, girls.

Alla pushed open her car door. "Very well, then," she told Charles. "Suit yourself." She fished his ticket out of her purse and threw it at him. "I'll see you in the tenth row. Or not."

The night air throbbed with anticipation. The sidewalks were too jam-packed to gain a foothold, so she stayed on the road and marched up Broadway.

As practical as this solution may have been, Charles had a point. Stars of Alla's stature were expected to step out of limousines resplendent in gowns designed to make female onlookers curdle with jealousy. And they must wave to the crowds with enough detached aloofness to maintain the mystery but imbue their smiles with a sufficient warmth to show how much they appreciated their fans.

But for Nazimova to walk up to the front doors of the Mission Theatre like she was a member of the hoi polloi? It simply wasn't done. And had this been any old premiere, Alla mightn't have stepped out of that automobile at all. But if she were to play opposite America's newest, steamiest, most seductive leading man, she needed to study what he did on screen so that she could counterbalance it to prevent getting upstaged—unintentionally or otherwise.

Dodging town cars, taxicabs, and the odd flivver, she made it as far as the twinkling lights without being recognized. And then she heard, "Oh, Madame! I was hoping to see you!"

Grace Kingsley was the *L.A. Times*'s first columnist to focus on the entertainment industry. Her appointment had signaled that the *Times* now took the film business seriously, and she had proved to be a skilled and popular reporter. Approaching fifty, with a faintly mannish way about her and no trace of a husband, did Kingsley share a clandestine trait with her, Alla wondered? It was hard to broach the subject without risking offense, and that was the last thing Alla wished to do.

The crowd—almost all of them female, their eyes glazed with hope—pressed in against them. Alla exclaimed, "What a commotion!"

Grace pulled a face of mock-horror. "These ladies look like they're ready to set their hair on fire. Oh, but you're not here unescorted, are you?"

"I seem to have lost my husband in all this hurly-burly." Alla made a show of looking around for Charles, even though he was probably still sitting in the limousine, having ordered their chauffeur to return home at the first opportunity. Alla linked her arm through Grace's. "Let's run the gauntlet together!"

She acknowledged the cries of "Madame!" and "Nazimova!" with a wave as they plowed through the hordes.

Then, suddenly, a chant broke out, rising in pitch with every iteration. "VAL-EN-TIN-O! VAL-EN-TIN-O!" And, like a dolphin surfacing, Rudy broke free of the mob. He was dressed in a smart tuxedo; his face glimmered in the light from the marquee above his head. The smile plastered on his face almost reached from ear to ear. Alla didn't blame him for drinking it all in like a vagrant lost in the desert. Since arriving in America, he had experienced more famines than feasts. A few times, he had faced an encroaching night without a bed to sleep in or a meal to fill his belly. And now all the world pleaded for him to bestow a wink or a kiss.

It took Alla a moment to notice the woman on his arm.

Natacha had wrapped her head in a turban of dark blue satin;

her long hair was braided into a tightly woven arrangement that hugged the nape of her neck. Her dress was several shades lighter; two thin straps of miniature pearls kept it from falling from her bosom—a rather risky design given how little it would have taken for the surrounding zealots to tear the whole ensemble asunder.

Much fuss had been made in the papers of Rudy and Natacha's public debut a few weeks before. They had attended a costume ball at the swankiest place in town: the Alexandria Hotel near Pershing Square. Dressed as tango dancers, they had captured most of the attention that night, and had made headlines in the newspapers the following morning.

Alla hadn't seen Natacha until several days later, when she had come knocking with four possible hairstyles for Marguerite Gautier. She hadn't brought up the night of the ball, so Alla hadn't either. They'd discussed the pros and cons of each hairdo and decided on the large fluffy halo.

In the days and weeks that followed, Natacha had peppered her conversation with references to Rudy. How she'd helped him shop for a top hat or how they had painted the living room of her rented duplex. But she had never sidled up to Alla and whispered, "You won't guess where Rudy and I went last night!" the way most women did with intimate girlfriends.

Now, underneath the Mission Theatre's marquee, Alla managed to catch Natacha's eye. She smiled her hello and raised her eyebrows as though to say, Well, now, isn't *this* exciting? Natacha lifted her chin as though to reply, It most certainly is.

Seeing Rudy and Natacha together came as more of a shock than it should have, leaving Alla to wonder why. It was hard to think clearly amid the pushing and shoving outside the theater, but Alla suspected these were twinges of jealousy she was feeling. Natacha had found someone special. They certainly made a striking couple. *And what do I have? A grumpy husband who isn't even that.*

Alla turned back to Grace. "Shall we?"

• • •

When THE END title card appeared on the screen, nobody in the audience made a sound. Alla shuddered with alarm: the hullabaloo in New York had sent Angelenos' expectations sky high, and Rudy's performance had failed to meet them. *Camille* was to commence shooting in four days and they had cast the biggest disappointment of the year.

Quel désastre!

But Alla should have waited three more seconds.

The audience needed to catch its collective breath before it unleashed a thunderous tumult.

"BRAVO! BRAVO!"

Soon, they were calling out Rudy's name, and their cries quickly coalesced into a rhythmic chant. A portly gent hustled him down the side aisle, up the steps and onto the stage. The audience maintained its applause as everybody rose to their feet. He pressed the flattened palms of his hands to his chest and nodded in appreciation, mouthing the words "Thank you!" over and over. Maybe it was fortunate that nobody had set up a microphone, Alla thought: the kid was too overwhelmed to string together a coherent response. He was now learning what Alla had grasped years ago: Sometimes words get in the way. It is better to let the adoration wash over you.

* * *

The exhilaration that followed the unleashing of *The Four Horsemen of the Apocalypse* upon the sex-starved movie-going public buoyed the *Camille* cast and crew through the first two weeks of filming. Every day brought news of box office records broken, avalanches of fan mail to the studio gates, and essays on how Valentino's redefinition of masculinity had shattered the Victorian-era model of what women wanted in a lover.

New Women had won the vote. New Women could seek out speakeasies and drink their male companions under the table if that's what they chose. And better yet, not be written off as guttersnipes and prostitutes. And this Rudolph Valentino, with his volcanic eyes that promised nights of guilt-free sin, was what the women had wanted all along but had been too demure to ask.

The bosses at Metro were, of course, rubbing their metaphoric hands with glee at the prospect of finding they had America's most-desired sex symbol under contract. Secretly, though, Alla suspected they were surprised that Rudy had rocketed to stardom amid an explosion of unprecedented fervor. In her experience, neither Maxwell Karger nor Richard Rowland had June Mathis's talent for spotting potential or her ability to foresee what—or who —was likely to spark the public's imagination. Alla herself had failed to see Rudy's potency. But it wasn't her job to discern such possibilities—it was theirs, and they had struck gold in places they weren't even looking.

Day seventeen of filming *Camille* was a Wednesday, but it wasn't just any old Wednesday; it was the day they were to film Alla's death scene. Marguerite Gautier was literature's most famous consumptive, so every detail had to be exactly right, every gesture truthful, every expression agonizing.

Natacha's boudoir set dazzled in its simplicity. She had taken her inspiration from the title of Alexandre Dumas's novel, *La Dame aux Camélias*, and made everything circular like a camellia: the bedroom, the bed, the bedhead, and even the cushions.

The crew fussed and fiddled with their responsibilities: curtains, lights, props. Alla sat on the edge of the bed, minimizing her movements. *Your consumption is killing you. Your lungs are filling with sputum faster than you can cough it up. Blood splatters your handkerchief. Your nights are sweaty, your appetite has receded, and fatigue burdens your every move. Time is slipping from your grasp. The shadow of oblivion stretches across you.*

"Madame!" Her director, Ray, dropped beside her with the enthusiasm of a teenager. He held a copy of the *Times* opened at Grace Kingsley's column. "Have you seen?"

She shook her head mutely and hoped that her glare was sharp enough to shut him up.

"*Four Horsemen* is on track to pull in a million dollars at the box office. And we have its star! It just goes to show that timing plays a big a part in the success of—" The rest of his sentence caught in his throat when the irritation on her face registered. "Oh gosh, Madame, I'm so sorry. You were preparing, weren't you?"

"I was trying."

"Your death scene. Of course. How insensitive of me." He tapped the newspaper. "It's just that we need *Camille* to be a big, fat hit."

"I know what's at stake, Ray. And if we don't get Camille's death right, the whole picture falls into a heap. So . . ." She made a flicking motion: *Run along now.*

Rudy strode onto the set. Lustrous in his snug black tailcoat, the weight he'd lost at Natacha's command—"Armand might come from the bourgeoisie but he's no sloth"—enhanced his appeal. It had been hard for a gourmand like Rudy to abstain, but whatever Natacha said was the rule of law in his world now. Fourteen pounds lighter, he was even more godlike than he'd been in *Four Horsemen*—if that were possible.

Rudy approached her with a quiet smile. "Madame," he said, sitting beside her on the bed. "Our big scene! Are you nervous?"

OUR big scene? This is Camille's death. It's MY big scene. You're here to cry and lament, and that is all.

She turned to glare at him, then did a double take. As soon as Metro's new darling had finished work on *Uncharted Seas*, Natacha had set about altering his appearance. She'd tweezed his thick brows into slender arches that metamorphosed into diagonals when he emoted sadness. She'd also decided his slicked-back, pomaded hair was wrong for the young provincial he was playing in this picture, so she'd refashioned it into a softer coiffure. Alla had been doubtful at first, but again, Natacha's instinct for this sort of thing had proved astute.

The *Four Horsemen*'s success had boosted Rudy's confidence.

No longer was he a scrappy hopeful knocking at doors, desperate to be noticed. Now, everyone from the East Coast to the West knew his name and recognized his face. Women wanted to be with him; men wanted the secret of his magnetism.

"I'm always nervous before shooting a scene," Alla told him. So much for preparing.

He recoiled. "A professional like you?"

"It's different when you're on stage. If you blunder or miss a cue, it's not the end of the world. Only the people in the first couple of rows are likely to notice. You will have a chance to get it right the next night, or the night after that. But the camera captures everything we do, recording it forever. If you don't get nervous about that, you don't care enough."

He nodded thoughtfully and was about to respond when Ray clapped his hands. "People," he called out, "Camille's death scene is the climax of our picture and Madame's job today is especially difficult. I would ask you to keep that in mind as you take your positions for the first shot."

Poor Rudy stumbled and bumbled through five unusable takes—tripping on the carpet, catching his ring on Marguerite's white lace coverlet—until Alla sat up in her deathbed and motioned for Ray to clear the set. She beckoned Rudy with a curl of the finger; he slunk toward her like a guilty cat.

"I'm sorry, Madame," he said. "I ruin so many takes."

She patted a space on the bedclothes. "It is I who should apologize to you." His glassy eyes filled with skepticism. "I should never have told you that the camera records everything for posterity."

"But you are right!"

"And you are too concerned with anticipating what's to come and are failing to live in the moment. Acting isn't about pretending to be someone else; it's believing that you are." She grabbed his hand and held it tight. "You *are* Armand Duval and you are in

Marguerite's inner sanctum, not in Hollywood but in Paris. I *am* dying of consumption and you are here to say goodbye with your heart bursting and your grief inconsolable."

He nodded and thanked her.

"And most important of all," she continued, "there is no camera. It doesn't exist and anybody who says it does is quite, quite mad." She straightened up and peered around them. "Camera? What camera? I certainly do not see it. Do you, Armand?"

A sliver of a smile escaped his lips. "Not one."

She spotted the silhouette of their director standing on the far side of the diaphanous curtains draped across the bedroom door and summoned him back. Ray gave Rudy an encouraging pat on the back as they passed each other.

"Everything okay?" he asked her.

Alla nodded.

Ray called, "Places, please, everyone."

Alla noticed Natacha had joined them. She didn't often come to the set when a film was in production. Why had she chosen this particular day to make an appearance? She and Rudy stood at the doorway, facing each other, their eyes locked, and their faces only an inch or two apart. Alla couldn't hear what she was saying, but his only response was to nod over and over. She lay back against the pillows once more, relieved that Natacha was here. Her preternatural poise was a welcome balm over someone whom she had inadvertently rattled. And the fleeting jealousy that had pricked her at the *Four Horsemen* premiere had now matured into delight that her closest friend had found love.

As she smoothed out the bedclothes, Alla told herself it was better that Rudy learn to ignore everything but his own performance now rather than appear in a succession of flops that would torpedo a promising career. She gave her fluffed-up wig a last-minute plumping and settled back, forcing herself to breathe lightly.

She heard him open the door. "Oh, Marguerite! My delicate bloom! Please, please, do not leave me, for I shall not bear the agony." His voice burned with anguish. His breathing came in raw bursts, louder with each step. She felt his weight as he pressed both hands to her mattress and fell to his knees. "I would give my life for yours; I swear it before God and all that is holy."

This is more like it. Alla sank deeper into the mound of soft pillows.

Rudy took a strangled breath and recited the speech June had written for him. The gist of it would end up in one or two title cards, but the exact words weren't important. They were a vehicle to help Rudy emote the right reaction to the encroaching death of his beloved.

It was a long speech, nearly a full minute, and Alla was impressed that he had taken the time to memorize it verbatim. More than that, the visceral sorrow with which he expressed every word pierced her like an arrow.

My goodness. He's better than I could ever have imagined.

Alla heard sniffles and muffled gasps from behind the camera.

He's so good that he's even affecting the crew!

On his knees and with his hands clasped in despair, he was stealing her death scene out from under her. Critics and fans wouldn't be praising the sensitive, delicate way she played Camille's demise; all the chatter would be about Rudolph Valentino's palpable, wrenching heartache.

And that's when Alla Nazimova, gasping her final tubercular breaths, transformed from the wise teacher and inspiring mentor she wished to be into the desperate, self-serving monster she abhorred in other actresses.

Have my life's experiences taught me nothing? Have not my successes and struggles, my triumphs and disappointments toughened the edges of my ego enough to repel any attacks, real or perceived? No. Apparently not. Apparently, *my* ego is made of fragile spider webs and my vanity stage manages everything, leaving me incapable of wresting control from its grip.

She could have put a halt to it. It wouldn't have taken much to hamper Rudy's concentration. She knew all sorts of tricks to distract him. She could make annoying little gurgling sounds, jerk her legs around with involuntary spasms, or clutch at the bedcovers.

But drowning in outrage and alarm though she was, she still knew what constituted professional behavior. Interrupting a fellow actor mid-scene was unacceptable, so she let him continue with his unrestrained wailing until the end of the scene, when he laid his head in her lap.

Ray called out "Cut!" and the crew broke out into applause as Rudy lurched to his feet. But it was to Alla that he directed his eyes, searching for approval.

"Well done, Rudy," she told him. "Very well, indeed."

"I did not think of the camera once!" His eyes were Christmas-morning bright. "I felt like Icarus with his wings of the feathers and the wax, flying, flying!"

Alla pulled back the covers and slid out of the bed. She held her admiring smile in place as her maid, Scobie, pulled a robe across her shoulders. She told Scobie to ask Ray to come to her dressing room. A few minutes later, when the knock came on the door, Alla had arranged herself in a regal pose, her long flowing robe spread out behind her, hair freshly coiffed, and backbone straight. "Come!"

Ray rushed in, his face flushed with enthusiasm. "We couldn't have asked for a better take than that. I don't know what Natacha said to him before we shot—"

"Natacha?" Alla drew back. "I was the one who gave him a talking-to."

"Yes, yes, of course you did," Ray said, although it was clear he hadn't seen their exchange at all. "I just meant that he and Natacha had a little chat, so whatever she said—"

"*I* said it!"

"What's important is that Rudy received the encouragement he needed to bring the scene what it required. You'll see what I mean when we print the—"

"I want you to cut him out." *You're a contemptible fiend, Alla*

Nazimova!

"You want—what?"

"You heard me." *What a mean-spirited self-aggrandizer you are!*

"You want me to edit down Rudy's performance?"

"I want him out of the scene altogether." *You're a desperate woman, scared to death of being over the hill.*

Ray pointed toward the set. "Nothing Rudy did in *Four Horsemen* compares to what he pulled out of himself just now."

"Why would I want anyone distracting the audience during my death scene?" *Your film career has reached dizzying heights and yet you haven't the room in your heart to let a talented newcomer have his moment. You make me sick to the stomach, you deplorable egotist!*

Alla averted her eyes to avoid having to acknowledge Ray's disappointment. "I'll do as you wish," he whispered, "but permit me to make one final protest. Cutting Rudy out is tantamount to sabotaging the picture. We've been lucky to cast someone who has caught fire with the public. You must have noticed how increasingly crowded the film market is becoming. Every month, more and more people are jumping in on the act, which means it's getting harder and harder to be noticed. Taking full advantage of what Rudy gave us today is the best way to maximize our chances of success."

It was a fine speech, and every word of it true. And in a day or two, or a week, or a month, Alla suspected she would regret how she had handled herself. But she was trapped in the grip of self-preservation. Male actors didn't have to worry about turning forty. Or fifty. Or even sixty, if they had a makeup man to help camouflage the ravages of passing years. But for a leading lady, every day past forty was another step along a gangplank of indeterminate length. Signore Valentino had a whole career ahead of him, whereas she had, what, another five years? Three? One?

I'm sorry, Rudy, but I've got a finite amount of time left in my career. Nobody is looking out for me any more than they'll look out for you. The sooner you learn this, the better.

She looked Ray in the eye. "My decision is final."

6

Alla tapped her manicured fingernails against her glass desktop. When the delivery boy had handed over the bulging envelope of reviews from her clipping service, she'd favored him with a ridiculously large tip. But now that she had read through its contents, she wished she hadn't been quite so benevolent.

She lit one of her perfumed cigarettes and wondered if the service had deliberately arranged the stack so that her most favorable *Camille* review sat at the top, the second-most positive one below that, and on down the pile to the most demoralizing one at the bottom. Did they think she'd only read the first half-dozen? Didn't they know that if you send an actress twenty-three reviews, she will read every last one of them?

She drew in another cloud of fragrant smoke and forced herself to hold it, fire searing her throat. She was punishing herself but wasn't sure why.

For putting in a lousy performance?
For sabotaging Rudy's?
For overestimating American audiences?

It had all started out so thrillingly well. She was pleased with her portrayal of Marguerite. Natacha's costumes and sets had photographed beautifully. The premiere at New York's Ritz-Carlton Theater had been a resounding success. Granted, there had been no calls for her to take the stage, but the picture earned a standing ovation and afterward, she'd been rushed with congratulations. She had nothing to complain about—well, except for those persistent, nagging misgivings about what she'd done to Rudy in the final reel.

If she had a chance to do it over, would she have done it differently? Perhaps. But he was stealing the picture out from under her. She had done what was necessary to preserve her star status. Little Miss Mary "America's Sweetheart" Pickford would have done exactly the same thing. That woman was nobody's fool.

And besides, Rudolph Valentino was doing fine. *Four Horsemen* had raked in four million dollars and he was now the spiciest leading man around. After Metro had released his final picture, he'd jumped to Famous Players-Lasky. They were only too happy to double his salary for *The Sheik*, which he'd spent the summer filming. June had orchestrated everything now that she, too, was working there. Alla missed her lively presence on the Metro lot but could hardly blame June for accepting the thousand-dollar-a-week paycheck Lasky had offered up on a silver platter.

Everybody was doing fine, thank you very much.

Until the clipping service packet arrived.

Screenland had applauded her "exotic, dazzling but baffling beauty." Alla wasn't sure what was so baffling about her beauty, but if it came with 'exotic' and 'dazzling,' she'd take it. The *Democratic Mirror* had called her performance "an unforgettable portrait." *Variety* had praised her for "the finest acting with which the silver sheet has ever been graced." That one made her smile. The next few hadn't showered her with roses, but they were supportive.

And then came *Photoplay*, a publication she had always counted on. But it had declared, "Never once does the picture touch actual humanity, largely because Madame Alla poses rather than acts." Oh, how that statement had stung. She read those last four words over and over until she could bear it no longer and pushed the clipping aside.

She should have stopped right there.

Each review had been more caustic than the previous one, until she reached the final critique: *Moving Picture World*, which had suggested that *Camille* "should be sold as a polite freak rather than a translation of the story."

Alla extinguished her cigarette on the word *freak*. "And that is what I think of *Moving Picture World*."

A knock on the doorjamb prodded Alla out of her sulk. "Madame!" It was the studio errand boy, Timothy, a fresh-faced youngster who looked like he had stepped out of *The Adventures of Huckleberry Finn*. "The big cheese wants to see you."

"Did he say when?"

"The word 'pronto' was mentioned."

Alla stared down at the pile of reviews in front of her and speculated on the reason for this unprecedented summons. Normally, Maxwell Karger would come to her, but now he expected *her* to go to *his* office? This was not a good sign.

Running right over there would pander to Karger's inflated sense of self-importance, so Alla took her time freshening her makeup and patting down her hair. She scooped up her hodgepodge of reviews and dumped them in the trash can. She was halfway down the corridor before she thought the better of it and returned to her office to slide them back into their envelope. They weren't *all* catastrophic. One day, when she was a dried-up old prune and life had squeezed out every last drop of her gifts, she would want to read about the time when *Screenland* had called her an exotic, dazzling beauty and *Variety* had considered her acting the finest to have ever graced the silver sheet.

Karger was on his feet, his hands planted on either side of an accounting ledger with pages a foot and a half across. It struck Alla as an artificial pose, as though he'd maintained this charade for the exact moment she entered his office.

Her custom-made perfume announced her presence, but he didn't look up, forcing her to play along. "You rang?"

Karger looked up from his balance sheets, feigning mild surprise. "Thank you for dropping everything to come see me."

His tone didn't drip with its usual superciliousness. Alla narrowed her eyes. What was he up to?

He picked up a red-leaded pencil and twirled it around his knuckles until it slipped from his grasp and bounced onto the wooden floor. Maxwell Karger was many things: authoritative, condescending, and a bit of a windbag with pretensions to megalomania. But he had never been—at least, not in Alla's presence—nervous. "Please, Madame, take a seat."

Alla lowered herself onto the chair. "What may I do for you?"

He bent over to retrieve the pencil. "As you are no doubt aware, your contract is up for renewal at the end of this month."

Alla swallowed the gasp that threatened to burst from her. *This* month? She did a quick mental count. Twelve days. The prospect of being cast adrift made her body tremble. But to show it to a man like Karger was a sign of weakness, so she crossed her legs and pressed her elbows onto her knees as she slanted forward.

Karger cleared his throat. "I stayed late last night examining the box office returns for *Camille*."

"And?"

"We did very well in nearly all the big cities."

Alla bunched her hands into fists. Her intuition about raising American filmmaking to an art was on the money!

"Not only New York and Los Angeles," Karger went on, "but Chicago, Miami, Seattle, Atlanta, Dallas, and Detroit reported very healthy numbers." He attempted a smile and almost pulled it off, but it crumbled at the edges. "You're popular in Chattanooga, it seems. *Camille* did better there than in Kansas City and Minneapolis—combined."

"Chattanooga?" Alla repeated.

"Tennessee. It's not a college town, so I'm not sure why *Camille* did so well there. The picture played real good in college towns, by the way. I guess because they teach Alexandre Dumas in their literature classes."

"It sounds like my picture did well all over." *Which means you're going to renew my contract.* Alla's own reaction puzzled her. She hadn't been happy at Metro for a while, but as soon as the prospect of being let go loomed bright and real, she was thrown into a panic. It was remarkable how swiftly a person could adjust her lifestyle to accommodate thirteen thousand dollars gushing into her bank account each week.

Karger cleared his throat again. "Like I said, we did well in the big cities."

"And college towns."

"However, the majority of movie-going Americans live in small country hamlets and rural areas. For a picture to be successful, it needs to appeal to both the big-city sophisticates *and* small-town hicks."

"How did we do among the small-town hick set?"

"In eighty-three percent of towns with a population of three thousand or less, *Camille* played only two days."

It was impressive how Karger could pull these figures out of the air. Alla had no idea that they took the trouble to analyze box office returns in such microscopic detail—or that they could. She had assumed they defined success by comparing how much a picture cost with its earnings and left it at that.

"Are there many towns with a population under three thousand?"

"Most of them."

Alla fell back in her chair. Evidently, 'dazzling but baffling beauty' and 'unforgettable portraits' weren't enough to carry the day. "Mr. Karger, I prefer to deal in broad canvases that—"

"*Camille* is a flop." He spat his words out.

The pronouncement felt like a sharp pebble to the chest. "How bad of a flop?"

"We've made back only fifty-nine percent of the budget so far."

"But Rudolph Valentino is the biggest name in pictures right now. I'd have thought he'd pull the crowds—"

"In big cities, yes. But they weren't enough."

"Trust me, Mr. Karger, women are women. Whether they live in cities or villages, they all respond to Rudy in the same way."

"If he's so hypnotic, why did you cut him out of the final scene?"

So there it was. Alla had suspected that Karger had spies everywhere. "I decided that Dumas was correct to not place Armand in the death scene."

"But you and June fought to write him *into* it."

"And when we played it, it struck me that we'd been wrong and he had to go." Alla had told herself this version of the events so often that she'd almost come to believe it. She met his eye. "If you agree that he's hypnotic, why did you let him slip through your fingers?"

"You sabotaged your own picture, and for what?" Angry dabs of spittle were collecting at the corners of his mouth. "He was upstaging you, and—"

"Four hundred dollars a week for the biggest name to hit motion pictures since Chaplin is insulting. You could have matched their offer. Or bettered it. One thousand per week is all it would have taken. But no. You had to be a bunch of cheapskates with the foresight of a housefly."

Alla knew Rudy was four thousand dollars in debt—and it was Metro's fault. Or partly. Before embarking for California to film *Four Horsemen*, Rudy had visited his tailor at 46th and 8th. Miserly Metro had only supplied his Argentine gaucho costume and the French soldier's uniform, so Rudy had been measured for twenty-five custom-fitted suits to wear as Julio. Did he need so many? Of course not, but his boundlessly open-hearted munificence was part of his charm and contributed to his on-screen appeal. And he never would have stepped foot in the tailor's atelier if Karger had done the right thing and supplied Rudy with a full wardrobe.

There was no mystery to why Rudy had grabbed Lasky's offer.

Karger yanked at the lapels of his jacket as though it were on the verge of blowing away. "If I had known that we were about to save ourselves thirteen grand a week, I would have made Valentino an offer he couldn't refuse. I would have gone to fifteen hundred, but that hot-headed dago jumped ship and signed with Lasky before we even had a chance."

Alla crossed her arms. "If you're going to start throwing around words like *dago*, you have no right to cry betrayal when Rudy signs with—" A sickening realization jolted through her body. *We were about to save ourselves thirteen grand a week.*

Karger pulled at his lapels again. "I asked you here to formally notify you that Metro Pictures is declining to renew your contract. Your last day at this studio will be October 31st, 1921."

Alla stopped by her office long enough to collect her handbag. She didn't say goodbye to anyone, told no one that she was leaving and wouldn't be back. Ever.

The end of October was less than two weeks away, so she was hardly going to sit there crossing each day off the wall calendar. The Great Nazimova had better ways to spend her time than mope around a studio that no longer wanted her. Plus, she could send her maid, Scobie, to collect her belongings later.

She marched out of the front gate and headed north up Cahuenga Boulevard.

She had never walked home from the studio. Not because it was too far, but because the thought hadn't occurred to her. Why would it, when she had a car and driver at her disposal? But Karger's rebuke had left her too agitated to stay still. How far was her home? Two miles? Five miles? Twelve, perhaps? No matter. The urge to keep in motion was stronger than her desire to keep her purple velvet slippers clean on Hollywood's dusty streets. All she had to do was walk up Cahuenga, then turn left when she came to Sunset. Sooner or later, she was bound to hit her Garden of Alla.

She had jokingly taken the nickname for her two-and-a-half-acre estate from the title of a Robert Hichens novel from fifteen years ago—*The Garden of Allah*. She loved how her oasis of greenery and birdsong welcomed her after a full day of cavorting for the cameras. It reminded her that there was more to life than discovering new eye shadow or a different way to fix her hair.

She could feel her garden beckoning her, promising comfort in the shade of her favorite Japanese maple with its firecracker-red leaves. But first she needed to think. To clear her mind. To figure out her next step.

Cutting Rudy out of her death scene had been unforgivably selfish; she could see that now. Truthfully, she had known it at the time, although she wouldn't have admitted it for all the vodka in Moscow. She could dress it up all she wanted. Career self-preservation! Prerogative of the star! Staying faithful to the source material! But jealousy and fear had been her taskmasters that day, and it was easier to confess when it was just her, alone, trudging along Sunset Boulevard with nothing but the mortifying torture of having been fired like some shop girl at I. Magnin.

Metro was never going to let her do what she wanted. They lacked a broad worldview. They were the morons who'd lost Rudolph Valentino. They had June Mathis, the top screenwriter in the business, and they'd lost her, too. And they had one of the biggest stars in Hollywood and after a succession of disappointing films, it was 'Metro Pictures is declining to renew your contract.'

The way he'd said it. So colorless. So remote. So glacial. Didn't he understand that she and Natacha and June had been trying to explore the human experience with so much more flavor and nuance than a tumble down rickety stairs or a frying pan to the skull?

Her thoughts turned to Natacha. What had she thought of Alla's order that her boyfriend be cut from the climax of the picture? She had never said anything at the premiere or during any of the times they'd been together since then. Alla saw now for the first time that her actions may have forced Natacha to choose between her lover and her friend.

But she's the most pragmatic person I know. She knows me better than anybody else. She must have understood my reasons for cutting Rudy out. Alla hoped against hope that was the case. If she couldn't turn to Natacha to help face crises like this, whom could she turn to?

Alla arrived at the corner of Highland Avenue just as a Lifebuoy Soap delivery truck roared past, leaving in its wake a plume of noxious exhaust. She took a step back, waving her pocketbook across her face to clear the air, but caught her heel on a discarded milk bottle. Her right knee gave out, and she toppled gracelessly to the ground.

The city had sealed this section of Sunset with concrete but not the sidewalks, if one could call dirt tracks running alongside a roadway 'sidewalks.'

The palms of her hands were now as filthy as her shoes. Her elbows, too. And her left knee. She cast furtively around, fearful that someone might recognize her, but it was the middle of the afternoon. The scattering of pedestrians peppering the streets had their minds on their own business and were unlikely to give a second glance to some scruffy ragamuffin rolling in the dirt.

A truck filled with Hoover suction sweepers thundered by.

Maybe it would have been better to follow the herd and become a housewife, she thought miserably. Spend the days scrubbing pots. Polishing the dining table. Tending to the children. Alla hoisted herself to her feet. Her attempts to brush away the dirt left trails of grime down her olive-green silk dress. Some housewife she'd make. At the first sign of drudgery, she'd be out the door.

Highland Avenue cleared of traffic in both directions and Alla started crossing the intersection. With every step, though, a solution came to her in one-word answers.

Housewife.

Children

Drudgery.

Door.

By the time she reached the other side, she knew what she should do.

* * *

Later that day, as the sun was sinking to the horizon through a sky of pink clouds, Alla's taxicab driver let her off out front of the Formosa Apartments near where Hollywood Boulevard met La Brea Avenue. The building was a world away from the Garden of Alla's luxury but was a decent enough place for a couple of kids gaining traction in a town strewn with professional potholes the size of Santa Catalina Island. She knocked on the door of the second ground-floor apartment on the right.

The jaunty melody of "I'm Forever Blowing Bubbles" floated through the door. A trio of voices, one woman and two men, warbled the lyrics more or less in tune. Dreaming dreams, scheming schemes, and building castles.

Alla knocked again, louder this time.

The sound of hurried footsteps on tile. The door swung open to reveal a smiling Rudy. "*Buonasera*, Madame!"

In the half-dozen or so times they had encountered each other since her decision to cut him from the death scene, he had showed no sign of disappointment. Not once. Not even so much of a glimmer of anger or resentment. Had their positions been reversed, she most certainly would have had a few choice words to say—and wailed like a bull elephant as she said them. But there had been no yelling, no silent treatment, no cutting looks. Rudy had continued to behave as he always had: his usual reverence mixed with his impetuous puppy-like charm, idiotic jokes, and recounting of his ardent search to find the ultimate *spaghetti alla Bolognese con polpette di carne*. Good God, but how that man loved his meatballs.

Alla wouldn't have blamed him if he'd set out to sabotage her the way she had vandalized his scene, but he always treated her with deference and welcoming smiles. In fact, she would have preferred a fiery confrontation. Fill the air with wild accusations. Get everything off their chests, *molto fortissimo*, until they had each emptied themselves of every scrap of remorse. But she wasn't going to get it. Rudolph Valentino, with those smoldering bedroom eyes that promised steamy nights of unrestrained passion, was just a happy-go-lucky guy not given to holding a grudge. And that, she had come to realize, was a sobering lesson in human behavior.

Rudy widened his door to let Alla into the small, circular vestibule and pointed down the hallway to his right. "We have almost finished with the photographs and have opened a bottle of chianti."

"Photographs?" Alla stepped into the living room. "What phot—"

The sight of Natacha Rambova with her hair down severed the rest of her query.

Natacha usually wore it parted down the middle and divided into two braids wound around each ear—even when it had only been the two of them, nibbling at Sunday morning toast and reading book reviews out loud. Not once had she worn it as she did now, cascading past her shoulders and almost reaching her elbows.

How different she looked! How relaxed and carefree. 'Informal' wasn't a word that Alla would ever have used to describe this island of a woman. But here she was, with a smile fresh as a spring breeze, her eyes *diamantes*, and a tinkling laugh bubbling out of her.

Natacha said, "We were calling it quits when you knocked."

They had dragged the chairs away from a small rectangular dining table loaded with envelopes arranged in eight stacks ten inches high.

Alla asked, "What is happening here?"

"Did I not tell you about our money-making scheme?"

Photographs of Rudy that Metro had taken to publicize *Four Horsemen* filled two large boxes at the right-hand end of the table.

In them, he wore his square-brimmed Argentine gaucho hat with tiny pom-poms dangling off the brim, and a leather strap outlining his jaw. He was staring straight at the camera, with his face partially obscured in shadow, and a tiny glint of light had caught his left eye.

"Paul came up with the idea," Rudy said. "My fans send twenty-five cents to our post office box and we mail them one of these, personally autographed by me." He let out a soft giggle. "Or one of us."

Alla drew back, slightly aghast that a star of Rudy's stature was wasting his energy with such a nickel-and-dime scheme. "Is this worth your while?"

"A quarter of a cent to print the photo, plus another quarter of a cent for the envelope, plus two cents for postage. That means twenty-two-and-a-half cents per autograph is pure profit."

"And how many requests do you get?"

"Around fifteen bags a day."

Alla's mouth dropped open. "*Every* day?"

"Every day that the post office is open."

"Aren't they open six days a week?"

"Si."

Natacha straightened the photos still strewn across the table. "In an average week, we pocket around two thousand dollars. But we split that three ways. Half for Rudy, with Paul and I sharing the other half fifty-fifty. It's a lot of work, but when we get going, the three of us are like a machine."

Alla had been vaguely aware that Metro Pictures received fan mail for her, but nobody had ever bothered her with it. What had become of it all? Was it too late to salvage it? Yes, she chided herself, far too late. You no longer work there.

"I am lucky that my New York tailor is a very patient man," Rudy said. "He sleeps better now that I send him two hundred dollars a month. I should pay my debt by this time next year!"

Rudy beamed his guileless smile, but Alla was glad that she wasn't his tailor. *If* Rudy continued to get fifteen bags of fan mail a day, and *if* he paid off his debt at the rate of two hundred a month, nobody would have anything to worry about. But this was a man who had bought twenty-five custom-made suits when half a dozen would have sufficed. He hadn't even tried to send the bill to Metro, who should have provided the star of their million-dollar movie with his wardrobe. Whoever heard of such a thing? For the first time, Alla was glad to be rid of those penny-pinchers.

"I had no idea!" she exclaimed. "But tell me, who is this Paul you mentioned?"

"That would be me," a voice behind her said.

A youngish chap in his early twenties stood in the doorway leading into the bedroom. With an easy smile and laughing eyes, he had an amiable face punctuated by a pointed nose that infused his otherwise congenial nature with intelligence. He bent deeply at the waist. "Paul Ivano at your service, Madame."

Alla extended her hand in a pose intended for a gentleman to kiss. Most American men missed their cue and shook it instead. But this Paul Ivano person scooped her fingers into the palm of his hand and brushed them with his lips. Alla shivered as a tingling spread down her back.

It had been a while since she'd felt any attraction toward a man. Yes, there had been men who had warmed her bed from time to time. Some of them she had welcomed willingly, some of them out of loneliness, and a few others had been an expeditious means to an end. But then she would tire of their rough manner, their body hair, their clumsy ignorance of the female body and oafish attempts to stimulate it. And so lately her eyes had been drawn to the female form.

But there was an air of easy familiarity about this Paul Ivano that threw Alla back to the time when she was twelve and had been packed off to boarding school—a traumatic event for most youngsters, but Alla had been overjoyed to find sanctuary from the cruelty of her father. Still, it had been so very far from everything she knew. Within weeks she had made an intimate friendship with Elena, a lonely girl from Volgograd. Boarding schools were filled with young girls like Alla and Elena, brimming with longings and emotions, and separated from familiar surroundings.

The two girls had clung to each other, whispering their hopes, their fears, their dreams. One night, Alla had blurted out her love for an older student, a raven-haired beauty named Katya.

Elena had dismissed Alla's confession with a swipe of the air. "We all do that. I can't keep my eyes off Miss Babkin, the history teacher. It'll pass."

In time, the daughter of the school groundskeeper had replaced Katya in Alla's affections, and after that, the new vice principal. The girl behind the bakery counter in the local village had supplanted the vice principal before Alla had grasped that this was not the phase Elena had talked about. On the bus back to Yalta after her final year at boarding school, comprehension had hit her like a mule-kick. She'd shrugged it off with typical teenaged defiance and told herself, "Who cares what people think? I certainly don't."

As the bleak Russian countryside had slid past her window, she waited for a sensible voice of reason to admonish her. "Of course you do. Everybody cares what people think of them." But a more profound epiphany had arrived instead: She *didn't* care. Not one little bit. Not what her father thought, not what her neighbors thought, or her siblings, or anybody. It was the most freeing moment of her life.

Natacha subtly cleared her throat to bring Alla back into the here and now.

"And what is it you do, Mr. Ivano?" Alla asked him.

"I was a technical advisor for *The Four Horsemen of the Apocalypse*."

"Indeed?" Alla accepted the glass of chianti that Natacha had placed in her hand and took a seat beside Ivano on the sofa. "And on what manner of technicalities did you advise?"

He smiled an aw-shucks grin that only heightened his charm. "Well, my parents are Serbian and Russian—"

"You're Russian?" Was this why she was reacting to him so

viscerally? She crossed her legs and squeezed her thighs together, as hard as she could.

"I was born in Nice, so technically I'm French, but my real name is Ivanisevich."

"That's about as Russian as can be." Alla broke into what she called her Charm Smile, which she usually saved for her leading men in their more passionate scenes. She rarely exploited it in real life, but had on occasion. Most recently on Jean Acker—and look how that had ended. But this Paul Ivanisevich sitting next to her was an entirely different situation. Surprising, but delightful. And intriguing.

The kid blushed slightly. "At any rate, my parents were gassed while serving with the French forces during the Great War."

"How awful!"

"Yes, it was. But it meant I was around a lot of French soldiers."

Rudy flopped onto the occasional chair in the corner. "So when Metro needed someone to check the later scenes in *Four Horsemen*, I make the suggestion of Paul. When shooting was finished, we were roommates."

Unless there was a back patio converted into a sleeping porch, Alla supposed this was a one-bedroom apartment, so what had the three of them done when Natacha stayed the night? She spied a pillow folded inside a checkered picnic blanket stashed beneath an expansive maidenhair fern. Behind it was a movie poster, artlessly glued onto a piece of pasteboard; it depicted *Eyes of Youth*, the Clara Kimball Young picture in which June Mathis had first noticed Rudy.

"But what I really want to be is a cinematographer," Paul said.

So this young gentleman was born in France to Russian parents, comes up with a lucrative scheme to sell autographed photos, and wants to be a cinematographer? And all wrapped up in an enticing package quite unaware of his appeal. *He must be half your age!* Alla turned away from him slightly. *But the desire to be a cinematographer—that shows drive and purpose.* Those were the sorts of qualities that made Alla's heart beat a little faster.

A couple of Sundays ago, Charlie Chaplin had invited her to a last-minute pool party. She hadn't felt much like going at the time, but Chaplin ran with an interesting crowd so one never knew who one might meet there. As it happened, Alla had met a young girl fresh off the bus from Cedar Rapids or Duluth or somewhere Alla had barely heard of. The girl had been pretty enough in an ingénue sort of way, and tempting enough to invite home for the night. But the girl had just lain there like a passive starfish willing to let Alla do whatever she had wanted, but unsure of herself or uninterested in taking part. Afterwards, Alla had rushed the girl out of the door, determined not to make that mistake again. She figured that she would choose better the next time someone interesting came along, but it hadn't occurred to her that such a person might be a mere lad of twenty.

"Ambition is an admirable quality." A loud ping rang out as Alla tapped her wine glass against his. "Otherwise, life slips by, and suddenly you're seventy and have accomplished nothing worth leaving behind."

"Madame." Natacha sat on the armrest of Rudy's chair. "When you called, you said you had something you wanted to talk about."

"Yes, but it's business, and here we are drinking this fine wine—" Alla raised her glass to salute Rudy's discerning taste "—and getting to know each other. Let's not talk about it right now."

A Beethoven symphony filtered through the wall of the adjacent apartment, highlighting the unwieldy silence that now descended on the room. Alla had sought out Natacha to sell her on the idea that had come to her as she'd plodded home from the Metro lot. She wasn't sure how Natacha would go about it, and didn't want to try in front of Rudy and this unexpectedly likable stranger.

"You don't have any plans for tonight, do you?" Natacha asked.

The assumption that she had nothing to occupy her time felt

like salt rubbed into the still-weeping wound of being fired. No! Not fired, Alla reminded herself. Liberated.

"As it happens, I don't."

"We're going to the Sunset Inn down in Venice."

"It's Photoplayers Night!" Rudy added.

Natacha slid off the armrest. "Well, good, then. It's settled. You're coming with us." She pulled at her long hair. "But first I must fix all this. Join me in here while I grapple with it."

The bathroom that lay off the bedroom smelled of macassar oil. It was painted a pretty shade of seafoam green with white trim to set it off. Natacha opened the mirrored cabinet over the basin, withdrew a brush and began grooming her long tresses. "Tell me what's going on, because obviously something is."

"I'm not sure where to begin."

"It takes me eight minutes to put up my hair."

"Metro has sacked me."

Natacha's brush stopped halfway down.

"Karger called me into his office and told me *Camille* performed well in the cities but that pictures need to succeed in the country towns if they have any hope of turning a profit."

The brushing resumed. "Which, I assume, *Camille* has failed to do."

"So he says."

"Do you believe him?"

Alla frowned. "You don't?"

"Karger strikes me as the type who doesn't like women with brains," Natacha said, then added in a stage whisper, "or talent. Or good taste. Or imagination."

Tremors of resentment began to churn Alla's innards. "You think Karger pretended *Camille* is a flop to rid himself of me?"

"I'm just saying that Karger is like all those guys in charge. They'll say anything to get you to do what they want, which of course is always in their best interest and not ours."

How true. All the men Alla had ever encountered in the entertainment business were like that: producers, directors, agents, bankers, casting guys. During the two-month run of *Comtesse Coquette*, one of her co-stars had talked over her funniest lines, blocked her spotlight, stepped on her dress, and failed to leave a teapot prop she was supposed to pick up later. But she had recovered from each attempt at treachery with professional adroitness, leaving the audience none the wiser.

Natacha handed Alla a fistful of pins, then twisted the right-hand half of her hair into a tightly wrung rope and wound it around her ear. "Why do they feel so threatened by us? They hold the power, they have the money, they get to make the decisions. And all because of that little doo-dad flopping between their legs. It hardly seems fair." She took a pin from Alla and inserted it. "I wouldn't mind so much if they were capable of making intelligent, perceptive choices."

"Speaking of choices," Alla said, leaning against the cool tiles, "I need to clear the air."

"Over what?"

"My decision to cut Rudy from the death scene."

Natacha went to take another pin but stopped. "I've been wondering if we'd ever talk about that."

Alla's courage faltered. She looked away. "Perhaps now's not the time."

"After you gave Rudy his pep talk, he came to see me at the edge of the set. I told him then and there that he needed to be a lot better, but if he was too good, you might cut him out altogether."

Alla's eyes found Natacha's in the mirror. They were as calm and composed as they always were. "You did?"

"None of us is in kindergarten anymore. We all have to look out for ourselves. It's called self-preservation."

"So you don't hate me for what I did?"

"I told him that he still needed to give the scene everything he had. We must always do our very best job at all times and in all ways. What you then might decide to do with his work was not up to him. His job was to give the best performance he possibly could."

The last three hairpins in Alla's hand started to bend as her heart pounded against her ribcage. "I can't tell you how pleased I am to hear that."

Natacha plucked one of the pins from between Alla's fingers. "Don't we share an identical philosophy when it comes to our professional life?"

"I'd like to think so, but now that you're dating Rudy, the line between professional and personal seems to have blurred."

"If that's your concern, then you can stop worrying. You and I —and Rudy too, for that matter—we're hunky dory."

The expression 'hunky dory' was so unlike her that Alla burst out laughing—although it may have been from the relief she felt that everything was actually fine.

Natacha started combing her bangs into a straight line across her forehead. "Six months ago, Metro Pictures had Alla Nazimova, Rudolph Valentino, and June Mathis, and now they have none of you, which tells us all we need to know about how clever Mister Maxwell Karger is. Meanwhile, he's still running a movie studio and you're out in the cold, but it should be the other way around. The question is: How did Pickford manage to pull it off?"

"She didn't form United Artists all on her own," Alla pointed out. "She did it with Charlie Chaplin, Douglas Fairbanks and D.W. Griffith, all of whom are men, and one of whom is her husband. And besides, she's twenty-nine and still playing Pollyanna. That is not the career I want."

Natacha started working on her lipstick. "Her *Pollyanna* grossed over a million."

"I didn't become an actress for the money or the fame."

"Why did you do it, then?" There was a slyness to Natacha's question, implying that she wanted Alla to say the answer out loud.

"To express myself. Explore ideas. Experience the world and everything in it. All I ever heard from my father was 'You're a child. Just a girl. A little nothing who will amount to nothing. You have nothing to contribute because nobody wants to hear from an insignificant little snippersnapper like you.' And every time he did, I said to myself, 'I'll show you.'"

"The little snippersnapper proved him wrong, didn't she?"

Alla rarely thought of her brutish father. And if he did force his way into her mind, she pushed him out again. The only act of kindness he had ever shown her was to hand-carve the miniature rocking horse that sat in her office. It was the sole memento of her childhood that had followed her from Yalta to Moscow to New York to California, which was amazing considering the only reason her father had made it himself was that he had been too cheap to go out and buy something. That's the sort of ogre he was. He'd even robbed her of the revenge she craved. "He died when I was seventeen, so he never saw any of my triumphs."

Natacha gave her reflection a last check. "The point is, you proved him wrong. You've made a marvelous success of yourself that many people dream of but very few achieve. Let's not forget that." Natacha wasn't naturally given to effusive praise, so Alla gratefully accepted it. "You must keep up the momentum. Have you any ideas?" Natacha stepped out of the bathroom, leaving Alla to follow her.

"As a matter of fact . . ."

"I had no doubt that you would." From out of Rudy's wardrobe she pulled out a floor-length dress in black wool with a stripe of tapestry sewn down the middle, and a gown in lilac chiffon with bejeweled shoulder straps. She held them both out and raised her eyebrows as though to ask Alla which one she should choose.

Alla pointed to the chiffon. "I'm not sure that you'll jump for joy over my idea, though."

Natacha laid the dress on the bed and asked her why not.

"I want to film *A Doll's House.*"

The lines between Natacha's eyebrows deepened with disapproval. "Ibsen?" she asked. "A bit Nordic and bleak and . . ."

Alla knew the word Natacha wanted to say but didn't wish to offend. "Domestic?"

"The whole play unfolds inside a Norwegian house, doesn't it?" Natacha slipped off her lounging pajamas with the stork motif and wriggled into a peach-colored suspender belt. "Isn't the main character just a little housewife who's keeping a secret from her dull husband?"

Aphrodite's story of courtesans in Alexandria had allowed Natacha's imagination to soar. And in *Camille*, she had French nobility and high-class girls with oodles of money to spend on clothes and jewelry and coiffures. But now Alla was presenting her with *A Doll's House*, whose action went only as far as the front door that Nora walked through at the end of the play.

"Aside from everything else," Natacha said, clipping her stockings into place, "you're a movie star with no studio. How do you plan on filming it?"

"I have Nazimova Productions."

Natacha's eyes glazed over. "I thought that existed solely on paper."

When Metro had approached Alla with a contract, it wasn't just the colossal paycheck that had convinced her to sign, or the stipulation that she could retain approval of her director, script, and leading man. What had really sweetened the pie was that the motion pictures would carry the same opening credit:

A
Nazimova
Production

"I insisted my lawyers insert a proviso that should I ever part company with Metro, the copyrights of all films produced under the Nazimova Productions shingle would remain with me."

Natacha's mouth popped open; the cogs of possibility churned behind those aquamarine eyes. Alla prodded her to spin around and had started fastening the buttons up the back of her gown when Rudy called from the other room.

"Will you be much longer, *tesoro mio*? We must leave soon if we will have a decent table."

Natacha collected up a small purse. "We should get a move on. If the maître d' shoves us in a corner, Rudy'll pout the whole night."

* * *

The Sunset Inn near the foot of the Santa Monica pier was a prosaic one-story rectangular box.

"A little drab, isn't it?" Alla asked.

"The drearier a place looks on the outside," Paul said, "the less likely it will come to the attention of the Feds."

"But the authorities must know what goes on here. A dreary façade isn't going to fool those men whose job it is to enforce the law."

"It's like the Ship Café. We all know what happens there, but you don't see anyone closing it down for violation of the Volstead Act. You keep it low-key and contained, you call taxicabs for the drunks, and maybe once in a while you need to grease a few palms to encourage them to turn a blind eye."

An ornate white-and-gold sign inside the doors welcomed them to Restaurant Française. The main room stretched the length of the building. Two-seater banquettes, upholstered in burgundy, lined the western wall. Overhead, cloth-covered lampshades shaped like upside-down umbrellas hung from the ceiling. Tables covered with starched linen filled the eastern wall and southern end in a tight geometric pattern. As Alla, Paul, Rudy, and Natacha walked in, a nine-man band launched itself into a jaunty version of an Irving Berlin tune Alla rather liked called "After You Get What You Want, You Don't Want It."

However, nobody's eyes were on the Abe Lyman Orchestra; instead, all were focused on the center of the dance floor. Buster

Keaton and Fatty Arbuckle were dancing the Black Bottom, each of them with a mop in their arms and their backs to each other. On every fourth beat, they stuck their rear ends out and pretended to be peeved when one of them sent the other reeling.

As Alla's party was being shown to their seats, Fatty threw his butt back as far as he could. It connected with Buster's hip. Buster leaped into the air like he was being shot out of a cannon. When he landed again, his knees buckled forward, sending Buster into a rolling tumble that ended only when he hit the bandstand. The crowd cheered its approval as Fatty yanked his comic partner to his feet and together they took exaggerated bows. Lyman's orchestra vamped the final bars until the applause petered out and couples invaded the dance floor.

"Is it like this every night?" Alla asked, taking her seat.

"Harold Lloyd was here last time I came," Paul said. "He entertained the crowd with a series of one-armed handstands. He must have done forty in a row and had us all egging him along—except Gloria Swanson. She'd made a big entrance wearing a gold-beaded gown in a fleur-de-lis pattern. It sure was a head-turner—or would have been if everybody hadn't been watching Lloyd's acrobatics. Miss Swanson was *not* pleased."

A waiter appeared and Paul ordered champagne cocktails. Alla's first choice would have been a vodka stinger, but with Prohibition blocking more and more access to liquor, nobody could afford to be too fussy anymore. She hadn't believed the law would ever pass, and now there was no way of telling how long it would stay in effect. Maybe forever? It didn't bear thinking about.

She also liked the way this Paul Ivano took charge. He wasn't belligerent, as though he was barking orders like a four-star general. His style was more gentlemanly than that. Like he'd been brought up to do the right thing. At a time that felt increasingly forgetful of its manners, his old-world appeal stood out.

He said, "Now that Fatty and Buster's act is over, it looks like somebody else is the center of attraction."

Alla snapped her cigarette lighter shut. A sea of faces turned toward her, eyes widened with excitement, mouths whispering behind raised menus. But all she wanted was a drink and to figure out how to bring Natacha around to her *Doll's House* idea. Rudy was smiling at her now. "Please tell me I'm not expected to sing for my supper," she told them. "What am I supposed to do, the can-can?" Out of the corner of her eye, Alla watched the maître d' approach their table. "I don't have a raft of party tricks to entertain the masses. And if I did, I certainly don't want to follow the likes of Fatty and Buster."

"Good evening, everybody. We couldn't help but notice your arrival." The maître d's sycophantic attitude set Alla's teeth on edge. "Although, I expect that must happen wherever you go." Alla cast a glance across the table, imploring Natacha to rebuff whatever request was coming. "But I've been approached by several patrons to prevail."

Alla tapped the ash from the end of her cigarette into a nearby glass ashtray. *Please go away.*

"I was there that night of the costume ball when you came dressed as tango dancers and cleared the floor with an exhibition dance." Why was this groveling maître d' talking about the night Rudy and Natacha had caused a sensation in the papers, forcing Jean to file for divorce? "So we were hoping you might favor us with one, too."

Alla's head shot up as the orchestra started playing a slow, sensual melody. Rudy's chair scraped across the floorboards as he pushed away from the table. He extended his hand to Natacha, who floated to her feet in a single, silken movement. Applause swelled around the perimeter of the dance floor as they took their positions at its center.

With their hips pressed as close together as public decency laws would permit—and perhaps a few steps beyond it— Rudy and Natacha glided around the floor with fire in their eyes, their limbs coiled around each other. It wasn't hard to see why they'd caused a sensation at the Alexandria.

Paul nudged her shoulder with his. "Not what you were expecting, huh?"

Her dismissal from Metro earlier in the day had been hard enough to take, but now she was being flat-out ignored. Alla donned her most stoic Ibsen-heroine face. "Being on display like a doll in a toy shop window gets to be onerous after a while."

The cocktails arrived. Alla scooped hers up but before she could make a toast, Paul said, "You're no doll."

Alla frowned at him, unsure of his meaning.

"You're a woman," he continued. "A full-blooded woman filled to the brim with deeply felt emotions that sometimes overwhelm you."

He was right, but she wasn't prepared to admit it. After a few champagne cocktails, perhaps. She cocked an eyebrow. "Oh, I am, am I? And how do you know that?"

"Because all great actresses are. You're born with the ability to access those surging undercurrents that the rest of us shy away from, fearing that if we dive in too deep, we might drown. But not you. You jump in, feet first, chest out, fists clenched. You meet the challenge of transmitting those primal emotions to your audiences on the far side of the footlights or the camera. You do it fully prepared to pay the toll to your soul." He clinked his coupe to hers. "And I salute you."

Alla could only stare at this youth. How old was he? Twenty? Twenty-one, perhaps? Twenty-two at the most. And yet he could come up with a potent speech like that? She shrugged off her Ibsen sang-froid and replaced it with Camille coquettishness. "How long have you been rehearsing that soliloquy?" The admiration in his eyes dimmed. *Oh my! He meant what he said.* Regretting her cavalier attitude, she tenderly squeezed his forearm. "I'm sorry. Please forgive me."

A glow of admiration replaced the disappointment. "I've seen all your movies."

His ability to spring from one emotion to another mystified

Alla—but it also made him that much more appealing. "I'm flattered."

"But you probably hear that all the time."

"Not really, but even if I did, it means more coming from you."

As soon as she had said it, Alla realized that she probably shouldn't have used such a come-hither tone. But he was unlike the men Alla usually encountered. Most of them in the picture business were preening cocksmen, or truculent billy goats, or overly articulate academics in love with their own opinions. This Paul Ivano, with his long face and Roman nose, his unguarded frankness, was exactly the medicine she needed to remedy the crushing events of the day.

"Thank you," he said. The Lyman orchestra started building to a crescendo, and Paul leaned closer. "I have something else I want to say."

Alla had a fair idea of what was coming. She also knew that she ought to close him down before he embarrassed himself. *But oh! Look at that earnestness. That naked yearning. And what woman doesn't like to hear what he's burning to say?* "Out with it," she told him. "Our tangoing duo are nearly done with their star turn."

"I think you're magnificent! You're real and authentic. You're flesh and bone and feelings and desires and aspirations and disappointments and failures and triumphs. You have a fierce intellect and a wide-open heart, and they need room to grow as well as be cherished for the rare birds they are."

The crowd around the dance floor exploded into applause as the music reached its climax.

"You have an uncommon gift for words," Alla told him. "Are you sure it's a cinematographer you wish to become?"

"I think you know what I wish to become."

Oh! Oh! What am I supposed to say to that?

Rudy and Natacha returned to the table, slightly out of breath and shiny with sweat. He waved appreciatively to the crowd and wiped his forehead with a napkin. "Did you notice how my toe caught on Natacha's heel?" Alla had missed most of their routine.

Her mind was now too filled with Paul's flattery to respond with anything but a shake of the head. "Good!" Rudy exclaimed. "They expect a polished routine, but we cannot rehearse every day in case someone asks us to perform."

"From the sounds of that applause," Paul said, "I'd say you went over real well."

Natacha slipped Alla a puzzled look. Alla distracted herself by pulling a cigarette from her silver case and took her time lighting it.

"You knocked it out of the park," she told Rudy. "Goodness me! Did I use a sporting term? That's a first!"

Natacha narrowed her eyes.

Rudy told Paul, "I must visit the men's room, but I need an escort to block the advances of some of my eager fans. There are at least three women who I know will corner me at the first chance they get."

"Let me guess," Natacha said drily. "The woman in the red dress, the one with the tiara, and the old cow in the hideous chintz disaster with the rose pattern. What does she think she is? Marie Antoinette's fainting couch?"

"Come on," Paul said, standing, "I'll play bodyguard." He bowed his head like he was Fitzwilliam Darcy from *Pride and Prejudice*. "Ladies."

Alla and Natacha watched the two men draw admiring glances until they were out of earshot. "He's quite taken with you," Natacha said, and took a deep gulp of champagne cocktail. "This afternoon as we were signing photos and stuffing them into envelopes, he went on and on about you." She withdrew one of Alla's perfumed cigarettes from the pewter case. They were past asking permission to raid each other's cigarettes. "I gathered from the dance floor that he declared himself."

"You don't miss a trick, do you?"

A slight shrug. "I try not to."

Alla signaled a passing waiter for another round. "I was taken completely unawares. You might have warned me."

"My money was on him staying mum, but he's braver than I gave him credit for. Good for him." She closed Alla's lighter with a decisive click. "And as for you . . ."

"As for me, what?"

"I think you and I are long past beating around the bush, so I'm just going to say this out loud. When it comes to your proclivities of the boudoir variety, I'd lay money that you're not exclusively one way or the other."

In all their meetings, dinners, walks along the beach, and leisurely mornings working their way through newspapers, the subject of Alla's inclinations had never come up. But it wasn't because Alla was afraid to risk what had become an essential friendship. She had sensed that Natacha was someone who didn't judge a person for their sex life. When it came to who went to bed with whom, and why, and how often, it seemed to Alla that Natacha gave it no thought. So this pronouncement about Alla's sexuality caught her unprepared.

"And you would win that bet. But I'm not sure how I feel about —" Alla fluttered her fingers toward the men's room.

"He's twenty. You must remember how positively *passionné* boys are at that age."

"Point taken. Now, about *A Doll's House*—"

"Not that again."

"I didn't get a chance to plead my case."

Natacha waved a smoking cigarette around as though to say, *Very well, then, plead away.*

"I think *Doll's House* is the right choice because that's the role I built my name on. When I opened at the Bijou in 1907, virtually every single reviewer—and certainly every significant one—said that my Nora Helmer was the finest portrayal ever witnessed this side of the Atlantic, and perhaps the other side as well. Unless the public saw me on Broadway or on tour, they will never know. But a motion picture version will allow them to see me in my finest role. I think they'll jump at the chance."

Natacha grimaced. "That's all very well, but doesn't Nora leave her husband and children at the end? I don't know that Mister and Missus Midwest are going to be too impressed with that."

"They aren't who we're making the film for."

"Didn't Karger tell you that for a picture to succeed, it must appeal to small-town folks as well as urbanites?"

"We'd be making this film for New Women. They want choices and options that weren't available to their mothers."

"We gave Camille a New Woman makeover and look what happened."

"That's because Marguerite Gautier was a whore, and housewives from Minneapolis cannot relate to her. But Nora is a housewife and mother—just like them." Alla could see the resistance in Natacha's face starting to crumple. "Nora wants to control her own destiny. Now that we can vote, more and more of us are insisting on taking control of our lives. You can't tell me you disagree."

There was a long pause before Natacha admitted that she couldn't.

"And this autographed photo stratagem," Alla continued, "I know it's a money maker, and you all could do with the cash, but you must admit, it's all rather tacky, isn't it?"

Another long pause. "Well, okay, yes. You make a fair point. But even a pared-down production will cost a packet."

Alla would have given up on *A Doll's House* had she not been struck with inspiration on the Highland Avenue corner, sucking in the exhaust from a delivery truck. "I'm going to finance it myself."

Natacha reared up in her seat. "You have that much money?"

Alla glanced towards the men's room and prayed that some fervent fan had waylaid the boys for a few more minutes. "It recently occurred to me that I still retain the rights to *The World's Illusion*."

"The novel by that Austrian writer? The one that everybody was nutty for?"

"It was a huge saga with great potential, so I snapped up the North American screen rights. I never did anything with it, but it came up in conversation with Karger about a year ago. He told me that if ever I wanted to unload it, I should give him first refusal."

Natacha's eyes skittered around the room as she sorted through the possibilities. Over near the front door, Rudy and Paul reappeared. They were laughing over some private joke as Paul pretended to straighten Rudy's tie.

"What do you think?" Alla pressed.

"*If* you can get Karger to buy the rights, and *if* you get enough money to finance a decent production of *A Doll's House*, then yes. Count me in."

Alla clapped her hands. "Marvelous!"

Natacha held up a cautionary finger. "Only if we can mount a polished production. Nothing cheap. Nothing half-baked. Nothing shoddy."

"Do I strike you as the cheap, half-baked, shoddy type?"

Natacha smiled. "No, you don't."

"So we're in business?"

Rudy and Paul were only a few steps away now. "Yes. We are."

A few hours ago Alla had felt as though she'd been run over by a steamroller, and now she had a new project she could sink her teeth into, *and* an ardent admirer who wanted to sink his teeth into her. She still wasn't sure how she felt about him, but there would be time to work out that later. For now, she was lighter than a helium balloon.

"Gentlemen!" With perfect, cinematic timing, their waiter arrived with fresh cocktails.

Alla instructed them to raise their glasses. "Here's to leaving boring Norwegian husbands!"

7

*A*lla handed Dagmar the plate of deviled eggs and told her she'd follow with the stuffed mushrooms.

Dagmar frowned. "I'm worried."

Alla dismissed her concern with a wave. "Miklos isn't the most punctual bootlegger God ever breathed life into, but he *is* reliable. He'll be along any minute now. He called me yesterday to say that he'd located twelve bottles of Stolichnaya! It's not as good as Moskovskaya, but we cannot be too fussy these day—"

"I'm not talking about hooch, ya chump." Dagmar slid the eggs onto Alla's kitchen counter and jacked a thumb toward the living room. "I'm talking about your two special guests in there."

"Eva and Mercedes?"

"Aren't you worried that one careless word and your lovely salon will turn into a Punch and Judy show?"

After moving to Los Angeles in the summer of 1918, Alla had discovered a dearth of highbrow stimulation. In New York there had been no shortage of academics and intellectuals with whom she could discuss Taoism, the dreamlike art of Henri Rousseau, the novels of Colette and the poems of Emily Dickinson. But Angelenos, she found, were largely a shallow lot, content to peruse the funny papers in the mornings and go see Ben Turpin stumble over a gopher hole in the afternoon.

But she chose to believe that in a city whose population was approaching one million, there must be at least a dozen educated people whom she could invite to a Saturday evening salon.

The first few had been sparsely attended, but as Alla established herself socially, word got out. Soon, 8080 Sunset was filled with University of California professors, playwrights accompanying touring versions of their plays, dramatists lured to Hollywood by profligate movie studios, European émigrés who had fled the Great War and savage pogroms, and artists keen to escape the confines of East Coast establishment rules. Before she knew it, she had created a West Coast version of Gertrude Stein's famous Parisian salons. More than the witty conversation that flowed like the sparkling champagne she served, Alla loved being surrounded by like-minded folks who packed her home with intelligence, camaraderie, and kinship.

But it was during her Sunday afternoons that the sisterhood she prized so highly was truly free to ripen. Whereas her Saturday night gatherings drew men and women in equal numbers, her Sunday socials were female-only affairs. If any Hollywoodites knew about them at all, they probably assumed they were sapphic in nature. But that wasn't the case at all. True enough, these poolside get-togethers had attracted the sort of women for whom the love of a man wasn't the be-all and end-all. Or even the preferred-but-not-exclusive option. And yes, perhaps more than a sprinkling of the predatory types who took a look at the gay young maidens also found their way to 8080 Sunset and licked their lips in anticipation of the chase. But at the same time, there were just as many women who found that the chance to luxuriate in a rare male-free environment offered the freedom to be who they truly were. And that's what mattered most to Alla. Not who sneaked into the shadows with whom, or who left the party with a new friend.

Even if the public did know about these get-togethers, what did it really matter? Alla had never seen her love life as being bound by the rules of 'being this or being that.' As far as she was concerned, what transpired between the sheets was a constantly moving target. Who really knew the mechanics that kicked into action when one person met another and thought to themselves "I find you very attractive"? The only thing that Alla knew for sure was that her Saturday night salons provided her with great intellectual stimulation and her Sunday afternoon socials provided her with equally valuable contact.

"Why would you say such a thing?" Alla asked Dagmar. "Mercedes and Eva have come to these salons in the past."

"But not *together*," Dagmar whispered. "You've had dalliances with both those ladies. Don't you think things could get a little—?" She seesawed her hand.

What Dagmar perhaps didn't know was that both these women had also attended several of Alla's Sunday afternoon socials. They'd never participated in the same one at the same time, but it felt inevitable that two headstrong and inventive individuals like Mercedes de Acosta and Eva Le Gallienne would meet. Alla had found each woman irresistibly attractive, so it made sense that Mercedes and Eva would eventually wind up in each other's arms, too.

"Really, Dagmar, if anything, you should be worrying that your father doesn't hog Mae Murray's attention. She came to meet Feodor and, if he doesn't arrive soon, she might leave in a huff." Alla lifted the deviled eggs off the counter and placed them back into Dagmar's hands. "Now, shoo!"

Feodor Chaliapin was a deep-voiced Russian opera singer of international renown. He was touring the United States with a repertoire of Russian composers, mainly Rachmaninoff, with whom Chaliapin had worked in St. Petersburg at the turn of the century. Alla had sent a telegram to the Hollywood Hotel, doubting that he would even reply. But later that afternoon, a return telegram had arrived saying he would love to attend one of Nazimova's renowned Saturday salons. Immediately Alla had telephoned Dagmar and asked if her father, Leopold Godowsky, the virtuoso concert pianist, would like to meet him.

Secretly, Alla hoped that somehow the two of them would end up at her piano. A social coup like that would cement the prestige of what some of her regulars had started to refer to as The 8080 Club.

Three liquor bottles sat on her counter: her last Stolichnaya, a Tanqueray gin that her new friend Lilyan Tashman had smuggled in from Canada, and a half-empty Negrita rum left over from a party Alla no longer recalled. But two-and-a-half bottles weren't going to last very long if her previous salons were anything to go by. She headed out the side door that led to the driveway.

West of the Crescent Heights cross-street, Sunset Boulevard devolved into a wide dirt track that made driving difficult once the post-Halloween rainstorms swept across the city. They'd come early this year and had transformed Sunset into a shallow swamp. Alla didn't know where Miklos lived nor the exact location of his inventory, because one never asked one's bootlegger where he stored his merchandise.

A jittery pair of headlights swung into view as a truck rounded the bend to Alla's left. It slowed down, charged into her driveway and screeched to a halt. Miklos leaped from the driver's cabin.

He was a prematurely gray Hungarian with the scrawniness of someone who had managed to survive the chronic food shortages of the Great War. "I apologize, Madame. A thousand times. The coppers, I think they follow me. So I must take the long route into L.A. County where they have no power."

"That's okay." Alla led him to the rear of his truck. "You did the right thing."

"I do not want them to know my customers." Miklos was a chronically anxious type, leaving Alla to wonder if he had chosen an appropriate line of work.

"I very much appreciate that." Alla would ordinarily try to soothe his jangled nerves but she had a house full of thirsty chatterboxes and a special guest who had gone missing. "Were you able to locate the Stolichnaya? Because if not, I'll take anything you've got."

"I have fifteen bottles but you no have to buy all if you no want. I can sell them to—"

"All fifteen, please, Miklos."

He reached into the back of his truck and pulled out a bottle with a long neck. "I have some Canadian Club whiskey, fresh off the boat."

She glanced westward down Sunset, but there were no headlights piercing the evening air. If the Feds were tailing a small-time operator like Miklos, it meant they were starting to take their jobs seriously. And if that were the case, perhaps this Prohibition insanity might be around for longer than Alla ever dreamed. It also suggested they were now going after not just the people who sold bootleg but their customers, too. "How many Canadian Club may I buy?"

"I can let you have six."

"Six it is, then."

His ragged teeth shone in the light hanging over Alla's door. "This is why I stop first with you, Madame. You never ask the price."

She hefted the carton of six Canadian Clubs, leaving him to deal with the vodka. "One must prepare for the long haul."

People had been drinking the hard stuff for centuries and no naïve law like the Volstead Act was going to stop that—no matter how well intended it might be.

The sorts of guests who came to Alla's salons were students of history and psychology. They read books on sociology and human behavior. They were the types who took a wider view of things and drew deep satisfaction from discussing it at length. They were not violent drunkards who chose to drink their weekly paycheck, yet had a wife and nine children at home.

Miklos's asking price of thirty-two dollars was on the steep side but there was no telling when she might get her hands on more good stuff so she paid it, plus a little extra for his trouble, and waved him from her door.

Back in the kitchen, Natacha was filling an ice bucket. "We were speculating what happened to you."

"Miklos said he was followed by the authorities, so he took the long way around."

"Via where? Albuquerque?"

Alla was relieved to see a faint smile crack Natacha's face. She had been awfully serious of late. Selling Metro the rights to *The World's Illusion* had been the easiest part of setting *A Doll's House* into motion. Karger had tried to haggle, but when she'd calmly gathered up her purse, he'd caved. The price she'd asked for was the same amount she needed, so she had walked out of the meeting with a check for the entire budget. But that was only because she had been forced to take a lean, stark approach.

She had told everyone that it was a bleak story that didn't require the lavishness of Camille's apartment or any sets depicting life at the Paris opera house. Nora's emotional life was barren and stark, and so the sets and costumes had to reflect that. It was all nonsense, of course. The set of her 1907 stage production had been crammed with authentic details of a middle-class Norwegian home from the 1870s: books, tapestries, an upright piano, a chaise longue upholstered in button-tufted velvet. Hemmed in by how much she'd got for *The World's Illusion,* she had instructed Natacha to keep the costumes simple and straightforward.

"Simple and straightforward" was the antithesis of Natacha's aesthetic, so she'd dashed off a few designs and left it at that, preferring instead to focus her energies on Rudy's career. Over the summer, he had shot *The Sheik* for Famous Players-Lasky, who were doing a masterful job building anticipation for its imminent release. Consequently, she'd had little time for Alla, who had missed the intimate camaraderie they had shared before Signore Valentino had diverted Natacha's interest away from a frustrated Scandinavian housewife.

Still, Alla was happy that Natacha and Rudy had come tonight. "I'd have expected Feodor here by now. I hope he didn't forget."

"Oh, you know those performers. So self-absorbed."

Among Natacha's narrow range of expressions, a smile tipped upward at the left-hand end of her mouth meant that she was only having a quiet dig.

"You couldn't be more right!" Alla pulled a tray of Parmesan-stuffed meatballs out of the oven and speared each one with a toothpick. "The world revolves around them and them alone. Performers are the worst kind of narcissist." She asked Natacha to pick up a bottle of each type from Miklos's delivery and follow her into the formal parlor, where Alan Hale was finishing off the last of his old fashioned. "There you are!"

He was a wide-eyed bear of a man who'd been making movies for almost as long as movies had been around. Alla had cast him as her husband, Torvald, mainly because his white-blond hair suggested Scandinavia. It also helped that he was soon to play Little John alongside Douglas Fairbanks in the upcoming *Robin Hood*, so the added publicity he might bring could only help her production.

"We were discussing your *Camille*," he said. "Do you think it failed because Marguerite is a courtesan?"

Alla bristled inwardly. No word in Hollywood carried with it a heavier load than 'failure.' One resounding flop and suddenly you were The Leper of Los Angeles. As Alla circulated around town, lunching at the Hollywood Hotel, cocktailing at Club Royale, and dinnering at the Cocoanut Grove nightclub, people still smiled and nodded. But they were beckoning her to their table a little less often now.

She placed the meatballs on to the coffee table. "As far as I'm concerned, *Camille* was an artistic triumph and the final product achieved exactly what I was reaching for."

"That goes without saying," Alan said, eyeing the whiskey bottle Natacha had brought with her. "And if it had come out several years ago, it may have done better. Or if Metro had released it before that appalling Fatty Arbuckle incident up in San Francisco last month. Everything has changed after that, especially now that he's been arraigned on manslaughter charges—"

"I've heard they might not even set bail." Dagmar's father sat in the corner, his fingers steepled together. Alla prayed to a God she didn't believe in that Feodor Chaliapin would ring the doorbell any minute and allow her to pilot the conversation away from *Camille*.

"It's shocking to see how ferociously the public has turned against him," Natacha said. "He's so universally adored and beloved, and then—" She snapped her fingers. "Fatty Arbuckle becomes America's most-hated pariah since the guy who locked the doors of the Triangle shirtwaist factory."

"He did rape that girl, if you ask me," Eva insisted. She wasn't sitting in Mercedes's lap, but the two women had squeezed themselves into the oversized armchair near the piano. Were they throwing their relationship in Alla's face, snuggling like a couple of moonstruck teenagers?

Well, the joke's on them when they find out that I'm sleeping with the fine young man standing next to Rudy.

During the preparation of a motion picture was hardly the right time to launch an affair. Alla would have preferred to focus on *A Doll's House*. But along had come sweet, smart, funny Paul Ivano, with his flattering speeches about her beauty and talent, and how he trembled whenever she drew near to him.

They had shared their first kiss a couple of nights after the Sunset Inn.

He had invited her to dine with him at the Sixty Club. The date —she hadn't even thought of it as a proper date—had gone swimmingly. The conversation had roamed across an expanse of subjects: Mother Russia, the Great War, migrating to America, learning English, being poor, being less poor, being famous and being in the shadow of fame. But when the check came, he had barely had enough money to cover half of it.

On the walk back to the apartment he shared with Rudy and

Natacha, he had impetuously taken her hand. She was surprised to find that they were rougher than she might have imagined—if she had taken the time to imagine them, which she hadn't.

"You don't strike me as the manual-labor type," she'd told him.

"Carpentry," he replied, rubbing a callus at the base of his index finger. "I'm quite good at it."

"Is there no end to your talents?"

She had meant her query as nothing more than a gentle salve to his bruised self-esteem after the business with the check, but it had emboldened him. He'd encircled her waist with his left arm and with his right, guided her into the shadows between a pair of ficus trees, where he'd planted on her the most tremulously tender kiss she'd ever received. It was clear from the way his lips tensed when they'd touched hers that he wanted more. She didn't resist, so he pressed himself closer, kissed her with the ardor of a screen lothario—and did a damned fine job of it.

So she'd kissed him back.

He had responded by wrapping his other arm around her waist, pulling her in more tightly. The two of them had stayed locked in a clinch until the wail of a klaxon from a passing police car broke the spell. He hadn't asked if he could accompany her home, but his eyes had held an unmistakable longing that his gentlemanly manners failed to disguise.

They hadn't spent that night together. She had been too disoriented by this unforeseen hairpin turn her love life had taken with someone twenty years her junior. And a man, at that. Until she was more certain of herself, she thought it prudent to keep Paul at arm's length. He had taken her rejection well and insisted on walking her home, where he'd left her with a gallant kiss to the hand.

She had spent the next three days wondering what she was waiting for. Take love where you find it, she kept telling herself, even if it comes charging into town from the most unexpected direction. Paul was sincere, intelligent, and enthusiastic. He was widely read, held his liquor well, had traveled extensively, formed his own opinions, and he bathed every day. His only possible drawback was his gender, which, in the face of a long list of assets, seemed inconsequential.

So she had invited him over for orange blossom tea and Russian butter cookies. The afternoon was a neutral time of day in which to make clear romantic decisions. But once they'd started talking about the fall of the House of Romanoff, the time had slipped away and soon it was dusk, which meant cocktail hour, followed by dinner. It had been Scobie's night off, so Alla had fixed them each a hearty dish of thick *solyanka* soup.

That night, Alla and Paul didn't get as far as coffee and cake.

Or the night after that.

Or the night after that.

And so many nights since.

What a peculiar thing it was to be dating a man! She had half-forgotten the fragility of the male ego when it came to things like paying for dinner or initiating sex. How desperate their need to be pacified if they seemed to come up short! None of those obstacles had been a problem during her affairs with women, but men were entirely different creatures. Alla bristled at the thought of appeasing the pompous ones like Charles, but Paul wasn't like that. Yes, it was a compromise, but, she came to see, it was a compromise she didn't mind making. And surely that was the mark of a good relationship?

Alla flickered Eva and Mercedes a quick glance as she handed Paul a whiskey on the rocks. "What do you think, *golubchik*?"

Golubchik was Russian for *darling*. Mercedes stirred in the armchair as she caught Alla's implication.

Paul cocked his head to one side. "Do I think Fatty raped that girl or do I think your *Camille* failed because the puritan public considered what Marguerite did to get by in the world too distasteful?"

"Either or."

"You and Natacha did a superb job bringing *Camille* to the screen. And if the sensibilities of those bluenoses who've forced

Prohibition on us are too delicate to cope with the tribulations of what they see as nonconforming eccentrics, they'll only be satisfied with Mary Pickford playing Rebecca of Sunnybrook Farm and Pollyanna over and over until her curls fall out."

Natacha clapped her hands together. "Bravo!"

"And as for Fatty?" Paul shrugged. "Who's to know what went on in that hotel room. Maybe he did. Maybe he didn't. Maybe he believed he had permission. Maybe he assumed it. Or maybe he was too drunk to tell the difference. I do hope he gets a fair shake when it comes to trial, but I can't see how. He's already been found guilty in the court of public opinion, thanks to those malicious journalists."

The slanderous press had exploited every possible angle to this tragic story. It had gotten so out of hand that Alla doubted Fatty's attorneys could find twelve unbiased jurors. "I agree with you one hundred percent, *liubushka.*

"What's happened to the presumption of innocence?" Mercedes asked. "Did we throw it out with the bathwater along with the baby called Prohibition?"

"You know what I've heard?" Alan said, helping himself to another generous splash of whiskey. "Rumors of an organization being formed to combat the bad press that the Fatty Arbuckle fiasco has generated. Hollywood and its lack of clean moral tone has become the puritans' favorite scapegoat for everything that's wrong with America. If Hollywood doesn't take action, there might not be any film industry to object to."

"I doubt that," Mercedes said. "It's too big now to be taken down by riled-up puritans from Shreveport, or Amarillo, or wherever these people are from."

"Don't underestimate a bunch of furious Bible-toting protesters. They're the ones who pushed Prohibition through. Now that they have, I'll bet my last dime they're looking around for the next problem to fix."

The room fell silent as everyone considered Alan's point.

What would those Victorian prudes think about Nora, who

leaves her family at the end of *A Doll's House*? Would they picket outside movie houses with placards and lobby to have her movie banned?

In her experience, people who brandished the Bible to justify their views rarely allowed for the possibility they might be wrong. Or that people with opposing convictions might have a valid point.

She had assumed that her *World's Illusion* payment would cover *A Doll's House*, but she had underestimated the cost of making a feature motion picture. The money had been enough for preproduction expenses with a little left over, but they hadn't started filming yet. She was going to have to dip into her savings. Fortunately, she still had most of her salary from a six-month tour of *War Brides*.

The Keith-Orpheum circuit had paid her $2,500 a week, and she had socked most of it away into a rainy-day account she hadn't bothered to tell Charles about. Behind closed doors, they led largely separate lives with circles of friends independent of each other, so it hadn't been hard to keep her *War Brides* money tucked out of sight. It was there to be used, and she felt no qualms about using it on *A Doll's House* because she would earn it back at the box office. But now that the Arbuckle scandal was starting to ripple across 1921 like an earthquake, Alla was less sure of the ground beneath her feet.

Right at that moment, she spotted Charles in the foyer, a light coat and bowler hat in his hands. He paused for a moment at the bottom of the stairs, studying the gathering from afar. They hadn't said but a few dozen words to each other in the six months since that night of the *Four Horsemen* premiere. What did they have to talk about? Her Sunday afternoon socials? The young man who made deep grunting noises in her boudoir late at night? She assumed Charles had someone tucked away somewhere, but she had no curiosity about who it was. He met her eye for the briefest moment before he donned his hat and strode out the front door.

"Do they have a name for this organization?" Alla asked Alan.

"The Motion Picture Producers and Distributors of America."

"And who are they going to get to head it up?"

"The current rumor is William Hays."

"But isn't he the Postmaster General?" Leopold let out a derisive grunt. "They're handing the top job *to a letter carrier*?"

"The post office has precise rules about what is and is not allowed to be transported through the mail," Paul said. "Plus, he's from Washington, so he has all the contacts necessary to ensure that the film industry doesn't get swamped with mobs of angry citizens demanding strict censorship."

Alla couldn't help but smile. Paul was the youngest person in the room by more than a handful of years, but he'd presented a balanced, informed opinion that had impressed hard-to-impress people. She wanted to rush right over and kiss the dickens out of him.

Natacha picked up the plate of deviled eggs and started passing them around. "That phrase—'clean moral tone.' It worries me. Who gets to decide what constitutes 'clean'? And whose morals are we talking about? I'm not saying that people have no right to be upset. What happened in Fatty's hotel room was tawdry and Virginia Rappe didn't deserve to die under circumstances like that, no matter what sort of person she was."

Rudy cleared his throat. "As I recall, she was a lovely girl."

Everyone in the room—Natacha included—stared at him. Virginia Rappe was currently the most famous victim in America.

"You met her?" Alla asked.

"We made a picture called *Over the Rhine*."

"I don't recall it," Alan said. "Who was the star?"

"Julian Eltinge."

"The female impersonator?!" During most of the 1910s, Alla and Eltinge had been among the highest-paid performers on the American stage. "You made a picture with Julian Eltinge *and* Virginia Rappe?"

"It was a nothing little film with a fly-by-night studio and never got released. I forgot it until I saw Virginia's photograph in the papers."

"What was she like?" Dagmar asked.

"She was nice. A regular girl." Rudy bit into a celery stick filled with crabmeat while everybody else grasped that they were tangentially connected to the Arbuckle scandal. The crunching sound he made was the only noise in the room. "She was pretty. And glad for the job like I was. Keen to do her best."

"So she wasn't the hard-bitten sybarite the press is making her out to be?"

Rudy frowned, unsure of the word 'sybarite.' Alla had forgotten that this was one of Mercedes's less-endearing traits: the use of two-dollar words designed to demonstrate the breadth of her vocabulary.

"She means hedonist," Natacha explained. "A libertine." Rudy took another bite, still frowning. "You know, the flapper type who likes to run wild."

"Oh, no!" Rudy insisted. "She wasn't like that."

"S'funny how the papers are portraying her as the Whore of Babylon while depicting Fatty as a satyr," Leopold said. "Either Fatty demanded sexual favors or Virginia gave them freely. They can't have it both ways."

"And yet they do," Natacha observed. "And that's what worries me about Rudy's new film."

The news that Natacha was worried about *The Sheik* made Alla's fingers twitch with nerves. Rudy's follow-up to *The Four Horsemen of the Apocalypse* was the most anticipated movie release of the year. If there was any such thing as a sure-fire hit, *The Sheik* was it. So if the implacable Miss Rambova was worried, what did that say about her *Doll's House*?

"Worried about it in what way?" Alla asked. "From what I hear, Rudy burns up the screen."

"Oh!" he scoffed. "I do not think I am burning anything."

"That's because you refuse to watch the dailies," Natacha replied. "But I've been in the screening room and I'm telling you:

Rudy is so good as Ahmed Ben Hassan that he will threaten the masculinity of all American men."

"Oh, my . . ." Dagmar whispered.

"I doubt American men will stand for that," Mercedes said. "It's one thing to play an Argentine like he did in *Four Horsemen*. At least his character was Caucasian. But now he's playing an Arab. That will be too much for the American male ego."

"Who cares?" Dagmar asked. "Rudy's job isn't to make *them* swoon."

"Because men control the money," Alla said. Mercedes, Eva, and Natacha all nodded; none of the men did. "And if Rudy gives women a reason to say, '*That* is how you should behave!', the menfolk are not going to like it. Not one little bit. This Arbuckle tragedy is pushing the movie-going public to become more conservative, and that spells doom for any picture that takes a controversial stand. I doubt anyone over at Famous Players-Lasky has thought about that."

"But Rudy is not playing an Arab," Natacha said. "The intertitles make it quite clear that Rudy's character is half English and half Spanish, and not Arab at all. So there's nothing to be worried about."

"Really?" Eva asked. She and Mercedes were sharing a cigarette now, pulling it out from between each other's fingers to take a puff. "'Ahmed Ben Hassan' sounds awfully Arabian to me. And the thought of Rudolph Valentino in desert robes carrying off a white woman to have his wicked, wanton way with her will be enough to send husbands into a temper. With the mental image of Fatty Arbuckle pressing himself on Virginia Rappe so fresh in everybody's minds, anything that doesn't reinforce the traditional status quo where the husband calls the shots and the subservient wife follows his orders—well, that'll go out the window, if you ask me."

Alla's front doorbell rang. "That must be Feodor!"

Leopold rocked forward in his chair. "Chaliapin? He's coming? Here? Tonight?"

"I had hoped he'd be here when you arrived," Alla explained. "I wanted to give you an early Christmas surprise." She rushed to her door and pulled it open.

On stage, Chaliapin had mastered the skill of transforming himself into Don Quixote or Mephistopheles. But standing on Alla's front steps in his bow tie and straw boater with matching trim, he looked more like a high school history teacher.

"Madame, I am so sorry to be late, but I could not locate a taxi with the ease I expected."

Though only a few decibels above a murmur, his voice held the deep-throated potency of a singer who could reach the back row of the Metropolitan Opera House without straining.

"Think nothing of it," she said, drawing him inside. "You've arrived now and that's all that matters."

He rubbed his hands together to warm them. "I do hope Leopold Godowsky is still here."

"You should have seen him when he heard you were coming."

"Perhaps we can offer your guests a musical bagatelle or two. It shall have to be extemporaneous, of course."

"We'll take it any way we can get it. And I, for one, will savor the diversion. Put movie people together, all we do is talk shop."

"It is the same with opera folk."

Yes, Alla thought, but your next project isn't threatened by newspapers who care more about selling lechery than reporting the facts.

8

*P*aul directed Alla's Rolls-Royce to the curb along Wedgewood Place and pulled on the hand brake. Every mansion that dotted the hillside behind them had a Christmas tree in its front window lit with tiny colored electric lights—whites, greens, reds, blues. Had she been in a better mood, Alla would have found the panorama quite charming in a fairy-tale, winter-wonderland way. But she was not in the cheeriest frame of mind for a party and several times on the drive over, she had almost told Paul to turn the car around.

The window of number 6770 was dark. *To match my mood. Maybe it's the best place for me to spend Christmas Eve.*

A week ago, Natacha had called her. "Rudy and I have scraped together a down payment on a house in Whitley Heights. It's in utter disrepair and will need tons of work, but we don't mind. We have so many plans! It will take a while, though. The place has no gas, no hot water, and no electricity. If you and Paul are free on Christmas Eve, we'd love to have you over!"

And do what, Alla had wanted to ask, pitch a pup tent? But Natacha's voice bubbled with exhilaration, so she hadn't. Being with Rudy had brought out Natacha's lighter side. It lit up her face and leavened her conversation, giving Alla a glimpse past that earnestness she usually presented to the world.

Paul kept his hands on the steering wheel. "We don't have to go in."

The flicker of a hurricane lamp penetrated the gloom beyond the front window. Alla sorely needed distraction from her surly temper. With any luck, Rudy and Natacha had built a roaring fire. Mulled wine would certainly hit the spot.

"We said we were coming," she told Paul. "We can't not show up."

"Of course we can. We're over the age of twenty-one. We're entitled to do as we please."

There it was again: their age difference. It didn't come up often, but when it did, it rarely ended well. Like when she'd told him the story about the Shubert organization paying for a language tutor, and how learning to write the English alphabet had made her feel like a twenty-seven-year-old schoolgirl. Paul had asked her what year that was. When she had replied "1906," he'd laughed good-naturedly. "We were learning how to write at the same time!" He hadn't meant anything by it, but the comment had felt like a dull blade slicing between her ribs.

"Rudy and Natacha will have seen us pull up. And besides, we have gifts that they desperately need. The poor things have spent every penny they had on their down payment."

Four large boxes sat along the back seat, each of them wrapped in brown paper. Alla had drawn little Christmas trees on them using her fountain pen and an old bottle of purple ink she'd discovered in her *secrétaire*. An array of household items filled the boxes: a cast-iron skillet, flatware, candlestick holders, a wireless radio set, a clock for their mantel—assuming they even had one.

The Sheik had been in general release for a month now and had sent the female population into a nationwide swoon. It was virtually impossible to pick up a magazine or newspaper and not come across an article, or an interview, or an editorial, or a photo of him in the rotogravure. Posters, lobby cards, billboards, advertisements—Rudy's face looked back at Alla everywhere she went.

She marveled at how adept he had become at the art of the inscrutable smile. Was Valentino laughing at you? Seducing you? Defying you? Tempting you? It was impossible to tell, and that, of course, was the goal. Oh, how every woman in the country ached to be kidnapped by The Sheik, spirited away to a romantic oasis and ravaged until his carnal needs were at last sated.

If only they knew that the object of their wicked desires was happy to stay at home and cook up a mountain of pasta while cracking silly jokes and bad puns. How horrified they would be to learn that he was up to his feverish eyeballs in debt and the only way he could piece together a deposit on a run-down dump was to sell his autographs at twenty-five cents apiece. And if only they'd been within earshot the time he'd told Alla with disarming honesty, "Women are not in love with me but with the picture of me on the screen. I am only the canvas on which women paint their dreams."

"Come on," Alla said, opening her car door. "If we don't ring their doorbell soon, they'll come out looking for us."

The house was as unprepossessing as Natacha had warned. Two stories tall with poky little windows haphazardly dotting the front, it had once been painted white but was now a dreary shade of boiled potatoes tossed in mud and left in the sun to flake off in chips the size of Alla's fingernail.

Natacha answered the door holding a hurricane lamp raised to her face. "Welcome to Wuthering Heights!"

Behind Natacha, Alla could make out the silhouette of an archway, and beyond it the fluttering light of a roaring fire. Natacha called out Rudy's name. Alla couldn't see him but heard the slap of leather against tile as he raced up the stairs. When he emerged into the light of Natacha's lamp, he wore a smile as wide as Westlake Park.

"*Buon Natale a tutti*! Come in! Come in!"

Alla pointed to the Rolls-Royce behind her. "We have gifts in the car. Perhaps you could give Paul a hand? They're a bit heavy."

As the men retrieved the packages, Natacha lit a couple more lamps deposited on a pair of battered wooden crates inside the doorway.

Natacha's upbringing had been well padded by all that money from her stepfather's cosmetics empire, and Alla couldn't help but wonder if her parents would be horrified at this bare-bones living—to say nothing of how Aunt Elsie de Wolfe would react. "Is it true you have no electricity? Or gas? Not even running water?"

"It all sounds so medieval, doesn't it?" Natacha handed Alla one of the lamps. "It's not so bad, though."

With none of the modern conveniences that everyone took for granted nowadays, she had still managed to coif her hair and wrap it in a dove-gray silk turban, fix her makeup with its customary precision, and dress in one of her serpentine caftans. This one was patterned in bold black and red stripes—but wouldn't it catch on protruding nails or warped floorboards, Alla wondered?

Alla stepped aside as Rudy and Paul appeared with the gifts in their arms.

Natacha held her lamp aloft and led them through a murky vestibule, under the archway, and into a spacious living room. To the left, a stack of flaming logs filled a cavernous fireplace. They threw out a significant amount of heat but not enough light for Alla to take proper stock of the room. From what she could tell, the walls were bare and had been painted about as recently as the brickwork outside. But the ceiling was eight or nine feet high, so at least they wouldn't feel cramped.

"We will paint these walls red," Rudy announced, "because it is the color I prefer above all others."

"And why is that?" Alla asked him.

"My mama used to grow begonias in her window boxes. That is the red I want."

Natacha murmured out of the side of her mouth, soft enough

for only Alla to hear, "Why not call it 'brothel red' and be done with it?"

Alla whispered back. "You're not going to let him, are you?"

"We don't even have the money for paint yet, so that's another battle for another day."

In front of the hearth, Natacha and Rudy had spread out half a dozen blankets and enough cushions to decorate a harem. Alla wasn't looking forward to spending an evening crouched on a pillow like a nomadic Bedouin, but that, she told herself, is what you get for socializing with people still in their twenties. Rudy produced a bottle and tore at the tinfoil wrapped around the cork. "I hope nobody has the plague!"

"And why is that?"

"We do not have proper glasses."

"Or any glasses at all," Natacha added. "I only had four and I broke them last week when I brushed them with the sleeve of my Egyptian lounging robe and sent the whole lot crashing to the kitchen floor."

Alla picked up the smallest of the boxes and told her to open it right this very minute. Natacha pulled away the wrapping paper and saw that the box contained a set of eight crystal champagne coupes. In double time, she removed the glasses from the box and filled them with what Rudy declared was the last of his stockpile.

"If I had known that," Paul said, as they clinked glasses, "I'd have asked my bootlegger to fix us up."

The champagne was domestic, but Alla was thankful that it was still cold, not overly bubbly, and, more importantly, contained enough alcohol to dull the thorny spikes of her *Doll's House* dilemma. She took a second, deeper sip. "You have a bootlegger?"

"My barber's brother runs a whiskey distillery out past Cucamonga. He's part of a whole network run by a guy called Frank Orsatti, who says he can get his hands on pretty much anything as long as you're willing to pay."

Alla regarded her lover with fresh eyes. His dewy-eyed outlook on the world was an irresistible antidote to the jaded ennui that beset her once in a while. What she especially appreciated about this boy—he hated it when she called him that, but at twenty-one he was barely out of short pants, for heaven's sake—was how he would find a way to remind her that he wasn't as green as all that. Like just now, for instance. He had his own bootlegger. How marvelous.

Rudy topped up everyone's glasses. "Somewhere around here, we have a peeka-nickuh basket." He had worked hard to improve his English, but he would occasionally twist a word like a wad of saltwater taffy. "What?" he asked. "A *scampagnata*—it is called this in English, si? A peeka-nickuh?"

"Yes, Rudy," Natacha told him, "that's what it's called. But if your fans could hear you, would they still see you as the swarthy lady-killer?"

Rudy grunted. "Lady-killer. I do not like this word. It sounds cruel, like I take them in my arms and stab them."

"When you think about it," Natacha said from behind her coupe, "there is a stabbing motion involved . . . but it's not your hand that's doing the stabbing."

Alla and Paul burst out laughing, but it took Rudy a moment to comprehend Natacha's ribald meaning. He threw his head back and let out a roar. "Si, si! You are right. The stabbing of a different kind, it is more enjoyable, no?"

"It is more enjoyable, yes," Natacha said. Then waved toward the dark at the far end of the room. "It's not much, but this palace of Versailles sucked up most of my *Doll's House* money. Speaking of which, have you found a distributor yet?"

Alla inched her cushion closer to the fire to help ward off the wintry drafts blowing through this white elephant. What had Rudy and Natacha been thinking? But her thoughts turned gloomily back to her own problems; Alla had worries of her own to ruin her sleep.

On the final day of principal photography on *A Doll's House* she had handed the editing process over to a guy named Lou. He had come recommended by Marshall Neilan, who'd directed Mary

Pickford in a dozen pictures. Lou hadn't a lot of experience but came cheap, which was helpful because by the time filming was over, Alla had exceeded her budget by an uncomfortable margin.

But at least filming had gone smoothly. Minimal sets had meant a quick preproduction, and a carefully planned schedule ensured that they had shot the whole thing in sixteen days. Alan Hale had put in a splendid performance, and the two of them had formed a mutually respectful bond that she felt had translated to a convincing relationship on screen. Really, it couldn't have gone better, so she hadn't been quite prepared for the brick wall she'd hit as soon as she started making the rounds to solicit distribution.

Setting up meetings hadn't been difficult. Not initially, at any rate. But it hadn't taken a genius to interpret the solicitous smiles glowing at her from behind the wide mahogany desks. Three-piece suit after three-piece suit had agreed to meet with her out of deference to her standing in the industry. Her first ten or twelve movies had been unqualified hits—an impressive run by anybody's standards.

But every meeting had ended the same way: "I'm sorry, Madame. However, . . ."

They had all been very nice about it. An empathetic tone. A kindly smile. A reluctant my-hands-are-tied pantomime. But it was uncomfortably obvious that some of them had only agreed to see her so that they could later brag to their wife or mistress or poker cronies that they had met The Great Nazimova. *But you should have seen how she begged. Talk about desperate.*

She presented Paul and Natacha and Rudy with an optimistic smile. "Not yet. But Hollywood is a town bursting with opportunity."

In truth, she had practically run out of worthwhile people to ask. Her final appointment had been with a pear-shaped man whose name she had already forgotten. He owned a chain of movie houses strung along the western seaboard. Thirty-seven in all. He had grimaced when she said the name 'Henrik Ibsen,' giving himself away as one of those anti-intellectual types looking for scanty bathing beauties until the next Mack Sennett film shipped.

Later that evening, she'd had to face how reckless she'd been to assume her film could acquire distribution by virtue of her name alone. She had presumed that it would open doors. And it had, but it was of little consolation when those doors had closed equally fast.

"All I have to do," she told them, "is knock on the right door."

Rudy reached behind him and grabbed a small, slim gift. Only half an inch thick and wrapped in white butcher paper, it wasn't much bigger than his hand. His smile was tentative, almost meek, as he offered it up to her. "I have not the money to buy you something so I make this."

"Oh, Rudy," Alla said, "you didn't have to."

Rudy shrugged away her admonishment. It was a book of some sort, but if he hadn't bought it, what had he done? Stolen it? She pulled at the rough string that tied the package together. The paper fell away to reveal a small notebook covered in black felt. "What is this?" she asked him.

Natacha told her to open it.

On the first page, Alla read the words written by hand in a careful, delicate scrawl:

A Book of Poems for
Madame Nazimova
by
Rodolfo Alfonzo Guglielmi

"Rudy!" She turned the pages over one by one. He had filled each one with poems: of love, of longing, of home, of the mother country. There was a poem about food; another one talked about standing in a spotlight; another one spoke about the shadows of three o'clock in the morning. And each of them was in dark green ink. "You wrote all these? For me?"

His smile turned remorseful. "I could not afford to buy a book of poetry, so I made one instead."

Alla pressed it to her chest as she blinked away the tears. "My darling Italian *golubchik*. I am touched beyond words."

"You cast me in *Camille* and give me the big break. This is my *molte grazie*."

Alla swallowed the sour taste curdling in her mouth. If she could have had a moment on the set of *Camille* to live over once more, she would have chosen not to sabotage Rudy in the way she had. She had come to regret her decision, but never so acutely as she did right at that moment.

"I shall treasure this till the day I die, truly I will." She watched him blush slightly.

"Honey," Natacha said, "before it gets too cold out there, perhaps you should show Paul your new Avions Voisin."

Rudy leaped to his feet like a gazelle, unabashed glee brightening his face. "Come!" He pulled at Paul's elbow. "You must see the sleeve valve Knight engine. A work of the art!"

The two men each grabbed a lamp and dissolved into the murk.

"Never have I known someone to tinker with a perfectly fine automobile the way Rudy does. Personally, I would have paid off the tailor first, but it's not my money." Natacha drained her glass, then lifted the bottle to the firelight to see how much champagne was left. Not much, but enough for two. She poured the remainder into their glasses. "So, you and Paul, huh?"

"I could say the same about you and Rudy," Alla replied. Natacha carried with her a remoteness that had prevented Alla from being able to picture her with anybody—man or woman. That she'd fallen for someone who skipped and capered through life with nary a thought for tomorrow made her choice all the more confounding.

Natacha stared off into the shadows. "I guess it's true what they say about opposites attracting." She shifted on her cushion. "He's a sweet man, though. Rather like Candide before Voltaire puts him through life's trials and tribulations. I worry that the bulldozers of this industry will steamroll over him. Look how Metro treated him. Though, of course, I hardly need to tell you."

Waves of nostalgia descended on Alla. Between the far-fetched scripts and Karger's reluctance to take on any material he deemed risky, she hadn't been at all happy working there. Then again, she hadn't needed to worry about the logistics of when or where her next movie would open, how many theaters would show it, how long it would take to turn a profit, or how it would play in small towns. After production was over, her most onerous task had been to choose a dress to wear to the premiere.

It's the price of freedom, she told herself. If you want the spoils, you have to earn them. Alla glanced in the direction of the garage.

"Don't worry about those two," Natacha said. "Once Rudy gets going on pistons and hood ornaments, it's hard to stop him. They'll be out there for ages. So, about *Doll's House*—is there a problem?"

The fire in the hearth was dying down now; the December chill of the place settled around Alla's shoulders, along with the house's creaks and moans. Knowing Rudy's love of Italian opera, Alla was surprised he hadn't lugged his hand-cranked Victrola to the house. "I've been trying to secure distribution, but all I've heard are variations on the theme of Thank You But No Thank You."

"It's like you said: Hollywood is bursting with opportunities. All you need is the right door."

"I've been to see every reputable company in town."

"Except the one you haven't tried yet."

Natacha's lack of bowl-of-cherries optimism had always appealed to the morose Russian buried deep inside Alla. It was, she suspected, part of the reason why they felt like they were fine-tuned bellwethers of the other's moods. So this attempt at buoyant positivity made Alla wonder if Rudy's innate everything-will-be-all-right outlook on life was rubbing off in the best possible way.

"Thank you for saying that," Alla said. "But it's all looking rather bleak, I'm afraid." She let out a deep sigh. "I bet Pickford doesn't have these problems."

Natacha slid a finger underneath the front of her turban and slipped it off. She reached around to the back of one of her coiled braids and withdrew a hairpin that had worked loose. "I wouldn't be too jealous of America's Sweetheart, if I were you. Look at what they've got her doing—*Little Lord Fauntleroy*! I hear she's about to film *Tess of the Storm Country* again. Nearly thirty and still playing twelve-year-old girls." She re-inserted the hairpin and pressed her palm against the braid to restore its shape. "Don't get me wrong. She's very good at what she does, and from what I hear she's a lovely woman, and obviously very business-savvy, but do we really need to go over again how that sort of approach is right for her but is the diametric opposite of what's right for you?"

The night Alla had come home from her meeting with the West Coast theater chain owner, Paul had done his best to bolster her spirits with a coq au vin dinner that he'd prepared himself. Delicious though it was, his efforts had fallen short. *This* was the reminder she needed. "God no! I'd rather take a job doing facials behind Elizabeth Arden's Red Door."

Natacha abruptly got to her feet. "Follow me."

Taking up a lantern, Alla followed her through a second archway, down a couple of steps and into a smaller room that, from its size and shape, appeared to be the dining room. Natacha shouldered a swing door that opened into a bare-bones kitchen. A line of four large windows revealed a lemon tree growing at the center of a courtyard. A three-quarter moon shone through its sparse branches and onto the tiled counter.

Setting down her lantern, Natacha pulled a small package from one of the cabinets. This, too, was shaped like a book. "When I saw it, I had to get it for you." She pushed their lanterns closer so that Alla could see her gift more clearly.

"But you are practically broke. You shouldn't have! Or did you make this, too?"

"Hardly!"

Alla tugged at the white ribbon holding the green-and-red-striped paper together. The left side of the dust jacket featured a drawing of a naked she-devil, large horns curling above her head and her lips pulled wide in a cryptic grin. A winged creature of some sort, probably female if the bulbous hair was anything to go by, knelt at the devil's feet, its hand pressed in prayer. On the left-hand side was the title:

SALOMÉ
A Tragedy In One Act
by Oscar Wilde
Translated from the French
With sixteen drawings
by Aubrey Beardsley

"It's a first edition of the English translation." Natacha opened the book at random, revealing a sumptuous Beardsley illustration of Salomé in a billowing cape with a peacock design. "Translated by Wilde's lover, Lord Alfred Douglas."

"Oh!" Alla could only manage a whisper. First Rudy's book of poetry and now this. The couple's thoughtfulness and generosity had stolen her voice.

Natacha flipped the pages to the start of the book and pointed out the dedication in large black letters: PIERRE LOUŸS. "I know you're an admirer of his, and of Wilde, so—"

Alla cut her off as she threw her arms out and wrapped them around Natacha's shoulders, tighter than a Gossard girdle.

The last few weeks she'd spent traipsing around, cap in hand like a Dickensian street urchin, pleading for someone to take her movie, had ground Alla's self-confidence to a nub. She had pinned hope against hope that maybe, just maybe, people would get to see

Nazimova in the role that had launched her into the American consciousness. Surely moviegoers would line up to see that! Or so she believed. But she had failed to convince one single three-piece suit that *A Doll's House* would be a moneymaker. And now she felt like the ghost of someone who no longer mattered.

For all her detachment, her reserve, her self-reliance, Natacha Rambova was the one person who understood how Alla saw the world. And that was because she viewed it through the same eyes.

"Thank you so very much. This gift means so very much to me. I'm exceedingly touched."

Natacha patted Alla on the back and pulled herself free of Alla's clasp. She closed the book and traced a circle around the word *Salomé* with a fingernail lacquered in dark red nail polish. "What if we filmed it?"

Alla drew back from the counter, fingers pressed to her mouth. A myriad reasons why this was an impossible idea flooded through her. She didn't know where to start.

Or was it such a crazy idea?

NAZIMOVA IS SALOMÉ! She could see the posters already. And the story was outrageous: a scorned princess dances the Dance of the Seven Veils to entice her stepfather to bring her the head of the man who has rejected her. Moviegoers devoured stuff like that. With Natacha in charge of costumes and art direction, and no Frowny-Puss Karger to tsk-tsk every decision they made, anything was possible.

For the first time in months, Alla's heart bulged with possibilities. But that's all they were: possibilities.

"I love your idea, truly I do, but we can't."

Natacha crossed her arms. "Give me three reasons why not."

"I don't have distribution for *Doll's House* yet, and until I do, I can't even think of starting another film."

"Everybody I know commences work on their next project as soon as they've finished their last."

"But—"

"I reject your argument. What's next on your list?"

"Theda Bara did *Salomé* already. It is too soon to release another version. And she did *Camille* four years ago. People will say that I am imitating her career—and who would blame them? Theda made that movie at the height of her vamping. Churches protested the immorality of her leaping across the screen in her unmentionables and now that this MPPDA and its code are on the horizon, we won't get away with doing another *Salomé*."

She shivered as the raw night air of this dump burrowed into her bones. Natacha hooked her arm through Alla's and led her back to the fireplace. "You may have a point about *Camille*, but I've been doing some research. Theda's *Salomé* was based on a relic called *Antiquities of the Jews* written in 90 AD by some crusty old-timer called Flavius. There is nothing modern or interesting about that."

Alla picked up a fresh log from the stack beside the fireplace and dropped it into the hearth. A string of loud pops and snaps rang out as it caught fire. "You can't be suggesting we update the Salomé story to modern times. We did that with *Camille*."

Natacha pulled their cushions together so that they were practically sitting kneecap to kneecap. "Our source material was written in the last thirty years and not two thousand years ago. We would end up with a more contemporary feel to the film, regardless of when we set it."

Alla sat quietly for a moment. *Salomé* wasn't a story that would have ever occurred to her, but Natacha's argument had merit. There was nothing mundane about the Dance of the Seven Veils, and if they could find a titillating way to lure moviegoers into theaters but not one so provocative that it would send the MPPDA into a flap, then maybe . . . maybe . . .

A name loomed over Alla like a rain cloud.

Sarah Bernhardt.

After Wilde had published his play, Bernhardt had announced that a production would be mounted on the London stage. They had been deep in rehearsals when the Lord Chamberlain had decided to ban it. Along with the Marquess of Queensberry's denouncement of Wilde as a sodomite, the incident had caused such a furor that it reached a thirteen-year-old girl mired in the backwaters of Yalta. Even now, thirty years later, Alla remembered it clearly, as well as the controversy that had fulminated around the opera that Richard Strauss had written a dozen or so years later. He'd based his libretto on Wilde's *Salomé* and the Germans had not been pleased.

"You may be right about giving *Salomé* a more modern interpretation," Alla told Natacha, "but performing this piece has never gone smoothly."

Natacha smiled obliquely toward the flames. "I've always seen you as a breaker of rules."

Her words were a salve to Alla's battered ego. If she had brought Natacha into all those meetings, she might not have had to face wholesale rejection. Alla began to tell Natacha that she would give the idea some thought, but her pragmatic Russian side asserted itself.

"Have you not forgotten that I'm forty-two?" she protested. "How could I possibly get away with playing a sixteen-year-old girl? I'd be a laughing-stock."

"Correct me if I'm wrong, but three years ago you played a fourteen-year-old Hedvig in *The Wild Duck*."

"I did."

"And nobody batted an eyelid."

Which was mostly true, although Alla recalled a couple of how-dare-she reviews. "In any event," she said, "you can get away with it more easily when your audience keeps its distance. But when the camera is *this* close and your face will be projected onto a screen bigger than a billboard? No, no, no, no, no!"

In the distance, a ripple of male laughter heralded the boys' return from the garage.

"Thank you, my darling dear," Alla said, giving Natacha's hand an encouraging squeeze. "It's a brave idea. A worthy one. And wholly in keeping with our ideal of producing films of high artistic quality, but *Salomé*—especially Oscar Wilde's version—is out of the question. But this book! It means the world to me."

The boys emerged from the dark, rubbing the cold out of their hands. "Come here and warm yourselves," Alla told them. "It's time to open your gifts!"

9

Alla tossed her hat onto a chair tucked into a nook on the perimeter of her foyer. Her aim lacked the verve it needed for the hat to hit its target, and it fell to the rug instead.

Her maid was whistling "Everybody Two Step" in the sunroom, which probably meant she was ironing. "Scobie!"

The whistling stopped. "How did it go?"

Alla tugged at the fingers of her glove. "You know those bank people. So hard to read."

Scobie appeared. She was a Scot of indeterminate age. Wiry almost to the point of emaciation, she was a thoroughly loyal and dependable woman on whom Alla relied to keep her household running by doing all the tasks Alla had neither the interest in nor aptitude for.

"Did you press my navy wool suit for this afternoon?"

"Doing it now, Madame. The cream blouse is already done." Scobie frowned. "You look like you could do with some tea."

"You're a mind-reader. As strong as you can brew it, please."

Scobie's frown yielded to a naughty grin. "How about a splash of that Canadian Club whiskey I found in the back of the pantry?"

Alla tugged off her gloves and headed toward the reading chair in the sunroom where she could kick off her shoes. Why on God's green earth had she worn new ones to a bank meeting? Her toes had started throbbing just as she had walked into the Hollywood First National.

"Didn't Viola and I finish off that stuff when she came over last week?"

"Or perhaps that's what I told you. Liquor is getting harder and harder to come by."

"Miklos told me I'd never have to worry."

Scobie bent down to retrieve the discarded hat. Alla pouted. Olive green with a contrasting ribbon around the base, the hat was one of Alla's favorites and she felt fleetingly guilty for flinging it aside.

"Ah, but here's the rub," Scobie went on. "It seems that Miklos has disappeared."

"No!"

"I should imagine that vanishing into thin air is not uncommon in his profession."

Alla unbuttoned the straps of her shoes and let out a deep sigh as her feet escaped their blue silk prisons. "That is a blow. How many bottles of the Stolichnaya do we have?"

Scobie dusted off the brim of Alla's hat some more. "We had four, but about an hour ago Master Charles left for a poker game, which means there's now three. So? Strong tea with or without a wee dram of Canadian Club?"

"Without." Alla wriggled her toes to revive the circulation. "This meeting I have later on—it's my last chance, so I must keep all my wits about me."

Having telephoned every reputable movie distribution company in town, Alla had spent most of January buttonholing the fly-by-the-seat-of-their-pants studios, two-bit movie exchanges, and second-string theater chains that she never would have approached a couple of years ago. Every rejection forced her to swallow her pride and contact the next rinky-dink operator down the list.

And then, the tiniest flame of hope had lit the encroaching darkness.

At Armstrong's Café on Hollywood Boulevard, one of the makeup assistants at Metro had approached Alla's table to say that she'd heard *A Doll's House* was "all dressed up with nowhere to go" and suggested a minor subsidiary of United Artists called Allied Producers and Distributors Corporation. A pal of hers had worked as a featured extra on a cowboy movie, *Perils of the West*, made by a Poverty Row studio named Primrose Pictures. They'd been having trouble finding distribution until they'd struck a deal with Allied. "You never know," the girl had said, "but it might be worth dropping a nickel into a telephone to find out."

Alla had wasted no time in tracking down this Allied outfit. She was put through to a Joe Farrington, who at first had sounded like every puffed-up suit she'd dealt with for months. But when she had explained the reason for her call, a burst of excitement had shot down the line.

"Yes, Madame! I would be most delighted to talk over this opportunity. Shall we say my office next Wednesday at four o'clock?"

Alla checked her watch; it was almost noon now. She called out, "I don't suppose we have any of the molasses spice cookies—"

"Master Charles polished off the last of them, too." Scobie disappeared into the kitchen.

Alla closed her eyes and wondered what she ought to do about Charles. He had always cooperated quite amiably with their arrangement. They both got what they needed out of it, so why was he acting pigheaded about everything now? She had noticed the first signs around a year ago on the night of the *Four Horsemen* premiere, when he'd stubbornly refused to get out of the car. Consequently, he had missed out on one of the most sensational evenings of the year. Ever since then, dry rot had set into the driftwood of their relationship. And now it was all about stealing bottles of Stolichnaya and hogging the last of the molasses spice cookies.

Her eyes flew open again.

Is he jealous? Of Paul?

Or if not Paul, then the idea of Paul? Did Charles see himself as being supplanted by a younger, more energetic version of himself?

But that was absurd! It wasn't like she and Charles had ever had a conventional marriage. They had slept together a number of times, and on occasion it had been quite agreeable, but it had been a long time since anything like that had happened. What did he have to be jealous of? Was it the Saturday night salons? He'd never attended any of them, but she'd never said he couldn't come. What was he waiting for? An invitation? Or was it the Sunday socials around the pool? Granted, he was plainly unwelcome there, but he knew of Alla's capricious nature when it came to that sort of thing. But why, after ten years, would any of this suddenly be a problem?

It was all so ludicrous that Alla put it out of her mind when the chime of the doorbell rang through the house.

Alla listened for Scobie but could hear only the ticking of the carriage clock on the mantel over the fireplace in the room next door.

"Scobie?" No response. Alla waited a moment or two in case her maid should appear and save her having to answer it herself. "SCOBIE!"

Another rat-a-tat-tat of knocks. They weren't going away, whoever they were. Alla got to her feet and contemplated putting her shoes back on but decided against it.

She opened the door to find Robert Florey, an actor she knew quite well, standing on her front porch. He was a six-foot-four Frenchman with the wide-open face of a Midwesterner but the *joie de vivre* of a Parisian. The way he commanded attention in any room he entered, Alla felt sure he was destined to become a director.

"Madame!" He greeted her with kisses to each cheek. "I know I should have telephoned ahead, but time is of the essence so I came knocking in case you might be *chez vous*."

She pulled him inside. "Always delighted to see you. My maid was fixing tea; however, she's disappeared, so I'm not sure—"

"I'm here!" Scobie called. "I was plucking a lemon from the tree in the backyard for your tea, Madame."

"It's tea for two now," Alla called back, and ushered Robert into the sunroom. Once they were settled on the sofa, she asked, "And to what do I owe this unexpected pleasure?"

He took off his dark brown trilby and unwound the woolen tartan scarf from his neck. He coiled it inside the hat which he laid on the coffee table in front of them. Adopting a more serious expression, he tried several times to speak but stopped himself. He was normally one of the chattiest people she knew and always had an entertaining anecdote to relate, an interesting book to recommend, or someone he wanted her to meet.

He finally managed to blurt out, "I don't wish to interfere." The shrill whistle of the teakettle shrieked from the kitchen. He waited until Scobie had lifted it from the gas. "I know about your appointment this afternoon. With Farrington at Allied."

"You do?"

"I am dating a new girl. Very sweet. And tall, which is convenient. Her roommate is the girl who approached you at the Armstrong Café. She told me about how she suggested Allied."

"I contacted Mr. Farrington as soon as I got home. Between you and me, Robert, I was expecting yet another rejection, but we made an appointment right away."

Robert sucked in a breath between his teeth. "Did you go?"

"It's at four this afternoon."

"So I'm not *trop tard*."

Oh God. What now? No wonder it had all been so easy. "Too late for what?"

Scobie marched in holding "the good tray" they saved for company. Lacquered in the blackest paint Alla had ever seen, it featured a Japanese maxim stenciled in red that translated roughly as "Love is everywhere"—or at least that's what Dorothy Arzner had told her when she'd presented it to Alla for her birthday. The tray held a Wedgewood china teapot and matching cups, creamer, sugar bowl, and a dish of lemon slices. Scobie had also set out a plate of animal crackers, which were hardly suitable for company but, absent the spice cookies, they'd have to do. Scobie set it down. "Do you want me to pour?"

"Thank you, Scobie, but no. That'll be all." Alla picked up the teapot. "You were saying?"

Robert shook his head. "This Allied outfit—do you know anything about them?"

"Not really, other than they're a subsidiary of United Artists."

"They are."

"So they're not dubious charlatans who mightn't be there in the morning."

Robert raised an eyebrow as he accepted his teacup. "You know what this business is like."

Alla's patience was starting to fray, along with her optimism that Allied might solve her problems. "Robert, dear, my appointment is at four, so if you've come to play the Prophet of Doom—"

"You know Max Linder, *n'est-ce pas*?"

It was a gratuitous question. Ten years ago Linder had been a huge star for Pathé in France—big enough to be known as 'The Highest Paid Actor in the World'—before crossing the Atlantic to start working for Essanay around the time Alla had signed her contract for Metro. His comedy shorts had been so successful that he had formed his own production company, much like Alla had done and for the same reasons: so that he could keep a fat percentage of the profits.

"What I mean is," Robert continued, "have you met Max?"

"Not in person. Why?"

"Well, you see, when he formed Max Linder Productions, he entered into a deal with Allied and—" He set his cup onto its saucer. "Let me put it this way: he used to put out five or six films a year. When was the last time you saw a Max Linder picture?"

Alla failed to recall what Linder's last movie was about. She picked up a slice of lemon and bit into it. The juice stung the inside of her mouth. "Are you telling me Farrington is not to be trusted, or that Allied is a disreputable company?"

"Having not dealt with them myself, I couldn't say, but the last time I dined with Max, he was talking about returning to France."

"But he's a Frenchman, so that's hardly surprising, is it?"

"Oh yes, he was always going to do that, but only after he'd conquered America. Crawling home defeated was not part of the plan. Look, Madame," Robert said, more gently now, "I'm not saying Allied will treat you the same way."

I'm a woman. If anything, they'll treat me worse.

"But as your friend, I felt it my duty to warn you. Step carefully. Based on what Max has told me, you're better off exploring all other options."

Alla smiled weakly. "Unfortunately, Mr. Farrington *is* my last option. I have nowhere else to turn."

Robert nodded slowly, the cheerfulness draining from his eyes. "In that case," he reached out and selected a tiger-shaped cracker and held it up, "be one of these, my bold Madame. Be a tigress!"

* * *

Joe Farrington reminded Alla of her first violin teacher. Dark brown hair starting to gray at the temples, parted down the middle, and brilliantined flat against his head. He had similar eyeglasses, as well: small, gold circles through which he peered at her with a mix of delight and awe.

Alla had been twelve years old when she began lessons with Professor Borovsky and had soon proved to be a prodigy. Whenever little Alla entered the room, Professor's eyes would shine with joy. After untold years of enduring the discordant scrapings of inept pupils, finally he had a student with real talent. It was that look in his eyes that made Alla want to please her professor and pushed her to excel, which, in time, had opened up a path out of her wretched life. She saw that same expression now in Farrington's face.

He came out from behind his desk, his right hand extended in front of him. "Madame Nazimova, what a delight to meet you at last."

Distracted to see Professor Borovsky's eyes staring back at her, she mechanically took his hand. It was warm to the touch, not clammy as she'd expected. In Alla's experience, studio men like Farrington often had dank hands. They went with the condescending smirks and the lascivious way they drank in a girl, picturing how she looked in her step-ins.

"How kind," Alla murmured.

He canted his head as though to say, *The pleasure is all mine*, and pulled out one of the visitor chairs in front of his desk. "Please, take a seat."

Robert had been a darling to forewarn her about this meeting. He'd had only her best interests at heart and she adored him for that. But this Farrington chap, with his reverential Borovsky eyes and his gentlemanly comportment, was the opposite of the portrait Robert had painted. Alla settled on the chair, unsure what to think.

"Your telephone call came as quite a surprise," he said. "After we hung up, I called my wife. Rose is a fan of yours and she'll probably castigate me for sharing this with you, but when she heard about our meeting she squealed like our little girl, Leatrice!" He reached for his blue-and-yellow-striped silk pocket square. It didn't need rearranging, but he adjusted it anyway. "I do hope you'll make my wife happy by signing an autograph?"

None of the men Alla had seen in her search to distribute *A Doll's House* had shown deference or displayed manners like this. And they certainly hadn't talked about their wives and daughters.

Farrington took out a blank sheet of expensive bond paper and a fountain pen from his desk drawer and slid them toward her.

"Your wife," Alla said, unscrewing the top of the pen. "Her name is Rose?"

"I can't begin to tell you how delighted she'll be when I present this to her."

Alla wrote her standard autograph greeting:

To Rose,
With love and affection,
Nazimova

She gave the final 'a' in 'Nazimova' its usual swooping embellishment.

"Do you enjoy sherry, Madame?"

"I do."

Farrington drew a bottle from the bottom drawer of the filing cabinet behind him and set it on his desktop. "You might know this one." He rotated it to show her the sepia-toned label of a tranquil mountainside. Two words ran along the top in dark red letters: MASSANDRA SHERRY.

Alla clapped her hands together. "Oh! But this is from the Crimea!"

"It is?"

"Massandra, close by Yalta, is where I grew up!"

Was this bottle of Crimean sherry leading to a larger ploy to win her trust in order to hoodwink her later? Alla wanted to give him the benefit of the doubt, but Robert's brows, furrowed in concern for her welfare, gave her pause.

"Come, come, Mr. Farrington." She dropped her voice into as close to a coquettish purr as a forty-two-year-old woman could manage. "You must have known that."

He gave the label a cursory glance as though reading it for the first time. "I thought you hailed from Moscow. Is that near Yalta?"

Alla saw no evidence of deception in his face. "They're a thousand miles apart. I trained at the Moscow Dramatic School. Perhaps that is what you're thinking of."

He took a couple of small crystal glasses from the shelf behind him and filled each one with a generous pour. "I should be more restrained; this is my final bottle."

"Prohibition is closing in on us all."

"I didn't think so, but my bootlegger has gone on the lam."

Alla frowned. Just when she felt she had secured a grip on the slang of her adopted language, along had come the 1920s with its flappers, its jazz music, and its relaxation of social norms. With the exception of Prohibition, Alla had welcomed all these brash changes, but alongside them, a vocabulary of jargon had sprouted like weeds after a summer rain and she was having trouble keeping up with them all.

"Where has he gone?" she asked.

"On the run. Taken a hike. Vamoosed. Disappeared with no warning."

"His name isn't Miklos, is it?"

Farrington lowered his glass onto the ink blotter. "Could be. I knew him as Hungarian Mike."

"That's Miklos!" Alla cried. "He supplied me, too, but my maid told me he has vanished."

"Well now, ain't that something?"

They each took a sip. American sherry was fine; Spanish sherry was better; but Russian sherry conjured memories of the Leventon family dining room with the landscape painting of the Caucasus Mountains above the sideboard, the faded Turkish rug under the table, and the tinny chime of the dinner bell her mother would ring ten minutes before she served the meager meal she had prepared on the paltry household budget Alla's father allotted.

"Damn that Miklos!" Farrington said. "I mean, I hope he's okay an' all, but what do we do now? Go dry? I don't know about you, Madame, but I find that alternative unacceptable."

"This is Los Angeles; Miklos is not the only bootlegger in town."

Farrington tapped his Moose Lodge pinkie ring against his glass. "You ever heard of a guy by the name of Frank Orsatti?"

"As a matter of fact, I have, yes."

"Through Louis Mayer, I suppose?"

Mayer had been with Metro Pictures but had left prior to Alla signing with them. Out of the fortune he had made by nabbing the second-round franchise to *Birth of a Nation*, Mayer had started his own studio, which, like most, had had its share of successes and failures.

"Someone else," Alla told Farrington. "Why do you ask?"

"I spent New Year's Eve at the Hollywood Hotel. They had so much champagne on hand you could've drowned in it. The good stuff, too—from Europe. Anyway, I overheard some grand old dowager type tell a friend of hers that she heard one guy had supplied everything and that his name was Frank Orsatti. Her friend pulled a face as if to say 'A foreigner? How distasteful!' But her friend said, 'If Orsatti's good enough for Louis Mayer, he's good enough for me.' I was hoping you might know him and perhaps call him."

"I'm sorry but I don't." Alla sipped at the Crimean sherry again. Velvety smooth. Sweet but not overly. Oh my, what liquid heaven! But she was loath to call anybody at Metro, even if they had a connection with Louis Mayer. "I'd imagine there is somebody in my broader social circle who—"

Farrington shook his head. "No need to go to all that trouble. I'll be joining an all-night poker game later this week. Someone there'll know him. Leave it to me. Now, I suppose we'd better get down to business." He pointed to her sherry glass. "Care for another?"

Alla's glass was almost empty. "Not if it's the last of your stock."

"If Mayer uses this Orsatti guy, I'm sure he can get his hands on more."

By the time Farrington had finished pouring, Alla was feeling a little lightheaded and wished she'd been more cautious. But oh, that label! And the flavor. It had left her with a craving she didn't know she had. That was the problem with Prohibition—now that drinking alcohol was a criminal act, everything tasted that much more delicious.

"And so to business," she said. Farrington sat up straighter in his chair. "You might have heard about town that I have filmed *A Doll's House*."

"Have you, indeed?" His face stayed neutral.

"Yes, and now I am seeking distribution. Your name came up—"

"May I ask how?"

"A friend of a friend worked on *Perils of the West*."

"In the normal course of events, I wouldn't have done a western. Let's be honest, that title is little on the nose. But the scenario was so well-crafted that I took a chance and it realized a healthy profit." Farrington was now threading his fountain pen around his fingertips with a dexterous skill born of hours and hours of practice. "So . . . *A Doll's House,* huh? That's an astute choice, I must say. The play in which you made your mark on Broadway, right?"

Alla's headline-making American debut had been fifteen years ago. How remarkable that this movie man would know that.

"As well as several successful revivals."

"But even hit plays can only accommodate a finite number of patrons. Motion pictures, on the other hand . . ."

Every previous distributor had shown Alla the door by this point in the conversation. "You wouldn't believe how many people don't see it that way."

"How many other distributors have you approached, Madame?"

Alla had lost count after twenty, but that was information he didn't need to know. The sherry had made her a little tipsy, but not *that* tipsy. She studied him more closely. Professor Borovsky's look of admiration had been replaced by . . . what? Suspicion? Wariness? Skepticism? She couldn't be sure. "You'll want to see the picture first, won't you?"

"What shape is it in?"

"Fully edited."

The pen slid through his fingers and clunked against his brass desk lamp. "I would love to see it. We have a screening room here on the lot."

Alla drew in a deep breath. The heady effects of the sherry were tapering off and Robert's warning came back to her. "I need to ask you about Max Linder."

Farrington's eyebrows shot up. "What about him?"

"He was producing half a dozen pictures a year before he signed with you. As far as I can see, he hasn't released a single one since."

"And you want to know what's happened to him."

"I believe it's called 'due diligence.'"

"It is," he agreed, "and I'm glad to see you're doing yours. I have neither the time nor the inclination to conduct business with people who aren't serious about their work."

Now that they had moved past social pleasantries, the man's geniality had fallen away. Was he praising her? Or insulting Max? Of course, it wasn't entirely out of the question that he might be doing both at the same time. "I'd have thought Max Linder would take his work seriously."

"And he does. But Monsieur Linder has yet to master the English language like you have. Negotiations took an ungodly amount of time because every point had to be translated, and clarified, and then translated again. And when we finally signed, preproduction took even longer because it's a period piece."

"So you've made a picture?"

"The Three Must-Get-Theres."

"What an odd title."

"I agree, but it's a parody of *The Three Musketeers*, so we're stuck with it. You'll be seeing advertisements for it in a month or two."

"That's encouraging to hear."

"When may I see your picture?"

"How about this weekend?"

"Two o'clock on Saturday?" He went to stand, but noticed she wasn't going anywhere.

Alla mentally crossed her gloved fingers. "Can you give me an idea of your standard agreement?"

"Generally speaking, it's fifty-fifty."

"I assume we're talking box office grosses?"

"Straight down the middle, yes."

Alla's heart sank a little. She'd been hoping for a seventy-five/twenty-five split. *A Doll's House* had gone over budget, not so much that it threatened to capsize her financially, but that's what this morning's appointment had been about: her bank manager had confirmed she had $300,000 in her various accounts. It was a decent amount of money, but between maintaining 8080 Sunset and her country house, Who-Torok, in upstate New York and her Manhattan apartment, as well as providing support for her sister, Nina, and her children, *and* her brother, Volodya, back in Russia, that amount could dwindle fast. It was enough to qualify her for a $100,000 loan, but only if *A Doll's House* secured distribution.

"Is there a problem?" Farrington asked.

The Allied Producers and Distributors Corporation was Alla's last chance. If this didn't work, *A Doll's House* would never see the inside of a movie house. And if that happened, Nazimova Productions was kaput.

"No, no," Alla replied. "Just curious."

10

*L*ois Wilson, an actress friend of Alla's, selected a slice of Gouda from a plate on the coffee table. She took a tiny nibble and settled back into the sofa in Alla's formal parlor. "The one I wish I'd seen on stage was Eleonora Duse. Apparently, she gave Bernhardt a run for her money. Even George Bernard Shaw said so, and he strikes me as being the sort who doesn't hand out praise like they're GooGoo Clusters. What I wouldn't give to have seen her perform in—well, anything!"

Lilyan Tashman picked out a larger slice and bit into it like it was the first chunk of food she'd had all week. The black-and-gray beaded flapper dress with the eighteen-inch fringing hugged her curves like a boa constrictor. "I know what you mean, but I would have *killed* to have been invited to the tea party that President Cleveland's wife threw for Duse. An actress had never been in the White House—through the front door, anyway—and Washington society was positively scandalized. Now, *that* would have been one interesting afternoon."

"Imagine the faces of those ladies when they learned that Duse later had an affair with Isadora Duncan!" Lois giggled into her highball.

"Now, now," Alla said, "we don't know for sure that they went bumper to bumper." In truth, her friend Eva Le Gallienne had confirmed the rumors but had sworn Alla to cross-your-heart-and-hope-to-die secrecy.

Lilyan held up a warning finger. "You can't say the same about her friendship with Yvette Guilbert, so don't even try."

Alla laughed and suggested to her friend that, with the rate she was going through the whiskey, she might want to pair the cheese with a cracker or two.

Lilyan shot her a withering look that the two of them had dubbed "Yes, Mother!" the night they had met. They were at an end-of-filming party at Famous Players-Lasky for a Richard Barthelmess picture called *Experience*. Richard and Alla had made their movie debuts in *War Brides,* and Alla had been touched that he had invited her now that he was a name-above-the-title star.

Lilyan had a hundred salacious stories, involving every profession: stage managers, chorus girls, casting directors, waitresses, dress makers. There was one particularly riotous story that had Alla crying with laughter, about a dentist with the unfortunate name of Dr. Torment and his penchant for excessive use of nitrous oxide. They'd had to withdraw to a secluded corner of the shooting stage until they'd collected themselves. They had been pals ever since.

It irked Alla that Allied had declined to throw a post-premiere party for *A Doll's House*, even though the New York opening had gone superbly well and the reviews had been excellent. Granted, *The New York Times* had called her "a jumping jack" in the earlier scenes with the children—but was that a compliment or condemnation? *Photoplay* had congratulated her for "curbing her Camille tendencies." Alla hadn't been sure how to take that until she burrowed deeper into the review: "As Nora, one of drama's most absorbing women, Nazimova really acts." That had been a delight to read, but the *Chicago Tribune, Philadelphia Inquirer, Boston Globe,* and *Charlotte Observer* had all published reviews that were a disconcerting concoction of tepid praise mixed with snide fault-finding.

By the time of the Los Angeles opening, she sensed that the tide was turning against her in the way that vague acquaintances never brought up her movie at cocktail parties or chance meetings at Hamburger's department store.

Paul believed that the New Women of the 1920s weren't identifying with her character, Nora. "You've won the right to vote. Bernice has bobbed her hair," he'd added, referring to a recent F. Scott Fitzgerald story that had caught the public's imagination. "She drinks and smokes in public; she dances on table tops and shows her knees. Women take freedom for granted now. They're thinking 'Of course Nora discards her situation, but what I want to see is how Mae Murray handles her liberty when she gets it.'"

It had been hard for Alla to hear Paul's theory, but she loved him for having the courage to say it. There was a distinct possibility that he was right, which made the L.A. opening and subsequent reviews crucial. She couldn't bear waiting for the morning papers alone, so she'd thrown this party to distract herself.

She felt Paul slip his hand into hers and give it an affectionate squeeze. "Was that a 'Yes, Mother'?"

"I'm afraid so," Alla replied. "Chilling, isn't it?"

"Pray that you're never on the receiving end, my sweet little pea," Lilyan told him. "I hear tell that it's not very comfortable." She shot Alla a look that said, *You're with a guy now? I don't get it.*

How long had Paul been standing there? Had he heard all that prattle about Eleanora and Isadora and Yvette? Lilyan's voice blared like a foghorn, so he probably had, but what did he think?

They'd never talked about the reasons why she was the black sheep of her family, and why none of her relatives beyond her sister, Nina, talked to her. To them, she was an immoral misfit whose infamy had brought only disgrace to the family. For a long time now, Alla had accepted it as the price she paid for being who —and what—she was. Charles had known the price of admission when he'd aligned himself with her, but Paul was a whole different situation.

Did he care about her history? Did he know her well enough by now to understand that she was someone who bedded the person, not the gender?

The past four months had been like an endless surprise party. How different it was to be with a man—and not just between the sheets, although that too had brought its fair share of marvels. She now had to deal with beard stubble and the smell of Barbasol shaving cream. He lacked the money to buy her jewelry or perfume or even flowers, so he made his gifts by hand: a tiny sculpting-wire tree to hang her earrings; a leather bookmark with her name tooled down the middle; a tall, thin, single-flower vase he'd glazed with vivid stripes of purple alternating with green. They were all so very masculine and each one had thrilled her to the core. And when it did, that thrill always took her by surprise.

"Where are Rudy and Natacha?" she asked him. "I'd have thought they'd be here by now. Rudy is back from Catalina Island, isn't he?"

Rudy had been on location filming *Beyond the Rocks* with Gloria Swanson. Any hopes that they could complete the movie in peace had been shattered when Elinor Glyn, the author whose novel the film was based on, had descended onto the set. Scandal followed Glyn like a shadow, and so the press chronicled her every move. As far as Famous Players-Lasky was concerned, Swanson plus Valentino plus Glyn equaled gold mine. And that was great for the guys in the publicity department, but a headache for the cast and crew trying to get a job done under the unruly circumstances of a location shoot.

"They were picking up June en route."

Alla hadn't seen June Mathis since she had moved to Rudy's new studio, where she was writing his next picture, *Blood and Sand*. It was based on a novel by Vicente Blasco Ibáñez, who had also written *The Four Horsemen of the Apocalypse*. That movie had done jaw-dropping business, so why wouldn't they repeat the formula?

Someone had put Al Jolson's recording of "Rock-a-Bye Your Baby with a Dixie Melody" on her Victrola; it rang out from the corner of the room. Alla checked her wristwatch as people sang along. It was now well past one o'clock. The morning papers would be out in about three or four hours. The local critics could turn the picture's fate around. Would they shower her with roses or pummel her with rocks? Was Paul right? Had she come out with this picture too late, before women had started taking their newfound freedom for granted?

She shook off her angst and told Paul that the icebox had a stash of Castellane—a brand of French champagne, care of Joe Farrington's new bootlegger—and would he be so kind as to retrieve two bottles and circle the room?

She excused herself and approached a couple of young actresses. Mildred Davis and Virginia Fox were grilling the Talmadge sisters, Norma and Constance, who, surprisingly, had appeared on Alla's doorstep *sans* husbands.

"Anita Loos. L-O-O-S," Constance was telling Virginia and Mildred. "I'm serious! The woman is a genius!" Constance's words had become slurred since the last time Alla had dropped by her conversation.

"You must have read her stuff in *Vanity Fair*," Norma insisted. "She's like Dorothy Parker—"

"Oh, that girl's poems do make me laugh out loud!" Virginia cut in.

"Anita's stuff is like that but less mordant. Sharp as a razor blade, though."

"She's written so many of my scenarios that I've lost count!" Constance declared. "At any rate, my point is this: once you get into a position of power and can dictate which writers you want, put Anita at the top of your list. You can't go wrong." It wasn't until she lifted her glass and found it empty that she noticed Alla standing there. "Did I mention how much I enjoyed your *Doll's House* this evening?"

Constance had told her twice already: the last time was when Alla was passing out the caviar—and that hadn't been too long ago. But as the time when the early papers would be available ticked closer, Alla needed to hear the praise Constance was intent on heaping upon her—even if it was the usual hollow acclaim one offers under circumstances like these.

Alla waved to Paul, who had appeared with an open bottle of Castellane in each hand, and beckoned him over. "What did you like about it, Connie?" she asked. "From one actress to another."

Constance thrust her glass toward Paul. "Your performance, of course, although that goes without saying. Those scenes with the children! Oh my goodness, the tenderness in your eyes said volumes. Absolute volumes!"

Alla had been pleased with how she had handled them, but they were the ones in which *The New York Times* had described her as a jumping jack. The ambiguousness of the description had dented her confidence more than she wanted to admit. But now she had one of the biggest movie stars in Hollywood singling them out without any prompting. Alla felt a rush of optimism and began to ask Connie how she felt about the climactic scene when Nora leaves her husband, but a commotion in the foyer drew everybody's attention.

"Sorry we're late! It's all my fault!" June pulled off her mushroom-brim hat of navy-blue stiffened silk and fluffed out her mob of loose curls. She spotted the champagne Paul was holding. "I hope that's for me. I've been giving my typewriter a right old walloping since ten this morning, so now it's time to tranquilize."

Rudy and Natacha appeared behind her, Rudy in his usual tux and Natacha in a dark gray floor-length sheath. As Alla approached to greet them, she saw it was made of bombazine. Trust Natacha to take a material that had gone out of fashion years ago and reinvent it with such effortless chic.

"I felt terrible that we couldn't make it to the premiere tonight." She landed a light kiss on Alla's cheek. "But Fred Niblo and his wife Enid threw a cocktail party and we were invited."

Rudy scowled. "What is the English word when you must do a thing you do not want?"

"Compulsory?"

"Si! I do not like being told what to do in my private life."

"We've been over this," Natacha said, her voice straining to maintain the party atmosphere. "Fred will be directing you in *Blood and Sand*. His last two pictures with Douglas Fairbanks were huge hits. This movie could catapult your career."

"Isn't that what *The Sheik* did?"

"You know how easy-come-easy-go movie careers can be. You can't rest on the laurels of *Four Horsemen* or *The Sheik* forever."

But Rudy was no longer listening. Paul had appeared and the two of them were talking about the unforgiving tightness of a toreador's uniform.

Alla guided Natacha to one of the sofas where Scobie had set out more caviar, crackers, and red wine. "Was Fred's party worthwhile, at least?" In Hollywood, cocktail parties were rarely just cocktail parties. Rather, they were places where one built relationships, maneuvered for introductions, flirted for attention, and made lasting impressions.

Natacha flicked an exasperated look in Rudy's direction. "He thinks that when you're at the studio you work, and when you're not, it's playtime. He just doesn't get that when you're an actor, you have to push, push, push. Remind them who you are. Show them what you're capable of. He might be America's heartthrob right now, but it won't always be the case."

"Rudy lives for the present."

"And don't I know it." She took a sip of the Bordeaux. "Delicious. From your new supplier?"

Alla nodded. "Did Rudy make a good impression?" If they had to miss her premiere, Alla hoped that it had at least been worth their while.

"I'd never met Fred Niblo before. Someone told me he can be a bit of a stodgy old bore, but I found him quite darling. I'm glad I pushed Rudy like a nagging old fishmonger's wife. The two of them discovered a mutual passion for mechanics and engineering. You know how Rudy is with his automobiles. They stood there for an eon comparing Duesenbergs to Bugattis. I barely understood a word of it, but they seemed to have a whale of a time."

Alla patted her hand. "Then it was time well spent. I was so besieged by people after the show that Paul Bunyan could have been wrestling with his ox and I wouldn't have noticed."

"Oh, but that's not why we're late," Natacha said. "We had to make a stop." The furtive way Natacha swept the room with her eyes made Alla nervous. "June has a contact at the *L.A. Times* who told her that if we dropped by some time after midnight, he could get us a sneak peek of their review."

"Did you?"

Natacha nodded.

"And?"

"Not great."

"Not great but good?"

"Barely even that."

Alla poured herself a full glass of the Bordeaux and wished Paul was close by to hold her hand. "Without the support of the *L.A. Times*, we're pretty much sunk."

"They loved your performance."

"Enough to outweigh what they thought of the overall picture?"

Natacha shook her head.

Alla now regretted throwing this party and wished she had the house to herself. "R.I.P. Nora Helmer." She drank deeply. This Orsatti chap sure knew his business. "I'm very well aware that you weren't a big fan of the idea in the first place, so I want you to know that I appreciate your support anyway."

Natacha set her glass on the side table next to her, then grabbed Alla's out of her hand and put it down. "Come with me." She guided Alla out of the room and into the foyer, where a hatbox stood on Alla's vestibule table. Natacha hooked her fingers through the cord. "This is the other cause of our tardiness."

"Your milliner must love you to keep such late hours."

Natacha mounted the stairs to the second floor and entered the master bedroom, where she pushed aside the hats and coats and bags that Scobie had deposited earlier in the evening. She placed the hatbox on the edge of the white coverlet.

"What is this subterfuge?" Alla asked.

"Your next picture."

"Now you've got my attention."

"*Salomé*!"

Alla sighed, disappointed. "We've already talked about that."

"I know we have—"

"None of my reasons have changed."

Natacha crossed the room to Alla's bookshelf and took from it the copy of *Salomé* that she'd given her at Christmas. Back at the bed, she opened it up to the first Aubrey Beardsley illustration.

Alla's patience drained away. "Yes, yes. I know his work is gorgeous and striking and inspirational, but—"

"Hush now!" Natacha pulled at the cord on the hatbox and slipped off the lid. A faint smell of paint wafted up as Natacha lifted out its contents.

It sat on a wig stand but it wasn't a wig.

Nor was it a hat.

But what was it?

It had short braids, long as Alla's index finger but thicker. They stuck out from the scalp but had some bounce to them. Attached to the end of each braid was a small white ball, smooth all over. It was one of the most glorious headpieces Alla had ever seen.

Natacha flipped the pages of the book in her hand and held it up to another one of Beardsley's extravagant illustrations, in which Salomé wore a headpiece similar to the one in Alla's hands.

"This is what you will wear when we film Oscar Wilde's *Salomé*."

Alla fingered the white balls. "What are these made of?"

"They're Venetian glass beads," Natacha said. "My wigmaker, Odie, suggested we paint them with white phosphorus so that they would glow in the studio lights during filming. I wasn't sure at first, but she was right. They'll look like tiny electric bulbs. Nobody will have seen anything like it on the screen."

The chattering babble of the party percolated up the stairs, contrasting with the shocked stillness filling Alla's bedroom. "You commissioned this wig to convince me to do *Salomé*?"

Rambova nodded. "I loved this book so much that I went back and bought one for myself so that I could study Beardsley's illustrations. I've been quite transfixed by them and couldn't work out why until inspiration hit me. The costumes, the sets, the whole look of the picture—I knew exactly how to do it all. But I wasn't sure if it was possible to pull off the image in my head. If we couldn't get it to work exactly right, I wouldn't revisit the idea with you. But look at the result."

The glass beads shone like tiny moons in the light of the bedside lamps as Alla rotated the wig around and around. The effect was mesmerizing. Alla could barely breathe.

Imagine what they would look like under the blaze of studio lighting.

Imagine what The Great Nazimova would look like!

"So?" Natacha pressed. "What do you think?"

It's been done before—but not like this.

You're far too old—but nobody will be looking at your forty-two-year-old face with this magnificent creation on your head.

Sarah Bernhardt tried to do this and failed—but who says that Bernhardt is the be-all and end-all?

Alla carefully placed the headdress back into its box. "I adore it."

"The wig or the idea?"

"Both!" Natacha pressed her lacquered fingertips to her mouth. "If there's one thing I've learned through my *Doll's House* experience," Alla continued, "it's that you might have made the best motion picture in the world, but it all comes to naught if you haven't means to distribute it."

"So where does that leave us?"

Alla replaced the lid on the hatbox and patted it twice. "I shall pay another visit to Mr. Joe Farrington of the Allied Producers and Distributors Corporation. He's not the clod that most of his colleagues are. If I can convince him to back *Salomé*, it's full steam ahead."

* * *

For her meeting with Farrington, Alla chose a suit of dark brown velvet. It had been a costume she'd worn in a play once upon a long time ago. *The Master Builder*? Or *Little Eyolf*? The years of those early plays in New York were starting to blur into a pageant of curtain calls, stuffy dressing rooms, closing-night parties.

She was quite proud of how the skirt still fit—her diet had certainly done the trick. But the jacket bore far too much fussy decoration down the lapels and around the edges. And the sparkling buttons were all wrong. They worked well on stage, where a thousand people were looking up adoringly. But for a business meeting, it projected the wrong image. So Alla instructed Scobie to strip away all the filigree and replace the buttons with utilitarian brown leather ones. Paired with sensible shoes—low-heeled, plain but elegant—Alla felt fully prepared to launch into battle.

Equipped with a purse on one arm and the cord handle of Natacha's hatbox on the other, she walked into Farrington's office all winsome smiles and isn't-this-lovely, but was confronted by a sourpussed version of the sweet talker from two months before.

"Take a seat." He pointed to it as though to say, *Either one. Or stand. I really don't care,* then crossed his arms and sucked a scrap of food from between his teeth.

Alla lowered herself onto the nearest chair, placing her purse on the other and the hatbox onto the polished floorboards. They had recently been waxed and the smell was a little overpowering. She anticipated a battle and had come prepared, but she hadn't counted on such a hostile audience. She pivoted to a new opening gambit.

"I haven't properly thanked you for introducing me to Mr. Orsatti. Goodness gracious me, what a treasure that man is. He located a crate of champagne in a trice. And some delicious Bordeaux. I forget the name of it right now, but if you like red wine, you should ask him about it. I threw a party after the *Doll's House* premiere. Nothing lavish, you understand. Just an intimate gathering of compadres. It would have been quite the dull affair without Mr. Orsatti's contributions, let me tell you."

Farrington's expression grew even more sour, if that were possible, and Alla groaned inwardly. Studios always threw the celebration that followed a movie premiere, but during a telephone call with Farrington the day before, Alla had made casual mention of a party and received flinty silence in return. Farrington had changed the subject to insist that she go out of her way to warmly greet the motion picture critic for the *San Francisco Examiner*, who had taken the train down to L.A. to see *A Doll's House*. And now she had opened with the very thing that he'd avoided. It must have sounded as though she were throwing it in his face: *You cheapskates thought so little of my picture that I had to throw the party myself!*

Should she keep talking? Change the subject? Or hold off until she could better gauge this prickly mood he was in?

Alla was deciding on her best tactic when Farrington said, "Now that your *Doll's House* has flopped, what disaster are you here to foist on me?"

So it's like that, is it?

"First of all," she said, "it hasn't been a complete disaster. *The New York Times*, *L.A. Times*, and *Washington Post* all published glowing reviews. And they weren't the only ones. The critic for *The Atlanta Journal* raved about my performance. And second, in New York, my film played to capacity houses for twenty-two straight days. I personally called the theater to check—"

"Be that as it may, Madame, I'm only concerned with the bottom line and *A Doll's House* failed to make back its budget at the box office."

"It's only been out two weeks."

"The picture flopped."

"There are flops and then there are flops."

"No. There are only flops."

"I'm talking about the difference between critical flops and commercial ones."

"We are not running a museum here. I had a meeting with Mr. Abrams."

Hiram Abrams had persuaded Mary Pickford, Douglas Fairbanks, Charles Chaplin, and D.W. Griffith to form an independent distributing company, which had become United Artists. It was a bold move, but there was something about Abrams that soured Alla's stomach.

"He raked me over the coals—" Farrington stopped himself with a sharp intake of breath and studied his manicured fingernails. "That's not entirely accurate. 'Raking over the coals' is putting it too strongly. But he did bawl me out for agreeing to our fifty-fifty split."

"What would he have preferred?"

"Sixty-six/thirty-three."

A percentage like that would have left Nazimova Productions even deeper in the red than it already was.

He leaned forward on his elbows, his fingers interlaced, his knuckles blanching. "I assume you're here to sell me on some idea of yours. It had better be good, because I'll have to take it to Abrams and he is not a generous man. Especially seeing as how United Artists hasn't gone according to plan."

UA had four of the most prominent names in the picture business, but somehow, they weren't able to produce enough films to keep their cash flow from dipping dangerously low. But that setback was not Alla's problem.

"Mr. Farrington," she said, injecting a full measure of confidence into her voice, "I want to film *Salomé*." Her announcement met with a blank face. She couldn't tell if he was shocked, horrified, impressed, or intrigued, so she charged forward. "Back in the nineties, Oscar Wilde wrote a one-act play about *Salomé*, the stepdaughter of Herod, Tetrarch of Judea—"

"I saw Theda Bara do it a few years ago. I didn't think she was all that great—"

"Exactly!" Alla slapped a palm on the desk. It was an old upstaging trick she'd learned. A sudden noise recaptured an audience she was in danger of losing. "Their approach was all wrong. They based their scenario on the writings of Flavius Josephus. Two thousand years ago, a donkey cart whose wheels didn't fall off was enough to impress audiences."

Her joke was a calculated risk that paid off. Farrington's lips curled at the ends, hinting at a smile.

"But Wilde's play is a one-act," Alla continued, "so the film won't be a sprawling epic that goes on for hours and hours like *Intolerance*. Plus, it only has two locations, which means two sets. And there are ways to suggest the rich pageantry of a royal court without replicating Versailles."

Farrington held up his hand. "Yes, yes, that's all very well, but *Salomé* is the story of a teenage girl who does her seductive Dance of the Seven Veils—"

"She's a courageous young lady who takes control of her life. Since women got the vote, they're going to college more, entering the work force in greater numbers, and are marrying later than their mothers and grandmothers. Some of them are even questioning whether they will get married at all." She saw how his eyes opened wider with every declaration, so she added, "I have researched all the statistics and can show them to you if you want." She was bluffing—but she was an accomplished actress whose job was to convince an audience.

"I can see for myself how society is undergoing a shift." His tone was more conciliatory now. "However, there's no getting around two important facts." He held up a finger. "*Salomé* does an extremely risqué dance. That in itself is problematic." He held up a second one. "But she does it to bring about the execution of John the Baptist. In the current climate I suspect it might be all too much."

"You're talking about Fatty Arbuckle?"

"Thanks to him, half the country thinks we're all a bunch of reprobates who indulge in orgies and drug binges as though life here is one long Sunday brunch."

"They have no idea how hard we work," Alla said. "The long, arduous hours we put in for nothing more than their amusement."

"And now we have this Hays guy." Farrington's face was flushing like a soapbox preacher's at Pershing Square. "Nobody's calling him a censor but that's what he is."

"We should be able to say what we want to say. That's free speech, if you ask me."

"Right. If we have to stick to a gosh-darned blueprint when we're making our pictures, you can forget creativity, forget innovation, forget variety, forget independence."

Alla recognized a cue when she saw one. She hooked the hatbox cord through her fingers and hoisted it onto his desk. "And besides, none of the previous Salomés have ever had anything like —" she removed the lid "—THIS!" She placed Natacha's wig in front of him and watched his mouth drop open. "Visualize how it will look with imaginative lighting and expert cinematography."

Natacha's ingenuity said more than any superlatives Alla could string together, so she took her seat and waited.

"Well, Madame, you do have a flair for the dramatic, I'll say that much for you."

"Thank you," Alla said, although she wasn't entirely sure he had meant it as a compliment. "Between this and the costumes and sets we've designed, cinema-going audiences the world over will have seen nothing like it and you will have brought it to them."

"No, I won't." His smile turned indulgent. "*You* will."

Was he giving her the go-ahead? "A motion picture is a collaboration in every sense of the word," she hedged. He tapped a fingernail against the top of his armrest. It was the only sound in the room and felt to Alla like a death knell. "So that's a yes?"

"It's a yes and a no."

A 'yes and a no' was better than a flat-out 'no.' "Care to elaborate?"

"Hiram Abrams will have my head on a platter like I was John the Baptist being served up for dinner." The tapping halted. "Which means that I cannot fund this *Salomé* project of yours. Not one Allied dollar can go into the production."

Damnation and hellfire. Producing *A Doll's House* herself had shrunk Alla's personal coffers by quite a margin and she wasn't sure she wanted to pay for *Salomé* out of her own pocket. Her next question was going to be 'Can we talk about co-funding this project?' but it had died a sad and quiet death. However, Alla sensed that Farrington had more to say, so she kept her mouth shut.

"However, I can rent you one of our stages to film it in, and I am willing to pledge whatever resources we have at our disposal to distribute it."

The other day, Alla and Natacha had drawn up a rough budget for *Salomé* and had arrived at a figure of around sixty grand. Maybe seventy. Eighty at the absolute most. She certainly had more than that socked away in the bank. She was reluctant to dip into it, but was prepared to if she must. And apparently she must. "Oh, Mr. Farrington! I could kiss you!"

"That won't be necessary."

Natacha's glass beads clanked and clunked against each other as she lowered the wig back into its box. She hadn't at all been sure if bringing it was a wise choice. But without it, she might not have struck a deal.

He jabbed a warning finger toward her. "If you run out of money, it's no concern of mine. Allied cannot, nor will we, contribute one thin dime to prop you up."

"Nor shall I ask you." Alla traced a cross over her heart. "Thank you! Thank you!"

"Thank me by providing us with a marketable picture."

Her mind was now a blur of possibilities. Alla Nazimova and Natacha Rambova were a team like no other operating in Hollywood. Together they'd show the world what two women could achieve.

11

The journalist from *Screenland* magazine wore a hat jammed with lavender silk petunias that jiggled up and down as she nodded. They were so distracting that Alla wanted to yank them out of the dark purple ribbon around the brim.

"So you agree with me?" she asked, handing over a steaming porcelain cup. What was this woman's name? Sophie? Stella? Sylvia? Or was it Shirley? She looked like a Shirley. More to the point, she looked like a sob sister.

"Oh, yes!" Maybe-Shirley replied. "Suffrage is just the beginning, don't you feel?"

"Quite so." Alla sipped her orange blossom tea and stole a glance at the clock. Scobie would be here soon with that glorious headdress. Had Natacha not taken a chance and commissioned it, she wouldn't be sitting here on the first day of filming. "Who says that women can't be directors? Can't produce their own movies? Can't run production companies?"

The journalist twittered like the pine warbler that had recently taken up residence in one of the lemon trees in Alla's backyard. "And that shall be the thrust of my article. Women hold their own in the film business."

"I would be proud to see my photo next to a headline like that."

"However, I do need to counter all these—well, I wouldn't call them rumors. Speculations, perhaps."

"About what?" Alla asked.

"It's just that ever since this whole disgraceful Arbuckle affair, Hollywood has changed, as I'm sure a smart woman like yourself has noticed."

"Given the shocking exaggerations that the yellow press serves up on a daily basis—"

"And not just the yellow press. Thanks to Fatty Arbuckle and Virginia Rappe, William Desmond Taylor and Mary Miles Minter, reporters falling over each other in the rush to print ever more outrageous headlines!"

Alla tsked like a small-town spinster who disapproved of everything. "I want to film *Salomé* to remind us that purity still exists."

Maybe-Shirley blinked as she tried to comprehend Alla's logic. "But isn't Salomé the one who dances the Dance of the Seven—"

"She was the one pure creature in a court where sin was rampant. Yet she remained uncontaminated, like a flower struggling to bloom in unreceptive soil. The first time she loved, she asked all, since she was willing to give all. It's my belief that women today ought to be reminded that they have forerunners who have been pushing society's norms for countless generations. I want to inspire them to believe that maybe this time we shall reach parity with men. It's worth striving for, don't you think?"

Maybe-Shirley placed her teacup onto the table next to them without making a sound, then shifted forward an inch or two. "Speaking of men, I don't mean to pry—" which meant that she did "—but can we clarify the issue of Mr. Bryant?"

Alla forced down a mouthful of tea. "Clarify?"

"I've been told that your husband recently moved out of your marital home and into the residential wing of the Hollywood Athletic Club. Is that true?"

This sob sister was sharper than Alla had bargained for. Magazines like *Screenland* had many pages to fill each month and usually rewrote whatever press releases the studios handed them, interspersed with pro forma interviews. But this old gal had done her homework.

Alla had been in the middle of preparing *Salomé*—an intense time in the life of any motion picture—when Charles had stormed downstairs and confronted her in the dining room.

"I'm out!" He'd pointed over his shoulder to the matching pair of suitcases at the bottom of the stairs. "I'm done. I'm finished. I'm through. We're through. You and me. It's over."

Alla had thought of all the recent times he'd snapped at her for no reason, the constant coming and going whenever he pleased without letting her know where he was, and how often he had returned home reeking of bootleg whiskey and bordello toilet water. When Charles had confronted her, she had been studying Natacha's costume sketches that were strewn across the table, so she'd straightened up and had replied, "Fine."

"What? Is that it? Ten years go down the drain and all you have to say is *fine*?"

There was a lot Alla had wanted to say. She'd wanted to remind him that theirs wasn't the first phony marriage in Hollywood. Nor was it the only one. Or the longest lasting one. That he had benefited from being married in a society that snubbed unmarried people. That he had gotten to enjoy the advantages of being on the arm of a celebrity. Paul or no Paul, they could have continued to present to the outside world as man and wife. Nothing had changed as far as she was concerned. She had wanted to say all that but wasn't sure that saying any of it out loud would have done either of them any good.

She was sad that what had been a beneficial arrangement was ending so angrily. But she had seen it coming so she was also relieved that things were resolving themselves one way or another. She regretted that she hadn't confronted what had been going on for quite some time and sought to find a compromise that both could live with. But she could feel herself growing surly and resentful that he hadn't done it either.

Unsure how to respond, Alla had said nothing, which had only antagonized Charles further. He had slapped his hands to his side. "Oh, so it's silence now, is it? You have your highbrow pals around on Saturday nights and you can't stop talking. You have those Sunday *playmates*—" he had said the word with a harsh sneer "—and it's all talk, talk, talk. But I only get silence. Well, I have my pride too, you know, and I cannot abide by this anymore!"

"Tell me, Charles, what exactly is it that you find so intolerable? That I got you cast in ten of my pictures? Or your director credit on *A Doll's House*? Not bad considering we both know who actually directed that picture."

Charles had jutted out his chin. "Oh, yes. Thanks for that, my darling wife. Now I'm known as a director of a failed picture. That'll look terrific on my résumé, won't it?"

If only he hadn't said that. If only he hadn't stooped so low. And if only she'd chosen to ignore the taunt. But the sting of *Doll's House*'s failure still jabbed at Alla's heart.

She had thrown the pencil in her hand at him. It hit him on the shoulder, making her wish she'd grabbed the scissors instead. "You ingrate! You selfish, miserable, little bastard! You don't even have the courage to say what's really bothering you."

"And what's that?"

"PAUL!" She had screamed his name with the full force of the vocal projection she'd learned after years in the theater. "He's younger. He's more handsome. And he's sure as hell more dynamic in bed. And that just kills you, doesn't it, Mister Nazimova? You're okay with your so-called wife sleeping with other women, but you think that if she's going to sleep with a man, it ought to be you. That's what this dramatic exit is about, and don't bother to deny it." She had suddenly felt twenty pounds lighter, twenty years younger, and really quite lightheaded! She had no idea how heavy the burden of a failing marriage had been until she had cast it aside. Emboldened, she had added, "You're free to move out any time you like, but if you do, there goes your *Salomé* screen credit."

"The hell it does!" he'd shot back. "My contract with Nazimova Productions calls for sole directing credit. If you renege on it, you'll hear from my lawyer."

Alla had wanted to laugh. As far as she was aware, he had no lawyer. Nor could he afford one. Mooching spongers rarely could. But with only days to go before filming on *Salomé* was due to commence, the fewer problems she had to solve the better.

"Have it your way, then."

"I fully intend to!" He'd turned on his heel and headed for his luggage.

She had called after him, "Everybody in Hollywood and New York will know that I directed *Salomé*, and when I've done it, they'll know that I am a force to be reckoned with."

That awful confrontation had been three weeks ago—enough time for Alla to calm down. And more than enough time to preserve a public face of confidence and conviction. She licked the orange tea from her lips and decided that flattery would be her best tactic.

"Most people in your line of work put as little effort into their job as they think they can get away with. But not *you!*" Alla wiggled her fingers at Maybe-Shirley. "I respect someone who takes their job seriously."

Maybe-Shirley should have known better than to fall for a line like that, but instead she blushed and squared her shoulders. "So it's true? You and Mr. Bryant have gone your separate ways?"

Alla was still formulating a palatable response when Scobie bustled into the dressing room holding Natacha's wig aloft as though she were presenting the lost Gospel of Mary Magdalene.

Alla shot to her feet. "Before you go, I'd like to show you this." She took the wig stand from Scobie's outstretched hands.

"Goodness gracious!" Maybe-Shirley set aside her notebook, her breaths coming in short bursts.

Scobie produced an invoice from the pocket of her apron and laid it on the table. "Miss Natacha asked you to sign off on this."

Alla checked the total—nearly $9,000. She glanced up to the top of the sheet and read out loud the name typed there. "Maison Louis? What's that?"

Scobie shrugged, but the journalist gave out a high-pitched yelp. "Maison Louis? In Paris? Why, that's one of the finest fabric stores in all Europe. They supply every great design house between London and Warsaw." She pressed her hands to her ample bosom. "Your costumes will be made from Maison Louis merchandise?!"

"Miss Rambova is designing all the costumes, including this." Alla gestured toward the headdress and signed the invoice. "It gives you a taste of the exceptional film we are making."

"Madame Nazimova, if this is what my readers can expect, I shall be writing up a glowing account of our rendezvous."

"How marvelous! I wish I could ask you to stay, but we've had to establish a closed set, so . . ." Alla flickered a well-practiced get-rid-of-her eyelid at her maid, who opened the dressing room door. "Miss Scobie will walk you out. Thank you so much for coming." Nazimova maintained her hostess smile until the woman was no longer in sight.

Filming wasn't due to begin for another week, but lighting tests with Natacha's wig had been scheduled for today. Normally, she was happy to leave camera lenses and lighting to her cinematographer, Mr. Van Enger. When it came to that sort of thing, he sure knew his onions, as those flappers were keen on saying, so why interfere when she had other matters to take care of? Phosphorus-covered glass balls had never been seen on screen, so the time it took to ensure they were photographed to their greatest advantage was time well spent.

Alla switched on the lights surrounding her makeup mirror and tucked stray locks into a hair net. She lifted the wig off the stand and pulled it on; it was heavier than she had expected. The heft of the glass beads made her feel almost regal. Yes, that was it.

Like a crown. But did she look like royalty? There was no precedent to shape her expectations because nobody in moving pictures had worn anything like this.

She faced the mirror. A silent gasp escaped her lips.

You look otherworldly, she told herself. No gender, no nationality. You could be from two thousand years ago or you could have come from a wild New Year's Eve party in DeMille's private ballroom. You are timeless! Another gasp popped out; this one made a noise. "You are ageless!"

Throughout the preproduction phase of *Salomé*, Alla had failed to fully convince herself that she could play a sixteen-year-old. She had stuck to her diet with the self-discipline of an ascetic and was now almost boyishly slender, especially in the one-piece tunic that Natacha had designed for her. Made of a loose, draping material that would shimmer under the lights, Alla felt better about playing a virginal stripling—but could she achieve the necessary suspension of disbelief that she would be asking of her audience?

But that was before she had understood the transformative nature of Natacha's creation.

Alla stood before the makeup table, transfixed by her reflection. What a revelation. She *could* play Salomé! She *knew* how Salomé walked and moved, how she stood when she addressed people, how it felt to be rejected by John the Baptist, and how to depict that betrayal using only her body, her face, her eyes. And if she could do this, then she could do anything. Play any part. Shepherd any movie to the screen. Produce pictures of high art and do it equally as well as those one-track-mind buffoons. The hell with them. The hell with them all. Who said she had to do it equally well? She'd do it better!

To the left of her makeup table was a window of frosted glass. It was often uncomfortably warm in her dressing room, so Alla had instructed Scobie to keep it ajar, even during wintry February. She also enjoyed hearing the sounds of a movie studio hard at work: the banging of hammers; crewmembers shouting across stages; idle extras chattering between takes; directors barking out orders through tin bullhorns.

On the far side of the window she heard the heavy footfalls of a pair of solidly built gentlemen. They were chuckling until the sound of their footsteps stopped outside Alla's dressing room.

"Who's in here right now?"

"Nazimova."

Alla didn't recognize the voice of the first speaker, but the second belonged to Joe Farrington. And she didn't appreciate his withering tone.

"*Salomé*, right?" the first voice asked.

"Yep."

"Why you okayed it is beyond me."

"Her production company is footing the bill. All we have to do is distribute it and take our percentage. It was a no-lose proposition."

The first voice grunted. "I wouldn't call a woman like that trying to pull off playing a juvenile a no-lose proposition. I mean, Jesus! What is she, fifty?"

"Mid-forties, I'd say."

"Christ almighty, give me strength. What is it with these women? Their self-delusion astounds me. Once they hit forty, they should pack it in and go be a housewife some place. I tell you, Joe, there ain't nothing sadder than a middle-aged woman who still thinks she can get away with playing the innocent maiden."

Maybe it was the freedom she'd felt following Charles's departure. Maybe it was this surprising affair with Paul that had shown her what was possible. Or maybe it was the transformative nature of seeing herself in the Salomé headdress that filled her with the grit it took to confront those two nasty oafs on the other side of the wall.

The white glass beads clanked and chimed as Alla snatched off the wig and set it onto the stand. She threw open her door and marched outside. Standing next to Farrington was a man she didn't recognize, but in a way she did. A large face, topped with an expansive forehead, a meaty nose, and drooping ears, he resembled every other man from her childhood. Alla knew a fellow Russian Jewish immigrant when she saw one. Worse still, he was around the same age as she was, but he had the gall to write her off as past her prime.

She jammed her hands onto her hips. "Hiram Abrams, I presume?"

The guy didn't even possess the humility to look embarrassed at having been caught out. "Madame Nazimova." His voice had taken on the velvetiness of a saxophone. "How remiss of me not to have made the effort to introduce myself."

"For someone who's never met me, you certainly have strong opinions."

"Well . . ." He rolled the palms of his hands around and around as though he were making meatballs.

"Don't you 'well' me." She fired off a contemptuous leer toward Farrington. *And I'm talking to you too, buster.* "We actors and actresses—our job is to turn into other people. Not variations on the people we are, but different characters cut from different cloth. Why shouldn't I play a sixteen-year-old? Just because I'm forty-three? What if the role called me to play seventy? Is that so unbelievable?" The scornful look that played out across Abrams's face was all the answer she needed. "Seventy is twenty-seven years from my present age, just like sixteen is. I can play both."

"It's different for women," Abrams replied. "You're there to be objects of desire. You're the prize, as long as you're in your twenties—and thirties, if you're lucky. But who wants to see a forty-year-old playing the vamp? Nobody wants to watch their mother trying to seduce John Gilbert."

"Maybe women do," Alla said. "Did you ever think about that?"

Abrams made a scoffing sound. Of course he hadn't. He and every man like him only ever thought of women as targets: of lust, of ownership, of power. Women were muddle-headed simpletons best suited to housework and childrearing, and better off leaving the important decisions to those with brains. In other words: men. Yeah, well, screw that. It wasn't like United Artists had set the world on fire. They'd had the odd hit, like *Way Down East*, but that was because of the three big names on the poster—Lillian Gish, Richard Barthelmess, and D.W. Griffith—and not because blowhards like Abrams were steering the ship.

"And why not shoot higher?" Alla persisted.

Abrams rolled his eyes. "Oh God, she's one of those. Moviemaking is an art form. Movies can elevate, educate, inspire, provoke. What a load of hogwash."

Farrington remained mute as a store-window mannequin. When it had been the two of them sitting in his office, he'd been a decent chap. But put him next to his boss and he was just another bootlicking toady.

"I have nothing against movies that entertain," she said. "But don't you think that they can serve a higher purpose—"

"NO!" Abrams shoved his face close to hers. She assumed it was supposed to intimidate her into backing down. Screw that, too. She stuck out her chin and flared her eyes.

"I do *not* think they can serve a higher purpose," he said. "They're the new vaudeville. A song-and-dance, a juggle, a comedy sketch; maybe a bit of melodrama." He flung his hands out and slapped them to his sides. "Nobody expects Shakespeare. Nor do they want it—any more than they want Ibsen." He drenched that last word in sarcasm.

Alla's right hand itched with the urge to slap the boorishness off the man's face. And if he hadn't been the head of United Artists, she might well have succumbed to the impulse. But why give him the satisfaction? Far better that she produce a superb picture that would make the whole town sit up and take note.

Alla drew herself up to her full five-foot-three. "You, sir, are talking out of the top of your hat."

"Which I shall eat if your *Salomé* becomes a hit."

"I suggest you stock up on salt and pepper."

She walked back into her dressing room and slammed the door.

* * *

"Abrams is a philistine," Dorothy Arzner said, helping herself some more rum. "But let's be honest, aren't all men?" She remembered Rudy was sitting next to her, and Paul next to him. "Present company excluded, of course."

"No offense taken," Paul said.

Rudy pouted "Philly—philis—what is this word?"

"PHIL-IS-TINE!" Dorothy barked. "It means an uncultured, unrefined, uncivilized, uncouth barbarian with no more brains in his head than he has in the tip of his teeny tiny—" she paused for shock value "—toe."

Adela Rogers St. Johns burst into a shower of wine-oiled giggles. A good pal of June Mathis and Rudy, Adela was a journalist for *Photoplay* magazine whom Alla hadn't met until June had insisted on bringing her to tonight's party.

Alla had forgotten about the dinner until she had arrived home to find Scobie setting the table for eight. Playing hostess was the last thing she felt like doing, but that had changed now that the meal was in full swing and they had plowed through most of her Bordeaux, some halfway decent gin that Paul had unearthed, and the bottle of Barbados rum that June had brought with her.

"You're absolutely right," she told Adela. "Joe Farrington is a philistine. If I didn't have to work with him, I would have slapped him from here to Easter."

Adela clapped her hands. "Bravo, Madame. You stuck to your guns. Pictures are the new vaudeville? Absolute tommyrot. *Camille*, *A Doll's House*, and now *Salomé*—by filming the classics, you shall inspire other filmmakers to lift their game. Truly, you should be heralded for your efforts and not dismissed like a Galatea. Who does he think he is? Pygmalion?" She gave an involuntary snort. "The man's a *pig* without the *malion*."

Adela was different from the typical movie magazine journalists like Maybe-Shirley with the jiggling petunias. Daughter of the famous trial lawyer Earl Rogers, Adela had a sharp tongue and a sharper mind, and the smarts to know when to use them and when to keep them concealed.

"Thank you!" Alla lifted her near-empty glass. "You're all such fine and dear friends who know how to boost a girl's spirits when they're in dire need of uplifting."

"I try not to look at this world with an 'us versus them' mentality," Natacha said, "but those men do their utmost to guarantee that we women can only view it one way." She turned to Rudy and Paul. "Present company still excluded, naturally."

"Thank you, my love." Rudy drained the last of his Cuba Libre and pushed his chair back. "And speaking of filming, I have my first *Blood and Sand* bullfighting scenes tomorrow, so I must have the good sleep."

People retrieved their coats, claiming to have a full day ahead of them, too. Alla didn't mind. First that interview with a journalist who wanted to probe into her personal life. Then the revelation that had come with putting on Natacha's Salomé wig. And then dealing with those two studio churls before subjecting herself to long, tedious lighting tests.

As her guests kissed her good night, Alla regretted having told Scobie she was free to leave. It was now past midnight and she hadn't anticipated how many dirty dishes eight dinner guests could generate. Paul had passed out on the couch, so he was no help. The last guest left was Dorothy, who appeared to be in no hurry.

"Let me help you with these," she said, hoisting a tall stack of dinner plates. Dorothy was a sturdily built individual—she could probably carry twice that amount all the way down to Santa Monica without breaking a sweat.

Alla followed her into the kitchen with glasses hooked around her fingers. "If I had the strength, I'd wash these myself, but I'm so terribly worn out that I must leave it for Scobie to deal with."

"I'm sure she's seen worse," Dorothy said, then added, "I am so very proud of you, by the way."

How queer it was to hear words like that from someone twenty years her junior. Especially someone with whom she'd had a brief but enjoyable dalliance that had lasted exactly as long as something like that should have, and no longer. "Thank you," she said, and waited for Dorothy to say what she had stayed behind to say.

"I have a question for you."

Alla leaned a hip against the kitchen counter for support against her encroaching fatigue. "Fire away."

"Who is Yakov?"

The sound of Paul's snoring blustered in from the living room, loud and rhythmic like a metronome. She had never heard him snore like that; evidently he must have downed more rum than she had noticed.

"Why do you ask?"

"When you were telling us about your nasty encounter with those Allied creeps, you said the name Yakov. I know Farrington's name is Joe, but the other guy—Abrams, is it? You said he looked like every Russian Jew you'd ever met in your life. Natacha said his name was Hiram, but you called him Yakov a couple of times, so I was confused. Or were there three men outside your dressing room?"

Alla didn't quite know what to say. There had only been Farrington and Abrams. Yakov, however, was her hateful father's name. But why would she have brought it up? It didn't make sense.

And then it did.

Suddenly, Alla is ten years old again. She's excitedly telling her father that she has a chance to play violin at the Hotel Russiya in a Christmas concert. Father! Father! You'll never guess who will be conducting! Nikolai Rimsky-Korsakov himself! Isn't that exciting? No, Yakov Leventon is saying. It is not. You cannot participate. Why, Father, why?

Because you are not nearly talented enough. But my teacher thinks so. He has already—Your teacher is not your father and your father says you are not talented and if you play in front of the great Rimsky-Korsakov, you will dishonor the Leventon name.

A fight ensues. Shouting. Screaming. Tears.

Little Adel runs to her room and picks up a novel she has been reading. Books are an escape from her miserable life. Children of the Streets *is her favorite. The name of the heroine is Nadyezhda Nazimova. Adel stares at the name, transfixed. She whispers it out loud. "Nazimova. Nazimova. Nazimova." She closes the book and jumps off her bed. As she races down the narrow stairwell, her cheap shoes slap against the wood.*

Father! Father! She finds him sitting near the fire, newspaper in hand. He doesn't look up. He doesn't even acknowledge her standing next to him. What if I go by another name? Her breath is short from the effort. There is a long pause. He asks what name. Nazimova, she tells him. What if my name is A—A— No, she thinks, I can't use Adel. She decides on another name. Alla Nazimova. If I am truly as terrible as you think, the only person I embarrass is myself. Another pause. Longer. Heavier. Suffocating. At last he nods. Anything but Leventon, he says.

Thank you! Thank you! Adel Leventon dashes out of the living room and up the stairs. She throws herself onto the bed. She is a new person. She is now Alla Nazimova, who will never speak to her father again. Not if she can help it.

"I don't know who this Yakov is," she told Dorothy. "Must have been a slip of the tongue combined with too much Bordeaux and dreadfully deep fatigue. Let's leave the rest of this to Scobie."

Alla walked Dorothy to the front door. Before stepping out on to the porch, Dorothy paused. "If you and Farrington and Abrams and this Yakov guy—"

"There was nobody called Yakov." Alla wished she hadn't sounded so defensive, but the resurfacing of this long-buried memory had thrown her off kilter.

"My point is," Dorothy continued, "if there was a screaming

match, news of it will have spread through the company by the time you slammed your dressing room door. You might want to think about giving your cast and crew a reassuring pep talk." She kissed Alla on the cheek and headed through the chill of a February night toward her black Model T parked on Sunset.

* * *

The next morning, Alla arrived at the studio earlier than usual, but wearier than she would have liked. After having left Paul snoring on the sofa, she had fallen into bed at one o'clock and dropped off to sleep. But she had not gotten the tranquil rest she craved.

She'd dreamed about the ugly scene outside her dressing room and the consoling dinner party that had followed. However, the two events had merged into a single, tumultuous delirium. The dinner party had taken place in her dressing room, which had also doubled as the set of Herod's palace, where they would soon be filming the banquet scenes. Abrams and Farrington had come knocking on the door to bawl her out, but the door they knocked on was the gate to the cage where John the Baptist would be kept prisoner.

But how can they be there? Alla kept asking herself as Abrams had catalogued his problems with her: You're just a woman. You're just a violin player. You're over the hill. But she was barely listening to him. How could the cage be here? They haven't even built the set. Or have they? Natacha's designs called for a domed cage of gold. This was a cube with dull iron prison bars. Meanwhile, Dorothy Arzner and June Mathis were singing "You Can't Give Your Heart to Somebody Else and Still Hold Hands with Me." It had been popular the year she'd made her debut on Broadway in *Hedda Gabler*. She must have heard that song a thousand times, but not in ten years.

She had woken up with the covers almost completely kicked away, her nightgown twisted above her waist, and her feet numb from the cold. Pulling the covers back on the bed, she had tossed and turned for hours before giving up at around five in the morning.

She'd hoped that by the time she was ready to leave for the studio, Paul would be awake, but no. Goodness, how that man could sleep. She'd left him a note and hailed a cab.

At her desk she'd set about studying the columns of figures her accountant had prepared for her. Try as she might, though, they made little sense. There wasn't any red ink on the page, however, so that meant everything was fine, didn't it?

The studio didn't stay peaceful for long. Hammers and buzz saws, trucks and alarm bells filled the air with a sense of purpose. Imagination! Creation! Inspiration! That's what they were here to do, and the comfort of being surrounded by people sharing a mutual goal warmed her heart.

Alla attended to the stray eyebrow hairs that had started to sprout in inconvenient places. *Nobody wants to see a forty-year-old prance around the screen playing the vamp.* "To hell with that!" *It's like watching your mother trying to seduce John Gilbert.* "It most certainly is not!" Pluck, pluck. "I've never been slimmer or felt more youthful in my life." Pluck, pluck. "And besides, isn't your mother entitled to romance? If she can get some physical satisfaction with John Gilbert, good luck to Mother, I say!"

"Who are you talking to?"

Alla hadn't noticed Natacha leaning against the doorjamb. "Abrams."

"Are you thinking of all the retorts you wished you'd said to him yesterday?"

Alla dropped the tweezers into her makeup case. "You're here early." Alla couldn't recall seeing her at the studio before ten.

"Sleep eluded me last night." Natacha slid the handles of a large tote bag out of the crook of her elbow and set it down on the chair inside the doorway. "Rudy and I had a fight. Or more accurately, I picked a fight with him."

"What was the purpose behind that?"

Natacha selected one of Alla's rouge brushes and ran the bristles across her knuckles. It took her a while to admit the truth. "Jealousy."

"Of what?"

"First it was *Four Horsemen* and then *The Sheik*, both of them huge successes, and now he's doing *Blood and Sand*. It's bound to be a smash."

"Nothing in this business is guaranteed."

"He's got Fred Niblo directing him, and June writing the scenario, which is based on a book by the same author as *Four Horsemen*; he's got two fabulous leading ladies, Nita Naldi and Lila Lee, *and* DeMille's cameraman shooting him. Rudy can't miss with this one."

There was that name again: Nita Naldi.

"But what have you got to show for your efforts?" Alla injected a little sting into her tone. "*Camille* and *Doll's House*, neither of which broke any house records at the Rialto."

Natacha put the rouge brush back and parked her behind on the edge of Alla's dressing table. "I'm sorry. I didn't mean for it to sound like that." She pressed the braids encircling her ears. "But when you're both in the same business, and only one of you is charging full steam ahead . . ."

"You're comparing yourself to two of the biggest successes in pictures in the last few years," Alla told her. "And you're right —*Blood and Sand* will likely be a huge hit, but after that, Rudy could have five duds in a row. Meanwhile, if our *Salomé* turns out the way we hope, we could be the ones all Hollywood is talking about."

Natacha smiled weakly. "It's all so quixotic, isn't it?"

"All that matters is the public. Thrill them, or make them laugh, or let them fall in love, and they'll gladly hand over their dimes."

"Easier said than done. But we're on the right track with *Salomé*, don't you think?"

Alla patted the top of Natacha's hand. It felt like old times, just the two of them, nattering away on a Friday night or a Sunday morning. Buttered toast, strong coffee, and a pile of newspapers. "I absolutely do."

"So you didn't mind that bill I sent over with Scobie?"

"The one from Maison Louis? It was rather high."

"I know it was, but hold on to your hat."

Natacha unzipped her tote bag and pulled out a length of cream silk. She dropped it into Alla's outstretched hands. "Maison Louis de Paris has the most renowned silk in the civilized world. Nothing comes close." Alla ran it through her fingers; it was the sheerest, smoothest fabric she had ever felt. "It's what you'll be using in the Dance of the Seven Veils."

Alla held it up to the light. "What's it made of? Moonbeams?"

"It's going to look so sensational on screen that I also used it to make this." Natacha reached back into her bag and fetched a tube perhaps two-and-a-half feet long. Alla couldn't begin to guess what it was for. "This is your costume."

"You mean a sleeve?"

"No, no. It's the whole thing. We might need to add some shoulder straps, but I'll make them so thin that they'll scarcely show up on camera. I used a special glue to fix the silk to the rubber."

Alla took the garment from Natacha and pinched it between her thumb and index finger. "This?"

"I had it made by a factory in Long Beach that manufactures tires. See?" Natacha grabbed the sides firmly and stretched it apart. Alla was surprised at how far Natacha could pull it, but was horrified that she'd be wearing a modified automobile tire.

"But haven't you forgotten that I'll be dancing under those hot lights? Natacha, darling, rubber and sweat do not a good combination make."

"That's what talcum powder is for. I figure if we can get you into a costume that streamlines your figure, and then waft bolts of translucent silk around, we can get away with the age thing." What had seemed like a mad idea now felt somewhat feasible. Alla's shoulders relaxed for the first time all morning. "I was right about the wig and I'm right about this. Now, quickly—put it on so that we can check it for size."

"But I don't have any talc—"

Natacha pulled out a tin of Watkins Egyptian Bouquet talcum powder and held it up.

"What else have you got in that bag of tricks?" Alla asked. "The *Aquitania*?"

Natacha shook the tin at her. "Use this liberally."

Alla disrobed to her step-ins and caked herself in powder until it fogged the air in her dressing room. She pulled the costume past her knees and around her hips. With Natacha's help, she inched it over her bosom and stopped when the top of the tube reached her collarbone.

Natacha stepped back to get a better view. "How does it feel?"

"No worse than a girdle that's one size too small." Alla caught Natacha's soft smile. "Do I look like mutton dressed as lamb?"

"Hardly." She pointed to the full-length mirror hanging on the back of the door.

Alla stepped in front of it. She barely recognized the svelte adolescent staring back at her. "Who *is* that little pipsqueak?"

"'Tis Salomé," Natacha whispered, her breath warming Alla's ear. "Daughter of Herodias and the stepdaughter of Herod, governor of Judea. Ah! The daughter of Babylon, with her golden eyes and her gilded eyelids!" She was now quoting one of the title cards Alla had written. "Salomé, Salomé, dance for me! And thou mayest ask of me what thou wilt even unto the half of my kingdom!"

Alla giggled. "I should never have doubted you'd come up with something extraordinary."

"Even if it might cost the earth?"

"Creating cinematic history doesn't come cheap."

The dressing room door swung open and Scobie poked her head in. "Madame, you said to come fetch you once the whole cast and crew have arrived."

. . .

When Alla walked onto the palace set, the image of herself in Natacha's rubber tube swirled around her mind. How young it made her look! How lithe! Like a ballerina! Perhaps not a sixteen-year-old ballerina, but certainly nowhere north of forty. Or even, dare she indulge, north of thirty? Her heart beat faster at the prospect of the possible.

Alla took the three steps to the dais where Herod's long table stood to address her company. Thirty or so faces stared up at her, some of them tentatively, some of them with impatience, and some with adoration.

"Ladies and gentlemen," she said, clasping her hands together, "first of all, thank you for joining me on this adventure. We are not just making another motion picture. Audiences will never have before seen the likes of what we're about to do."

Applause rolled through the crowd.

"Even though I have written this picture, produced it, will star in it as well as direct it, I cannot do it alone. I need *your* support and *your* commitment and *your* passion to create the very best movie we can. Even if it means working late into the night, which, I'll warn you now, will probably happen. Great art can sometimes come at a great cost—including a full night's sleep."

The company responded to her little joke with scattered laughter, although it may have been more to indulge the boss. If the only memory they took away from her little monologue was a feeling that they were all in this together, Alla didn't mind.

"So," she continued, "whatever you need to do to achieve our goal, I want you to feel as though you can ask me. I can't promise I'll make it happen but I do promise that I'll try."

A solitary arm extended itself above the crowd.

"Yes?" Alla called out. "Speak up!"

It was one of the men Alla had cast as a palace guard. She guessed he was twenty. If drinking were legal, he probably wouldn't even be allowed to do that.

"Seeing as how most of us are going to be half naked in this picture, do you think we could get this soundstage heated? It's freezing in here, and it will be worse at night. I'm already catching a chill and I haven't even taken my clothes off yet!"

The young man had a point. Natacha's costumes for the guards required them to be bare-chested with only a chunky necklace of pearls the size of golf balls around their necks. Instead of pants, they would be wearing black silk stockings on which Natacha had painted a large fish-scale pattern in absinthe green. And on their feet, thin ballet slippers.

Mercifully, this first request was an easy fix. "I shall ask that Allied supply us with heat," Alla told the group. "None of us can afford to catch cold."

* * *

It took sixteen heaters to keep the stage warm enough to ensure that everybody didn't freeze off their bubs. Thanks to Natacha's daring imagination, hardly anybody in the cast was fully garbed from crown to toe. Mitchell Lewis, who played Herod, had been the luckiest of the bunch. Natacha had given him a patchwork robe that covered a damned sight more than the palace guards' outfits did. All they wore on their torsos was a mixture of rouge and Vaseline applied to their nipples.

But it was the musicians Alla had engaged who probably most appreciated the heat. They were a string quartet who played the Zinnia Grill at the Ambassador Hotel down on Wilshire Boulevard. Rather than the typical repertoire of inoffensive and oftentimes soporific minuets by Beethoven and Haydn, and a Mozart sonata or two, they played that new jazz music, as well as some ragtime and blues—often with a syncopated rhythm, and sometimes with no rhythm that Alla could discern. Alla had gone to hear them one night and when they took a break, she'd sought them out in their dressing room next to the kitchen and grilled them about the music. They'd explained that they took a basic tune and improvised.

"You make it all up?" Alla had asked. "As you go along?"

"Pretty much."

"Tell me, have you ever played for a motion picture company?"

It had long been a frequent custom in movie studios to employ musicians to play as the actors emoted. It was generally felt—and Alla agreed—that directors could get far more out of players if music filled the set. She had requested musicians on *Camille* and *Doll's House* but Allied had said no. Secretly, Alla thought that the failure of those two pictures was due, in part, to how the actors had had to play to the camera on a set that had been silent as a morgue.

The quartet was made up of skilled musicians, which meant they didn't come cheap. But Alla was determined to avoid the mistakes of her last two pictures and had paid their steep price. In frigid filming stages, however, musicians' fingers worked less than ideally. Poor music meant poor performances from the actors, so, if for no other reason, Alla had provided heating to protect the players against the cool March weather. And she was glad she had: their harmonized tintinnabulations had provided exactly the right ambiance.

All in all, filming had gone swimmingly. Well, perhaps not *swimmingly*. There had been problems with close-ups in which she wore the beaded wig. They required different lighting, special lenses, and extra-careful makeup. The wig had worked fine in the tests, but nothing was the same when actual filming got underway.

She also hadn't counted on her cinematographer, Mr. Van Enger, insisting on six takes for every shot.

"Six?" Alla had asked, taken aback. "Whatever for?"

"To give you the pick of the best, Madame. I guarantee that you will thank me when it comes time to edit this picture together."

His face had remained impassive, but his tone had suggested that this was what she had hired him for and if she were going to ignore his counsel, she was wasting his time. But she wanted to work with the best, and that was him. If six takes kept him happy, that's what they would do, even if it meant throwing the entire schedule out. Instead of taking eighteen days to complete the picture, it would now take at least twenty-five, or possibly more.

But that was fine, because the daily rushes were showing Alla that the *Salomé* they were making was every bit as good as the *Salomé* she had envisioned—and in some ways even better.

Yes, oh yes, things were progressing well—that is, until just recently. She was taking a break in between shots and, trapped in Natacha's silk-covered rubber sheath, caked in sweat and talcum powder, she was bitterly regretting having sent Scobie to the nearest Owl drug store for more Watkins Egyptian Bouquet instead of asking her to stay and help her out of the constricting tube. She groaned when the telephone rang and gingerly stretched out an arm.

"This is Madame."

"Good afternoon. This is Mr. Blumenthal calling from the Hollywood First National Bank."

Alla slumped against the edge of her desk. Blumenthal belonged in the previous century: handlebar mustache, pince-nez, and a whey-faced complexion that rarely felt the sun. Conversations with bankers like him were seldom fun, but especially while encrusted with damp globs of lavender-scented powder. "Mr. Blumenthal, this is a surprise."

"We need to talk, Madame."

Alla picked a ball of congealed powder from her cleavage. "Unfortunately, right now isn't a good time. You see—"

"I really must insist." He rattled some papers at the other end of the line. "I've been reviewing your account."

"Nothing amiss, I hope."

"I'd like to bring your attention to a series of recent withdrawals, both large and frequent."

"Yes, Mr. Blumenthal." Natacha's rubber tube was made for standing in, not sitting. The Owl wasn't too far away, but it was a busy store at lunchtime. There was no telling how long Scobie would be. Alla slumped down farther until she was lying on her back. At least she could breathe properly now. "They're expenses for the picture I'm filming. It's *Salomé*, and—"

"You're not financing the picture yourself, are you?"

Alla didn't appreciate the supercilious shading he'd applied to his question. "Yes," she snapped. "It was my only option—"

"But you must know what a chance you're taking."

"Mr. Blumenthal, you told me that if I were able to find distribution for *A Doll's House*, you could extend me a one-hundred-thousand-dollar overdraft based on having at least three hundred thousand dollars in deposits. Do you remember saying that?"

"Yes, of course I do." The patronizing tone had disappeared.

"Whatever did you think I was going to need the overdraft for?"

"The usual things, like building a new house or—or—"

"I'm a filmmaker, Mr. Blumenthal. It's what I do, it's who I am, and it's all I think about."

"I see." It sounded like poor old Blumenthal was choking on his own words. "How deep into production are you?"

"About halfway."

"Are you aware that there is now only a shade under two hundred and twenty-seven thousand dollars left in your account?"

Alla jack-knifed to a sitting position but her costume squeezed the air from her lungs and forced her back onto the horizontal. "But that doesn't include the overdraft?"

"Yes, Madame, I'm afraid it does."

But that meant they had burned through over a hundred thousand dollars. That couldn't be right. "Are you positive? Did you double-check the arithmetic?"

"I did."

Her costume now felt like a straitjacket. She pulled at the neckline to give her lungs room to expand. She couldn't catch her breath. Sweat broke out along her hairline.

"Madame? Are you there?"

Alla told him she needed a minute and then dropped the telephone. Gripping the top of her costume with both hands, she wrenched it down over her breasts and gulped at the air until she could feel her heart begin to slow. She picked up the candlestick telephone again.

"At the current rate of outgoing expenses, when do you suppose I shall run out of money altogether?"

The taps and thuds and whirs of Blumenthal's adding machine filtered down the line.

The bolts of French silk. The real gold paint covering John the Baptist's cage. The slaves' fans of ostrich and peacock feathers. Pewter shields. Belgian lace. Six takes for every shot. *One must spend money to make money. Every penny will be on the screen and people will see it.*

But the bromides offered scant comfort. Even freed from the grip of Natacha's tube, her lungs burned with panic.

"Seventeen days," Blumenthal said.

Alla swallowed, her throat dry as the Palm Springs desert. "I see."

"What on God's green Earth—?" Scobie stood at the doorway, a tin of talcum powder in each hand and her purse tucked under one arm.

"Thank you, Mr. Blumenthal," Alla said into the telephone. "I do appreciate your call."

"You need to get your house in order, Madame." He now sounded like a stern father admonishing a wayward child.

By cutting back what? The costumes were all made. The props and sets, too. They were already working with a bare-bones crew. Perhaps the musicians? Oh, but they had been doing such a sterling job, inspiring everybody.

"Thank you, Mr. Blumenthal, but I really must go now." Alla hung up.

"I'm gone twenty minutes and look at the sight of you!" Scobie scolded. "Half undressed, covered crown to heel in this glutinous muck, lying on the floor like it's the Black Plague all over again." She tugged at the costume, which was now wrapped around Alla's hips. "Let's get you out of this and cleaned up. Blimey, I do hope

Mr. Ivano never sees you like this. No gentleman wants to see his sweetheart looking like the wreck of the *Lusitania*."

It wasn't until Alla was in the shower that she came up with a possible solution to save *Salomé* and what was left of her finances—not to mention her pride.

Paul was sitting by himself in the miniature English garden hidden in a rarely visited corner of the studio lot. He had told Alla once that he liked to go there when he needed a break. She could smell the pungent aroma of the Abdulla Egyptian Blend cigarettes he smoked. It was a habit he'd picked up from Rudy, who had discovered them on the SS *Cleveland* as an eighteen-year-old Italian immigrant with no idea what the New World had in store for him.

"There you are," she said softly as she approached.

"Hello, my sweet!" He shifted along the bench to make room for her and kissed her cheek as she sat next to him. "But aren't you filming? It's 'I Demand the Head of Jokanaan' Day, isn't it?"

Oscar Wilde had called John the Baptist "Jokanaan," so Alla had kept it. Later that afternoon, they would be filming the scene where Salomé demands his head on a platter, but she had told Scobie to tell the company that she needed a few minutes to prepare.

"I'm about to get into costume," she replied, "but first a question."

He crushed his cigarette on the gravel beneath their feet. "What do you need?"

What she needed was to ask something of him that she had no right to, even though they'd been sleeping together for months now. And what a delightful few months it had been. Even more so after Charles had left. Since then, the atmosphere around 8080 Sunset had been so much more tranquil. More like how she imagined life on a South Pacific isle. Finding fulfillment, satisfaction, and companionship with a man was a development Alla could never have foreseen.

"It appears we've burned through more of my budget than I realized."

He read the concern on her face and took her hands in his, protecting them against the March chill. "Is it bad?"

She nodded.

"Can you finish the picture?"

"By hook or by crook it *will* be finished!"

"But not without sacrifice?"

She nodded again. His brown eyes were like warm pools of chocolate that she wanted to swim around in until all this was over. "I'm going to ask a favor of you."

"I'll do anything that's in my power. I hope you know that."

"You've edited a picture, haven't you?"

"Three of them. But only if you count being an assistant editor. Why?"

"How would you feel about editing *Salomé*?"

He squeezed her hands in excitement. "I'd be honored. And a little flabbergasted. You would be entrusting me with your prized picture."

A lock of hair had fallen across his forehead and into his eyes. She brushed it back into place, her touch as tender as a rose petal. "You think I don't trust you?"

"It's not that." A twinge of doubt wrinkled his face. "Maybe a little. I know about your past romantic life, and . . . trusting men . . . is something that . . . doesn't . . ." His words slowed as he took more and more care to select the right one.

"You're not just any man," she told him. "You're like no man I've met before." In truth, Alla's life had been filled with more women than men but that didn't mean her statement was untrue.

"Thank you!"

"Hold on. I haven't asked you the big favor yet."

"I'm listening."

"I need you to continue directing the second unit as well as taking on the editing duties."

"Is that all? I can do both."

She mounted a hopeful smile. "No, the big favor is that I need to defer your pay until after *Salomé* comes out and I can recompense you from the profits."

In the distance, a bell rang out, calling for the end of the lunch break. The cast and crew would be reassembling on the set and here she was, not even in costume.

When they had first met, Paul was living off the proceeds of their fan-mail scheme. Thanks to work he'd picked up via Alla and at Famous Players-Lasky, his financial situation wasn't quite so precarious. But now that the studio had taken over filling requests for autographed photos, he was only a few paychecks away from insolvency. Alla cringed at the idea that she was the one prevailing on him to risk sliding into poverty.

"I see."

"It's a lot to ask, I know."

They sat in silence as Paul thought it over. She should have been in her dressing room, wiggling into her costume like a sausage as Scobie choked her with talcum powder. But aside from letting the musicians go, Alla didn't know what else she could do. If there had been alternatives to choose from, she would have. And if this romance of theirs had never happened, she probably wouldn't be sitting here now. But it had, and that meant she had options, so here they were.

When he finally spoke, tears glazed his eyes. "I'm prepared to do whatever it takes."

She pulled him into a hug and squeezed until her strength gave out. "Thank you! Thank you, my sweet, dear man!" She got to her feet. The entire company was waiting for her and, as Mr. Blumenthal had made quite clear, she couldn't waste one more dime. She kissed the tip of her finger and pressed it to his lips. "It'll all be worth it in the end."

He attempted a smile but it curdled slightly at the edges.

"What's wrong?" she asked.

"You're placing your film in my hands, but I've never led the editing of a picture before."

"You've worked in an editing room."

"I know how to do it—" his fingers were now fidgeting with the end of the necktie she'd given him for Christmas "—in theory. I'd hate to let you down."

But I can't afford anyone else. I can scarcely even afford to pay you out of my profits, because there might not be any.

"I trust you, my little *liubushka*."

"Thank you, my love, but I don't trust me quite yet. So how about this: Give me a week to organize the footage and see what we have."

This wasn't what she wanted to hear. She wanted him to say, *Your job is to be the best Salomé you can be, knowing that I've taken charge of the editing. Leave it all to me.* But he was being sensible and cautious. Maybe if she had been both those things, she wouldn't be in this mess.

A week sounded like a year. "Do you need all seven days?"

"Two-thirds of the picture is already in the can, multiplied by six takes for every shot. That's a lot right there."

Her hands quivered like feathers. Paul couldn't know that the gesture meant *But in a week's time I could be out of money.* She debated telling him, but he had a mammoth job ahead of him so she didn't want to add to the pressure.

But she really did trust him, and not because she was out of options. "You have marvelous taste, so go forth and edit!"

She left him with a thank-you kiss on the forehead and followed the stone path back toward her dressing room, feeling lighter with each step. In the beginning, trying to look like a sixteen-year-old had consumed her. Lighting. Costumes. Wigs. Camera angles. Posture. How do adolescents walk? Stand? Hold their torsos? Life's worries had yet to pummel them. The shattering of their illusions still awaited them. They approached everything with nimble liveliness born of the confidence that all will work out fine—just like in the movies.

But while she had focused her attention on fooling the audience, a change had taken place within her.

Spoiled and headstrong though Salomé may have been, there was a strength to her that Alla had come to admire; Salomé wants what she wants and she goes after it. And when it's denied her, does she whimper, "Oh well . . . doesn't matter . . ." and slink into the background? No sirree, she does not! Anyone who gets between Salomé and what she wants pays a price. A head-on-a-platter price—that's what Salomé demands. And nothing less will suffice.

Somehow portraying this mettlesome adolescent had filled Alla with a power she'd never felt before. It was like the girl had opened the top of Alla's neck and slid a steel rod down her spine, then screwed it in tight.

Alla reached her dressing room and was immediately engulfed in Scobie's reprimands. "Where have you been? They're all waiting and you're not dressed yet!" But Alla didn't mind. She felt like she could breathe for the first time in weeks.

* * *

During the week that followed, Alla clung to the hope that everything would work out. She negotiated with Van Enger to reduce the six takes down to four, and on days when they had to work late, she ordered sandwiches from a diner on Ivar Avenue instead of the caterer she'd been using.

It became, however, a little harder to fly on the wings of optimism when an envelope with the Allied Producers and Distributors Corporation logo landed on her desk at the end of a long day on the set. She stared at it for the longest time. Most likely it contained an invoice. But for what? She told herself to stop being paranoid and opened it in a single swift motion. When the number printed at the bottom of the page sank in, she let out a strangled gurgle.

Scobie sat her iron onto the ironing board, her stoic face crinkly with alarm. "You look like someone's been kidnapped."

"They're charging me." Alla rattled the paper in her hand. "For the heaters."

"But without them, your cast would have frozen to death."

"Nobody said anything about a charge." Alla shook the invoice at her maid. "Almost twelve hundred dollars!"

Scobie took the paper from Alla's outstretched hand and ran her eye down the page until she read the words written in red ink: PAYMENT DUE IMMEDIATELY. "I bet some dolt from the accounting department has made an error. They've added an extra zero."

Alla dropped into her chair. Despite cutting corners wherever she could, the expenses of a film in production had continued to slip through her control. Not to mention all her other weekly costs.

A few nights ago, after Paul had crawled into bed and assured her that the editing was going fine, she had waited until his breathing slowed to a regular cadence and then sneaked downstairs, where she had made a list of every expense she could think of and married it with every dollar left in her back account. Through some stringent economizing and prudent delaying of bills, she had figured out how to survive this scary money predicament. At four in the morning, she had crept back to the bedroom and drifted off to sleep, praying that she'd be okay as long as nothing unexpected landed at her feet.

And now it had.

A hundred and twenty dollars would be hard enough, but twelve hundred may as well have been twelve million.

"An extra zero?" Alla asked Scobie.

"It's all figures in columns with those people. Put a number in the wrong one and it throws out the whole caboodle. I'm sure if you go see that Mr. Farrington, he can sort it out in two shakes of a lamb's tail."

Alla groaned. She had spent the day blocking out Salomé's Dance of the Seven Veils. It had been painstaking work, but they had to get it right. The *Salomé* story worked up to the dance; if they got it wrong, the entire picture might fall into a heap. Alla really didn't want to confront Farrington with this damned invoice, but if she didn't, there would be no sleep for her. And a sleepless night was the opposite of what she needed before filming her dance the following day.

From the anteroom out front of Farrington's office, Alla could see the man hunched over the paper in front of his desk. She knocked on the doorjamb.

Surprise glinted in his eyes.

"Burning the midnight oil, I see," she said.

"The motion picture business is not for folks who want only to work a regular eight-to-six day."

"Indeed."

He motioned for her to take a seat, so she ventured inside and withdrew the invoice from its envelope. "I received this." She hoped for a response but he kept his expression poker-face blank. "When we talked about those heaters, you didn't say there would be a charge."

"You thought they were free." His response came out as not so much a question but as evidence of idiocy.

Now that he had put it like that, her naiveté made her cringe. "This is an outrageous sum."

"Which is why few companies do it."

"But it's winter. Even with filming lights on, it's like an icebox inside those stages. And my poor cast. Their costumes were—" she groped for a more polite word than *skimpy*— "sparse, so the heaters were essential."

"I suppose you ought to have either filmed during the summer or designed more substantial costumes. You had options, Madame, and you chose the heaters. They do the job, but they're expensive to build, expensive to maintain, and expensive to run."

"But twelve hundred—"

"Let's see now." Farrington pulled his infernal adding machine closer. "You've been in production since March eighth. It's now

April twenty-fourth, which is forty-seven days." That wasn't the type of information one knew off the top of one's balding head. Someone had been anticipating this conversation. "Forty-seven days at twelve dollars per heater per day—"

"Twelve? Per day?"

"One dollar thirty cents per hour to run. Let's simplify matters and assume an average shooting day of ten hours." He arched an eyebrow. "Even though there have been many days when you've filmed deep into the evening. So that's thirteen dollars per heater per day—" tap tap tap "—times forty-seven days—" tap tap tap "—on top of the rental total of five hundred and sixty-four—" tap tap tap "—comes to—" Each number felt like a hammer blow to Alla's temple. He hit the final key with what struck Alla as being an excessive measure of satisfaction and pulled the strip of white paper out of the machine. "One thousand, one hundred, and seventy-five dollars. I can take a check."

This Farrington wasn't the same guy with whom she had negotiated *Doll's House*'s distribution. He was more like the one who had stood out front of her dressing room as Hiram Abrams talked about how women were nothing more than Kewpie-doll prizes on the Atlantic City boardwalk of life.

He smiled, but there was no warmth to it. And his eyes were dead, too. No depth, no humanity, no compassion, just like—

Alla gripped the armrests of her chair.

Yakov Leventon.

A month ago it had been Abrams, with his supercilious attitude, oozing contempt and scorn. But now Farrington sat in front of her, the same disdain bleeding from every pore.

You're not twelve anymore. You're not only older now, but smarter.

Alla felt that shaft of steel buttress her spine.

And you've got Salomé on your side.

What was Salomé's chief skill? Seducing men into doing what she wanted. Specifically, Herod, her stepfather. In a revolting sort of way, Farrington was a father figure, too, insofar as he called all the shots.

Alla asked herself what Salomé would do. The answer came to her at once.

"The money simply isn't there."

"In that case, we have a grave problem."

"But I do have a remarkable motion picture."

"You want to guess how many producers have told me that?"

She smiled prettily at him. "I know you've visited our set. You've been very discreet about it, but I've seen you standing all the way in the back, watching us work." She patted the invoice she couldn't afford to pay. "Putting this aside for one moment—"

"I'm not putting anything aside. Not even for a moment."

"Now come on, Mr. Farrington, you must admit that you've never seen anything like what we've been doing on stage number four."

She paused to let him picture the *Salomé* set filled with Natacha's outrageous costumes: priests in turbans shaped like enormous beehives, ladies-in-waiting wearing capes with four-foot shoulder pads, transvestite bodyguards, courtiers with golden hats and painted nipples, women with beards, and dwarfs in Arabian fairytale shoes and Viking helmets.

"No offense, Mr. Farrington, but you and I know that Allied is a second-string subsidiary of an also-ran studio." She watched him bristle. "You're not Famous Players-Lasky. You're not Universal. Or Biograph, or Fox, or First National. You're not even Warner Brothers, because if you were, you'd have Rin Tin Tin. Oh, I know, I know. United Artists has Charlie, Mary, and Douglas. But they're not exactly churning out the hits like Abrams expected. In fact, they're not churning out much of anything—hit or miss. You need to make your mark." Alla pointed a finger at his heart. "And by 'you,' I don't mean Allied and I don't mean Abrams. You're no dummy; that much is clear. And you're ambitious. You need to get people talking about you. And that's not going to happen with a run-of-the-mill melodrama in which some insipid virgin gets carried away in a flood, or kidnapped by natives, or pines for her long-lost Confederate soldier. Making one's mark in the world takes nerve. Daring. Rule-breaking innovation and imaginative risk-taking."

"And you think your *Salomé* is all that."

"Don't you?" she asked, bold as Salomé herself.

Through his window, Alla could hear the steady clop-clop-clop of a horse pulling a hansom buggy with mulberry-colored upholstery along Cahuenga Boulevard. Carriages like that were becoming rare on the streets of Los Angeles these days, but someone near the studio still drove one. Whenever Alla saw it, she would always wave to the gray-haired farmer-type who drove his old nag with a leisurely touch. He looked like he belonged to a bygone era and had failed to notice that the modern world had passed him by.

"What do you want, Madame?" Farrington asked.

The scorn in his voice had dropped away, which was all that Alla needed to hear.

"I have no budget for your heating bill."

"How do you propose we settle the matter?"

He had every right to seize *Salomé* and hold it as collateral until the bill was paid, but she was counting on him knowing that a picture couldn't make money if it didn't get distributed.

"You take a bigger piece of the pie."

"In what form?"

"Instead of your distribution fee, you extend us a loan to cover expenses necessary to finish. Nazimova Productions will pay you a percentage of the box office."

"Twenty percent."

"I was thinking ten—"

"Twen. Ty. Per. Cent." He spat out the syllables like they were thumb tacks.

There were more scenes yet to be filmed than there was money left in the bank. And that didn't include marketing and advertising. Or Paul's salary.

"If you could see your way clear to fifteen percent, I would—"

"My offer is twenty percent. Gross, not net. And I claim first dollar."

'First dollar' meant that she wouldn't see a penny until that loan was paid in full.

Well, Nazzy, ol' girl, you wanted to be in the movie business. This is what it's like. Nobody plays by the Marquess of Queensberry Rules.

Farrington's offer, though severe, would let her finish *Salomé* without the ignominy of declaring bankruptcy. Once word got out that her picture was astonishing, people would line up around the block. There would have to be a lot of them, but there were over a hundred million people in America now. Only a fraction of them would need to see *Salomé* to make all this worthwhile.

"You've got yourself a deal, Mr. Farrington."

He tugged at the cuffs of his snuff-brown suit. "Give me a figure and I can make the check out right now."

"Fifty thousand."

He reared back. "You can't be serious."

"Most of that is just a cushion for unanticipated expenses. You know, such as heating bills." He didn't react. "Whatever I don't use, I shall return as soon as I've completed the picture."

"Thirty thousand is as high as I'm willing to go."

"Fine." She wouldn't be able to pay Paul everything she owed him, but she could at least let him have some of it.

Farrington unscrewed the top off his fountain pen and retrieved a checkbook from his attaché case. "Shall I make this out to Alla Nazimova?"

"This is a business transaction, Mr. Farrington, so naturally you must make it out to Nazimova Productions." He didn't need to know that she deposited all checks into the same account.

He smiled the businessman's smile of approval and signed the check. "I'll need to write up a contract. Nothing fancy, plain language, but clear about what we've agreed to."

"I wouldn't dream of doing it any other way."

"My secretary shall deliver it to your office by close of business tomorrow. Two copies. Sign both, and return one to me."

She got to her feet and extended her hand. That was what businessmen did, wasn't it? Shake hands on it?

He got to his feet too and grasped her hand. "I hope you're right about this *Salomé* of yours."

"I am," she assured him. "It's going to be remarkable."

Alla bid him good night and swept from the office. She didn't look at the check until she was back in her dressing room. She wouldn't need all of it. Hopefully, she wouldn't even need half. But she now had it there, just in case.

* * *

Alla was caressing her costume with a distracted air. The silk lining was so soft, so delicate. But oh, that rubber tube. Even with handfuls of Egyptian talcum powder, it was still an effort to squeeze herself into it. She was thankful when a knock on the door—two slow followed by two fast—delayed the moment.

"Come in, Natacha, dear. It's open."

The two-slow-two-fast knock was their private code they used to alert each other of their presence in case one of them didn't feel like being interrupted.

Natacha opened the door with an almost surreptitious air and closed it behind her with a stealthy click. A tremulous smile played on her lips. Almost mischievous.

"Who are you?" Alla asked. "Mata Hari?"

She slid into the chair next to Alla's vanity. "I have an idea." Alla knew from experience that whenever Natacha started a conversation with those four words, it was time to pay attention. "And I want you to hear me out before deciding one way or the other."

"Very well."

"It's about your Dance of the Seven Veils. I was thinking—what if we used just one veil?"

Natacha was a virtually bottomless font of ideas. Almost

always those ideas were startlingly innovative, and Alla had adopted most of them. But not this time. "Just one? But it's—"

The hesitant smile had dropped away now. "I asked you to hear me out, remember?" Alla gestured for her to continue. "It's just that seven veils are a lot. It's a lot to choreograph; a lot to organize; a lot to keep track of while you're dancing around. By the time you get down to the last one, there will be six of the damned things on the floor. That's six times the likelihood of you tripping on one and having to start over. That's more expense than I suspect you can afford right now, not to mention the danger of spraining an ankle—or worse."

"In other words, I'm no spring chicken and I'm in danger of breaking a hip."

"Now, now," Natacha tsked, "that's not what I said. Nor did I imply it."

They both knew that was exactly her implication, but what Natacha had brought up was no trivial matter. How clever and how kind she had been to cloak it in the disguise of a wholly different concern. Alla was no trained dancer, and she would be prancing around on a concrete floor, blinded by overhead lights. Now that Alla had had a moment to think through Natacha's suggestion, she could see it had a lot of merit. But what was she supposed to do? Spin around and around with one silly little length of flimsy material flapping behind her? "Exactly what do you have in mind for my Dance of the Single Veil?"

"One veil, yes, but a *big* one."

"How big?"

"I've measured it out, and we have enough silk to make a veil the size of three double beds. Your four handmaidens could each take a corner and flip it up like a parachute. You could duck under it—artistically, of course—and then they could let it float down on you like a shroud. If we light it from behind at just the right angle, it would glow like the beads in the headdress you wear in the first half. It's theatricality we should aim for, not historical accuracy."

And it would hide my age beautifully.

Alla had been so preoccupied with juggling all the other balls in the air to keep this production going that she hadn't given the most important part of the picture the attention it deserved. But Natacha had.

"I like it," Alla declared. "And it does save a lot of time and effort."

Natacha shot to her feet. "I knew you'd agree, which is why I've gone ahead and used the last of the French silk to make it."

"Without consulting me?"

"If I had any doubts about it, I would have run this by you first."

"But you knew I'd say yes."

A coy, sphinxlike expression suffused Natacha's face. "Need I even reply to that?"

"No, you don't," Alla admitted. "Now do me a favor and go find Scobie. Getting me into this torture chamber you've devised is a two-woman job."

Alla walked onto the set still brushing the excess powder from her skin. The air was noticeably cooler without the heaters, but absent other options she could only pretend everything was splendid. "Good morning, everybody! I first must tell you that things have changed with the Dance of the Seven Veils."

Natacha stepped out from behind the camera. "I explained the change while you were getting into costume, and we've come up with this." She made a swooping motion with her hands, which sent the handmaidens marching backward into a square. They each held a corner of the huge veil Natacha had made, and when she gave the signal, they swooped each corner above their heads. The expanse of translucent material mushroomed above them like something that extraordinary Spanish painter, Picasso, might conjure in a fever dream.

A rapturous wave washed through Alla as she bustled over to the four women cast as Salomé's ladies-in-waiting. Natacha had been right to reconceive the Dance of the Seven Veils. Alla had been dreading it for all the reasons Natacha had listed, and she had scarcely been aware of it. She turned to her ladies-in-waiting. "Let's get to work."

Natacha had created one of the most striking costumes in the whole picture for them. Each woman was dressed in a clinging suit of sparkling hose, and to set these off, Natacha had somehow dreamed up the most remarkable capes. Suspended from balsawood yokes that extended two feet from their shoulders, they hung like black curtains to mid-calf and were decorated with large, circular geometric patterns the size of dinner plates.

"How do they feel?" Alla asked. "Not too cumbersome, I hope?"

"We've been practicing," one of them said. "As long as we plant our feet well apart and keep them flat on the floor, we won't tip over."

The girl had an Olive Thomas look about her. Penetrating eyes that hinted at an incisive mind. Her chin came down to a delicate point, raised slightly, almost in defiance. She probably used to wear her hair in the same mass of Pickford curls as everyone else, but, like all young women nowadays, she had pruned most of it off, leaving just enough for a Marcel. Her last treatment must have been a few weeks before, because her hair had softened into a series of loose blonde waves.

Has she been here all along? How have I not noticed her before? Alla pressed her hands to her chest to stop them from trembling. "I don't believe we've met."

"My name is Odette."

Odette. Odette. Odette. Alla repeated the name in her mind as though it were the mantra of a Buddhist monk sequestered high in the Himalayas. And every time she did, she savored the way it made her tongue tap against the roof of her mouth. It was poetry. Music. Dance.

"Odette." The name felt even more joyous when she uttered it out loud. "As in the princess from Tchaikovsky's *Swan Lake*?"

The girl's response was a silent grin coupled with an unhurried blink.

How enchanting! How hypnotic! I could look at this girl all day long!

Natacha tapped her shoe on the stage's floor. "Perhaps the rest of you could introduce yourselves?"

Her prompting made Alla realize she had been staring at this honeypot too long and hadn't given the other girls the time of day. "How rude of me not to get to know you better before now!" she exclaimed, and turned to the three others. "And the rest of you?"

Odette's fellow ladies-in-waiting—Norma, Merle, and Edith—were each pretty enough in their own standard-issue, chorus-girl ways, but none of them possessed a fraction of this girl's spunky verve. None of them looked unblinkingly at Alla like that. And the smile! Knowing but not overly self-confident. A little bit saucy, and tart as a gin rickey.

Alla pulled herself away from this captivating Odette before she made a fool of herself. It took more effort than she expected, but they had a pivotal scene to film. *But all I want to do is study every line, every dimple, every wave of hair, every contour of her face!* She shook away the vision of Odette. "We must film the dance this afternoon, so we have only three hours," she told the cast. "We have a special guest coming to the set today whom I can't turn away, more's the pity. When Elinor Glyn knocks, you'd better open the door."

Alla told the four girls to enter two by two. "I like what you've done . . ." Her voice trailed off as her imagination started to stir. "But let's try this: approach me as though you're in a wedding procession. Step-and-pause, step-and-pause. When you get to me, two of you go to the left and two to the right. Form a square, shoulder to shoulder, so that the audience can no longer see me."

As the four girls did as she commanded, Alla tried not to stare at Odette, but how could she not? That glistening skin! Those crème-de-menthe eyes! That lissome figure! That sassy manner!

"Slow down a little," she told them. "Now, cross in between each other and as you do, turn around—don't hurry! This has to feel like a pageant. Salomé is about to perform her dance. This is a spectacle. She wants the head of Jokanaan, and if any of her ladies-in-waiting messes it up, she'll have *their* head on a platter, too—and they know it." Facing her now, the girls inched the edges of their wide collars closer and closer until they touched. "Perfect!"

Alla crouched until she had disappeared from view. Lowering herself wasn't too taxing, but straightening up again was more difficult than she anticipated. She was halfway up before she started losing her balance. Instinctively, she reached out. A hand grabbed hers. Soft but firm, and warm to the touch.

"I've got you."

Alla looked up to see Odette beaming.

You most certainly do.

* * *

Back in her dressing room, Alla pulled at the bottom hem of her rubber costume. Re-choreographing the dance had taken longer than she had expected. Elinor Glyn was going to arrive any minute and Alla wasn't nearly as prepared as she wanted to be. There were few people who intimidated Alla, and this woman was one of them.

Glyn was an imperious author of scandalous romance novels with titles like *The Damsel and the Sage* and *The Vicissitudes of Evangeline*. That is to say, they had been deemed scandalous by a general public who had not led the morally ambiguous life that Alla had led.

Not that Alla felt her life had been immoral, but her family equated 'actress' with 'whore,' and her extramarital affairs only proved their point. But she felt it was her life to do with what she liked. And she had. *And* enjoyed it. If the consequence was that few of her kin talked to her, that was beyond her control. Somehow, Alla sensed Elinor Glyn would approve.

She could tell by Glyn's titles and florid covers, however, that those novels weren't for her. Dorothy Parker, Sinclair Lewis, Anita

Loos, and Sherwood Anderson were more to her taste. Several years ago, a clever doggerel had done the rounds, which had told Alla all she needed to know.

> *Would you like to sin*
> *With Elinor Glyn*
> *On a tiger skin?*
> *Or would you prefer*
> *To err with her*
> *On some other fur?*

Still, title after title had been a bestseller, so it was clear that she was giving women—and William Randolph Hearst—what they wanted. As soon as her stories and articles had appeared in his various publications, Hollywood had shown interest.

Clever girl, that Elinor. She had written into her contract that movies based on anything she published with Hearst remained her copyrighted property. And Hollywood studios loved to film her brand of melodrama.

Alla threw the costume at Scobie. "What time is it?"

Scobie turned it inside out to clean off the sweat and talcum. "You've got four minutes."

Glyn was known for being punctual to the minute, so there was no time to dress in the suit Alla had planned. She pulled on the satin kimono-style robe Natacha had given her a year or two before. It was blood-red with Japanese characters in bold, black calligraphy, and the wide lapels were the same shade as Alla's violet eyes. She fluffed out her hair and was coating on lipstick when a set of sturdy knuckles rapped on the door with three slow knocks. An orotund British voice boomed, "It's Elinor Glyn here. May I enter?"

Alla tightened the sash around her waist and motioned for Scobie to open the door.

Glyn wasn't tall, but she moved like a battleship: slow, but with deliberate forward motion, impossible to thwart. Dressed in a claret-colored velvet suit with a black collar, matching leather buttons, and a fox fur arrayed around her shoulders, she took in Alla's kimono. "If I had known it was a casual affair, I would have worn my pajamas. I don't suppose you have a spare set lying around? I'm wearing a new girdle that my dressmaker foisted on me and it's more uncomfortable than a hair shirt."

Alla shook her hand—the woman had the grip of a lumberjack—and apologized that there were no handy sets of pajamas and asked her to take a seat. Sending Scobie out to clean her costume, Alla told her, "I was surprised to get your call. I didn't think movie interviews were your specialty, Miss Glyn."

"First of all, it's Elinor." She withdrew a long pin from her hair —a henna-rinsed crest of flaming red—and placed her black feathered hat on Alla's table. She possessed piercing eyes that Alla was more used to seeing on domineering nuns and Russian generals. "Secondly, the word is out, my dear. This production of yours. Ever since I arrived in Los Angeles to write the screenplay of *Three Weeks* for Mr. Goldwyn, all I keep hearing about is *Salomé, Salomé, Salomé*! What better excuse to finally meet the redoubtable Madame Nazimova?"

Alla had never thought of herself as redoubtable, but rather liked the sound of it. Did Joe Farrington find her redoubtable? Did Hiram Abrams?

Her thoughts turned to that Odette girl. Did *she* find Nazimova redoubtable? What a charming pixie. So full of vivacity and bounce. She would be fun to attend a party with. A couple of drinks and the bon mots would start flying. Witty asides and droll observations about other guests and their host's décor choices. Neat little figure, too. Curvy but not excessively so. Athletic, like an ice skater or tennis player—Alla liked that. Yes, oh yes,

Madame liked that very much. But her thoughts soon turned to Paul, and a pang of guilt skewered her conscience.

"You're at Goldwyn Pictures?" Alla asked, brushing her thoughts aside. "Have you bumped into my good friend June Mathis? She's toiling away on their film version of *Ben-Hur*. I don't envy her, though." She bulged her eyes in mock despair. "How Goldwyn or June think they can adapt a six-act play is quite beyond me." *Salomé* was going to clock in at around seventy-five minutes, and it was taking everything Alla had to keep body, soul, and bank account together. She had burned through Farrington's $30,000 faster than she'd expected. A lot faster, in fact. There hadn't even been enough to pay Paul all that she owed him, and he had had to make do with a smaller check than she'd hoped. And his job was far from over.

"Goodness gracious me, yes! June and I had a very long lunch during which she suggested that your filming of *Salomé* would make an interesting story—especially seeing as how it's the talk of the Hollywood grapevine." Her rings clunked as she folded her hands in her lap like she was Queen Victoria preparing to make a public pronouncement. "I don't listen to gossip, but I must confess that I am frightfully intrigued."

Completing her movie had been so all-consuming that Alla hadn't paid much attention to what was going on in the outside world. "What exactly has the grapevine been saying?"

"Well," Elinor said, suddenly playing it coy as a milkmaid, a role that hardly suited her dowager duchess persona, "I've heard it said that everyone in your cast is—" she lowered her voice to a stage whisper "—homosexual. Is it true?"

Not only did Natacha's outrageously scanty costume designs reveal more skin than they covered, she had also dressed the male courtiers as women and instructed the guards to paint their nipples. In addition to which, Alla had based the scenario on the work of Oscar Wilde, the nineteenth century's most flagrant invert.

Many times, Alla had been asked if the habitually serious Natacha Rambova was "that way inclined." Then again, Alla had thought of herself as "that way inclined" until the sweet, adoring Paul had come along. But now Odette had popped up in front of her like some light-filled nymph that had her heart beating ever so slightly faster, and in ways that Paul had never done.

She dismissed the thought as soon as it came to her, but it refused to be swatted away like a mosquito. Paul was like an anchor, but in a good way. A safe harbor. Dependable. Reliable. He possessed a fine pair of arms. Strong. Protective. He was a considerate lover, too. Unhurried. Selfless. But her attraction to Paul had never involved butterfly stomachs or clammy palms or flushed cheeks the way this Odette had. What did that mean? And why was there now a cold lump sitting at the bottom of her stomach?

"Well?" Elinor pushed.

"I can see why people might speculate," Alla conceded, "but I haven't gone from cast member to cast member and questioned them about their love lives, so I really couldn't say."

Elinor arched a dissatisfied eyebrow. "Not that I care who puts what where in the boudoir, but when people learn that I've been to the set of Nazimova's *Salomé*, well, they're bound to ask."

Through the open window of her dressing room, Alla could hear the cast and crew returning from their lunch break. "Would you like to see the set for yourself? Get a feel for what we're doing?"

Elinor was positioning her hat back onto her head before Alla's feet had found their slippers.

She ushered her guest onto the set where she would be performing the dance later in the afternoon. The first cast member she saw was Odette standing to one side, already dressed in her giant dark cloak with the two-foot shoulders. When she spotted Alla heading toward her, she straightened and presented a sunny face designed not so much to impress the boss as to reflect genuine delight. This girl had thrown Alla so far off balance that she wasn't sure if she could trust her own instincts.

"Odette, isn't it?" Alla asked, feigning breeziness that might have fooled Elinor Glyn but didn't deceive this self-possessed imp.

"That's right. Odette Finch." She threw Alla a playful wink.

Good lord! Just when I thought she couldn't be more winning. Look away from her! Look away! "May I present Elinor Glyn?"

"The authoress?"

"She's doing a story on us for one of the Hearst magazines."

"I'm very honored to meet you, ma'am." Odette bobbed down into a self-conscious curtsy that revealed a patch of décolletage. By the time she managed to right herself again, a hearty blush was filling her cheeks, which only enhanced her youthful glow.

"Your costume," Elinor said. "It's remarkable. May I caress it?"

Odette stepped forward and opened the flap of her cape, offering Elinor a corner to feel. Underneath it, Alla caught the outline of her sylphlike frame swaddled in the glittery fabric that Natacha had found somewhere—Maison Louis, in all likelihood—and that had no doubt cost a small fortune. Ironic, as the audience was probably not going to see it. But my, oh my, how it suited her.

Elinor fingered the edge of the cape. "Do you know what this is made of?"

"I'm not sure," Alla answered. "By any chance, do you know, Odette?" *What a lovely name. And how perfectly it suits her.*

"It's cretonne."

"Cretonne?" Elinor pulled the cape closer to her face. "I've only ever seen it used for upholstering."

"Miss Rambova imported several bolts of white cretonne from France, dyed it black, then stiffened it with a light coating of carpenter varnish to give it that formal look."

Elinor started asking about the wide yoke hanging from Odette's shoulders over which the cape was suspended, but Alla's mind had wandered.

There was an attractive mixture of humility and confidence, reserve and liveliness to this girl. It shone out of her like a night flare.

How have I not noticed her? I must have been more preoccupied than I realized if a girl like this has been within touching distance. Alla thought once more of Paul. *Oh, but even he's not enough to blind me to a creature like this. Look at her. Cheeky without being impertinent. Sassy but not brazen.* Alla knew she shouldn't be having these sorts of thoughts. Not with Paul in her life. And in her bedroom. *But oh, this Odette. This lovely, sassy, cheeky elf!* Alla crossed her arms, then uncrossed them and clasped them behind her back. But she still wasn't comfortable, so she pressed them to her sides. It felt unnatural and self-conscious, but she didn't know what else to do.

"Your outfit is a credit to Miss Rambova's ingenuity!" Elinor announced. "Such creativity! And you wear it well, my dear."

"Wait till you see Salomé's headdress," Odette said. "It has glass balls attached to the ends of little braids. I suggested to Miss Rambova, 'What if we paint them with phosphorus? Imagine how they'll glow under the studio lights.'"

Alla confronted the girl. "That was *your* suggestion?"

Odette smiled modestly. "I'm a wigmaker by training."

"Are you telling me that you made my headdress?"

"After Miss Rambova came up with the design, she approached me to construct it. It was the most challenging task I've ever undertaken, but I'm sure Madame will agree: when people think of *Salomé*, they'll be thinking of The Great Nazimova in that headdress."

Alla felt the color drain from her face. She cast her mind back to that conversation with Natacha in her bedroom when she had first produced it like a magician pulling a live rabbit out of his hat. *Odie*. That's what Natacha had called her wigmaker. "Your work is the main reason I agreed to this movie in the first place."

Odette blushed the shade of a pale American Beauty rose. "That was the plan all along, which is why I took extra great care in its creation. I've been a fan of yours since *War Brides*. But not the movie, although I enjoyed that too. I'm talking about when you did it at the Palace Theater in New York. I saw it twice more when you toured it around the Keith-Orpheum circuit."

This girl couldn't have been the youngster Alla had assumed, then. She had to be closer to thirty than twenty. "If you're a wigmaker, how, pray tell, did you come to be in this movie?"

"By shamelessly begging Miss Rambova to find me a place in the cast."

The second half of the sentence—*so that I could be near you*—hung unspoken in the air. Alla could feel heat bloom across her own cheeks now. Her fingers fidgeted like Mexican jumping beans; a thin streak of sweat broke out along her hairline. "Well, I'm sorry it's taken us this long to meet, but now I can thank you for creating such an unforgettable headpiece for me." She lifted a hand toward her dressing room and said to Elinor, "Perhaps we can talk further while I dress. We begin shooting soon."

Scobie was waiting for Alla, the rubber costume freshly cleaned and powdered. She had attached the twin drapes of gauzy veils to the waist for this afternoon's shoot.

"And now comes the unglamorous side of show business," Alla said with a laugh in her voice. "Getting into preposterously tight costumes!"

Elinor lit a cigarette and inserted it into an eight-inch ivory holder. "That wig girl has a certain *je ne sais quoi*, doesn't she?"

"Yes, I suppose she does." Alla adjusted her costume with more care than it needed. Of all people who could have witnessed that exchange, did it have to be Elinor Glyn?

"There's no supposing about it." Elinor wagged a finger with a matching pair of ruby-encrusted rings on it. "I am an expert on romance and passion. Quite frankly, I'm surprised I came away from that encounter without my fox fur getting singed. Don't deny it, Madame, for I know you felt it. Unless I miss my guess, that little minx felt it, too. And I mean 'minx' in the best possible way."

Alla shot Scobie a 'help me' look.

"I'll call your makeup man in," Scobie said brightly. She opened the door and let out a sharp whistle that must have come in handy calling sheepdogs in the Scottish Highlands.

"I assumed The Great Nazimova did her own makeup," Elinor said.

"Often I do, but there will be several close-ups today and you know how it is—even the greatest acting in the world won't hide that I'm no longer sixteen. But makeup experts more skilled than I can get me in the general vicinity. Such as Herr Baumann here."

Alla's makeup guy was a no-nonsense German émigré whom Lilyan Tashman had recommended. He rarely spoke as he worked, but he had the commanding presence of a Prussian field marshal that Alla hoped would discourage Elinor from pursuing the subject of Odette until Alla had a chance to sort through the tumult of her feelings.

Baumann was as efficient as he was capable and soon had Alla camera-ready. He had applied her makeup more thickly than she'd ever needed, but if it made her look twenty years younger on screen, nothing else mattered.

Scobie pulled out the other wig Natacha had designed for the picture. It was a helmet of white hair, cut short above the shoulders and flaring out at the sides. As startling as the one with the glass beads was, Alla couldn't go through the entire film wearing only one wig. "And white will help you look younger," Natacha had added. "All that reflected light will do the trick." Pulling the wig into place, she checked herself in the mirror. Natacha had been right—this one carved off years.

"You must excuse me," she said to Elinor, "but the camera calls." ·

"Of course." Elinor stubbed out her cigarette. "I have everything I need."

Alla thanked her for her time and hurried onto the set, where the cast had already taken their positions. The four handmaidens were standing in a square. Odette smiled as she stepped aside to let Alla into the formation.

Alla sank to her knees, taking her out of sight of the camera until the handmaidens parted to reveal a transformed Salomé ready to dance her single-veil dance. As she did, her eyes locked with Odette's, who returned her gaze with a searing look that penetrated Alla's heart.

I've been waiting to meet you, Odette's eyes said. *There is palpable heat between us and we would be fools to ignore it.*

Guilt backwashed through Alla's chest. She had asked Paul to work without pay, editing together the movie that could save her career and set her back onto the path of financial stability. But when the first pretty girl came along, suddenly Alla was all doe-eyed peepers and virginal blushes.

What kind of heartless monster am I?

But this Odette wasn't the first pretty girl to come along. The *Salomé* set was filled with them. And so were the Zinnia Grill, the Ship Café, the bar at the Christie Hotel, and the Cocoanut Grove. You couldn't swing a bottle of Pimm's in this town without hitting a smoky brunette, a sunny blonde, or a blazing redhead. But none of them had caught Alla's eye the way this Venus of loveliness had.

Paul didn't deserve this. He was a good guy with nothing but love and adoration in his heart, but the emotional connection they shared was shallow waters compared with what seemed to be simmering between her and Odette. This was no passing fancy. Just drinking in the sight of her had ignited something deep inside Alla.

Have I been fooling myself all this time? Telling anyone who will listen that I was this free-thinking, free-flowing sensualist who loved the persona for who they are, regardless of what may or may not be hidden inside their undergarments?

Alla had never believed in the concept of love at first sight. Attraction at first sight—yes. Lust at first sight—oh, yes. Absolutely. But love? No. In Alla's opinion, such a thing was a myth. Romantic, to be sure, and everybody could agree that it sounded marvelous. To read about it in an Elinor Glyn novel was one thing, but in real life, love took time. It took time to know somebody and to love them in spite of the parts you might not like. That was love.

But now . . .

But now . . .

Along had come someone who had challenged all of that. One look was all it had taken. One glance. One very special person. And her name wasn't Paul Ivano.

Natacha called out, "Roll camera!"

Alla lifted her arms over her head, letting the fabric fall across her face.

"And . . . action."

Her thighs burned as she rose slowly to her feet until she emerged between the capes like a white-hot volcano. The handmaidens rotated around her before parting to reveal Salomé in her clingy tunic for the first time.

DANCE! Alla told herself. *Dance like you've never danced before.*

* * *

It was one o'clock in the morning when Alla dismissed the company. Twelve hours was a long time in front of the cameras. A long time to be on your feet, a long time to fill the camera with energy, a long time to pretend your legs weren't killing you and that your stomach wasn't ravenous.

"Thank you," she told the cast as they tottered toward the exit. "I know it's been an excruciating day, but it'll all be worth it. You'll see." She was still waving good night to the last of the stragglers when Scobie called from inside the dressing room.

"Ready to go?"

"Not quite," Alla told her.

Scobie's face was a mask of shock. "But you've been dancing for twelve hours. How are you even upright?"

Because I could have danced till dawn! That's what Alla wanted to say. Because Odette fills my mind every second. Because she already makes me tremble when I'm near her, and I suffer when I can't look at her. Because meeting her has made me see how far I've strayed from who I truly am. Because the realization of what I want has made me feel as though I'm filled with helium!

"Because I love what I'm doing and I'm doing what I love."

Scobie shrugged in that I-don't-understand-show-business-folks way of hers as she collected her belongings, muttering about damn fools and the benefits of a good night's sleep, and stepped into the corridor. "Oh, I almost forgot." She pulled a Western Union envelope from her coat pocket. "This arrived a while ago." She handed it over and said that she'd see her in the morning.

Alla sliced along the envelope's edge with a knife. The telegram was from Blumenthal, her bank manager.

AT CLOSE OF BUSINESS YESTERDAY YOUR CURRENT BALANCE IS 2907 DOLLARS 23 CENTS STOP AT CURRENT RATE OF WITHDRAWALS YOU WILL BE OVERDRAWN BY NEXT WEDNESDAY STOP

That gave her four days to complete filming—an unlikely prospect.

She left the telegram on her makeup table and wandered outside to the set, where a pair of working lights cast long shadows. She approached the golden cage that served as a photogenic prison for Jokaanan and ran her hands over its bars.

Alla had helped Natacha design the cage and had been proud of what they'd come up with. But now the bitter irony it represented made the metal freezing to the touch.

This project had become a prison. She had mounted a movie that she couldn't afford. And why? To prove herself to a father whose approval she never would have received even if he'd lived to see what she had become.

"You don't look happy."

Alla spun around. "Where did you come from?"

"I waited until everybody had gone."

"But you knew I'd still be here?"

"I always know where you are." Odette's smile faded quickly. "No. Wait. That came out a bit creepy, didn't it?" A silvery tinkle of a laugh popped out of her. "What I meant was—"

"Come, let's have a drink." What Alla really wanted to do was embrace the girl with all the strength her arms possessed, but even though nobody else was around, it seemed too forward. God knew she'd been forward during any number of her Sunday socials, but this was different. This was her place of work. And Odette was different. She wasn't a one-time fleeting fumble in the dark.

Alla motioned for the girl to follow her past Herod's banquet table and into her dressing room, where she poured a couple of brandies and handed one to Odette. She switched off the lights around her vanity mirror, bathing the room in a warm pink that was more forgiving to a face over forty.

Odette sipped her brandy. "I've been worried that I gave you the wrong impression."

"And what impression is that?"

"That I'm just a crazy fan who idolizes a stage and screen goddess. But it isn't the case."

Fan worship wasn't what Alla needed right now. She watched Odette trace a finger around the lip of her glass. "I'm glad to hear it."

"I have something to tell you, but I'm fearful that it'll sound like the sort of bizarre coincidence that if you read it in one of Miss Glyn's novels you'd scoff and say, 'Oh, that would *never* happen.'"

"I have read none of Miss Glyn's novels, but I suspect they're filled with implausible happenstance."

Odette's eyes were large, like Colleen Moore's, and could have served her well if she'd wanted a career in the flickers. But she gave off the aura of someone too sensible for that. *Is that what I'm responding to? So many girls I meet in Hollywood are so flighty, so scatterbrained, without two brain cells to rub together. But this one, oh, this one is anything but.*

Odette furrowed her brows together. "Do you remember Caroline Harris?"

The Shubert organization had engaged Mrs. Harris to teach Alla how to speak English before making her Broadway debut in *Hedda Gabler*. Alla had proven to be so adept at languages that she had mastered English in less than six months, causing Mrs. Harris to declare her 'the sharpest pupil I'm ever likely to have!'

"Of course I do, but how do you know her? Are you a fan of Richard Barthelmess?" Richard was Caroline's son, which was how he'd ended up in Alla's first film, *War Brides*. "I could get you an autograph—"

"No," Odette said, "nothing like that. We used to live next door."

"Right next door? To the Harrises?"

"Uh-huh. The walls were quite thin and I used to listen to you practice your vocabulary. I remember Mrs. Harris telling you to get your vowels right. They're the key—"

"—to ensuring that your future audiences will understand you."

"American 'o,' not Russian 'o'!"

"She must have said that to me a hundred times."

"Until you finally got it. And she said, 'Today we celebrate—'"

"'—with peppermint schnapps!'"

Mrs. Harris could bring language alive more skillfully than all those dreary school textbooks combined. One of Alla's happiest days was when Mrs. Harris had told her, "Alla, you are ready. Now go and give Broadway the gift of Henrik Ibsen!"

Alla led Odette to the sofa, where they sat close. Not close enough to touch, but almost. Alla wanted to reach out and grab this lovely girl by the hand but held back for fear of ruining a precious moment like this. "Were you in the apartment that always smelled so deliciously of baking bread?"

"Yes! That was us!"

The girl's smile melted Alla's heart. Not because it was perfect like Paul's but because she had a snaggletooth on the left that only revealed itself when she smiled. The imperfection made her perfect.

"I can't tell you how many times I was tempted to come knocking on your door, begging for a slice."

"I wish you had, even though I would have been quite tongue-tied, so maybe it's just as well."

"Oh, but what an extraordinary coincidence!" Alla's head began to swim. "It feels like—"

"Fate?"

Fate? Yes, Fate! That's how it feels. "I was going to say one of Elinor Glyn's improbable flukes, but I like your word better."

"You're the reason I became a wigmaker. I knocked on Mrs. Harris's door one day and confessed that I wanted to be an actress like Madame Nazimova. She sat me down and laid out a few facts about employment among theatrical folk, and then suggested one of the trades associated with the theater. My grandmother had suffered terribly from alopecia, so I helped her maintain her collection of wigs. It seemed like the obvious path . . . and here we are."

Here they were, indeed.

"Your work is marvelous." Alla laid her hand on the worn velvet upholstery, barely two inches from Odette's. *Oh Paul, dear, sweet Paul. Forgive me, but I can't help myself.* "And for the record, I think you're pretty marvelous, too."

Odette deposited her brandy snifter on the side table next to her. "I'd say we have a mutual admiration society."

Suddenly, their lips were touching. Yielding softness at first, then inquisitive tongues as their ardor grew. Alla ran her fingers through Odette's glossy curls. They felt like strands of Chinese silk. A hand encircled the back of her neck, pulling her closer and closer until Odette's firm breasts pressed against hers.

Alla had almost forgotten what it was like to kiss another woman. How smooth and supple everything was: cheeks, neck, hair, hands. No late-afternoon beard, no callouses, no guttural groaning. Women were all perfume, subtlety, grace. With men it was a battle of submission; with women it was a negotiated exchange. Men felt like business; women felt like home.

"I had a feeling you'd still—oh!"

Alla yanked her hand from inside Odette's blouse. Paul had never visited Alla in her dressing room. Let alone in the middle of the night. She closed her eyes but couldn't pretend he wasn't there. She forced herself to look up at him.

His face was suet white and his jaw hung open. "I'm—I'm—sorry—I didn't—I would have—"

"Paul, I just—" But what could she say? He was working late into the night editing a picture for no pay, and here she was making love with a woman.

She got to her feet but he thrust out a hand. "I should have knocked. I shouldn't have—have assumed that—anything." He jammed his derby onto his head. "Rudy and Natacha—their guest room has a bed in it now." He dashed out.

Alla buried her face in her hands. *I am a monster. A heartless, self-absorbed beast. Without Paul around to finish the film, I'm lost. And I deserve to be. I'm thoughtless. Selfish. Cruel. I'm—*

"If that was your boyfriend, you should go to him."

The sharp edges of Alla's fingernails bit into the palms of her clenched hands. She pushed harder and harder. *Punishment. It's what I deserve.* "I wouldn't know what to say."

"You'll figure it out. Don't let him get away."

Alla dashed onto the shooting stage. Paul was nowhere in sight, but there was only one exit. She ran toward it, calling out his name. She made it outside the building in time to see his faded red Marmon screech past the security gate and disappear into the night.

She trudged back to her dressing room, tormenting herself for the choices she had made, the urges she had given in to. When she stepped inside, she found Odette reading Blumenthal's telegram.

"I'm sorry," Odette said, looking up. "I wasn't snooping, honest injun. When you rushed out of here, the backdraft sent it flying to the floor. I picked it up and, well, I couldn't help but read it. Which, now that I think about it, sounds like snooping."

"Of all the crimes committed tonight, reading someone else's open telegram doesn't even reach the top five." Alla slipped it back inside the envelope. It was almost impossible to finish the movie by Wednesday, but without Paul continuing to work on it, 'almost' became 'absolutely.'

"Are you really out of money?"

Alla nodded. "I wanted to create a motion picture that would stand the test of time. One that would prove to the champions of the lowest common denominator that films are art, too."

"But the film's almost done."

Alla wasn't looking at Odette now, but she could smell the florals in her perfume. "Wednesday is my deadline, and we have at least six more days of filming left. The money will have run out well before then."

"Unless you get an injection of cash to tide you over."

"I had to fight Allied to fork over the money they've already given us. They're not going to loan—"

"But you're good friends with Rudolph Valentino, aren't you?"

A gravelly sigh escaped from Alla. She sat down on the sofa. "Let me tell you about Mister Rudolph Valentino. Next month, he is legally required to make a twelve-thousand-dollar alimony payment to Jean Acker; however, he barely has half that in the bank. Which means he will have to borrow thousands from Famous Players-Lasky to meet his obligations. His current contract with them pays him much more than Metro did, but when he left Metro last summer, he was deeply in debt. Even at double his Metro salary, he's swimming against the financial tide. And probably always will be. It's the way he's built."

But she herself wasn't much different, she thought glumly. When Metro was paying her thirteen thousand a week, she had spent it as though they were going to keep paying her that for the rest of her life. *And now look at you. One week's salary is all you'd need to pull yourself out of this hole.*

Odette joined her on the sofa, tucking one leg under the other and laying an arm along the back. Her fingertips reached for Alla's hair and toyed with it tenderly. How reassuring it felt. Paul's touch had never made her feel quite like this. "What happened to your *Aphrodite* project?"

Turning to look at Odette would have brought a sudden halt to the way she was caressing Alla's hair, and that was the only thing that felt good right now. She stared straight ahead. "The studio canceled it after the Supreme Court ruled that motion pictures were a profit-making industry and therefore not covered by First Amendment guarantees of freedom of speech. My *Aphrodite* was shaping up to be quite provocative, which sent those yellowbellies at Metro into fits. And that was the end of that." *What am I going to tell Paul? What does one say in a situation like this? He deserves the truth. He won't finish the movie, and who would blame him? I've brought this whole mess on myself.* "Why do you ask?"

"The other day I was reading an interview in *Variety* with Nita Naldi. She wants to return to Broadway with *Aphrodite* but this time taking the lead role."

"How can she be sure she'll get it?" Alla asked. "Broadway people don't look too highly on motion picture stars. Trust me, I know."

"Because she's one of the producers."

Smart move, Nita. It's a sure-fire way of getting the role you want. "Why are you asking about this?"

"I did a couple of the *Aphrodite* wigs for Miss Rambova. And I saw the costumes she was overseeing. They were of a remarkably high standard."

"Everything Natacha does is remarkable," Alla said.

"Once your production got shut down, what happened to all her costumes, and wigs, and props?"

"In storage somewhere, I suppose."

Odette's eyes shone with eagerness. "Could you sell them to Nita for her production?"

"Well, now, there's an idea!" *So you're not just heaven to look at but smart, too.*

"Nita is currently making *Blood and Sand* with Valentino. Perhaps you could get him to ask her?"

"And if not, I know June Mathis, who wrote the screenplay, and Dorothy Arzner, who's directing additional footage."

"At least one of them must know how to reach Nita, don't you think?"

After months of struggling to get this production completed,

Alla had felt on the precipice of disaster with no prospect of backing away from its edge. But now? Good God, it just might come together! And she had this gorgeous, enticing, exciting woman to thank for it. Alla grasped Odette's hands in hers. They were so warm, so soft. She could already feel them running all over her body.

12

Alla crushed her cigarette butt with the heel of her shoe and peered down a deserted Sunset Boulevard. Did they really have to leave town so early? She had made the ultimate weekend sacrifice and gotten up at five-thirty, and now it was eighteen past seven.

She pulled the chinchilla collar of her coat around her neck to ward off the cold morning. "If you knew how to drive," she muttered out loud, "you could've told Rudy and Natacha that you'd meet them in Palm Springs. You could have slept till a decent hour."

Seven twenty-two. Where were they?

Not that she was in a hurry to get this road trip underway. It was going to be an excruciating five-hour drive. She and Paul. Alone. She on the passenger side clammy with regret and guilt; he behind the wheel radiating hostility.

She didn't—couldn't—blame him for feeling that way, but here they were three weeks later and he had blocked every attempt she had made to talk.

At least the sale of the *Aphrodite* costumes had gone smoothly. Once Alla had explained to Natacha about the financial pickle she was in, Natacha had agreed to sell them. Strictly speaking, they belonged to Metro, but the movie had been tossed overboard by the halfwits in the studio's front office. Consequently, Alla and Natacha had felt justified in taking them as payment for all the work they'd done. That *Aphrodite* business had happened two years ago, so Metro would have forgotten about those costumes. Nita had purchased them all, and the sale had brought in enough money to finish *Salomé*. As soon as Alla had banked Nita's check, her spirits had soared again. It's all going to be fine, she'd assured herself. More than fine, in fact. *Salomé* was shaping up to be everything she'd hoped it would be.

Editing the picture, though, had been painful. For the final week of the shoot, Alla had given Paul time and space to calm down. As she endured the long days necessary to get the picture in the can before the money ran out, he had cocooned himself in the editing room sorting through Van Enger's mountain of takes.

By the time shooting was over, he had hired a young kid to help him. Was he an apprentice? Did he expect to be paid? She had left the matter unaddressed and was thankful to have a buffer between them. Perhaps that's why he'd hired an assistant. With the kid always there, it had been impossible to bring up that delicate matter of Odette until a few days ago, when Paul had sent his trainee on an errand to get more adhesive tape at a hardware store on Hollywood Boulevard.

Alla had taken it as a sign that he'd cleared the room on purpose.

"Paul, darling, we need to clear the air—"

He had thrust out his hand like a traffic cop. "We have a job to do. And not much time to do it in. I agreed to edit this movie, and I shall. Maintaining our professionalism is how we will get through this."

And now they had to drive to Palm Springs together. What were they going to do for five hours? Sit in silence? The whole way?

This was supposed to be a happy occasion. Two days ago, Natacha and Rudy had appeared on Alla's doorstep with a bottle of Pol Roger champagne in hand. And not just any old bottle, but 1897—the year Natacha was born.

"We are getting married!" Rudy's eyes had twinkled with undiluted joy. "I asked her one hour ago and you are the first we tell. It is *meraviglioso*, no?"

"It certainly is." Alla had led them into the parlor and produced her best crystal coupes from the mahogany sideboard. "When is the happy event?"

"This weekend," Natacha replied. "We're all driving to Palm Springs, where we'll stay overnight and then on Sunday, we'll drive across the border to get hitched. Where's Paul? I hoped the four of us could celebrate together."

Alla had replied, "Editing," and left it at that.

She hadn't brought Odette home with her that night at the studio. It just hadn't seemed right. Not until she had cleared things with Paul. She owed him that, at least.

But he'd prevented them from talking over the situation, and, well, she wasn't made of stone. She had feelings. Keenly felt longings. She was only human, after all, and couldn't be expected to keep at bay the overpowering desire she felt for Odette and that Odette felt for her. And so eventually, inevitably, she had welcomed the girl into her bed.

And when she did, their lovemaking confirmed every suspicion that Alla had been harboring: all those protestations that she bedded the person and not the gender were a load of bunk. She looked back at all her great loves: Katya from boarding school, Mercedes De Acosta, Eva Le Gallienne, and yes, Alla had to admit, even Jean Acker. Each of these women had been different from one another in almost every possible way except one: they were women.

Had she really bedded those men merely to satisfy the expectations of society. Russia, New York, Hollywood. The locations may have changed, the language may have differed, but the expectations were the same. A man with a woman was accepted, natural, normal.

But who in their right mind wanted to be normal? If that was the goal, she would still be Marem Adelaida Leventon. She would have remained in Yalta and married the local cobbler or the blacksmith. She would have popped out the requisite four or five brats and then slid into old age, crocheting doilies and cooking borscht until her arthritic fingers could no longer hold the battered wooden soup spoon.

That path was not on Alla Nazimova's map. It had never been. But somewhere along the way, her true path to happiness had become muddled. That is, until Miss Odette Finch had shown up, her hand extended in friendship and in love. And Alla had Salomé to thank for it. Without *Salomé*, she might still be stumbling around in the dark.

Alla stamped her feet on the dirt path that ran along the side of Sunset Boulevard to fend off the morning chill.

When Rudy and Natacha had arrived to celebrate their betrothal, Odette had been gone a quarter of an hour and Alla had had enough of awkward scenes. But as the three of them had clinked their glasses, she felt she ought to address a problematic hurdle. "Your divorce from Jean has only just gone through. The interlocutory decree won't be final until well into next year—are you sure you can get married again so soon?"

"That's what I asked," Natacha had said from inside her glass.

Rudy ignored her. "The man in the publicity department, he tells me —*promises* me— that they had an actress in the same situation. She got married in Mexicali and there was no difficultness."

"Don't you think you ought to double-check this with an attorney?" Alla had suggested. "One that specializes in divorce?"

Natacha had made a motion with her right shoulder that was a smidge shy of a shrug. "Rudy figures it must be okay if someone in publicity says it is. The studio's P.R. department is hardly going to relish dealing with its biggest star being charged with bigamy. Which makes sense, when you think about it."

That night, bathing in Rudy's adoration and marinating in more than a little champagne, Natacha had been fuzzy around the edges, so Alla hadn't pushed the matter further. The two of them were deeply, happily, hungrily in love. Who was she to wet-blanket the occasion just because her own love life had taken a turn she hadn't seen coming?

So they had drunk the French champagne and toasted to the success of the forthcoming marriage, to *Salomé*, to *Blood and Sand*, and to everything else they could think of.

But now that she was standing in the Sunset Boulevard dirt at an ungodly hour, the whole thing felt like a mad folly. Especially if it meant sharing a car with someone who refused to even so much as look at her.

The roar of far-off engines broke into the serenity of the deserted street. Rudy's light gray Avions Voisin and Paul's red Marmon appeared from the west. They came to a stop at the curb and Rudy jumped out.

"We are sorry we are late!" he exclaimed. "But Douglas, he has the car trouble. Yesterday it was everything fine but today? Pffft! It is kaput."

Paul sat behind his steering wheel looking straight ahead. Douglas Gerrard, an Irish actor whom Alla had met several times, sat in the back seat, waving at her. He was awfully fun to be with, in that mischievous-leprechaun Irish way. If Paul still wasn't prepared to talk, at least they had Douglas to cushion the antagonism.

"But everything is hunky dory!" Rudy picked up Alla's suitcase and headed toward Paul's trunk. "Natacha and I will drive in my car and you will be with the boys, si?"

Alla opened Paul's passenger door. "You've had car trouble, I hear."

Douglas had the typical rust-colored hair and pale skin of his countrymen—not an ideal combination in the harsh desert sun. "Probably just as well. It's a clunking old jalopy and might not have made it there and back. Better to conk out in my driveway than ten miles past the middle of nowhere."

"How true." Alla took her seat and closed the door. "Good morning, Paul."

He kept his eyes on Rudy's car in front of them. "Morning."

Rudy climbed into his sleek Voisin and took off. Past Crescent Heights Boulevard, they were on paved roads, which made for a smoother ride. As the stores and houses along Sunset slipped past them, nobody said a word until Alla could bear the silence no longer. "Tell me, Douglas, what are you filming at the moment?"

His was a conventional face that was neither blessed with handsomeness nor cursed with mediocrity, and could be inserted in any picture, regardless of location or époque. Consequently, he was the rare actor who was always working.

"I'm doing a picture called *Omar the Tentmaker*."

Alla spun around. "What a lovely coincidence! Two of my *Salomé* co-stars, Rose Dione and Nigel De Brulier, are in it, too. Poor old Nigel! He played the prophet and was dressed in rags for almost the entire picture—and not many rags, at that."

"I heard about the heaters you had installed to keep everyone from freezing to death. He was mightily appreciative. In fact, he told me that the whole cast and crew adored you for it."

Alla faced the front, smiling to herself. It was nice to know that at least they'd been thankful for a decision that had helped push her close to the brink of financial ruin. "What else did he tell you?"

"That you've crafted a picture like no other. I can't wait to see it, nor am I the only one. Your film is the talk of every Hollywood party I attend."

It was the fourth or fifth time someone had told her about *Salomé* being a popular topic of conversation around Hollywood. This was exactly the news she needed to hear. With the recklessly extravagant amount Alla had shelled out, she would need every box office dollar she could get. And so if Hollywood was talking about it, Hollywood would probably go see it.

"Isn't that encouraging, Paul?"

He nodded curtly but said nothing.

"Who else is in your picture?" she asked Douglas.

"You know Patsy Ruth Miller, don't you?"

"She was in my *Camille*!"

"And Boris Karloff, too. Heard of him?"

"I don't believe so."

"He gets stuck with exotic roles: henchmen, Arabians, maharajas, and the like. It's a shame, because he's got a certain uniqueness about him."

"After that?" Alla asked. "Do you have anything lined up?"

"Aye, but it shoots in San Luis Obispo."

"Is that bad?"

"'Tis a sweet town, sure enough, but it's all the way up the coast. If you get to Santa Barbara you're only halfway there. And now that my car's had it, I don't know how I'll get my sorry arse up there."

"I'm sure you can fix it before shooting starts."

"I doubt it."

"Nonsense!" Alla wanted to look at Paul but couldn't rally the courage. "Everything is fixable."

"Not everything."

"I refuse to believe that. Maybe it's difficult, and maybe you'll have to work at it, but there's a solution for every problem and a path around every obstacle."

Paul stifled a grunt that was loud enough for Alla to hear but too low for Douglas to catch. If they had been alone, she would have confronted him, blurted out everything she needed to say. She didn't care if he hurled every cuss word in his vocabulary until his voice was raw and the veins in his eyes had popped.

But they weren't alone. She couldn't provoke Paul into blowing his top, so she encouraged Douglas to do most of the talking, and pretended as if everything was fine and fair as a summer day. Fortunately, Douglas was the chatty type, with a store of witty and self-deprecating tales. And that was enough to fill a road trip that might otherwise have been as stony and desiccated as the passing desert scenery.

* * *

Neither Natacha nor Rudy had told Alla how they knew Dr. Florilla White, but the woman was a welcoming hostess who had opened her sprawling ranch house to the wedding party with plenty of bedrooms, fresh linen, food, and booze. "It's like Prohibition never happened," the doctor told them. "We drive down to Mexicali, load up, and are back by cocktail hour!"

The night air was a little on the crisp side, but the sky was clear, revealing a blanket of stars that made a romantic canopy for Dr. White's pre-wedding buffet dinner, which they ate al fresco on the patio by the pool.

Alla could scarcely believe they had escaped L.A. without tipping off the press. She half-expected photographers and reporters to come charging out from behind the clumps of prickly pear and saguaro cacti that stood at the rim of lights surrounding the property. But no such invasion took place and, after finishing the evening with icebox cake and port wine, each member of the party headed off to sleep. Alla trailed Paul to his room, but he closed the door with an unambiguous thud.

The next morning, Florilla's chef prepared a pancake breakfast for them before they piled into their cars for another five-hour drive to the town of Mexicali, which sat across the border from Calexico. Someone had decided it would be bad luck for the bride and groom to arrive together, so Natacha and Alla, Florilla and her sister Cornelia traveled together in Florilla's fire-engine-red LaFayette touring car.

The four women filled the cabin with gay laughter and lewd observations about the male sex and all its faults. Alla's only disappointment was Odette's absence. The girl had revealed herself to be a well-read woman with a sharp wit and commanding intellect. How very comfortable she would have been in this carful of formidable women.

Mexicali was a typical border town whose single-story houses, uniformly painted white, filled a maze of streets baking in the hot sun. Children played on the cracked sidewalks beneath tall, thin Mexican fan palm trees that quivered in the negligible breezes. But they were the only sign of the locals that Alla could see.

Cornelia pulled up behind Rudy, who'd parked out front of a vast yard filled with locals dressed in their Sunday best: men in black and white suits embroidered with gold thread, vibrantly dressed women with flowers and mantillas in their hair. There must have been a hundred people milling about. A wide gravel path cleaved the garden into halves. Six miniature jelly palms on each side lined the path leading to a large two-story house with a wide colonial veranda running its entire width. More people had assembled around the veranda, and at the right-hand end, a five-man mariachi band—two guitars, a violin, a trumpet, and an accordion—were playing a lively tune that Alla didn't know but the crowd was singing along to.

"This is the home of the mayor of Mexicali," Florilla explained. "His name is Otto Moller. A darling fellow, so accommodating, and quite the Valentino fan. When I told him what our plans were, he insisted we hold the wedding here. I accepted on your behalf because it's far and away the nicest address in the whole town, but good golly, I had no idea there'd be all these people. I hope you didn't have your heart set on a quiet wedding, because apparently word got out!"

Alla checked her friend's face for signs of dismay. Women like Natacha rarely savored the spotlight when it came to the more intensely personal experiences like weddings. But she saw neither disappointment nor annoyance tarnishing Natacha's composure. Alla hoped this meant that she had sensibly resigned herself to the reality that if she were going to marry the object of American female passions, she might as well get used to the blinding lights of fascination and envy.

A flurry of excitement fizzed through the crowd as the wedding party approached the banquet table on the front porch.

Someone—the mayor's wife, Alla guessed—had gone to a great deal of trouble trimming it with garlands of alternating pink, magenta, and fuchsia set against the alabaster-white tablecloths.

A round-faced man with a large graying mustache approached them with outstretched hands. "Señor Valentino! And Señorita Rambova! What a delight! We are excited to help you celebrate your love!"

Rudy had chosen an open-necked white shirt, paired with tight cream pants and a light tan linen jacket with matching knee-length riding boots. He beamed the mile-wide smile of the eager groom who couldn't wait to wed his beloved. He grabbed Natacha by the hand before following the mayor up the porch steps.

Natacha wore an equally casual ensemble. Her dress was brown, too, but darker. A simple pattern of squares ran down the front. It had elbow-length sleeves and a portrait neckline cutting straight across her collarbone. She had eschewed all jewelry and wore only a matching cloche to protect her from the sun. It wasn't a traditional wedding outfit by any stretch of the imagination, Alla decided, but it was very Natacha.

The mayor spirited the couple away to meet a tall gentleman with a stern face. He appeared to be wearing a uniform. Police? Military? The crowd had grown too thick for Alla to see him properly, but he did carry the air of authority. The four of them spoke for a few minutes before the mayor led the bride and groom to the center of the veranda. The mariachi band struck up a jaunty version of Mendelssohn's "Wedding March" and the crowd pressed in closer.

Mayor Moller raised his hand to call for quiet. He didn't get it —the gathering was too stirred up over being witnesses to the marriage of a real-life American movie star—but he waited as long as he could.

It was a standard ceremony with the requisite promises and declarations, and ending with the "I do's." When the mayor told Rudy that he could now kiss the bride, the gathering let out a booming cheer. Rice rained down on them and the mariachi band filled the air with high spirits and revelry. The giddy cheerfulness ratcheted up a notch when a line of señoritas appeared from the back of the house with trays of drinks alternating with dishes of guacamole-loaded enchiladas and stacks of corn tamales. When twenty platters of carne asada came out, Alla was tempted to ask who was paying for all this. She hoped that Rudy and Natacha weren't going to be presented with a bill at the end of it all. Those two were as poor as she was.

Bottles of tequila and beer were passed around as everybody sang along to the music. The band strolled around like a quintet of wandering minstrels, encouraging people to sing along and dance wherever they stood.

It had been a long time since Alla had appeared in public and nobody paid her any attention. Being invisible like this would have unnerved her five years ago, but things were different now. Was it this high-quality tequila? Whatever the reason, Alla felt almost like she was on a vacation from herself.

Her thoughts turned to this backbreaking movie of hers. Now that it was nearly finished, she'd soon have to drum up interest using every method at her disposal. Favors to be called in, magazine interviews to be offered, advertisements to be created. And paid for how? With dreams and hopes and wishes? Maybe she and Rudy weren't that different, after all. They both spent, spent, spent until there was nothing left and then couldn't work out where it had all gone.

What a couple of fantasists we are.

She watched the celebrations around her until she noticed Paul by himself at a table on the periphery of the front lawn. He slouched over his glass tumbler of tequila, his mouth drooping into a frown. He was drunk, but not so drunk that he couldn't listen to reason. She wended her way through the maze of guests and, without asking permission, pulled out the wooden folding chair beside him and sat down.

"What a delightful wedding. And here was I thinking the six of us were going to the town hall, or whatever they have down here for civil ceremonies. But this!" She waved a hand across the festivities. "It's so much better, don't you think?" He said nothing. "It'll give Rudy and Natacha fond memories to look back on." Still nothing. At least he hadn't walked away and left her sitting alone. It wasn't much to cling to, but it was all she had.

"Rudy looks so relaxed and happy, doesn't he?"

Rudy and the mayor were deep in conversation, or rather the mayor was and Rudy simply nodded. "He does."

Two whole words!

"That jacket looks familiar. Did he borrow it from you?"

A long pause. "Yeah." A longer pause. "Playing a toreador in *Blood and Sand* meant he had to drop some weight. The suit he had planned to wear hung off him like cheap drapes, so we had to make do with whatever fitted best in my closet."

"Did you tell him what happened?" Alla ventured. "At the studio that night?"

Paul picked up a half-burned Dutch Masters cigarillo, which sat smoldering in a brass ashtray. After a while, it became obvious that he had no intention of responding to her question, so she changed tack.

"Will I be able to see a final cut soon?"

He sucked a loose strand of tobacco out of his gums and spat it into the bed of Aztec marigolds behind them. "Nearly done."

"What do you think of it?"

The mariachi band launched into a high-spirited number—the first one Alla recognized—and the crowd sang along: "*La cucaracha! La cucaracha! Ya no puede caminar . . .*"

Paul smiled bleakly. "I haven't ruined your movie, if that's what you're afraid of."

"It isn't." She could have done a better job at convincing him that the thought had never crossed her mind, but now was not the time to be stretching the truth. "But I do want to hear your opinion."

"It's unlike any movie I've ever seen. And I mean that in the best sense." He kept his focus solely on the dancing guests. "I know you were horrified when Van Enger wanted to do six takes, because the expense exploded the budget. But as your editor, I can tell you it's been a huge gift. The final film has benefited enormously, and it could well be its saving grace, which might be a bitter pill to swallow seeing as how his demand was born out of jealousy." He met her with a sharp look, prickly and accusatory. "You know that's why he wanted all those takes, right? He saw you giving Natacha everything she wanted, so he felt he had to stake a claim. Men are like that, you know: we're territorial."

Ouch! Touché! "I know you are." She hoped her smile registered as a winsome white flag. "Can we talk about what happened that night? I had only met Odette—"

He jerked away from her as though she'd punctured him with a cattle prod. "I don't want to know anything about her."

"But Paul, darling, we have to—"

"I'm not your darling. Not anymore. If, in fact, I ever was."

"Please don't think—"

"You don't get to call the shots about what I think." His chair scraped against the gravel as he tottered to his feet. "I'll finish the movie to the best of my ability and deliver the final cut when I'm done. Other than that, do not talk to me." He scooped up his glass and drained what was left of his tequila. It must have burned, but he didn't show it. "Catch a ride back to Los Angeles with Rudy and Natacha."

He dissolved into the crowd of merrymakers.

"That didn't go so well, did it?" Natacha dropped into the vacant chair beside Alla, a tall glass of bubbles in her hand.

"I was hoping that maybe with a few drinks inside him he'd be more open to . . ." She shrugged away the rest of her reply.

"He told us what happened," Natacha said. "That is to say he told Rudy, who told me." She nudged Alla with her elbow. "So, you and Odie, huh? I didn't see that coming any more than I could have predicted you and Paul. I must say, though, you and Odie seem like a more natural fit."

Alla quietly blessed Natacha's unwillingness to take sides. Mrs.

Valentino was more right than she ever could have guessed. The previous morning, Alla had woken up with Odette whispering in her ear about how they fitted together like jigsaw puzzle pieces. She would have been blissful if this blossoming love affair hadn't come at the cost of wounding Paul so deeply. *But everything comes at a cost, doesn't it?* "Let's talk about you. This is your big day. Are you happy?"

"I am—now."

"What does that mean?"

"I've had misgivings about marrying Rudy ever since he asked me."

"Why would you say yes if you weren't sure?"

"I wanted to marry him but I was far from confident that he was legally free to marry me. And I wasn't so convinced on the say-so of some movie studio publicity hack."

"What changed your mind?"

"I insisted that we get an informed opinion, so Mayor Moller took us to speak with Sheriff Silver from Calexico."

"The tall fellow in the uniform?"

"He assured us everything was in order. I figured he'd know better than anyone here, so we went ahead."

"And now you're married!" Alla exclaimed.

"And now I'm married."

"To Rudolph Valentino!"

"Yes," Natacha said, giggling now. "I am married to—" she took a deep breath "—Rodolfo Alfonzo Raffaelo Pierre Filibert Guglielmi di Valentina d'Antonguolla."

"You've been practicing."

"And I thought Winifred Kimball Shaughnessy was a mouthful."

Alla lifted her glass. "Let's drink to that."

They clinked glasses as the mariachi trumpeter hit a long, high note that floated over the crowd and soared into the purplish haze of the encroaching dusk.

13

Newspapers filled Alla's dining table. Not just local papers like the *Examiner* and the *Times*, but ones from further afield: the *San Francisco Chronicle*, *The San Diego Union-Tribune*, the *Denver Post*, and the *Seattle Times*.

Scobie walked into the dining room with four more in her arms. "The eastern papers have arrived. I've got the *Chicago Tribune*, *The New York Times*, *The Washington Post*, and *The Boston Globe*."

Alla looked up from the *Hollywood Citizen*. "Same headlines?"

"More or less. Coffee, anyone?"

Alla nodded.

"Coming right up." Scobie dumped her load on the end of the table and headed back into the kitchen.

Alla abandoned her *Hollywood Citizen* for *The New York Times*.

Odette asked, "Did he make the front page?"

Alla read the headline:

VALENTINO CAUGHT UP
IN BIGAMY SCANDAL
QUICKIE MEXICAN WEDDING
DEEMED ILLEGAL

Under it was a photo of Rudy and Natacha at the Mexicali wedding.

"Yes." Alla skimmed the headlines of the three East Coast papers.

> HOLLYWOOD'S BIGGEST STAR
> CAUGHT UP
> IN WEDDING OUTRAGE

> LOVE TROUBLES
> SCREEN'S PERFECT LOVER

> IS VALENTINO'S MARRIAGE INVALID?
> SHERIFF SAY YES BUT JUDGE SAYS NO

"Poor Rudy. He must be crushed."

"There must be something more important going on in this world than the dubiously legal marriage of a movie star," Odette said. "I dunno, like maybe the Teapot Dome scandal?"

"I wager that President Harding and his cronies are glad that Rudy has edged them off the front page."

Scobie appeared with her coffee pot in hand. "Have neither of you eaten yet? And here it is nearly eleven o'clock. How about I fry up some bacon and eggs?"

Alla had always taken care to be discreet when entertaining her overnight guests—especially the women—escorting them to the door before any of her staff arrived in the morning. A faithful Presbyterian, Scobie preferred to have her Sundays off, which had suited Alla, especially after her Sunday socials had become as regular as her Saturday salons. She had been less vigilant with Paul, and now that Odette had replaced him, Alla had grown tired of living in a French farce. If Scobie disapproved of her unorthodox dalliances, Alla figured she could speak her mind, but Scobie hadn't so much as lifted a disapproving eyebrow.

"Sounds delicious," Alla said, and picked up *The New York Times* again. Hardly any of the papers had gotten the facts right, but she hoped that the *Times* would at least have made a decent stab at it.

Despite the unpleasantness of her attempted tête-à-tête with Paul, the trip to Palm Springs and Mexico had been a delightful weekend. Florilla had been a superb hostess, and that wedding at Mayor Moller's house had been such a picture-perfect fête that it could have been from a movie.

But the romantic idyll hadn't lasted long.

Within a day or two, Rudy had received a call from the studio warning him that the district attorney's office was investigating the legalities of his Mexicali marriage. By the time Rudy and his manager met with the studio legal team, it had become clear that the Los Angeles district attorney, Thomas Lee Woolwine, was planning to showcase Rudy's prosecution. He was running for reelection amid a distracting rumor that a disgruntled female employee was bringing charges against him. Whether or not Woolwine's motivations were political had mattered little, however, when he'd announced that Rudy would be charged with two counts of bigamy, the penalty for which was one to two years in the state prison and a $5,000 fine.

Until the day before yesterday, Alla had known only what she had heard from Natacha, who had called her a couple of times from upstate New York. Natacha hated to be separated from Rudy when he needed support, but he had insisted she take sanctuary in the secluded safety of Foxlair, the retreat in the Adirondack Mountains built by her stepfather.

Rudy wasn't returning Alla's calls, so now she could only get her information from the papers, which were indulging in a gleefully aggressive free-for-all. They raced each other to print the story as it unfolded, rarely taking the time to double-check the facts. Who cared about the truth when a headline like VALENTINO'S FIRST WIFE SAYS "NOT SO FAST, MISTER!" could sell ten thousand more copies?

Rudy had pleaded guilty to the bigamy charges, and his $10,000 bail had to be paid in cash. How very suspect, Alla thought, that this drama had played out on a Sunday, when the banks were closed, forcing Rudy to spend time in jail. America's hottest movie star guilty of bigamy *and* thrown into the clink until somebody could pony up the funds? Call downstairs and get 'em to print up an extra twenty thousand copies.

Fortunately, June Mathis, Douglas Gerrard, and an actor friend of Rudy's, Thomas Meighan managed to cobble together the ten grand needed to set him free. The next day, the date for his trial was set.

Those big shots at Famous Players-Lasky must have been livid. First, they'd had to deal with the Fatty Arbuckle rape, then one of their directors had been murdered, and now their biggest star was charged with bigamy. It wasn't often that Alla felt sorry for studio heads, but even they didn't deserve a trifecta like that.

Odette folded her *San Francisco Chronicle* and read out loud, "Will Hays, the moral watchdog of Hollywood, has weighed in on the latest uproar to shake the film industry, proclaiming, 'These scandals must stop.'"

"That's all he said?"

Odette ran her eyes farther down the page. "Pretty much."

The aroma of bacon drifted in from the kitchen. "This Hays character doesn't have what it takes to censor a Sunday school class."

"Uh-oh!" Odette jumped up from her chair, rounded the table, and dropped the *Chronicle* in front of Alla. She pointed to the headline: ACTRESS WANTED IN BIGAMY TRIAL. Next to it they'd printed a photograph of Alla in *A Doll's House*. The caption read: *Subpoena for Alla Nazimova as witness in Valentino bigamy trial has yet to be served.*

Alla pressed her face into her hands. "They want *me* to testify?!"

Odette nodded. "It seems they do."

Alla returned to the article. "'Madame Nazimova's name was mentioned and her picture was shown to Mrs. Remalda Lugo, an Indian squaw. Mrs. Lugo recognized that bobbed hair, those eyes, that wide, fascinating smile.'" Alla looked up. "Nobody has called my smile 'fascinating' before."

Odette tapped the paper. "Keep reading."

"'She identified the picture as that of the woman in silk pajamas and kimono whom she saw one day lying on a bed in the little three-room bungalow at Palm Springs, where Valentino and Miss Winifred Shaughnessy, stepdaughter of Richard Hudnut, the perfume magnate, spent the honeymoon that followed their marriage in Mexicali, Mexico. Since early morning Deputy District Attorney James J. Costello and a number of investigators armed with a subpoena had been seeking the foreign movie actress. She will be called as a witness if she is found.'"

Alla let the newspaper fall back onto the table. "*If* I am found? They make it sound like I've fled! It's not like nobody knows where I live."

Odette laid a comforting hand on her shoulder. "You know what those men can be like—running around thinking they're cleverer than Sherlock Holmes, and then they overlook the obvious."

Sooner or later, Costello's investigators were bound to come knocking, and when they did, what should she do? Appearing at a sensational trial could generate countless inches of publicity in the papers. Normally, that would be a good thing. But the Arbuckle / Taylor / Valentino hat trick had pushed the needle of Hollywood's moral barometer into the danger zone. The public's appetite for lurid melodrama would never wane, and that was fine as long as it was happening to someone else. But Alla couldn't afford to become engulfed in Hollywood's next P.R. fiasco.

She couldn't *not* accept a subpoena . . . could she?

Scobie appeared, holding two plates piled with food. "How about you push aside all those papers and make room for a decent breakfast? I know Rudy and Natacha are your friends, and 'tis only natural you're concerned for their well-being, but—" The doorbell rang. "Who can that be, calling so early in the morning?" Scobie set down the bacon and eggs and headed for the foyer. "If I don't recognize them, I shall send them on their way."

Steam from the fried eggs rose from the plate, but Alla's appetite had dissipated. As she wrapped her robe more tightly around her waist, it dawned on her that it was the same kimono mentioned in the article.

Scobie's voice shot through the foyer. "You've no call to be spying through windows like some Peeping Tom. An outrageous invasion of privacy is what it is. Wait here." Scobie closed the door with an exasperated yowl and was soon back in the dining room.

"A horrid little man is asking for you. I didn't recognize him, so I said you weren't at home. He told me that he saw you through the window and that I'd better come fetch you."

Alla rose from the table and smoothed down her famously bobbed hair and straightened the cuffs of her infamous kimono. She considered changing her clothes, but that was only delaying the inevitable.

The man standing on her front step wore a suit of dark brown tweed that he'd bought when he was twenty pounds lighter. He sported the thick mustache of a villain from a *Perils of Pauline* serial. What a predictable cliché.

Alla was only five-foot-three, but she had spent years on the stage playing women of towering majesty. She drew herself up now and used her chest voice. "How may I help you?"

"Alla Nazimova?"

"Come now, let us not play games." She watched him reach into the inside pocket of his jacket and retrieve a sheet of paper, folded into three. "Is this the part where you tell me I have been served?"

His smile revealed a row of tobacco-yellowed teeth. "Not till I place it into your hands."

"And if I refuse?"

"The law is the law and nobody can evade it. Not even you."

Alla snatched the subpoena out of his hand. "Happy now?" She stepped back and slammed the door.

Odette was waiting for her, hidden by the potted maidenhair fern sitting on a wooden stand inside the doorway. "I've never seen a subpoena," she said, her eyes on the folded paper.

Alla thrust it toward her. "Be my guest." She hadn't seen a subpoena either, but was in no hurry to look at this one.

Odette opened the page. "The trial starts next week. Woolwine must have pulled strings to get it moved up."

Alla didn't like the sound of that. Not one little bit. The district attorney was obviously keen to maintain the momentum he'd whipped up in his grandstanding press conferences. "I wish Rudy would return my calls. We need to get our stories straight."

"What about June?" Odette suggested. "She might know—"

A second knock on the door took them by surprise.

"Do you think it's him again?" Alla whispered. "Was I supposed to sign for it?"

Odette shook her head. "They don't sign for subpoenas in the movies. Or do they? Maybe it's Paul? He's probably on their list, too."

It was a hell of a way to get Paul to start talking to her, but better this than nothing. She opened the door and immediately wished she hadn't.

"Mr. Farrington. This is a surprise." Hiding her left hand behind her back, Alla shooed Odette away. Seeing the two of them together in their pajamas on a Sunday morning implied there had been a Saturday Night Before. There had been, of course, but now, more than ever, Alla needed Farrington on her side, and confronting him with her lesbian lover was in nobody's best interests.

Farrington took off his fedora. "I'm sorry to barge in like this, but tempus fugit and all that. It's rather urgent."

Alla led him into the parlor and motioned for him to take a seat. The four mother-of-pearl combs Alla had pulled from Odette's hair the previous evening lay strewn across the coffee table. She discreetly snatched them up and slid them into the pocket of her kimono.

"What can I do for you?"

"I take it that you've seen the Valentino bigamy situation in the papers?"

"I have."

"Are you aware that you have been identified as one of the witnesses to his bigamist marriage?"

"I am."

A fleeting hint of horror swept across his face. "So it's true? You accompanied Valentino and Rambova to Mexico?" Alla nodded. "And you were physically present for the ceremony?" When she nodded again, he pinched the top of his nose in what struck Alla as unnecessarily histrionic. She waited for this little performance to end, which it did with an exaggerated sigh.

He said, "It's only a matter of time before some grubby little subpoena server takes you unawares, Madame. Those people know a hundred ways to trick you. I suggest you leave town altogether. Have you been to the Hotel del Coronado near San Diego? Or up north, perhaps? I know a charming little inn near Santa Barbara. I suppose it doesn't matter where you go, just as long as you keep out of sight."

Alla folded her hands across her lap in an attempt to look calm and demure. "I wish you'd been here ten minutes ago."

"Why?"

"Did you not see the chap in the drab tweed?"

Farrington pinched his eyebrows together. "I passed him on the street as I was coming here. Why? Oh God, don't tell me." He slapped the brim of his hat across his kneecap. "Damnation!"

"I believe refusal is not an option."

"This is disastrous!"

"Mr. Farrington, if I had known there was any chance their marriage was on shaky legal footing, I wouldn't have participated. But Rudy and Natacha spoke to a sheriff who—"

"I'm not talking about the trial. How you handle yourself on the witness stand is your own affair. I'm talking about *Salomé*. I'm sorry, but with this Valentino business coming so soon after the Arbuckle rape and Taylor's murder, we can't release it."

Alla gripped the upholstery to steady herself. She had counted on releasing *Salomé* as soon as Paul had delivered the final cut, which she hoped would be very soon. As close as she could figure, she had about two weeks' money left. "Until when?"

"Not in the foreseeable future."

"But now's the perfect time. With Hays coming to town, everybody's talking about the place of censorship in society and who has the right to exercise it. A picture like *Salomé* will add to the conversation. It's bound to fuel the fire, which will only drive people to the box office to see what the fuss is all about."

"You insisted on making a picture about a girl who performs an erotic dance designed to seduce her stepfather into getting the head of a scorned lover served up on a platter. Your *Salomé* won't add fuel to the fire—it'll add gasoline." He jumped to his feet and jammed the fedora back onto his head. "*Salomé* cannot be released until Valentino's misadventure has faded from the public's memory.

"But that could be months from now."

"Or years."

"Years?!"

"You want to turn a profit, don't you?"

"Of course!" *Otherwise, I'll have to sell what decent jewelry I have left or rent out my house to make ends meet. Dear God, I might even have to let Scobie go!*

"The very worst time to release a film like yours is amid a furor over morals and decency." He held up his hand to brook no further discussion. "The decision is mine, and my decision is final. Good luck at the trial. I fear you're going to need it. I'll see my own way out."

Alla watched him trek from the parlor to the foyer. He stepped outside and closed the door without looking behind him.

*　*　*

Alla could see the mob from blocks away. Wide-brimmed sun hats with bright ribbons dangling down the side. Black velvet appliqued with gold thread. Strings of pearls looped around long necks. Zigzag patterns. Checks. Stripes. Candy-apple reds. Jade greens. Butterscotch yellows.

Of course the flappers had turned out in droves. *Of course* they had wanted to show their undying love for their idol. Perhaps catch a glimpse of him in the flesh. And maybe—*just maybe!*—get a chance to even touch that celebrated flesh. Wouldn't *that* be a thrilling memory to hold close for the rest of their lives?

The press had gorged themselves in a feeding frenzy over the news of Alla being a member of the wedding party and of how she had been the last witness to receive her summons. But she'd been far too preoccupied with her testimony inside the courtroom and hadn't spared a thought for the unruly melee she might encounter outside it. "Oh, Scobie! We're going to have to hack through all that."

The street was now starting to congeal with traffic. Scobie tsked. "I expect there'll be a mighty scuffle when you get out of the car." The outskirts of the crowd had spilled over the curb and onto Grand Avenue. A reed-thin girl with frizzy hair held up a placard above the cloches and headbands: *WE BELIEVE VALENTINO!*

Scobie braked as the rusty Buick and white Studebaker ahead of them ground to a halt. "You'll have to hoof it from here; otherwise, you might be late."

"But I'll be mobbed! I'll enter the courtroom looking like a bedraggled hobo."

Scobie unwound the black scarf coiled around her neck and handed it to Alla. "Drape this over your face. You'll be able to see well enough, but with any luck they won't guess until you've made it through the door."

Resembling a widow en route to the reading of a will would likely draw as much attention as going bare-faced, Alla figured, but it was worth a shot. She slung the scarf over the brim of her hat like she was the femme fatale out of a Poverty Row B picture and opened the car door.

As she closed it behind her, a flapper in pastel-blue georgette angled her head to one side and squinted. Who was that mysterious veiled lady who had exited her Rolls-Royce driven by a female chauffeur?

Alla panicked. *What made me think I could sail inside the courthouse like I'm Nellie Nothing from Nowhere?* There was little else she could do but brave the crowd and get through it as unobtrusively as possible.

The girl in the blue georgette approached her. "It is Madame, isn't it?"

Alla nodded.

"Even buried beneath that veil, I knew it was you." She waved her hand down Alla's suit. "That's the Paul Poiret you wore for that *Photoplay* interview last year."

The black wool was the most conservative garment in her closet and the best choice to convey to the judge that she was a serious person. "I'm flattered that you follow my career so closely."

"Oh, but I adore everything you've done—on stage, on screen, and in life. It may not look like it, but I'm all of a-quiver on the inside!"

A cool head was what Alla needed. She took the girl's gloved hand in hers. "What's your name?"

"Corinda."

"Tell me, Corinda, is there another entrance?" Alla pointed to the crowd still thronging the court's front doors. "I don't know that I can face—"

"Goodness me, no! You don't want that." Corinda led Alla away from the crowd until they arrived at the corner, where she pointed down the side street. "The first alleyway you come to is how they deliver the accused."

Alla flinched. Sneak in like a common criminal?

Then again, she was about to commit perjury. Right there in open court.

As soon as the date for Rudy's trial had been set, they'd all gathered together: Rudy, Natacha, Paul, Thomas Meighan, and Douglas Gerrard. With district attorney Woolwine out to hang Rudy from a flagpole, it was imperative that they got their stories straight.

The sheriff from Calexico had been dead wrong. Rudy's interlocutory divorce decree was still in effect, so Rudy's lawyer, Mr. James, had decided that the best strategy was to insist that the marriage hadn't been consummated, and therefore available for annulment. But that meant everybody had to stretch the truth.

Alla felt it was bad enough that she'd been swept into the undertow of this deteriorating situation—but lie under oath? "I doubt that I have the nerve to pull it off!" she had told the group.

"You're an actress," Mr. James had said. "Treat it like a scene from one of your movies."

It had taken a couple of hours to thrash out a five-point story:

One: Someone at the studio had told Rudy that his Mexico marriage would be valid, even though the twelve months determined by the interlocutory decree said that no marriage was possible until that period was up.

Two: Deputy Sheriff William Silver had agreed that any marriage that took place south of the border would be legal, which had allayed Natacha's concerns that the union might not be on firm footing, even though the sheriff was ill-informed.

Three: The wedding took place at Mayor Moller's house with everybody in attendance, including Deputy Sheriff Silver.

Four: After the celebrations, they drove back to Palm Springs. However, the drive to Mexicali had been more than four hours in each direction and everybody had arrived home bone-tired. On top of which, the day had been unusually warm and Florilla's house was still unbearably hot. So Paul had helped Rudy move a single bed onto the porch, where Rudy had passed the night alone.

Five: In the morning, the wedding party drove back to Los Angeles whereupon Rudy had been arrested.

Rudy had pointed out that four out of five of those points were true. "All you have to do is stretch the truth and say that me and Natacha, we did not sleep together."

Alla had nearly laughed aloud: the great movie lover, Rudolph Valentino, gets married and doesn't sleep with his bride on their wedding night? Who was going to believe that?

Poor Rudy—so pale, so drawn. All he'd wanted was to marry the woman he loved, and now he was trapped in a nationwide firestorm born of one man's ambition to be elected California governor. Technically speaking, Rudy had committed bigamy, but not on purpose, and he was genuinely regretful about the whole affair. Couldn't Alla help out a pal and be a teensy bit elastic with the truth?

The court's back alley ended at an unmarked door. Alla pulled the veil from her hat and coiled it around her throat. She was soon standing in a dimly lit, deserted corridor. A sign, *PRISONER DETENTION*, pointed to the right; a second one, *COURTROOMS*, pointed left. The echoing din of an unruly crowd grew louder as she approached a swing door at the end.

It opened into a huge vestibule filled with dozens of people: women of all ages, reporters, photographers, a sprinkling of serious-faced lawyer types, and so many security guards that Alla couldn't count them all. She tapped one on the shoulder and asked where the Valentino trial was to be heard.

"The biggest one."

Courtroom B was packed to capacity; murmuring filled the air. A burly bailiff in a khaki uniform stopped her. "Only persons with business before the court are allowed—" His mouth formed a tight little circle. "Beg your pardon, Madame." He stepped aside. "Anywhere in the first two rows."

She had been careful not to look anybody in the eye, but now that she was seated and the trial was about to begin, she furtively searched for a familiar and comforting face. Truthfully, what she wanted was a Sheriff Silver of her own to reassure her that what she was doing was the right thing, even if it wasn't exactly legal. *Exactly legal?* What she was about to do wasn't at all legal!

She spotted Douglas sitting with Thomas, who had helped cobble together Rudy's $10,000 bail. But they sat on the other side of the aisle and were talking to June and Paul in the row in front of them. She wished she'd taken a better look around when she'd come in, and she would have chosen a spot near one of them. She would have felt less alone now.

As the clock behind the judge's raised desk hit eleven, the bailiff called for quiet and announced the entrance of the case's presiding judge, Justice J. Walter Hanby, who, after warning the visitors' gallery that he'd stand for no hysteria in his courtroom, wasted no time in getting the proceedings underway. The prosecuting attorney, Mr. Costello, called Rudy to the stand.

Rudy wore a pressed suit, his hair trimmed and slicked back. The prosecutor tried to trick him up using long sentences in complex English, which for the most part failed. But now and then he flummoxed Rudy, who only had to look to the gallery for support. His fans weren't shy in calling to him until Hanby silenced them with a thump of his gavel.

Jean Acker took the stand next to testify the circumstances of their marriage. She spent most of her time in the witness box with downcast eyes, demure as a novitiate. Everything she said could have been proved with photographs of her marriage certificate and divorce decree, but the prosecution had cannily realized that their case needed faces.

Douglas was next, followed by Paul; they both stuck to the agreed-upon script. Sheriff Silver's testimony paralleled what Rudy, Douglas, and Paul had said, and nobody had asked where Rudy had slept on his wedding night. Had Alla been worrying for nothing?

"The prosecution calls Madame Alla Nazimova."

An excited twittering burst from the gallery as Alla headed for the witness stand. She barely looked at the court registrar as he commanded her to swear to tell the truth on a careworn King James Bible.

Costello had that lean, hungry look of a prosecuting attorney intent on amassing as many wins as possible. "Miss Nazimova," he said, presenting her with a cheerless smile, "you were a member of the Rudolph Valentino/Winifred Shaughnessy wedding party, correct?"

"Yes, I was."

"And the events as presented in this courtroom today—the drive from Los Angeles to Palm Springs, the overnight hospitality of Dr. Florilla White, the drive to Calexico, then on to Mexicali, where a wedding ceremony took place at the home of Mayor Moller—do you disagree with any of them?"

"No, sir, I do not."

Costello leaned on the wooden beam surrounding the witness stand. "If there's anything you feel needs clarification, or doesn't line up with your memory of how the events played out, we could go through each event, one by one."

"That won't be necessary." Alla relaxed into the chair. She was merely here to confirm the facts and no more. "Everything described by the previous witnesses tallies with my memory of what transpired."

Costello held for a dramatic pause. "Everything?"

A stony hush settled over the room. The only sound Alla could hear was the swift scratch-scratch-scratch of the court illustrator. "Yes," she told him more firmly.

"Miss Shaughnessy and you are great friends, are you not?"

"We are professional colleagues and close personal friends."

"Sufficiently close to recommend she abscond from California so as to avoid attending this trial?"

It was time to treat this like a movie scene. "Miss Shaughnessy is quite capable of making up her own mind."

Costello paused again, long enough for Alla to realize that perhaps her statement had led the judge to believe that Natacha had been fully aware of the hole she was leaving Rudy in when she'd left the state—and that she didn't care.

"With specific reference to the wedding night," Costello said, "we've heard testimony saying that after the wedding feast, everyone returned to Palm Springs, but that Mr. Valentino chose *not* to share a bed that night. His *wedding* night. With his *wife*."

Everybody in that room—as well as tomorrow's newspaper-reading public—was supposed to believe that he wouldn't do the deed? It sounded to Alla as preposterous in court as it had at Rudy's house that night. What was she supposed to say?

"Feel free to disagree with me, Miss Nazimova, but I put it to you that this version of the story stretches credibility. I mean, we are talking about Rudolph Valentino here."

A twittering giggle broke out at the back of the room, halted only by a single, forceful thwack of Judge Hanby's gavel.

"I suggest you ask Mr. Valentino," Alla retorted. "He's sitting right there."

"Miss Nazimova, did Mr. Valentino spend the night separated from his brand-new spouse?"

Alla needed an immediate solution that was plausible enough to preserve Rudy's status. And it needed to be something that this pompous blatherskite couldn't refute.

"It wasn't Mr. Valentino's choice, I can assure you," Alla said in the same voice she'd used at the end of *A Doll's House* when her character, Nora, was declaring her intention to leave. "This was, after all, the day he had wedded his radiantly beautiful wife. Of course he wanted to—er . . . do what all bridegrooms wish to do on their wedding night." She paused to let the fresh outbreak of chuckling peak and fall away. "But the decision was taken out of his hands."

"Oh?" Costello jumped in. Alla could see resentment building in his eyes. "What sort of red-blooded male allows his wife to call the shots like that? Or are you saying that Mr. Valentino is not the red-blooded male that his notorious reputation would have us believe?"

Alla made a show of turning away from Costello and rotated in her seat until she faced Judge Hanby. "How indelicate may I be, your honor?"

"We are all adults here, Madame," Hanby said. "You can be as indelicate as you need to be. However, I will caution you against saying anything that will turn my court into a circus. Do that and I shall find you in contempt."

"Thank you, your honor." Alla confronted Costello again. "On the drive back to Palm Springs, Miss Shaughnessy confided in me that her wedding day had unfortunately coincided with her monthly cycle."

Costello's face blanched. "Oh."

"And that she would be quite incapable of fulfilling her nuptial duties that night. As I'm sure you can appreciate, this was a state of affairs that embarrassed her deeply. And this was further complicated by the fact that she found herself without a Lister's Sanitary Towel with which to—"

"Thank you, Miss Nazimova."

Alla presented him with a face of mock surprise as though to say *But Mister Costello, I haven't finished yet.*

He hurried back to his table. "No more questions, your honor."

*　*　*

Alla braced herself as June Mathis pulled her aubergine-colored Studebaker to the curb outside 8080 Sunset. She could see Paul seated up front but was unable to interpret the neutral look on his face. She opened the rear passenger door and climbed in beside

Rudy. He greeted her with a European kiss to each cheek. "Are you dreadfully hungover?" she asked him.

"Not so bad." He looked a little pale, but after what he'd been through, Alla wasn't the least bit surprised.

After she had finished her testimony, Judge Hanby had needed no time to deliberate on a verdict. "I am dismissing the bigamy case brought against Mr. Valentino on the grounds of insufficient evidence." The viewing gallery had pitched itself into a shrill cheer as Rudy shouldered a path through the well-wishers who crowded the courtroom, the foyer, and finally the sidewalk. Fortunately, his lawyer had planned ahead; a car and driver were waiting for them.

"I assume there was some celebrating when you got home?" Alla asked.

Rudy pointed to the back of Paul's head. "We finished two full bottles of chianti, didn't we, *mio amico*?" Paul nodded without turning around. "I had to pack my traveling trunks, so we made the celebration as I chose shirts and trousers and neckties."

"You must be looking forward to seeing Natacha again," June said. At seven in the morning, the traffic along Sunset was very light. "How will you get to the Adirondacks?"

"I will take the train to New York, then another to Albany. The chauffeur of Natacha's stepfather will be waiting for me."

"That's assuming we get you on at Pasadena in one piece," Paul said.

There was something about his voice that raised Alla's hopes. Was it just her imagination, or was he no longer radiating resentment like he had during the whole trip to Palm Springs? She let out a quiet sigh. Maybe this trip wasn't going to be quite so icy after all.

"But nobody will think to look for him there," she said. "Won't they assume that he'll board at the La Grande station in downtown?"

"Most of them will," June said, "but Rudy's fans are something else again."

Their enthusiasm for Rudy's exoneration had been so boisterous that it had allowed Alla to slip away unnoticed. "I got a taste of them at the trial yesterday." She patted Rudy's hand. "Your fans would go to the ends of the earth for you."

"Or Pasadena, at least." There was no buoyancy in Paul's voice, but he was talking, so that was something to peg the wisp of a hope on.

"We're making good time, so listen up," June said. They were already past Los Feliz and heading into Glendale with nothing behind them but a dejected-looking horse pulling a milk truck. "We can only relax if there's nobody around when we get to the station, but I'll bet my last plug nickel that there'll be some of Rudy's rabid fans camped out there just in case."

Alla felt a light tap on her wrist. "Thank you for what you did yesterday." Rudy's voice was so soft that Alla could barely hear it over the roar of June's engine. "Telling the lies in front of the judge was a terrible risk."

"Think nothing of it," she told him, and meant it, too. The less she dwelt on committing perjury, the better.

"Oh, my stars!" June laughed. "When you said that Natacha was having her monthly cycle, it was all I could do to stop myself from falling on the floor!"

"I could have told him that Natacha was too drunk to respond to Rudy's advances, but I decided that would not play well in Prohibition America."

"And when you said 'Lister's Sanitary Towel'? Jesus! I almost passed out!"

"I needed to say something that would shut that little weasel up."

"It brought the whole trial to a screeching halt. Priceless, darling. Priceless!"

Rudy's eyes burned with gratitude "I will never forget what you did for me."

"Let's put the whole thing behind us. Four days on a train will give you lots of time to recuperate. And at the other end, Natacha will be waiting for you with open arms and nobody around to bother you." She changed the conversation to the Egyptian-themed theater that Sid Grauman was building and how excited Natacha, a devotee of all things Egyptian, would be when it opened in the fall.

They pulled into the parking lot of the Atchison, Topeka and Santa Fe Railroad's station ten minutes ahead of the scheduled pit stop. A dozen vehicles filled most of the available slots. June drummed her steering wheel. "This is more than I was expecting."

Paul opened his door and got out. "I'll scout for fans."

"And reporters," June called after him.

He nodded and disappeared inside the building.

"When was the last time you heard from Natacha?" Alla asked.

"I got four telegrams from her yesterday."

Rudy's handsome face took on an adoring glow. It was the same sort that often filled Odette's face, and Alla couldn't wait to see it again. At Alla's insistence, she had kept her distance during Rudy's trial.

"The nearest town to Foxlair is twenty minutes away," he said. "The only place to send a telegram is at the local dry goods store. Knowing that she made the trip four times in one day fills my heart with love."

"You shall drown that girl in kisses."

"Yes, I will."

Paul hurried out of the depot and slid back into the car. "The good news is no reporters."

"Is there bad news?"

"A clump of six or seven girls is standing on the platform. They're all eagle-eyed, surveying every direction, with Valentino love written all over them."

"I suppose that's my cue." Alla adjusted her cloche so that it sat farther back than she preferred but exposed more of her face. "How long until the California Limited arrives?"

June consulted the watch hanging from a chain pinned to her lapel. "Six minutes. Rudy's booked a Pullman at the front of the train, so lure them toward the south end."

Alla kissed Rudy on the cheek and told him to give Natacha her love. She slid out of the Studebaker and strolled past the ticket booth and onto the platform. Halfway along, a covey of girls stood in a watchful circle. She approached the platform's edge and looked southward as though searching for a locomotive that wasn't due for a few minutes.

She checked her watch, then stole another glance at Rudy's fans. A streak of pastel-blue georgette caught her eye. This was going to be easier than she thought, but what was the name of that girl outside the courthouse? It was a lovely name, slightly unusual. Corinna? Cordelia?

Alla waited for the girl to recognize her, but the knot of budding womanhood stayed on alert.

So this is what it had come to? Once celebrated as the American theater's most-lauded interpreter of Ibsen, The Great Nazimova was now proffered as a decoy. *I'm merely here to distract over-zealous fanatics away from a nice Italian boy saddled with the ability to project a raw eroticism not previously seen on the screen.*

She closed her eyes and imagined the premiere of *Salomé* at one of the fancier theaters. The end credits roll . . . the applause builds to a deafening roar . . . people start calling for her . . . "Nazimova!" . . . "Madame!" . . . She appears on stage and takes a bow . . . humbled but grateful . . . "Thank you! Thank you all!" but nobody can hear her over the thunderous ovation . . .

A distant train whistle pulled her out of her fanciful daydream. *Don't be such a selfish so-and-so. Rudy's been through the most awful scrape, and once this train has whisked him out of town, he'll be able to put the whole debacle behind him. And if it means I have to deal with these squawking chickens, so be it.*

She opened her eyes and made a grand gesture of pulling off her hat and raking her fingernails through her hair.

"Madame! Oh, Madame!" The sound of running feet. "How thrilling to see you again." The girl in blue georgette led the pack. Soon all six of them surrounded her. "You remember me, don't you? Corinda? From yesterday?"

"Of course I do, my dear. You were my savior!"

"I can't believe my luck. Twice in two days I get to see you." A brief frown flashed across the girl's face. "How come you're here?" A soft gasp. "You're not here to meet Natacha Rambova, are you? Is she returning to L.A. now that Valentino's been exonerated?"

"No," Alla told them. "I'm here to meet a friend, but her telegram was vague so I'm not sure I've got the right day." The other girls began to search the platform. "Did Corinda tell you how she saved me?" Alla asked, lassoing their attention back around to her.

"Yes," one of them said, "but we weren't sure we could believe her."

"After all," another added, "you *are* Nazimova."

"See?" Corinda said, pouting now. "I swore it was true. I told you it was her." She swung back to Alla. "We've all loved you for as long as we can remember. But even more so now."

"Why?" Alla asked. "Whatever did I do?"

"You saved Valentino!" Corinda blushed slightly. "I mean, your testimony was a little bit shocking." Behind them the California Limited train pulled alongside the platform amid a gush of steam and smoke, and a loud blast from the locomotive's whistle.

One of the girls broke into a cackle. "When I told my mother what you said, she was scandalized!"

Down at the far end of the platform, Rudy hurried for the first carriage, flanked by June and Paul, leaving a porter to haul the five traveling trunks Rudy had brought with him.

"Now listen to me, girls," Alla commanded in her best schoolmarm voice, "what I said in court yesterday was nothing to be embarrassed about. Half the population goes through menses every month. There's nothing scandalous or shocking about it, and the sooner men realize it, the better. You girls are entering womanhood at the most exciting time in history. You can now vote, smoke cigarettes, drive automobiles, go to college, have a career. Promise me this one thing." As the girls nodded in rapturous reverence, Alla snuck another peek. June and Paul now stood alone. "You are all New Women and, as such, you are beholden to nobody. Take charge of your lives. Some of you will fail and some of you will succeed, but trust me when I tell you that there is great satisfaction in knowing that you did it on your own terms."

The whistle announced the train's imminent departure. A surge of steam enveloped them as it slowly pulled away.

* * *

June braked to a stop under the porte-cochère of the Huntington Hotel.

"What are we doing here?" Alla asked, surprised.

"I said we should celebrate getting Rudy through his mess and sneaking him aboard with no one the wiser. What better place than this?"

Paul said, "Because it's only open during the winter months to give those poor East Coasters a break from that vile weather they have to put up with."

"Exactly!" The harsh wail of June's klaxon filled the archway. "I know someone who knows someone who runs a gin mill from out of the main bar. The police think the place is closed down until November, so they won't come snooping." She blasted the klaxon again. "Around the back, maybe? We're bound to find an open door someplace." She started up the engine and followed the driveway to the right. "You have to admit, running a saloon inside a deserted hotel is pretty ingenious, don't you think?"

"Oh, it's a cunning idea, all right." Paul let out a soft bubble of a laugh. It was the first sign of humor Alla had seen coming from him in months. Its appearance gave her a sliver of optimism.

The driveway led to a graveled lot with fifty spaces for automobiles, twenty of which were filled.

"See?" June cried out. "I told you!" She parked the car in one of the vacant slots and they climbed out.

An early promise of summer warmth filled Alla's face. "I felt like I haven't had a decent gin since . . . I can't even remember when."

June grabbed them each by the arm. "Shhhhh!"

The hotel was far enough from the bustle of Colorado Boulevard that the only sounds Alla could hear were the swish of the wind and the twitter of birdsong. "What are we listening for?"

The lament of a solo trumpet floated toward them. June pointed down a flagstone path. "Thataway!" The path led to a door marked *EMPLOYEES ONLY*. Bright chatter and a long, low note from a saxophone spilled out when Paul opened it. They skulked down a short passageway that opened into a large room paneled in a rich, dark cherry wood. Two of the walls held intimate booths for four, and the bar filled a third wall. Tall stools ran its entire length; every one of them was taken. Tiny cocktail tables for two filled most of the floor. At the center of each one sat a tiny lamp, shedding a circle of light the size of a small dinner plate. In the far corner, a trio of musicians was playing a slow version of "The Wabash Blues."

A waiter with a starched napkin folded over his left arm appeared. "Welcome to The Hunt," he said. "Table for three?"

June scanned the crowd. "That's right."

"It'll be a bit of a squash," the waiter said without apology.

"Fine, fine. We're pals."

He led them toward the perimeter of the room. June's pout indicated that she would have preferred one closer to the center of the action, but Alla didn't mind. At a table built for two, they'd need as much elbow room as possible.

As they were getting settled, June asked the waiter if they had Cointreau. He assured them that they were fully stocked. "In that case, a round of Singapore Slings, if you please, kind sir." As he departed, she dropped her purse onto the polished parquet flooring. "That day in court! I've never been so on edge in my entire life. When the judge announced he was dismissing the charges, I felt like dancing the Black Bottom right there on his desk."

Paul laughed. "I'd have paid good money to see that."

"If scenario writing doesn't pan out, perhaps I could have a second career on the burlesque circuit!" She barked out a laugh, but cut it short. "So he *does* come here!" She stared at a well-fed gentleman in his early sixties. He had very little hair and no visible neck, but exuded the well-heeled prosperity of a successful businessman.

"Who's that?" Alla asked.

"Abraham Erlanger." June flattened her chaotic hair. "He was the original producer for the stage version of *Ben-Hur*. My esteemed boss, Mr. Goldwyn, got himself all caught up in a protracted and very heated battle with him for the film rights. In the end, Goldwyn had to offer him a generous profit participation deal, which of course almost killed Goldwyn." She rattled around in her purse and pulled out a little pot of lip rouge. "I don't know how he did it, but Erlanger also got approval over every detail of the production. Including casting." She dabbed at her lips with the tiny brush. "And now that Rudy's troubles are behind him, I'm starting my campaign to get him the lead role." She dropped the pot back into her purse and got to her feet. "Wish me luck, kids!"

And suddenly she was gone.

"That gal, she sure is a force of nature, isn't she?"

Though rhetorical, it was the first time Paul had voluntarily addressed Alla in months. Taking it as a sign that enough time had now passed, she lit a cigarette to marshal the courage she needed, let out twin plumes of smoke through her nostrils, and inched herself out onto what felt like a perilously flimsy limb.

"We can't not talk about it forever," she said. "That night on the set when you walked into my dressing room. I know it must have been a shock. To tell you the truth, it was to me, too. A shock, I mean. I didn't see it coming."

She toyed with the lighter, hoping it would calm her nerves. It didn't, but it was better than nothing. Paul kept his gaze on June as she approached Erlanger, bold as a lioness. But Paul hadn't cut her off or walked away, so she persisted.

"I was very happy with us. Honestly! You've seen enough of

the world to know that it takes all types. I'm sure you know what I mean. But this girl. Odette. She's touched my heart as few before her have. That's not a slight against you. And I hope you don't take it personally. Although, of course, I'd understand if you did."

The waiter arrived with the Singapore Slings. He placed them on the table and asked if they'd like to start a tab.

"Yes," Paul told him. "It looks like we might be a while."

Feeling brave, Alla held out her cocktail glass for him to clink. Slowly, he raised his eyes. He took his sweet time about it, but eventually he met her eye as he clinked her glass. He did it so gently that she couldn't hear the sound over the din filling the room, but she felt it through her fingertips.

He took a sip of his cocktail and swirled it around his mouth before swallowing it. "I'm not bitter. And I'm not angry. In fact, I don't feel betrayed."

Relief gushed through Alla like a dose of Epsom salts. "I've felt terrible about—"

"That is to say, I don't feel those things *now*. I *was* bitter, and angry, and felt completely betrayed. I resented you for a very, very long time. But then Douglas Gerrard took me aside and asked what was going on with me. When I told him, he pointed out that surely I knew of your penchants before you and I started keeping company. I told him that I did, but that I believed—or at least wanted to believe—that you hadn't met the right man yet. Watching Rudy and Natacha at their wedding, so bright and gay and happy, I was quite envious because I wanted it to be you and me some day, and the realization that we wouldn't, well, it upset me. To say the least."

Given their age difference, Alla felt that such an outcome was a little unrealistic, but it was a beautifully romantic notion, so she couldn't fault him for that.

"But then I spent all day in that courtroom," he continued. "And I realized we were only there because Rudy had rushed headlong into marrying Natacha. Even though it turned out to be an ill-considered wedding, and he should have stopped to ask the right questions of the right people, I thought he ought to be congratulated for his actions—not punished. And then you got up in court and said what you said. It wasn't true, and you took a terrible risk. Perjury is no laughing matter, but you sat on the witness stand and you sold it to the entire room like only The Great Nazimova could. And I said to myself, She's not a bad person. She's not two-faced. She's not a fraud or a ruthless destroyer of hearts."

"Is that how you saw me?"

"It's what I told myself while I was nursing my broken heart."

"And now?"

"I watched you on that train platform, surrounded by those adoring fans. I couldn't hear what you were telling them, but I could see the look on your face."

Alla sipped her cocktail. It was strong, but strong was what she needed. "How did I look?"

"Like you were in your element." He put his drink down and moved over to June's chair so that they could be closer. "I get it now. Some people prefer men; some prefer women. And there are some who have no preference. I do think you've been fooling yourself that you're one of the latter when in reality you're not. You've made your choice, so go be with her. You've lived your life on your terms, my dear, and I don't want you to stop now. Certainly not on my account."

The look in his face was so gentle, so understanding, so full of love that she wanted to kiss him. Not in *that* way, of course. But she didn't know how to kiss him without sending the wrong message, so she smiled back and trusted that it carried the message she hoped.

"WELL!" June flopped down in the chair Paul had vacated. "That was a waste of time. Mr. Erlanger is most certainly not agreeable to the idea of casting Rudy as Ben-Hur. I may as well have suggested Beelzebub, whom I suspect Erlanger thinks Rudy is closely related to." She picked up the third Singapore Sling and scrutinized the dreamy looks on their faces. "What did I miss?"

14

The elevator cage rattled and clanged and shuddered. Each time it passed another floor, a metallic *CLUNK!* filled the air. Alla fanned her face with her beaded purse. "I hope this is safe."

Odette told her, "Natacha said the whole building is a storage facility."

"All ten floors?"

"And so they built the elevators, not for humans, but for sofas and boxes and machines."

Another *CLUNK!*

Alla winced. "Did she say why she wanted us to meet her here?"

"Only that it'd be worth it." Odette landed one of her dainty kisses on Alla's cheek and pointed to the needle sweeping clockwise around a brushed metal disk above the doorway. "Nearly there."

"What did you say the name of this place was?"

"Elysium, as in Elysian Fields, the final resting place of the heroic and the virtuous in Greek mythology."

A final *CLUNK!*

"Thank goodness." Alla pulled the rough iron door handle all the way to the right and stepped forward.

Dark royal blue—the hue that fills the sky for a few evanescent moments before dusk surrenders to the night—covered the entire space: floor, walls, ceiling. Stars smaller than the glass balls on the Salomé headdress sprinkled the ceiling and had quite possibly been painted with the same white phosphorus paint. Windows reached from the floor to the ceiling on three sides. Beyond them, the lights of Hollywood twinkled like a fairytale landscape.

The more cunning rumrunners had figured out how to circumvent the Feds, because booze now seemed to flow again in such volume that it was as though the Volstead Act had never taken effect. Life these days seemed to consist of driving from one furtive speakeasy to another with barely a break long enough to sober up. In Alla's mind, they were all starting to blur together. But this place was something else again.

The maître d' was dressed in an all-white tuxedo and on his back a pair of papier-mâché angel wings reached out a little wider than his shoulders. He clicked his heels together in the fashion of a Prussian field officer. "Welcome to Elysium."

"What a breathtaking establishment you have here," Alla exclaimed.

A string quintet over to the far right, also with wings on their backs, was playing "The Sheik of Araby." It was a novelty song inspired by Rudy's movie, but this ensemble had re-orchestrated it to make it sound more like Puccini.

"We're meeting someone here," Alla told the maître d'. "I don't know if she—"

"Miss Rambova arrived a few minutes ago. Please, ladies, if you'll follow me."

He led them to a table positioned in a corner, offering up views of the Hollywood Hills to the north and, in the distance to the west, the lone lights of the Beverly Hills Hotel surrounded by the inky darkness of all those lima bean fields.

In contrast to her usual sinuous wardrobe of kimonos and capes, Natacha wore a tailored suit of dark summer-weight wool with cream piping. She had pulled her hair into a bun that rested at the nape of her neck. How different she looked without the braided coils bracketing her face. But that was probably the point.

It had been two or three months since the bigamy scandal had filled headlines and driven Natacha to seek the safe haven of her stepfather's mountain retreat, where Rudy had later joined her. It wasn't long, though, until Famous Players-Lasky conscripted them back to Hollywood so that Rudy could pull double duty: participate in the publicity rounds for the upcoming *Blood and Sand*, as well as film his next picture.

Natacha hadn't said as much, but Alla knew that the glare of publicity around the bigamy situation had made the girl's life unbearable. She wouldn't have returned to Los Angeles so quickly, but the studio had hired her to design Rudy's costumes for *The Young Rajah*. This was the first time Alla had seen her since Natacha had snuck back into town. After everything she'd been through, was it all that surprising to see that she wanted to change her entire look?

"I assumed that sidecars would be okay," Natacha said, "but it's not too late to change our order."

"That'll be fine," Alla told her. "I do want to hear about the *Blood and Sand* premieres. It was at the Rialto, wasn't it?"

"The Rivoli in New York and the Rialto out here."

"How did they go?"

The waiter arrived with their drinks. Natacha didn't bother to clink her glass with theirs and threw back a sizable mouthful. "Some front office bigwig told Rudy that there's every expectation it'll be in the top ten box office champions for 1922. Perhaps even the top five."

Natacha's Pacific-blue eyes had lost their sparkle. "Is that not a good thing?"

"It would be nice to think that the success of the picture is due to Rudy's performance."

"I've heard he's terrific in it," Odette put in.

"He is, but I suspect that our—" she stopped short of saying 'bigamous marriage' and settled instead on "—predicament is what drove people into the theaters. Is it too much to ask that art should carry the day?"

It was a fanciful question whose answer—a resounding yes—was embedded in the doleful way Natacha had asked it. Alla said, "A success is better than a flop."

"I suppose so, yes. I mean, I don't wish to sound ungrateful. Nor do I want any movie of Rudy's to fail—" She shook away the rest of her sentence and replaced it with a warm smile. "It's nice to see you both again." Natacha reached down to the large saddle-bag-style tote at her feet and pulled out a *New York Herald*. "Which brings me to this." She unfolded it to a page she had previously selected, then took a sip of her drink and read,

"'Watching how the Valentino picture, *Blood and Sand*, is sending movie palace cash registers into a frenzy forces one to speculate about efforts of the briefly Mrs. Valentino, aka Winifred Shaughnessy, aka Natacha Rambova. Last we heard, she was working on an unusual cinematic project. However, members of the film gentry are eloquently silent concerning the present whereabouts of Nazimova's *Salomé*, or its ultimate destination. What, we wonder, has happened to it? Is it too flagrantly artistic to be profitable?'"

She laid the paper on the table. Way off in the distance, the headlights of automobiles snaking along Santa Monica Boulevard merged into a long, thin line.

"I met with Mr. Farrington," Alla said, "and he told me in no uncertain terms that they wouldn't even think of releasing it until the controversy surrounding it had died down."

"Which controversy?" Natacha asked. "The part where the heroine does a seductive dance and demands a decapitation? Or where the woman responsible for the artistic landscape of the picture becomes caught up in a scandal not of her own making?"

"Probably both," Alla admitted. "He brought up Will Hays a number of times."

A packed assemblage at the newly opened Hollywood Bowl

had welcomed President Harding's hand-picked censor. It had been, Alla suspected, an empty exercise in artful showboating.

"What else did Farrington say?" Natacha asked.

"That they dare not release it without the approval of a leading industry authority like the National Board of Review, and they dare not submit it as long as there is any association with the Valentino bigamy scandal."

The Board wasn't an official governmental body, so it possessed no political clout like Hays did. But they were an elite group of filmmakers, cinema enthusiasts, and academics who regularly met to watch, review, and discuss whichever new releases they deemed worth their while.

"For what it's worth, here's what I think." Odette pushed aside her empty cocktail glass. "If the public thought Valentino was a degenerate, they wouldn't be going to see *Blood and Sand* in droves. Now that it's doing bang-up business, the whole bigamy scandal has become a moot point. The public doesn't hold anything against Rudolph, so in my opinion the case is closed. Hays is an unknown quantity, but sooner or later he'll have to start singing for his supper. And *Salomé* is tailor-made for him *unless* the movie gets a thumbs-up from the National Board of Review."

Natacha ran a fingernail up and down the edge of her lapel. "But Allied won't be submitting our movie to the NBR."

"Can't you do it yourselves?"

Alla and Natacha stared at each other. *Can we?*

"Do you have your own copy of the movie?" Natacha asked.

Alla sighed. "My meeting with Farrington didn't exactly end with hugs and kisses."

"Are either of you aware," Odette asked, "that the studio workshop where the costumes and wigs and props are made sits right next to the lab?"

"I don't suppose you've befriended anyone who can make us a duplicate?" Alla asked.

Odette shook her head. "Not necessary. It's standard practice to run off three or four copies. They keep the negative and an extra in a cupboard, and the rest of them in a separate storage shed."

"Where?" Alla asked. "On the lot?"

"You know that English garden down the back where hardly anybody goes? It's right near there."

"You're not suggesting we just waltz in and take one?" Natacha lit a cigarette. "And anyway, they probably keep it padlocked."

"Nope. I always stashed a pack of Lucky Strikes there for when I was on a break. I often went in there and poked my nose around to see what I could see."

"Heavens to Betsy." From the way that Natacha took a long, deliberate drag of her cigarette, Alla could tell she wasn't completely in accord with this radical plan. But Alla was. She had to be. She was running out of options.

She'd spent the summer laying off most of her staff, and pawning all her valuable pieces of jewelry. When that hadn't been enough to cover the bill, she'd sold her Rolls-Royce and had taken to catching taxis and eating at home most nights. She hadn't checked her bank balance in a couple of weeks for fear of having to face the harsh reality of letting Scobie go too.

For the first time in months, Alla felt the glimmer of good news peeping over the Hollywood Hills. She told Natacha, "Leave it to us. If anything goes wrong, you can claim blissful ignorance." The waiter deposited a fresh round of drinks on their table. Alla pinched his sleeve. "Do you offer a food menu? Suddenly I'm quite starving."

* * *

Alla checked her watch again. The second hand ticked toward the twelve. Soon it would be seven-thirty. Only half an hour to go and still nobody had shown up. The toe of her shoe tapped against the dark brown tiles of the Hunley Theater foyer as doubts gnawed at her innards.

Natacha's *New York Herald* article had only confirmed Alla's suspicions that Hollywood had been gossiping about what had happened to her *Salomé*. Filming had finished in the spring and now it was late summer, so why hadn't it seen the light of day, or rather, the dark of movie theaters? Had Nazimova exceeded the bounds of decency, even by Hollywood's lax standards? Was the cast truly made up of inverts and sapphists? Alla still wasn't sure how that rumor had got started, but it did give the picture a certain cachet of notoriety—and as everybody knew, the worst fate for a motion picture was for nobody to be talking about it.

Seven-thirty-two.

Had she left her run too late? Had interest peaked mid-summer and, when no *Salomé* had surfaced, had everyone's curiosity been rerouted by a new Clara Kimball Young picture? Or Colleen Moore? Or, worse—Nita Naldi? Why did she always feel as though she were in competition with that girl?

Purloining *Salomé* from Allied's storage vault had been as simple as Odette had promised. Nobody had stopped them driving onto the lot. Nobody had looked twice at the pair of them lugging heavy cases to the dilapidated Ford that Odette had borrowed from a friend. And the security guard had bid them farewell with a tip of his peaked hat as they drove away.

After they had stashed the reels in the bottom of Alla's closet, she'd searched for the right theater in which to hold the preview.

The Hunley was down at the eastern end of Hollywood Boulevard and had only been open for a few months, so its owner, Otis Hunley, a savvy chap in Brooks Brothers suits, was keen for the business. His theater was a classy operation, first-run movies only, so Nazimova holding a preview of *Salomé* there was, she hoped, all that people needed to hear. To secure sole use for the evening, she'd had to sell off her final piece of jewelry: a pearl necklace she had bought with her first paycheck from the Shubert Theater Organization. It had been a painful transaction. But that was okay. She could dine out on that story for months after *Salomé* became a big hit. And when that happened, she would buy another necklace.

The next day, Alla and Odette had compiled a list of people to invite. Scobie insisted they stop at nine o'clock and eat the beef stew she'd been keeping warm. By then, they had a list of around a hundred.

Alla had handwritten a note to each critic, columnist, and journalist inviting them to the preview on September 22nd. It wasn't until after they'd been mailed out that she realized that she should have requested an RSVP; otherwise, how could they know how many to expect? All of them? Half? A couple of dozen? Anyone at all?

She stood in the foyer of the Hunley wearing her Madeleine Vionnet suit. She had bought it in Paris prior to the Great War, so it was a little old now. But, she'd told herself, it would have to do.

The preview was scheduled for eight o'clock. It was now seven-thirty-five. Her hopes began to wither away like the last wildflowers before winter's first snowfall.

Odette stood at the doors into the auditorium to welcome their guests. She mounted her bravest smile and called out, "They'll be along any minute. I'm sure of it." Only the roar of passing traffic prevented the foyer from being silent as a catacomb. She abandoned her post and hurried to Alla's side. "I thought Natacha would be here by now. Whatever's delayed her is also probably delaying everybody else. Perhaps there's been an accident and it's blocking traffic. That intersection at Western Avenue's been getting mighty busy."

"Natacha said she'd come after eight o'clock, once the movie's started. She didn't want to be a distraction."

"It's just that—" Odette cut herself off. "Look out! Man the battle stations!"

Please, dear God, let this be somebody on my guest list. Alla plastered a convivial smile on her face as a cluster of seven or eight people trooped in. Recognizing six of them—two critics and four columnists, plus a couple of wives—she pulled a handful of questionnaire cards from her jacket pocket. "Welcome! And thank you for coming. We so very much appreciate it."

"I wouldn't have missed this for the world," the *Los Angeles*

Times columnist, Harry Carr enthused. Carr wasn't an entertainment reporter; rather, he was a generalist whose profile had soared after filing an eyewitness report of the San Francisco earthquake in '06. Consequently, he had a large and varied following, which is why he'd made the list. "But Madame, you might want to let the management know that parking around here isn't as freely available as it needs to be."

"But the streetcar passes right outside."

"And that's fine, I suppose, for the public, but the caliber of people I imagine you've summoned tonight will be coming via private automobile."

Alla winced inwardly. Earlier that evening, having sold her beloved Rolls-Royce a week earlier, she had taken her first streetcar ride. In the flurry of emotions surrounding that tearful farewell, combined with the business of getting ready for tonight's premiere, she hadn't stopped to think where people might park. She mentally kicked herself; it did explain why hardly anybody had shown up yet. They were all still circling the block!

Well, never mind all that now. Chin up. She handed out the questionnaires and explained that their feedback would be invaluable.

To her relief, more people began to arrive, and soon the foyer was filling up. If enough of them liked her film, she would have a strong case to accompany her submission to the National Board of Review. All she had to do now was stop herself from smoking too many cigarettes as *Salomé* unfurled for a bunch of people who had little idea that her entire future depended on their opinions.

* * *

The Normandie Corner Bakehouse sounded like a swanky French patisserie but was just an ordinary diner a couple of notches above a greasy spoon. But it was open until late, so Alla didn't care. Besides, it was the best she could afford for now.

She and Odette were sliding into a booth when Natacha burst

through the door, her loose hair cascading around her face. She swept it behind her shoulders as she sat down. "I meant to be here an hour ago," she said, throwing the blue velvet turban in her hand toward the end of the table, "but Rudy's been unmanageable since we got back from New York. The papers have been mocking him for saying that $1,250 a week isn't enough, and of course Zukor and Lasky have been stoking those fires with predictable comments about actors and their egos and their greed. So now Rudy's decided that he doesn't want to work for Famous Players-Lasky at all."

Natacha's perfume swirled around her. Alla was fairly certain she was now wearing Guerlain's new fragrance, Shalimar. Its floral notes mixed with vanilla suited Natacha, but why had she stopped wearing Three Flowers from her stepfather's line?

Alla straightened the pile of response cards. "But didn't Rudy sign a new contract with them?"

"Yes, but this next picture they've forced him into—all I hear, morning, noon, and night is how he hates it, and how he longs to be free."

In *The Young Rajah*, Rudy played an Indian prince who comes to America and becomes a football star at Harvard. It sounded to Alla like the ridiculous sort of picture Metro had imposed on her. On the other hand, although Rudy's salary was a fraction of what she had been making a couple of years before, her circumstances were entirely, shockingly, disturbingly different now. Anything more than five hundred a week sounded appealing.

"So?" Natacha asked. "How did it go? How many people showed up? Did they enjoy themselves?"

Alla pictured the looks on the faces of the audience as they'd exited the theater with their response cards filled out. She had learned how to recognize the faked smiles offered by people who said they'd enjoyed a performance when they hadn't at all. The edges of their mouths were pulled wider than was natural and held longer than was necessary. Alla had seen some of those among the guests, but only a sprinkling.

"For the most part, yes." She tapped the stack of cards in her grip. "But it's the numbers that matter."

Alla had counted the cards they had received after the preview. Of the hundred or so invitees, she guessed that around sixty had shown up. And of those, fifty-seven had taken the trouble to fill out the cards. Nearly everyone! Not that it had been a chore: there were only three questions, and all they'd had to do was circle 'yes' or 'no.' Still, Alla was thrilled.

But did they like the picture?

Natacha flagged down the waitress and ordered coffee and three slices of pineapple upside-down cake as Alla read out the responses and Odette kept a tally. By the time they were finished, they had demolished the cake and were on their second cups of coffee.

Odette laid down her pencil, then pressed her palms together and made baby claps with her fingers. "Ladies, I think we have a winner."

"Numbers!" Natacha said. "What are the numbers?"

Odette consulted her totals. Question one: 'Is *Salomé* an exceptional picture?' Fifty-one replied yes."

Alla pressed her fingers to her mouth. *So it wasn't my imagination or my vanity or an over-inflated ego. You give people quality and they really do gobble it up!* "And the next one?"

"Question two: 'Do you believe *Salomé* realizes the greater possibilities of the motion picture as a medium of art?' Fifty replied yes."

Natacha's eyes shone with optimism. "So much for custard pies and pratfalls. Philistines: zero. Cosmopolitans: two. And the third?"

"Number three: 'Would legal censorship be justified?' To that question, fifty-six replied no."

Alla fell back in her seat and slapped her hands against the Bakelite tabletop. She might be practically broke, but at least she was right. "Vindication at last!"

"Those numbers are consistent," Odette said, "which makes

them reliable. I don't know what the National Board of Review requires, but they look awfully impressive to me."

"What's our next step?" Natacha asked. "Go back to Allied and—"

"Damn them and their narrow-minded ways," Alla said. "I'm sure they'd rather we take *Salomé* with us and slink off into the night, never to be heard of again. We need to build a case Allied can't ignore, so we're going directly to the National Board of Review."

"And we're positive that individuals can apply, right?" Odette asked. "Not just studios?"

Alla had read the rules. Nowhere did it say that submissions had to come from studios. She pressed her thumb to the pile of cards now sitting at the table's center. "I'm sure they don't accept every picture that applies, but with numbers like these, I'd say we stand a very good chance."

* * *

Alla hadn't seen Grace Kingsley since the night of the L.A. premiere of *The Four Horsemen of the Apocalypse*. That had been a year and a half ago, when an interview with The Great Nazimova carried the weight and prestige of a papal audience. Who would have guessed what a difference eighteen months could make? Alla now needed Grace and her high standing at the *L.A. Times* much more than Grace needed her.

She called to Scobie in the kitchen. "Please tell me your cinnamon raisin cookies came out perfectly."

"I'm insulted that you asked."

"Everything must be—"

"—must be perfect today. But not obviously contrived within an inch of its life. Casual. Spontaneous. Informal. Got it."

"And the tea?"

"Oolong. Miss Kingsley's favorite. I've also made shortbread, cucumber finger sandwiches, and fruit scones. Unfortunately, my clotted cream didn't turn out quite as planned—"

A tremor of panic juddered through Alla. "Scobie!"

"'Tis tricky, that clotted cream, but not to worry. I've got some of the regular stuff left over and I'll whip it into picture-perfect peaks. Miss Kingsley won't even notice."

Alla adjusted the placement of the teaspoons an inch to the left. What a ridiculous fussbudget she was being! Nobody but the head butler at Buckingham Palace would know where the teaspoons lay at what was supposed to be a casual, spontaneous, and informal afternoon tea. Winning Grace over was step two in her three-part plan to convince Allied to release *Salomé* for public exhibition, and now that step one had been accomplished, Alla was so very close to making all her sacrifices worthwhile.

The doorbell rang.

"She's prompt, I'll give her that." Scobie emerged from the kitchen untying the apron from around her waist. "I'm used to your show business pals, for whom a starting time is merely a suggestion. But here it is, right on two o'clock."

"Put the kettle on and start whipping the cream," Alla told her. "I'll answer the door."

Scobie stopped halfway into the foyer. "But I thought the whole point was to impress this woman."

"Casual, remember?" Alla shooed her maid back toward the kitchen. She let the doorbell ring a second time, then counted to three before she opened the door. "Grace!" She laced her voice with a carefree indifference as though she had only half-expected the woman to show up at all. "How lovely that you were free to join me."

Alla wasn't sure which side of fifty Grace occupied, but she dressed as though she were heading into church circa 1902: a conservative suit, low-heeled shoes, a cream blouse with modest ruffles, and a wide-brimmed hat filled with bows and feathers that had been the height of fashion in 1897.

But that was why Alla had chosen her. Grace was a serious-minded journalist who shunned the spicy scandals that rocked Hollywood from time to time. She refused to write of boudoir escapades, barroom brawls, marital separations, or sob-sister desertions. She was a plain-facts reporter who preferred to supply answers to the what, where, when, and for-how-long questions that applied to the moving picture business. This trait made her unusual among her Hollywood-centered colleagues but perfect for Alla's purposes.

"I must confess," Grace said, stepping inside, "I was surprised to receive your invitation." She peeked around the foyer. Alla didn't need to ask why.

Grace was bound to know 8080 Sunset as a place where persons of high intellect and flexible morality met to discuss and debate all manner of subjects. Usually with free-flowing alcohol. Sometimes around the pool. Sometimes *in* the pool. And not always with their clothes on. At least those were the rumors, so Alla didn't blame the woman for fearing that this might be one of those afternoons.

"I've been thinking about that night we bumped into each other at the *Four Horsemen* premiere, when we were besieged by Valentino fans."

Grace withdrew a long pin from her hair and removed her hat. "Goodness! What a night that was. I felt like I was standing in the eye of a hurricane."

"Although from what I hear, the eye of a hurricane is where everything is calm and tranquil, which was hardly the case." She led Grace to the dining room, where Scobie had laid out the silver tea service. "I feel as though you and I have been circling for years but never had the chance to get to know each other."

Grace eyed Alla with the wariness of a duck during hunting season. *And why would we?* her raised eyebrows asked. *You're Alla Nazimova with exactly the type of infamy I prefer to avoid.* Alla pretended not to see it.

"A friend of mine in London sent me a birthday package that

included a tin of oolong tea, and I immediately thought of you and how often you mention it in your column."

"Twinings of London?"

Alla reeled in her prey. "Your favorite brand, is it not?" She motioned for Grace to take a seat. "My maid is Scottish, so I've left the brewing to her."

"It'll be there in two shakes!" Scobie called from the kitchen, delivering her line exactly on cue.

"Unless you would care to do the honors."

"No, no," Grace said, unfurling her linen napkin. "I'm sure a Scot can do it better than I."

Alla had prepared a list to carry the conversation along like a cork on a country stream, and launched into it as Scobie brought in a Wedgwood teapot covered with a knitted tea cozy—not because it kept the oolong warm but because it covered an awful crack and Alla lacked the funds to replace the teapot.

Amid cups of tea and steaming fruit scones, they talked of the Hollywood Bowl ("You wouldn't want to be seated too far away from the stage, would you?"); the impenetrability of James Joyce's *Ulysses* ("I gave up before page twenty."); how Irving Thalberg at Universal had worked up the nerve to fire Erich von Stroheim from *Merry-Go-Round* ("Can you imagine the fireworks that must have ignited in that office? I bet a hundred ears were pressed against the door."); and whether Metro's two-strip Technicolor picture, *The Toll of the Sea*, was going to be an innovation or a gimmick ("It'll only work if Anna Mae Wong doesn't end up looking like she's been filmed through a cheap kaleidoscope.")

If Grace had come to Alla's home half-expecting / half-fearing that a semi-naked orgy would be spilling over the diving board, she let those suspicions go and was happy to natter about any subject that came to her. And that, too, was part of Alla's plan.

As her carriage clock chimed the quarter hour, her doorbell rang.

As arranged, Scobie scuttled out of the kitchen, through the foyer, and opened the door.

"How odd!" Alla pushed a plate of buttery shortbread toward Grace. "I'm not expecting company." She waited for Scobie's tentative "You have a telegram, Madame" before she stage-whispered, "Unexpected telegrams make me anxious. Is it going to be a pleasant surprise or news of an awful tragedy?" Scobie placed the telegram in front of her.

In truth, it had arrived a week ago. After shipping *Salomé* and their response cards to the National Board of Review, Alla had waited four weeks until she had heard from them. It had been a long and taxing interval, during which Alla had sold off her one remaining valuable piece of art, an original painting by Russian artist Konstantin Makovsky. It was a minor work, but now that Makovsky was dead, the value had escalated, so it had fetched a generous price. What a shame she didn't have an attic full of Makovskys to peddle.

But the wait had been worth it. A telegram had arrived from the NBR informing her that they had viewed *Salomé* and awarded it their approval.

Alla made a show out of positioning the telegram next to her plate.

"A birth in the family?" Grace asked around a cucumber sandwich.

"You've probably heard about my new picture."

"*Salomé*?" The woman's detached tone was hard to read. If Grace didn't approve of the subject matter, this whole charade would have been a waste of time.

"I held a preview last month."

"So I heard. Was there a reason I wasn't invited?"

Alla blinked in surprise, then covered it quickly by looking down at the plate of sandwiches. She had been saving Grace for this afternoon's tête-à-tête. What she hadn't counted on, though, was that word would have spread about her preview. She waved her fingers airily. "There were only a dozen or so of us."

"I got the impression it was a larger group than that. I know three or four people who attended."

"That's what I meant about circling each other for years, which is why I wanted to invite you here today. Anyway, virtually the entire audience thought *Salomé* a fine picture and encouraged me to submit it to the National Board of Review." Alla opened the telegram and made a show of reading it and registering surprise. "This is from them telling me that it's received their stamp of approval."

"Congratulations. That *is* good news." Grace smiled, and then frowned as she spotted the tentative sulk Alla had arranged on her face. "Isn't it?"

"I fear I may have been a little rash."

"How so?"

"Not until after I had shipped the film off to the Board did someone tell me that it ought to have come from Allied."

"You didn't send it under your own name, did you?"

"I submitted it under Nazimova Productions." Odette had suggested it, and Alla had been very grateful that she had.

Grace wiped the edges of her mouth. "Yours is a legitimate company; I don't see why there should be any problem."

"Not as far as the Board is concerned, but now I'm worried about stepping on men's egos. You know how fragile they can be."

"Whose in particular are we talking about?"

"Joe Farrington. He heads up Allied, and he can be quite the prickly pear."

Grace rolled her eyes toward Alla's pressed iron ceiling. "Aren't they all?"

"You'd think there'd be one or two who don't find us threatening or intimidating."

"If there are, I've yet to encounter them. And I've met them all: Fox, Goldwyn, Griffith, Selznick, Laemmle, Schenck. I'm sure you have, too, so you must know what I'm talking about."

"Some of them do have one or two good points," Alla said, "but on the whole, they're a sorry bunch. You know those anthills you see out in the desert? Monstrous piles, seven feet tall? That's how I see them. Quite intimidating from a distance, but get up close and you see they're filled with holes and all these ants are scurrying around like terrified neurotics, petrified that the exterminator is coming."

Grace let out a whoop of a laugh. "Oh, that *is* funny, Madame. You've got it exactly right. And we women are the exterminators, determined to usurp their power!"

"You understand, don't you?"

"I'm a lady journalist. Of course I do."

"So now you understand the position I've put myself in. I'm very proud of *Salomé*. I've got the approval of the National Board of Review, but the male of the species who can give me distribution might turn me down out of spite."

Grace rested her arms on the table. "What can I do to help?"

The sound of smashing glass shot toward them from the kitchen.

"Scobie?" Alla called out. "Are you okay?"

"I—um—yes—Madame—I—oh!"

This was not part of the plan. Alla pushed back her chair. "If you will excuse me, it appears that I need to check on my maid."

She entered the kitchen to find Scobie ignoring the glass shards scattered around her feet. In one hand she clutched a *San Francisco Examiner,* and with the other she was beckoning Alla to join her.

The glass fragments crunched under Alla's shoes as she approached. "Whatever is the matter? You know how important—"

"Look! Look!" Scobie shoved the paper under Alla's face and rapped a fingertip against a headline: SALOMÉ NOW DEEMED LEGITIMATE

"But we didn't invite anyone from San Francisco to the preview."

"Not your *Salomé*," Scobie replied. "The opera by Richard Strauss. The one he based on Wilde's play, like you did."

Strauss had written his opera fifteen years after Wilde had published his play. It had been mounted a couple of times in Germany and Austria, but was banned in England. A few years later the ban had been reversed, but by then opera patrons in New York had decided that Strauss's *Salomé* was immoral and decadent and all manner of things that infuriated those New England puritans. The controversy had been raging when Alla had first landed in New York, so she remembered it well.

She scanned the article. A cluster of progressive opera enthusiasts had successfully campaigned for the ban's reversal. Strauss's *Salomé* was now acceptable fare for consumption by American audiences. It could also be, if worded correctly by a certain Miss Kingsley of the *Los Angeles Times*, a well-positioned thumb in the faces of those who believed that moving pictures should be heavily censored.

"Well," Alla whispered to Scobie, "if this isn't perfect timing, I don't know what is." She refolded the newspaper so that she could present the headline to Grace and marched back into the dining room. "I would have dropped that glass too if I had—"

But Grace was no longer sitting in her chair. She was standing at the end of the table now, the National Board of Review telegram in her hand. "Since when does Western Union employ female messengers?"

Alla's mouth went dry. "Whatever do you mean?"

Grace pointed through the parted drapes in the parlor window. "After your maid took the telegram, I saw her walk around to the back of the house."

Alla collapsed into the nearest chair, mortification swamping her. It was Odette who had "delivered" the telegram. "I've known about the Board's approval for a week," she said quietly.

"I can only assume therefore that today—" Grace gestured a hand over Scobie's elaborate afternoon tea party "—was a ruse."

"Truth be told, I'm utterly desperate." Alla's voice faltered as she struggled to keep the tears at bay. "*Salomé* has cost me virtually everything, including my jewelry, my automobile, my artwork. Anything to stay afloat long enough to get *Salomé* distributed. I thought that if I could get the Board's approval, it would be enough to persuade Allied to give it the go-ahead."

"You thought you could go over their heads and then bullyrag them into agreeing afterwards, didn't you?"

Alla nodded.

"I doubt that's going to be enough." Grace's voice was now soft and surprisingly compassionate.

Alla took in a deep breath to steady herself. "But the National Board of Review—"

"But fragile male egos. They trump everything, my dear." Alla had expected her to sweep out of the house in a grand huff at learning that she'd been hoodwinked but instead she returned to her chair. "They also hold all the cards. Well, most of them, anyway. Women—especially us professional women—must band together if we're ever going to redress the imbalances."

"So—so you'll help me?" Alla asked. Considering the contrivance she'd used today, it was more than she dared hope for.

Grace stroked the fine fuzz on her cheek. "When I first arrived in Hollywood, the place was teeming with strong, intelligent women. Lois Weber, Bess Meredyth—I could be here all day naming names, but my point is that as this industry has grown in stature, influence, and income, the men have muscled their way in. They have different techniques, but they're all sending the same telegram: thanks for laying the groundwork, girls, but we'll take it from here. Well, phooey to that, I say!"

Alla dabbed at her eyes with her Irish linen napkin. "I'd like to say that, too, but I fear I have no alternative."

"Balderdash!" Grace declared. "However, I don't think a rubber stamp from the NBR and some response cards are going to do it. You need to hold a proper preview."

"I've already invited everybody I could think of to my private viewing."

"Well then, isn't it lucky for you that I have an extensive list of contacts? Give me a few days and I can provide you with names and addresses. As for the venue, have you ever been to the Rosemary Theater?"

"The one on the beach, down past Santa Monica?" Alla quaked at the thought of filling such a huge place.

"I belong to the Ebell Women's Club. It's the only organization run by women for women because those men? Ha! They aren't going to look out for us, so we must look out for each other. I'm on a committee with someone whose husband manages the Rosemary." She leaned over and patted Alla on the wrist. "Don't you fret, Madame. We'll build a case that Allied can't ignore."

Alla squeezed her fingers together to stop them from trembling. "I don't know how to thank you! Or how I can ever repay you!"

"Your success is all the payment necessary, because if one of us succeeds, we all do. Rising tide and all that. Getting the vote was just the beginning. It's all onward and upward."

"But the Rosemary will need payment up front, won't it?"

"I would expect so, yes."

Alla's heart sank again. The Rolls-Royce was gone. And so were the diamonds, the sapphire earrings, the pearl necklace. The Makovsky portrait. The stock and bonds. What did she have left?

"You haven't tried these yet," Alla said, offering the silver platter Scobie had piled high with her cinnamon raisin cookies. "I can't let you leave without tasting them."

A shaft of afternoon light now slanted across the platter. Scobie had spent most of the previous day polishing the entire silver service to a blinding sheen. Alla's eyes moved from the platter to the creamer to the cutlery to the jam bowl to the butter dish to the salt and pepper shakers. When she landed on the cake stand, she knew that the whole set had to go.

* * *

Alla paced the length of the dining room, back and forth, back and forth. "I can't look! I simply cannot!" If she had any rings left to twist around her fingers, she would have, but they were naked now. As naked as her self-confidence. Stripped of its armor. Raw and vulnerable.

Odette let out a tender laugh.

Alla gripped the pocket doors leading into the formal parlor. "How much longer?"

"Stop being so melodramatic."

"Please, my sweet *dushenka*, show an old woman some mercy."

"Old woman? You're not even forty-five yet, for heaven's sake. That hardly makes you Whistler's mother."

The age disparity between Paul and Alla was approximately the same as that between Alla and Odette. The difference was that Alla never thought of it. Or at least, that was what she'd been telling herself until she'd heard the snip-snip-snip of Odette's scissors and the rustle of paper. It was like listening to the devil's secateurs hack away chunks of her soul.

Odette was right. What a histrionic ham she was. But if Alla could have sat calmly at the dining table and watch Odette go about her business, she would have. This was her last chance. She had sacrificed everything, right down to the silver service she'd been given as a wedding present. *Oh well. The marriage to Charles wasn't authentic. We were never really married. Not in a legal way. Not in any way. What does it matter that the silver service is gone?*

She would have given anything for a drink. Brandy. Scotch. How she would gladly have killed for a shot of Stolichnaya! But she could barely pay the milkman let alone a bootlegger, so her bar was empty. Her nerves were shot.

She had devoted every iota of energy she possessed to calm herself during the press preview. The Rosemary Theatre was sandwiched between the merry-go-round and the Skee-Ball gallery next to the Pacific Ocean Park pier. The screams from the Blarney Racer roller coaster had pierced the foyer as Alla greeted every last invitee on Grace's list.

What a gift of manna from heaven Grace Kingsley had revealed herself to be. Within forty-eight hours, the Rosemary had been booked for the third Sunday in October, and that had at first given Alla pause. Weekends were the busiest time for cheap-thrill amusement parks. Wouldn't it bring down the whole film-as-art tone that she was trying to set? But when she arrived, Alla had found the bustle and tumult added a festive touch to the day.

Grace had worked her address book from A to Z, and all her counterparts in a five-hundred-mile radius had shown up: Reno, Bakersfield, Sacramento, Phoenix.

As they had filed out of the theater afterwards, the audience *seemed* to have enjoyed it; their smiles *seemed* genuine enough. Their congratulations hadn't *seemed* contrived. But there was only one way to know for sure: she had to wait until they had published their reviews.

And that's what Odette was doing now: clipping reviews out of newspapers that had been shipped to Los Angeles and laying them across the dining table.

"I'm done!"

Odette's announcement made Alla's stomach collapse in on itself. "Oh, God!"

"Come in here." Odette sounded like an impatient kindergartener now.

"I can't bring myself to do it. Read them out to me. From best to worst—no! From worst to best. Yes, that's it. Save the best till last."

"I think you ought to read them yourself." Odette's warm hand tugged her toward the table. There must have been at least fifteen reviews lined up. Like a firing squad.

"All right," Alla conceded. "But tell me, which one should I read first?"

"It doesn't matter."

"Are they that bad?"

"Oh, for crying out loud, you can be so maddening." Odette pointed to a clipping from the *Arizona Daily Star*. "Start with that one and work your way west."

Two hours later Alla marched into Farrington's office like she was Hannibal conquering the Alps. "Is he in?" she asked the secretary, but it was a superfluous question. She didn't break her stride until she stood in front of the man himself.

"I have something to show you. In fact, I have fifteen somethings."

He looked up from the contract he'd been reading. "Is this about your *Salomé* preview at the Rosemary?"

"Ah, so you heard about that?"

"You don't give up, do you?"

"No, sir, I do not."

"I won't ask where or how you even got a copy of the movie to show, because it's an irrelevant question."

Thank heavens! "I've come because—"

"You've wasted your time."

"I've done no such thing. The preview—"

"*Salomé* is a lost cause."

"No, it isn't. I've come here to—"

"Will Hays and his cronies have won. No reviewer between here and Maine will go see it. And if they do, they won't review it. And if they do that, they won't dare give your picture a favorable review."

Alla opened her attaché—a prop from a long-ago play that she had retrieved from a box in her backyard shed for the specific purpose of impressing Farrington. She pulled out the fifteen articles and laid the top one in the pile in front of him.

"The *Arizona Daily Star* begs to differ. The word they used was 'great.'" Before he had time to read the whole article, she laid the *San Francisco Bulletin* on top of it. "The key phrase in this one is 'high and eloquent beauty.' They're talking not about me but the picture." She slapped down the *Sacramento Bee* and quoted, "'*Salomé* is an amazingly fine piece of art on the screen.' And here's *The San Diego Union-Tribune*, which talks about the satisfaction of an artistic craving." Alla especially liked that one. "And in case you think it's all highbrow stuff, this one is from *Screenland*. May I read it out loud?" She didn't wait for a response. "A painting deftly stroked upon the silversheet in which poets and dreamers will find imaginative delights."

She kept the *Screenland* review clamped in her hand because that particular reviewer had gone on to talk about "weird settings and the still more weird acting" before saying that sitting through *Salomé* was "worth something to watch Nazimova balance her Christmas-tree headdress." Farrington didn't need to see that, and besides, from the resigned look on his face, she could see that her arrow had hit its bull's-eye.

15

A light flurry of snow dusted Broadway as Alla and Odette's cab inched toward midtown Manhattan.

"You're awfully quiet." Odette squeezed Alla's hand. "Feeling nervous?"

Pulling up at the Criterion in a regular taxi was going to be mortifying enough, but dressed in this absurd get-up was beyond the pale. The eyes of the cab driver in the rearview mirror were filled with bemusement and, Alla feared, scorn. And why wouldn't he be laughing at her?

"I feel ridiculous!"

"And *I* think you look stunning."

Alla clutched Odette's forearm with her free hand. "You always know the right thing to say."

"It's easy." She smiled that tenderhearted smile of hers that warmed Alla's chest. "We just have to say what's true."

"Here's the truth for you," Alla said. "I feel like a trussed-up Thanksgiving turkey, which wouldn't be so bad except that it's New Year's Eve—"

Odette squeezed Alla's thumb and tugged at it firmly enough to get the message through: *Hush now, my love.* "You're heading to the premiere of the picture you've been working on all year and that you've poured everything into."

A weighty look passed between them. 'Everything' was right: here she was, hours from the finishing line, and The Great Nazimova was drained: creatively, emotionally, artistically—and financially. As of yesterday morning, she had less than one hundred dollars in her bank account.

How had this happened? Falling so low and in such a short amount of time? She hadn't ever set her sights on conquering Hollywood—moving pictures hardly compared to the theater—but who would have thought it possible that anybody would offer her such a staggering salary? And had it only been four years since she'd arrived in Los Angeles feeling a little like Cleopatra making her triumphant entry into Rome?

Snow continued to scatter on the cab's windshield as they entered Columbus Circle. It was a powdery snow. Quite pretty, really. The cinematic type that lands on the angelic maiden selling matches to buy medicine for her sick mother right before she encounters the chimney sweep who's found a twenty-dollar bill in the street and brought it straight to her.

Maybe that's the movie I should have made. Audiences eat up tripe like that with a soup ladle.

What a lumpy-headed dolt she had been to assume that Metro's money spigot would always be open full bore. They had only been willing to pay her that outrageous sum for as long as her movies showed a healthy profit. And as soon as they'd stopped doing that, it had been a boot to the behind and out the door.

But she'd been far too preoccupied with *Salomé* to see it. Far too caught up in the self-induced hallucination that, if she compromised on nothing, insisted on first-rate everything, stayed true to her vision, the critics and the public alike would recognize what she had been trying to do and would come flocking to her picture.

And maybe they would. It was impossible to know. But she had overreached herself to the tune of $350,000. *Salomé* would have to do *Birth of a Nation*–level box office to recoup her outlay.

You fool! You boneheaded, birdbrained boob!

"Oh, no you don't!" Odette yanked Alla's thumb, more rigorously this time. "I can see 'despair' written all over your face."

Alla pulled her hand away. "Claiming psychic abilities now, are we?"

"You might be God's gift to the stage, but I don't have to be psychic to know when you're giving in to your worst fears as you're entering the home stretch."

"What am I? A racehorse competing in the Kentucky Derby?"

"Aren't you?"

"WHAT?"

"In a manner of speaking, isn't *Salomé* your Kentucky Derby? Your one-hundred-meter dash in the Olympic Games? Your Pulitzer Prize in drama?"

A giggle bubbled up. "Oh, my sweet angel, you do know how to uplift an old girl like me."

"Again with the 'old?' You're in your prime. And what a glorious prime it is, too." She held up her hand to silence Alla. "May I remind you that *Tarzan of the Apes* earned one million dollars a couple of years ago? It was a decent enough picture, but a million bucks worth? I think not. Your *Salomé* is leagues ahead of Elmo Lincoln running around in a loincloth and a cheap wig."

"I'd like to think so," Alla said, "but—"

"But me no buts! You may have been gamboling about in Natacha's little scrap of silk-covered rubber, but let me tell you, that *Salomé* wig—" she reached up to Alla's head and flicked one of the glass beads with her fingernail "—it wasn't cheap."

For a few precious moments during Odette's cheerleader speech, Alla had all but forgotten about her outlandish costume.

"It's just an idea, Madame," Farrington had said. "Naturally, we cannot force you to do anything against your will." But, of course, he had employed a supercilious tone that had taken an order and dressed it up in the brightly colored wrapping paper of a nonchalant suggestion.

"You want me to wear my *Salomé* wig and that tight little costume?" Alla had asked.

"Think of the publicity. The photographic opportunities will be without parallel."

"To the New York premiere? In front of everyone?"

"I don't see why you're getting so riled up. You wear that wig for half the goddamn picture."

Alla had wanted to explain the vast chasms that separated screen costumes from street wear, but she would have been wasting her breath. "So you want me to show up to my movie premiere in what amounts to a one-piece Jantzen swimsuit, *in* winter, *in* New York?"

"You want your picture in the paper, don't you? Get people talking about you again? About *Salomé*? And besides, you look like a ripe tomato in that get-up. I mean, all that skin! What red-blooded American male wouldn't want to see that?"

Farrington had missed the whole point of the picture. In demanding the head of John the Baptist served to her on a platter, Salomé was saying 'I need neither the approval of men, nor their acceptance. I don't need men at all. Refuse me and you shall pay for it with your life.' To put it another way, Salomé was rejecting the whole male-based patriarchy upon which civilization was based.

Of course, it was no great surprise that the raison d'être of *Salomé* had sailed right over the pointy head of a barbarian like Farrington. And so she expected that it would sail over the heads of most American men. And that would have been fine with her, except that even if one hundred percent of American women over the age of sixteen went to see the picture, it wouldn't be enough to raise *Salomé* out of the red.

Alla needed Farrington and Allied on her side. As aghast as she had been at the prospect of wearing the Salomé outfit in public, she had given in. But not without a compromise: she would wear the movie's flamboyant cape over it. It had seemed like a victory at the time, but now she was watching the corner of 51st and

Broadway pass outside the window of a somewhat shabby taxicab. The mounting uncertainties were beginning to bury her alive.

She reached up and adjusted the wig so that it sat more securely on top of her head. "Your handiwork still marvels me."

"I like to think that Oscar Wilde himself would have approved."

"I have no doubt about that." *I don't remember it being this heavy.* "He probably would have asked to borrow it." *I'm going to have such a headache by the time this evening is over.* "Be honest with me, my pet. Do I look silly?"

Genuine surprise filled Odette's face. "On the contrary, you cut a striking figure. All five-foot-three of you."

"Plus heels!" To give herself as much stature as she could manage for the night, Alla had borrowed a pair of shoes from Scobie. Although what a maid was doing with three-inch heels was beyond Alla's comprehension. It was bad enough that she was wearing her maid's shoes tonight, so the less she thought about it, the better. At least she still had a maid. Although for how much longer was hard to say. "Along with the extra inches your wig gives me."

"Not to mention your sheer physical presence."

There you go again, knowing the exact right thing to say. Alla laughed ruefully. "Oh yes, let us not forget that."

They were at 52nd Street now. Less than ten blocks to go. The snow had petered out. The doors of a diner opened and a couple of flappers stepped out, giggling as they pulled up the collars of their ocelot coats. A deep longing overtook her. Pastrami on rye with a dill pickle. And maybe a little coleslaw on the side. She couldn't very well show up to the Criterion with deli meat on her breath, but she'd had nothing substantial since the black coffee she'd poured herself at breakfast.

"Is it what we talked about the other day?" Odette asked.

Alla pulled away from her pastrami daydreams. "What, my love?"

"Remember when you came home from your meeting and told

me that Farrington had booked a New York theater but then badgered you into attending in costume?"

"What about it?"

"What did you tell me next?"

"That I feared my appearance would undercut my desire to be taken seriously as a purveyor of bona fide art, and as the woman responsible for legitimatizing Wilde's play."

"Is that what all this trepidation is about?"

"I suppose so."

Odette seized Alla's hands in hers. "If this premiere were taking place during the daytime, I wouldn't blame you for feeling frivolous. However, your *Salomé* will be premiering at midnight. And not just any midnight, but midnight on New Year's Eve. A special moment like that requires a special ensemble." She took in Alla's skeptical expression. "You think Mary Pickford could get away with this wig, this cape, this everything?"

Alla went quiet for a few moments. When Farrington had sent her a telegram confirming that he'd secured the Criterion for December 31st, 1922, Alla had been overjoyed. She had half-expected that he would book some seedy little hall below 34th Street—or worse, below 14th. But at Broadway and 44th, the 1000-seat Criterion was only three and a half blocks from Times Square. Perfect!

But then she'd read the second sentence, which had seemed like an afterthought. The showing would be at midnight, after the current picture playing there was finished for the night.

What an insult! Who was going to turn up at that hour?

However, once again, she'd relented: there wasn't much she could do about it but make the best of the hand she'd been dealt.

And perhaps Odette had a point. A midnight screening did hold a certain allure. She wished she could lean across and give her girlfriend the full-on-the-lips passionate kiss that she deserved. But instead Alla could only say, "Thank you, my turtledove. Whatever happens tonight, I'm so very glad you're here by my side."

Odette returned her declaration with a muted smile. But there was no time to decipher it. They had arrived. Odette paid the driver and exited the cab as Alla gathered up the hem of her voluminous peacock cape with one hand and gave the Salomé wig a final adjustment with the other.

The Criterion was a seven-story theater with an enormous vertical neon sign lighting up the Broadway and 44th Street corner. The marquee read, *"SINGED WINGS" – STARRING BEBE DANIELS, CONRAD NAGEL, ADOLPHE MENJOU*

"Singed wings, indeed," Alla muttered.

"Look!" Odette pointed to a sandwich board on which someone had pinned a poster:

TONIGHT!
SPECIAL PREVIEW!
ALLA NAZIMOVA
IN
"SALOMÉ"

It was handmade, but at least they'd taken care to make the lettering even and presentable.

A man with a perfectly round face, gold pince-nez hanging from a chain, and wearing a black serge suit hurried toward them.

"Madame Nazimova! How pleased I am to meet you! I have been such a fan of yours ever since *Hedda Gabler* at the Princess."

A stranger hadn't gushed over her like this in a long, long time. Alla hated to admit it, but it was a much-needed boost to her ego. "How kind of you."

"I was there on opening night!"

"You don't say?"

"I was way up in the back, of course, but it was an evening I'd never forget."

"And you are . . .?"

He bowed his head at a slight angle. "David Gishman, general manager of the Criterion."

So he's a fan! "This is my assistant, Miss Finch."

What to call Odette in situations like these had been the subject of a long discussion over pecan pralines. 'Girlfriend' was unacceptable. 'Partner' sounded like they were in a law practice. 'Associate' was almost as bad. 'Friend' felt dismissive. In the end, they had agreed on 'assistant,' though only by default, as it seemed the least troublesome solution.

"Shall we?" Gishman asked, gesturing to the glass doors. "We get such a chilling wind whipping down Broadway." Muffled music seeped out from the auditorium. "*Singed Wings* still has about a quarter of an hour to go, so let's relax in here."

His office was spacious. A large wooden desk sat to the left, and on the right a three-seat sofa of worn blue damask lined the far wall. "Please take a seat." As they did, he grabbed a sheet of paper off his desk and sat opposite them on one of the occasional chairs. "I do have some excellent news regarding your *Salomé* showing tonight: the house is completely full." Out of the corner of her eye, Alla saw Odette's hand move for an encouraging squeeze but stop halfway along. "Every motion picture critic and entertainment journalist I have ever heard of has asked for tickets. The demand has been so strong that I had to turn some of them away. Tonight's showing has set a new house record of—" he checked the figures tallied on his paper "—$1,311.25!"

Alla's legs twitched from the urge to leap on the man's coffee table and dance a merry jig. "Mr. Gishman! You don't know what a reassurance it is to hear that because, you see, *Salomé* isn't run-of-the-mill."

"Your pictures rarely are, which is why I agreed to the showing tonight. And tomorrow night, too."

"You'll be running it a second time?" Odette asked.

"Already sold out." He checked his sheet. "And the total is $1,318.75. Another record! I'd be a fool not to, don't you think?"

Alla's heart pounded against her ribs. She wouldn't have been at all surprised if it burst out of its cage and through the window behind Odette. "You're in the business of hit pictures, Mr. Gishman." Alla struggled to keep an unruffled professionalism to her voice, and wasn't sure she was succeeding. "It's your job to give the people what they want."

He jerked his head toward the theater. "And it ain't *Singed Wings*. Don't get me wrong. It's okay, but it's not breaking any house records." He pulled a fob watch out of his jacket pocket and checked it. "Speaking of which, it's about to finish up."

Alla gathered her cape around her. "I should be out front to greet guests as they arrive for our showing and—"

He shut her down with a shake of his head. "Now that I see how you've dressed for the occasion, I think a better plan would be to bring you out on stage, where you can make a speech. In my experience, it's best to keep it brief. Thank them for coming out at midnight, tell them you hope they enjoy it, and then exit, stage right." He stood up. "I'll call for you when it's time."

The door closed behind him with a gentle click.

"A house record!" Odette squeaked.

"*Two!*" Alla interlaced her fingers through Odette's and squeezed them tight.

"Oh, ye of such little faith."

Three hundred and fifty thousand dollars was a colossal amount of money to recoup, but now it didn't feel quite so insurmountable. But first she had to get up on that stage and zing them right between the eyes. And here she was, wearing the perfect outfit.

* * *

Alla plucked at the edges of her cape so that each side hung straight down from her collar to the tips of Scobie's shoes. "How's the back?" She felt Odette flatten the train against the grimy floorboards. Alla guessed that nobody had swept the stage of the Criterion in quite some time, so the cape would end up caked in dust, but that was okay. The audience wouldn't see it from the seats. Their focus would be on Odette's headdress. Alla had never worn it for such a long stretch, and the headache she had predicted was starting to throb.

"Perfect!" Odette stood up and brushed her hands clean. She circled around Alla until they stood face to face. "And I do mean perfect."

Alla gave her shoulder an affectionate slap. "Enough with the flattery, young lady."

Gishman walked out onto the stage and raised his hands to quiet the crowd. "Ladies and gentlemen, before we begin, I have a surprise for you. She's traveled from Hollywood, California, to be with us tonight, and I've coaxed her into coming out to say a few words. Please put your hands together for the star of tonight's exclusive preview, Madame Alla Nazimova!"

She lifted her chin, pushed out her chest, and commenced a measured, rhythmic walk, each step led by a swaying hip. Left, then right, then left, then right. Not so slow as to grow boring, but not so fast that the audience was deprived of the opportunity to drink in her startling appearance.

She held her elbows close to her waist and her hands pressed together in front of her. If the audience had been any closer, they might have seen the whites of her knuckles, so maybe the Criterion's dim footlights weren't such a drawback.

She let the cheering wash over her like baptismal water. As soon as she sensed it beginning to peter out, she cleared her throat to ensure that her voice would project to the back rows. "Thank you! Thank you!" she said. "It is my hope that you shall give *Salomé* as warm a greeting as you gave me just now. But of course that's up to you. I'm so appreciative that you chose to greet 1923 by being among the first to see my new picture."

She took a half-step back and opened her arms wide. Grasping the edge of the cape, she swept it around her. "What do you think? Crackerjack, huh?"

'Crackerjack' wasn't the kind of slang Alla normally used, but her eyes had adjusted now and she could see past the lights to rows of faces that belonged to people who did. It brought a thunder of applause mixed in with wolf whistles. She raised her right hand and toyed with the glass beads in her headdress. "And what about this?" More applause. Louder wolf whistles. "As soon as I saw it, I thought to myself, 'Now, *this* is a character I must play and a story I must tell!'"

She waited until the clamor began to subside.

"Seriously, though, never have I worked so hard or poured so much of myself into any of my previous projects as I have with the motion picture you're about to see. My hope is that Salomé speaks to you as she spoke to me. She might be a princess, but she's still just a girl without the power to control the course of her own life until—" Alla held her right index finger high in the air "—she decides 'I don't think so!' She wants what she wants and won't accept anything less. She rejects how things are done! She declares that she and she alone is in charge of her life! She says no to the men and yes to what her heart tells her!"

This time the response wasn't quite so thunderous, but what applause there was came from the women in the audience, and they outnumbered the men.

"And that's why I felt compelled to bring Oscar Wilde's *Salomé* to the screen. Unlike theater and opera and concerts and these new radio broadcasts, films occupy a unique position in the arts. What they capture is preserved, not solely for contemporary audiences but also for future generations. I know, I know! This thinking goes against the view that motion pictures are a minor and transitory art form and belong on the lowest rung of the ladder. Filmed yesterday, shown today, forgotten tomorrow. But I disagree. The images caught on film are preserved forever, and we artists working in motion pictures owe it to current and future moviegoers to work at the peak of our potential. That's certainly what I did when making *Salomé,* and I hope it shows. Thank you, everybody, for coming tonight. I sincerely hope you enjoy the motion picture that's about to unspool on the screen behind me."

* * *

It was three o'clock in the morning when Alla shook the last of the congratulatory hands, posed for the last of the newspaper photographers, and beamed the last of the thank-you-so-much-for-coming smiles. It was three-thirty by the time Gishman had put them into a taxicab heading north up Broadway. And it was three-forty-one when Alla saw that the 52nd Street Diner was still open. She yanked off her Salomé wig and shook her hair free. God, that felt good. She nudged Odette. "Let's duck in there for a late-night nosh."

"Aren't you exhausted?"

"I'm still worked up over this whole evening." She told the driver to pull over and paid him with what few coins still jingled in her purse.

Alla pressed a shoulder against the deli's doors and breathed in the fug of freshly carved meat and egg bagels intermingled with cigarette smoke and nighttime banter. They were soon seated in a corner booth, and sent the waiter away with two orders of pastrami on rye.

"You were fabulous up there tonight," Odette said. "On stage, I mean."

"Thank you." Alla offered her one of the perfumed cigarettes, but Odette shook her head. These were Alla's last and she would soon be going back to drug-store brands. "I felt strangely at home."

"Of course you did! You're a creature of the theater."

Alla smiled and drew in a lungful of scented smoke. She was going to miss these. "I suspect you're right, my dear. But the screening went well, didn't it?" After she had finished her speech, she'd had every intention of slipping into a seat to get a sense of how the audience was reacting. But courage had deserted her at the last minute, so she had sent Odette inside instead and passed the time leafing through copies of *Paris Vogue* and *Photoplay*.

"Oh, yes!" Odette's eyes blazed with the enthusiasm that comes so effortlessly to the young. "They lapped it up."

Alla flicked open her pewter cigarette case with her nail. She had already finished her first one and was desperate for a second, but there were only six left. *If tonight isn't worth celebrating, what is?* She lit up.

Odette frowned. "You don't look as elated as I expected."

"No, no, I am."

"But?"

It was confession time, and, aside from perhaps Natacha and Scobie, Odette was the only person whom Alla felt she could say this to and not feel judged. "I've recklessly sunk nearly every dollar I own into producing this movie."

"If the preview in L.A. and this one tonight are anything to go by, I'd say you've got a hit on your hands."

There was that youthful American optimism again, and exactly the tonic Alla needed. But she didn't have the nerve to admit how much she had spent on *Salomé*. The arrival of their sandwiches saved her having to reply. The pastrami was piled two inches thick. Steam curled upward in unhurried whorls, and the spicy brown mustard oozed out from the rye and drooled a single droplet onto the white china.

They said nothing for a few minutes as they bit into their early-morning feast.

Finally, Odette sat back and said, "Alla, my sweet?"

"Mmmm?" was all she could get around her mouthful of delicious warm comfort.

"I have some news."

It wasn't what Odette said but the somber tone of her voice that made Alla look up. "Good, I hope."

Odette wiped away a mustard smudge. "I've had a job offer. A pretty good one, actually."

What a blissful, unexpected, but beautifully well-timed relief. They had never had the 'Who Pays for What' talk. They hadn't needed to; Odette hadn't ever sat back and waited for Alla to pay for everything, even though she usually did. Breaking free of the mental habit of thinking that she always had plenty of money on hand had been difficult. But Odette had picked up checks and paid cab drivers, and had done so without displaying any need to draw attention to what she was doing. Now that Alla's bank account was barer than the cupboard of Old Mother Hubbard, this news couldn't have come at a better time.

"How wonderful!" Alla pressed her fingers together as though in prayer. "Which studio?"

"As a matter of fact, it's the Ziegfeld Follies."

"Ziegfeld? How perfectly thrilling!"

Odette smiled for the first time. "Yes, it is, rather. And I have you to thank."

"Me? What did I do?"

"Well, you and Natacha. Mr. Ziegfeld saw some of the advance publicity material that Allied sent out for *Salomé* and told his secretary 'Find me that wigmaker.'"

"And she did!"

"He's bringing back Fanny Brice to star in his next season, and their wig supervisor is retiring. It'll be my job to oversee all those wigs and headdresses."

"For a Ziegfeld show?" Alla asked. "That's a lot."

"Almost a hundred."

"If anybody's up for a job like that, it's you, my darling. I'm so proud of you! If we could order a bottle of champagne like in the olden days, I would." Of course, paying for it was another matter entirely. She lifted her sarsaparilla. "This will have to suffice. Here's to you!"

Odette clinked her glass against Alla's, and Alla looked at her curiously. This was a big job, an exciting one, and Flo Ziegfeld himself had sought her out. So why didn't she look excited?

"You want the job, don't you?"

"Yes, I do."

"And who doesn't look as elated as she deserves to be now?" Public etiquette be damned—Alla reached across the table, took

Odette's hand in hers and kept it there. "Is it because you'll have to be in New York? Darling, you must go. I'm not sure what my future holds. It all depends on what happens with *Salomé*. But we'll make it work. I could come back to New York perhaps, or if they give you a vacation, you could catch the fastest train heading west—"

"It's not just for the season," Odette blurted out. "The job is— it's more than that."

Alla withdrew her hand and steadied herself for the news to come. "How much more?"

"After the New York season ends, Ziegfeld is sending Fanny Brice and the whole company out on the road. It's a year-long tour and if I prove myself, I could be promoted to head wardrobe mistress. The pay's incredible, and it's a tremendous opportunity. I —I would be—be—"

"—a fool to turn it down."

The reality of the situation lay on the table like a dying sparrow, wheezing as the last signs of life seeped away. No money. No career. And now no girlfriend. Was this what rock bottom felt like?

It appeared so, yes.

Alla mentally counted off the months they'd had together. Seven. It felt like seven days. And yet at the same time, it felt like it had been seven years since that day on the *Salomé* set. Alla smiled to herself. *That's irony for you. It's been a May–December romance that's actually lasted from May to December.*

"I'm relieved to see you smile," Odette said. "I'd like to think that you're happy for me despite what this means for us."

There was nothing to be gained by boo-hooing fat tears of self-pity all over Odette's big break. She deserved it, and anything but rainbow-colored gaiety would be selfish and uncharitable.

"Of course I am!" Alla said, force-feeding sparkle into her voice. "I was just thinking that I wish I'd told that taxi driver to drop us off at some speakeasy. If any occasion calls for a bottle of Pol Roger, this would be it."

Odette's chin crinkled and wobbled.

"No, no," Alla told her. "I forbid tears. Not tonight. *Salomé* is on her way and so are you. This sarsaparilla is miserably inadequate. How about we celebrate with a slab of cheesecake the size of Madison Square Garden?"

* * *

If Scobie's three-inch heels hadn't been so gosh-darned comfortable, Alla wouldn't have insisted on walking back to her apartment in the Hotel Des Artistes on 67th Street. But after Odette's bombshell, she needed some time in the cold, pre-dawn air to clear her head.

She would have preferred that the two of them stroll the fifteen blocks with their arms linked, but her cape got in the way so they'd walked side by side, their shoulders pressed together, but saying little. What was there to say? They had precious little time left. Filling it with small talk was a waste of a crisp Manhattan morning with streets so deserted that it felt like they had New York to themselves.

They arrived at Alla's building as the bells of the nearby Holy Trinity Lutheran Church began to peal. Alla counted seven chimes as she pulled the keys from her purse. So much had happened since she'd left her apartment yesterday evening.

As she opened the building's front door, Odette's hand grasped her elbow.

"I won't come up."

"Neither of us has slept all night. You must be as exhausted as I am."

But that wasn't true. Alla didn't feel the least bit tired. The *Salomé* preview had gone as well as she could have expected—perhaps even better. And if her delivery service had done its job, there should be a stack of morning papers sitting outside her front door with the reviews. Maybe it was better that Odette wasn't there. Raves or raspberries, she needed to do this by herself.

"I want to surprise my mother," Odette said. "I haven't even told her that I'm back in the city. I guess you could call it a 'Happy New Year, Mom' kind of thing."

"I understand," Alla said, and pulled her into a hug to hide her disappointment. She had been hoping for one final night together, but she was to be denied even that. She brushed her lips against the girl's creamy-smooth cheek. "I want you to know that I'm so very, very happy for you."

"Thank you." Odette's response came out a hoarse whisper. "I'll call for my things."

"No rush. You know where to find them."

A final peck to the cheek and Odette walked down 67th Street. The heels of Scobie's shoes sounded extra loud to Alla as they clicked against the foyer tiles. The metal gears of the elevator clanged as the lift climbed upward. Alla stepped from it into the deserted corridor. Even in the dim light, she could see the pile of newspapers. They were heavy and difficult to hold as she slid the key into her lock. Wearing an outlandishly theatrical cape didn't help.

Fifteen papers were more than she was expecting; they would take a while to wade through. A pot of extra-strong coffee was called for. After dumping her burden on the kitchen table at the window overlooking Central Park, she lit the gas under the kettle.

The sun was peeking over the buildings that lined the east side of the park when Alla opened *The New York Times*. Her heart beat harder as she flipped the pages. Breathing deeply didn't calm it as she hoped. She scanned the page until the word "Salomé" caught her eye.

Oh, God. Please let it be good.

She stopped reading the review at "an exceedingly tame and not remarkably graceful performance that Herod wouldn't have given standing room in his kingdom for."

She reached for the next paper.

When she got to the entertainment section, she saw that their critic was Robert E. Sherwood. Hooray and hurrah! This was more like it. She didn't know Sherwood personally, but she had met a number of his Algonquin Round Table friends, like Dorothy Parker and Edna Ferber. His take on her film would undoubtedly be sympathetic.

It was the review she'd been hoping for: "*Salomé* is exceptional in every noteworthy sense. The person responsible for it deserves the whole-souled gratitude of everyone who believes in the possibilities of the movies as an art."

Maybe *Salomé* wouldn't be the cinematic sinking of the *Titanic*, after all.

Maybe the situation was salvageable.

Maybe there was hope.

She held her breath as she read the *New York Tribune* review and let it out again in a low whoosh. It was far from a rave. She pushed the paper aside and consoled herself by rereading the Sherwood review again. "Exceptional in every noteworthy sense." She read that part several times before she plunged into the next one.

Halfway through the pile, she saw that she'd built her expectations on cotton candy. The reviews in *The Newark Ledger*, the *Buffalo Courier*, the *New York World* and the six after that were peppered with all the words she feared the most.

Bizarre.

Misguided.

Unintelligible.

The *Hartford Courant* described it as "thematically muddied and visually inexplicable." The *Pittsburgh Post-Gazette* pronounced the picture "a fine idea ham-fistedly executed with callow amateurism."

The next review flowed from the pen of Thomas Craven, whose articles and essays Alla had enjoyed and admired. He was now writing for *The New Republic*. Not yet ten years old, the magazine's influence on culture was almost without equal. Even if the other papers hated her *Salomé*, if Sherwood and Craven both liked it, that might be enough to cloak the advertisements in enough glowing reviews to put it over. The magazine's politics were liberal and progressive. If anybody was going to get what she was reaching for with this movie, it would be *The New Republic*.

Alla found Craven's byline and began reading.

"*Salomé* is degrading and unintelligent."

Alla might have stopped right there, but her name appeared in the next sentence so she forced herself to continue.

"Nazimova has attempted a part for which she has no qualifications. She flits hither and thither with the mincing step of a toe-dancer; she has the figure of a boy, and in her absurd costume, a satin bathing suit of recent pattern, she impresses one as the Old Tetrarch's cup-bearer. Try as she will, she cannot be seductive—the physical handicap is insurmountable; she tosses her head impudently, grimaces repeatedly, and rolls her eyes with a vitreous stare. The effect is comic. The deadly lure of sex, which holds the Wilde drama like a subtle poison, is dispelled the instant one beholds her puerile form."

Alla sat back and pushed the paper away from her. There were other reviews, but what was the point of reading them? She picked up *The New Republic* and slammed it onto the floor. It thwacked against the polished wood. But that wasn't satisfying enough so she stomped on it with all the force that Scobie's shoes could marshal. Take that, Mister Craven and all the Cravens like you! She threw the *Philadelphia Telegraph* against her icebox.

"You don't like my picture! You don't get what I was trying to do!" *The New York Daily News* followed. "All right! I get it! Shut up! Shut up! SHUT UP!"

She hurled and tossed and pitched, paper after paper, until her kitchen floor was ankle-deep with newsprint.

She felt like *Salomé* at the end of the movie when the guards surround her with their long spears and stab her to death. With these reviews, Allied wasn't going to put any marketing support into her movie. Without that, it would limp along at an embarrassing pace until it died a natural death.

It had all been for nothing.

She had risked everything and lost.

The only sounds in her apartment were her panting breaths from the exertion it had taken to hurl fifteen newspapers into oblivion. As they subsided, she looked around for her cigarette case. She found it buried under the sports section of the *Washington Post*. There was one last perfumed gasper left in it.

How apt.

She lit it and stood at the kitchen window of the New York apartment she'd probably have to sell. What a shame. She did so love this place.

She gazed at the cigarette tip's orange glow until a calming serenity came over her.

Salomé was to be her immortal masterpiece, but it had thrust her to the brink of bankruptcy and had probably ended her motion picture career.

And yet . . .

And yet . . .

And yet she found that she didn't really care.

But you must, she told herself. *Your life is in tatters. What sort of emotionless ogre doesn't care when her world disintegrates—OH!*

The vision of her sixteen-year-old self riding the bus from boarding school came rushing back to her. That was the moment when she'd realized that she didn't care what anybody thought of her. That startling insight had freed her from the need for anyone's approval, and she had never looked back. And now, standing in her apartment, her kitchen floor thick with disapproval, she wondered what, exactly, she was being freed from?

She continued to smoke the cigarette until it burned her fingers. Turning her back to the window, her eye found a framed poster for *Stronger Than Death* hanging on the wall of her living room. It featured a drawing of her in a long burgundy gown. It was her favorite of all her movie posters. The confident pose, the vivid colors, the flattering illustration.

She walked toward it.

Stronger Than Death was before *Salomé*.

Before *A Doll's House*.

Before *Camille*.
Before Rudolph Valentino and Natacha Rambova.
Before the Allied Producers and Distributors Corporation.
Before failure.

She had finished filming *Stronger Than Death* the day of that Ship Café party in Venice. The longer Alla thought about the woman she had been that night, the less she recognized her. That Nazimova had been so preoccupied about her weight. So ridiculously jealous of Nita Naldi. She had been at the apex of her film popularity and yet she had been so restless, so dissatisfied with her life.

But that Nazimova couldn't have handled the coming pennilessness with such composure. She would have been completely undone by a scathing review in *The New Republic*.

A rush of happiness filled Alla with giddying swiftness.

Was this what it was like to be creatively fulfilled and not give two hoots about anything else?

She sifted back through the years to find the period when she had felt as content as she did right at that moment.

The answer wasn't slow in coming.

She had mastered English in less than six months, and then had attacked *The Master Builder* and *Hedda Gabler* and *A Doll's House*. And she had managed it so superbly that they had hailed her as the greatest interpreter of Ibsen in the English-speaking world.

"You *are* a creature of the theater!" she told the figure in the poster. "Not motion pictures. Not Hollywood. Not claustrophobic cameras and outrageous costumes."

She didn't remember shedding the *Salomé* cape and tossing it on the sofa, but it lay there now, discarded like an old snakeskin she had outgrown. A handful of glass beads painted in white phosphorus peeked out from underneath. Alla reached it in four strides and pulled it out from under the folds. It felt even heavier now, a dead weight in her hands.

She held it up to the morning light slanting through the windows. "You convinced me to make *Salomé*," she told it, "and brought Odette into my life. For that, I thank you." She stared at it some more. "And you've helped me see how far I've strayed." She tossed it back; the beads clunked dully as they hit the cape.

There was a time when she wouldn't have treated a piece of costume like that so indifferently. But it represented the past and everything she no longer was. Or, she saw now, had ever been. The path ahead of her was straight and flat and smooth. She would return to her true home: the theater.

THE END

Did you enjoy this book?

You can make a big difference.

As an independent author, I don't have the financial muscle of a New York publisher supporting me. But I do have something much more powerful and effective, and it's something those publishers would kill to get their hands on: a committed and loyal bunch of readers. Honest reviews of my books help bring them to the notice of other readers. If you've enjoyed this book, I would be so grateful if you could spend just a couple of minutes leaving a review.

Thank you very much,
Martin Turnbull

AUTHOR'S NOTE

Whenever I read a biographical novel like the one you've just finished (and thank you for reading it, by the way), I often wonder how much of the book is factual and how much of it was the invention of the writer. I'm going to assume that you've made it this far and you're now wondering which elements of *Chasing Salomé* were real and which bits did I invent?

The events in Alla Nazimova's life between October 1919 and New Year's Day 1923 played out for the most part as I've described. Nazimova first met (and rejected) Valentino at the Ship Café and then was forced to re-evaluate her opinion of him when her friend June Mathis became Valentino's chief booster. Nazimova met Rambova, and Rambova in turn met Valentino as I described, and together they made a tight foursome when Nazimova embarked on an affair with Valentino's roommate, Paul Ivano.

For most of her life up to and including the period covered in this novel, Nazimova had affairs with men and women. Terms such as 'gay,' 'lesbian,' 'bisexual,' and 'queer' were not around during the period covered in this novel. Nor, generally speaking, did people delineate their sex lives and sexual orientation along the clear and distinct lines that we tend to do nowadays. From the research I did for this novel, it struck me that the concept of sexuality was more fluid back then, which is ironic considering how we in the twenty-first century have reverted to viewing it along much less structured lines. I think Alla would approve.

During the early 1920s, Nazimova was also conducting an affair with Sam Zimbalist, at the time an assistant editor at Metro and who went onto become an important producer at Metro-Goldwyn-Mayer. (He was not, as far as I can tell, related to the concert violinist Efrem Zimbalist Sr., actor Efrem Zimbalist Jr. or actress Stephanie Zimbalist. But if anybody reading this knows otherwise, I'd love to hear from you.)

Nazimova's relationships with Paul and Sam were of the on-again-off-again variety, and conducted on both coasts. I chose not to include Sam in this book because I felt it would muddy the narrative. More importantly, I included only Paul Ivano because he was the final significant relationship Nazimova had with a man. After their affair came to an end, Nazimova dated only women.

In April 1927, she met Glesca Marshall at Eva Le Gallienne's Civil Repertory Theatre in New York. Within a year or two, they were a couple and would remain together until Nazimova's death in 1945.

The making of *Camille*, *A Doll's House,* and *Salomé* (and the canceled *Aphrodite*) happened pretty much as I described, including the uphill battle Nazimova fought to get them made and released. The men who ran the burgeoning moving picture business did not take kindly to a woman trying to join their ranks. It's hard to know if they intentionally set out to put obstacles in her path, but, typical of their sex and the era, they would not have taken a woman seriously.

In my opinion, it's a miracle that these three movies got made at all. What Nazimova went through to get *Salomé* produced played out more or less how I described, and the reviews she reads in this novel were taken from the actual reviews of the day.

With *Chasing Salomé*, I wanted to explore the themes of "Art" versus "Commerce" and the delicate balance between "Show" and "Business" that played out so starkly in Nazimova's efforts to bring *Salomé* to the screen. You can't have art ("show") without the money ("business") to make it, nor are you going to make money without some type of art to sell. Had Nazimova kept a closer eye on her *Salomé* budget, she might have actually made money. Or at least not lost money to the verge of bankruptcy. But she got carried away making the art and paid scant attention to the enormous amounts of (her own) money that she was pouring into the production.

By the time *Salomé* came out, Nazimova was at the end of her emotional, creative, and financial rope. She did go on to make three more movies: *Madonna of the Streets* (1924), *The Redeeming Sin* (1925), and *My Son* (1925), but they fared poorly at the box office and sent Nazimova back to the theater again. According to Gavin Lambert's 1997 biography of Nazimova, an April 22, 1929, article in the *Los Angeles Times* announced that "Nazimova will be the first actress in Hollywood to make 'talkies' in any other language than English. This is expected to set a precedent which may force Hollywood to go poly-lingual." It's a grand shame that nothing came of it.

In hindsight, Nazimova probably should never have left the theater. By all accounts, she was riveting when performing live—but what are you going to do when the movies offer you $13,000 a week? And that's 1918 dollars, which is the rough equivalent of around $200,000 in 2019—without income tax, which didn't take effect until the mid-1930s. Nazimova didn't appear in the movies again until 1940, when, thanks largely to David O. Selznick, she had a late-career renaissance and acted in five movies before her death.

In a way, it could be said that *Chasing Salomé* is an origin story to my Hollywood's Garden of Allah novels. After *Salomé* had left Alla virtually penniless, one of her chief assets was her beloved Garden of Alla manse at 8080 Sunset Boulevard. In 1924, she appointed Jean Adams as her "business representative" in Los Angeles as she toured the United States in a long succession of theatrical productions, including a stint in vaudeville. It was Jean

AUTHOR'S NOTE

and her husband who proposed that Nazimova turn her home into a hotel, thus ensuring a regular income that would protect her from the financial vagaries of the acting life.

The hotel opened on January 8, 1927 (by which time the city had changed its official address to 8152 Sunset), and became a touchstone of Hollywood's social scene for the next three decades and, not coincidentally, the central location for my series of novels.

The irony of *Salomé*'s failure is that if the movie had been a hit, Nazimova would not have later so desperately needed a reliable source of income. There would have been no need to convert her home into a hotel. And so there would never have been a Garden of Allah Hotel, which means that all the events, parties, chance meetings, torrid affairs, and endless shenanigans would never have taken place. At least not there. Consequently, the Garden of Allah Hotel would never have become a central part of the fabric of Hollywood during its heyday. And that, in my opinion, would have been a grand shame.

Valentino and Rambova legally married a couple of months after the events of this book, but their union lasted only a few years. Their divorce was finalized in January 1926. In August of that year, Valentino died of peritonitis following an operation he'd undergone for acute appendicitis and perforated gastric ulcers. His funeral in New York became the stuff of legend. In the late 1920s, Rambova moved to Spain, where she remarried and later became a respected Egyptologist.

The personal feelings and thoughts and reactions of Nazimova as described in this novel were largely my own invention, but gleaned from various biographies and copies of Nazimova's letters to her sister, Nina, which can be found in the Library of Congress. Maxwell Karger at Metro and Hiram Abrams at United Artists were real people, however Nazimova probably did not deal with them on a day-to-day basis. I was unable to find who her actual contact was, so I invented Joe Farrington to fill that gap.

The only other main character I invented was Odette. One of the most famous images of Alla Nazimova is of her in that remarkable headdress with its glass beads coated in phosphorescent paint. The identity of the person who made it has been lost to the mists of time. It's unlikely that Nazimova, Rambova, and the wigmaker realized what an indelible image they were creating, but in planning the novel, I did wonder who made it. After all, it was around this time that Nazimova's true sexual nature reasserted itself. The first woman whom she became attached to after Paul and Sam is unknown. Perhaps it was a gradual series of relationships that cemented her romantic future. But for the sake of a clear narrative, I decided to merge all those women into one person, and who better, I decided, than the person who constructed the wig that made Nazimova immortal?

Incidentally, that wig still exists. It was discovered in one of Nazimova's traveling trunks in Columbus, Georgia, in 2014. You can read about it here:

http://bit.ly/nazimovatrunk

FURTHER READING:

You can learn more about my Hollywood's Garden of Allah novels here:

http://bit.ly/gardenofallahnovels

(I offer the first novel in the series, *The Garden on Sunset*, free in ebook format at all the major retailers.)

About the Garden of Allah Hotel here:

http://bit.ly/aboutgardenofallah

The Garden of Allah's Wikipedia page has an extensive list of famous people who stayed there or visited there over the years:

https://en.wikipedia.org/wiki/Garden_of_Allah_Hotel

AUTHOR'S NOTE

The website of the Alla Nazimova Society contains information about and many photos of the singularly extraordinary life of Alla Nazimova:

http://www.allanazimova.com/

Specifically, you can see images of *Salomé* here:

http://www.allanazimova.com/tag/films-salome/

If you'd like to know more about the main players in this story, I can recommend the following biographies:

Nazimova: A Biography, by Gavin Lambert

Dark Lover: The Life and Death of Rudolph Valentino, by Emily W. Leider

Madam Valentino: *The Many Loves of Natacha Rambova*, by Michael Morris

You can read and download Oscar Wilde's one-act play, *Salomé*, complete with the Aubrey Beardsley illustrations here:

https://ebooks.adelaide.edu.au/w/wilde/oscar/salome/index.html

It's no small irony that Nazimova's two most notorious flops are the only ones we can now watch. They are both available on YouTube.

Camille: https://www.youtube.com/watch?v=WmdMP2OIidg
Salomé: https://www.youtube.com/watch?v=BkMq_Cs3OUs

ALSO BY MARTIN TURNBULL

Hollywood's Garden of Allah novels:

Book 1 – *The Garden on Sunset*

Book 2 – *The Trouble with Scarlett*

Book 3 – *Citizen Hollywood*

Book 4 – *Searchlights and Shadows*

Book 5 – *Reds in the Beds*

Book 6 – *Twisted Boulevard*

Book 7 – *Tinseltown Confidential*

Book 8 – *City of Myths*

Book 9 – *Closing Credits*

The Heart of the Lion: a novel of Irving Thalberg's Hollywood

All the Gin Joints: a novel of World War II Hollywood (Book 1 in the Hollywood Home Front trilogy)

Thank Your Lucky Stars: a novel of World War II Hollywood (Book 2 in the Hollywood Home Front trilogy)

Rave reviews for Martin Turnbull's *Hollywood's Garden of Allah* series:

What a marvelous series! I tore through all nine books in record time and plan to go back to the beginning and start over.

I loved this whole series. One of the best book series I have ever read!

If you start The Garden of Allah series from the beginning you will be treated to not only a great story but an accurate history of Hollywood from the 1920s Silent Era through the late 1950s.

I would give every one of the nine books more than 5 stars. This was a wonderful series that I wish did not have to end. I LOVED reading this series! They were so well-written, thorough, detailed, and really really interesting. I would love to read more, as I enjoyed these characters so much, and loved learning about the development of the industry and the area.

ACKNOWLEDGMENTS

Heartfelt thanks to the following, who helped shaped this book:

My editor: Jennifer McIntyre for her keen eye, unfailing humor, and the willingness to debate every last letter and comma placement.

My cover designer: László Kiss

My beta readers: Vince Hans, Nora Hernandez-Castillo, Beth Riches, Royce Sciortino, Steven Adkins and especially Bradley Brady and Gene Strange for their invaluable time, insight, feedback and advice in shaping this novel.

My thanks, too, to Tracy Terhune for his guidance on some of the finer points of Rudolph Valentino.

And finally a great big thank you to my extraordinarily eagle-eyed proofreaders: Bob Molinari, Susan Perkins, and Leigh Carter, whose final polish raised this manuscript to gleaming perfection.

ABOUT THE AUTHOR

From an early age, Martin was enchanted with old movies from Hollywood's golden era – from the dawn of the talkies in the late 1920s to the close of the studio system in the late 1950s – and has spent many a happy hour watching the likes of Garland, Gable, Crawford, Garbo, Grant, Miller, Kelly, Astaire, Rogers, Turner, and Welles go through their paces. It feels inevitable that he would someday end up writing about them. Originally from Melbourne, Australia, Martin moved to Los Angeles in the mid-90s where he now works as a writer, blogger, webmaster, and tour guide.

www.MartinTurnbull.com

CONNECT WITH MARTIN TURNBULL

Website
https://martinturnbull.com/
Facebook
https://www.facebook.com/gardenofallahnovels
Blog
http://martinturnbull.wordpress.com/
Goodreads
https://www.goodreads.com/author/show/5444454.Martin_Turnbull

Be sure to check out the Photo Blog for vintage photos of Los Angeles and Hollywood on Martin's website:

https://martinturnbull.com/photo-blog/

To hear about new books first, sign up to my mailing list:

http://bit.ly/turnbullsignup
(I promise (a) I won't fill your inbox with useless drivel you don't care about, (b) I won't email you very often, and (c) I'll never share your information with anyone. Ever.

Made in United States
North Haven, CT
24 January 2023